Donal O'Neill

Crucible

Macdonald
in association with Lilliput Press

A Macdonald Book

First published in Great Britain in 1986 by
Macdonald & Co (Publishers) Ltd
London & Sydney
in association with Lilliput Press, Gigginstown, Ireland

British Library Cataloguing in Publication Data

O'Neill, Donal
Crucible.
March of a nation
Rn: Eoin Neeson I. Title
823'.914[F] PR6064.E4/

ISBN 0-356-12326-X

Printed in Great Britain by
Redwood Burn Ltd, Trowbridge, Wiltshire,
Bound at The Dorstel Press

Macdonald & Co (Publishers) Ltd
Greater London House
Hampstead Road
London NW1 7QX

A BPCC plc Company

for my friend Darach Connolly

Acknowledgements

My thanks are due to many people who provided help and encouragement. I am particularly grateful to Senan Crowe, O.P., who guided me through the pitfalls of forgotten Latin syntax, to Tony Mulloy who kindly lent certain source material at considerable inconvenience to himself, to Antony Farrell whose dedicated editing was as enthusiastic and professional as one would expect and, above all, to the two people who were the inspiration for the book and who guided me through it. Notwithstanding the help and advice so readily available it was necessary sometimes to travel a different path. Any errors and mistakes, consequential or otherwise, are entirely my own.

—Donal O'Neill

Map of Ireland showing some places of significance

Prologue

Between the first coming of the Celtic people to Ireland* and the Coming of Christianity to this most remote island of the west, stretches an age of vaulting occurrence which lasted close on a thousand years. During that time - from the age of the gods to the coming of God - the homogeneous race who inhabited the island were cut off from the rest of the world in many respects. Contact with Britain, Gaul and the Mediterranean was, at first, for trade and commerce and, essentially, remained like that throughout. In isolation they developed a civilisation of a sort; a sophisticated agriculturalism in which art and the things of the mind had an unusually high place; and from which reports of ritual cannibalism and sacrifice come side by side with accounts of extraordinary respect for law. Might and right, blood and judgement, flourished equally. During this time, too, the great myths and legends of the Gael, conceived in fact and nurtured on fancy and requirement, became part of the mother-lode from which issued the lore and traditions that nourished generation after generation.

The three great cycles of Irish legend are the Mythological Cycle, the Ulster Cycle and the Fenian Cycle. Roughly they span the period in question in that order and they demonstrate the three classic human faculties, thought, will and feeling. The Mythological Cycle illuminates intelligence and knowledge, the Ulster Cycle willpower and the 'man-sized' Fenian Cycle' human warmth of feeling'.

This story deals with none of them directly. The meaning and origins of the Mythological Cycle have already been explored.* The Ulster Cycle is heroic and should remain so. Our story concerns the people who lived in Ireland when it stood at the apogee of its barbaric, half-civilised splendour, a threat and irritant to the western provinces of the disintegrating Roman Empire and the only nation of the west not to have been conquered by Rome – yet, itself, teetering on the brink of savage decadence for lack of inspiration, either from within or without. The burst of physical and intellectual energy that (apparently, for to think otherwise is to euhemerise twilight figures) characterised the period of legendary Cormac Mac Art and the Fianna (c.250 A.D.) dissipated itself in the extraordinary fleets of successors like the warrior-kings Criffan the Great and Nial of the Nine Hostages, who rule as our story begins. As the Vikings were to do to their country also some 500 years later, they burned and looted across Britain and Gaul. But they brought back with them that missing dynamic, particularly in the person of one humble slave who escaped and returned again to fuse the past with a vision of the future and lay the foundation for one of the greatest bouleversements du mystiques in western history and for an efflorescence of devotion and learning that, in western Europe, was unsurpassed until the Renascence 800 years later.

The notional fourth cycle, the Cycle of the Kings, a late compilation of convenience purporting to recount the lives and activities of historical figures, touches on some of these events. But here is the story of that miraculous time, between the year 370 when the barbaric, pagan Scotts were lords of Scotia Major, Scotia Minor, Western Britain to the Ictian Sea and Mann, at constant war with the empire, and the year 570 when their war-fleets were hulks and Christianity had distilled and overtaken their battle-shrouded intellects.

—Donal O'Neill

* *See Of Gods and Men, Donal O'Neill*

Principal Characters

Fergus Mac(Mock – son of) Ceil – sea-captain and old soldier of the warrior king, Nial of the Nine Hostages.

Aidan – his son, friend of Sucatus (later Patricius).

Nial – (of the Nine Hostages), Ri Eireann (Ree Erin), King of Ireland (2).

Criffan – his uncle-in-law and predecessor (1).

Mongfin – Nial's step-mother, Criffan's sister.

Brian)
Fiachra) – (Feeuchra) her sons
Aillil) – (Al-ill)
Fergal)

Corc – (Curk) Prince of Munster.

Ibar Mac Sitchenn – (Eebar) a dawlee, a learned man one degree below the rank of ollamh or brehon (sage).

Cartan – Nial's mother.

Torna – (Tore-nuh) a poet, Nial's foster-father.

Oscar - king's champion.

Sitchenn - A smith and mystic.

Stilicho - Roman general, legate, nephew-in-law of the Emperor Theodosius.

Salthus - his clerk.

Festus - Pirimpilaris.

Potitus - a Christian priest.

Calpurnius - his son.

Sucatus - *his* son, later called Patricius - Patrick.

Colman - a warrior.

Mweelcu - owner of the slave, Sucatus.

Aethius - a scholar.

Con)
Eoghan) - seamen.

Celestine - the Pope.

Germanus - Bishop of Auxerre.

Loman)
MacCartan) - disciples of Patrick.
Benen)

Duach (1) - (Doo-ach) a chieftain.

Brigit - his daughter.

Fiac - (Fee-ach) a chieftain.

Laoire - (Lay-reh) Ri Eireann (3).
Blaheen - his consort.

Durrach - his major-domo.

Erc - his nephew.

Lochru - (Luck-roo) a druid.
Lucht Maol - (Luckt-Mwayle) a druid.

Duach (2) - chief Poet of Ireland.

Ibar) - (Eebar)
Declan)
Ciaran) - (Kee-rawn) Irish bishops.
Ailbe) - (Al-beh)

Failbhe - (Fal-veh) Aidan's daughter.

Orla - (Ore-lah) *her* daughter.

Phelim - (Faylim), King of Garton, a petty kingdom of Ulster.

Crimthan - his son, later Colm 'Cille' (of the churches).

Aine - (Oynya) his cousin.

Dermot O (grandson of) Donal (Doh-nal) - her son, friend of ColmCille.

Aoife - (Eefa) a girl.
Bran - her father.

Berkan - an abbot (Mo Bhi - muh vee).

Finian (1) - a monk, Abbot of Clonard.

Finian (2) - a monk, Abbot of Moville.

Ge'Olf - a Saxon prince.

Ruadhan - (Roo-awn) a monk and abbot.

Mugint - Abbot of Whitehorn.

Drustic - Northumbrian princess.
Rioch - (Reeuck), student at Whitehorn.

Talmuc - a prince, student at Whitehorn.

Diarmuid - Ri Eireann (4).
Curnan - (Currnawn), Prince of Connacht.

Tadhgh - (Tigue), son of Diarmuid's steward.

Donal (2)
Fergus - Mac Murray, joint Kings of Ulster.

Cathal (Cahal) Maol - Chieftain of the Dal Riada.

Laib - King of the Dal Riada.

Ferdia - a chieftain of Connacht.

Brendan - Abbot of Birr, ColmCille's confessor.

Cormac - (Currmuck), Abbot of Ardstraw, prosecutor.

Molaise - Abbot of Devinish.

Conal Gulban - King of the Irish Colony of Albyn (Scotland).

Brude - King of the Picts.

Aodh - (Ai - Hugh) Mac Ainmire (Annmirra), Ri Eireann (5).

Aidan - Mac Gowran, successor of Conal Gulban.

Dallan Forgaill - chief Poet of Ireland.

Baithin - (Beheen), monk, ColmCille's nephew.

Caitlin - (Kathleen), consort of Aodh Mac Ainmire.

Conal)
Donal (2)) - her sons.

Chapter 1

It was cold and the almost motionless sea was grey, the colour of old iron. White rime glistened on the sheets and planks of his ship and the slippery deck was as yet unmarked by anything save the footprints of the solitary black-backed gull that flapped grudgingly from beside the taff rail. It was the paddling of the gull - splat, splat, splat - across the deck above his head that had wakened Fergus.

He rolled from his bunk, raised himself on an edge of the cargo bulkhead until his bald crown touched the hide-covered hatch, and pressed upwards. One end of the cover rose on his head like a huge hat and he looked bleakly across the slanting deck, and beyond to where the lifeless sea merged with the lifeless sky. His eyes watered. The tide was well out, but had turned, and between him and the gentle ripple of white foam marking the water's edge there was an expanse of cold sand. No sun was visible and he guessed the time to be about an hour of the second *cadar*, or somewhere about the middle of the *hora prima*, as the Romans calculated it in their careless and unreliable fashion. 'Six hours or so - a full *cadar* - before the tide,' he mused. By then his cargo must be aboard and stowed and he and the ship ready to sail. He glanced again at the thin line of foam marking the water's edge, above which a few gulls soared over a small scurrying group of waders.

The ship - a fine and proud vessel, once, that had carried Aesold, daughter of King Aengus of the Liffey, to marry the

King of the Tin Coast – lay tilted to one side, high and dry, close to the high-water mark and aslant from the pier of rocks, trampled earth and timbers that jutted out from firm ground. From there a frosty *togher*, or corduroy road, led to a *bowher*, the substantial road winding from the invisible settlement two miles inland to the pier head.

The inside of his mouth felt like old leather. He manoeuvred a thick tongue over sparse teeth to moisten them. Not a spit! He grimaced, as much at the results of the night before as at what he saw, shivered suddenly from the neck down, changed his mind about climbing on deck for his purpose, and dropped back into the cabin, allowing the hatch-cover to fall into place. In the confined space he heaved himself awkwardly to the cabin window and unlatched the frame of the leather cover. He stood on tiptoe to reach the opening, at the same time crouching uncomfortably due to the low headroom, and with much relief emptied his bladder onto the sand below, grumbling to himself the while. He itched at the belt line and scratched, noting with irritation an accumulation of fat on his belly and hips. By the time he finished he felt better, more alert. He pulled on trews and a pair of Roman boots and went on deck. He squinted landward again. As far as he could see everything was as pale and lustreless as to seaward; pale sand, pale sky, pale countryside with pale, indistinct, hills in the distance. He hated winter. He hated this particular day of it most of all because he had a hangover, and he hated the flat Wexford shoreline he was on and the largely Christian, and therefore, suspicious, settlement beyond. And he hated his crew who should be here instead of there.

'Curse them, wherever they are,' he swore, 'may their anuses close up and fester – not meaning them any harm,' he added hurriedly. He scanned the shoreline, but there was no sign of the crew. In the distance, towards the settlement, he thought he detected a fudge of smoke, but it was too indistinct for him to be sure and, in any case, what of it?

'Women, I suppose!' He spat dryly, his anger with the absent crew, to say nothing of his absent - and only - son, Aidan, totally unfettered by any foolish and intrusive recollection of his own rather startling gymnastics in the cabin the night before. Afflicted with seven daughters and two wives, Aidan, who appeared late and unexpectedly eighteen years ago when Fergus was past fifty, was the apple of his father's eye; he was also spoiled crooked and tended to be both cheerful and unreliable, qualities in which Fergus placed small trust. He lifted a lean and forlorn wine flagon from the scuppers and shook it. Frost glimmered on one side of it. But there was a faint, positive, gurgle from within and he pulled the wooden plug from its leather neck. He raised it over his head, supporting it with both hands, and allowed the jet to fill his mouth. Then lowered the bottle, swallowed and grimaced. He lifted it again at arm's length and squinted at it, tasting the resin in his mouth still.

'Falernian my arse!' He spat again, this time with more satisfactory volume, and returned to the cabin where he produced some bread, cold sausage and dripping from a cupboard. With his knife he cut the sausage and spread dripping on the bread. He half filled a wooden cup with wine, topped it up with water from the water-skin and ruminatively ate breakfast. His mind was inclined to wander this morning - he grinned as he chewed, passing the food from one infrequent tooth to another, in congratulatory recollection of the previous night - and he let it meander where it would. He settled comfortable in the warmth of the little cabin. His belly rumbled and he belched silently. He put his feet up on the bunk, took an indifferent swig from the cup, cocked an ear, but to silence, and then leaned back, closing his eyes.

'By the gods,' he muttered aloud, 'they wouldn't've farted around like this when I was with Nial . . . '

But it was many years since he sailed with the King. Time, activity and continued exposure to the elements had eventually stiffened and slowed him until, almost without realising it, he started more to tell of past activities than participate in new ones. He began to remain on board to command the guard of a squadron of the fleet when they landed and attacked a foreign coast. After that it seemed a short while before he remained behind to 'guard our own shores' when the great fleets of a hundred or two hundred boats put out to sea. Their oars would beat the tide so that their threshing echoed back to him on shore, and the songs of the warriors accompanied it as the sea host moved away, their sails coasting the blue ocean to the horizon and beyond in moving patterns as the courses changed. Then came the day when he finally quit; bought a ship of his own with what little remained of the vast booty that had passed through his hands, and became a trader. And he hated and resented it. But when he first served the king, and before that his uncle by marriage . . . by the gods! He well remembered the day Nial took the throne – that would be, what? 379 by the Christian calendar – as if it were only last week instead of sixteen years ago. At the Fair of Tara, so it was Samhain, and he rode his great horse onto the chariot course that morning merely the fifth son of a long dead king, followed by four other lords, and strode onto it that night to marry the world as King of All Ireland, Alban and Britain to the Ictian Sea.

Chapter 2

THE great Fair of Tara had been summoned by the King, and every lord and noble in the land - as well as multitudes of freemen, entertainers, merchants and slaves - was on the move. It would last six weeks in all, the first two being devoted to public games and celebrations, and the remainder to private meetings in solemn and formal session of delegates from all parts, considering and deciding on legal and public issues. It was held every three years or, more recently, at the command of the king. But not oftener. Nial's first concern when he reached Tara was to ensure that his mother, who had preceded him in answer to Criffan's summons, was secure and safe. He had come with four companions, three of his four half-brothers, and Corc, son of the King of Munster, who was closer to him than any of the others for they had been brought up together, foster children of the poet Torna, who was also Nial's saviour. The young man disliked Tara and having anything to do with it.

His own father, Ochy Moyvane, had been King and that had nearly cost him his life. Criffan who succeeded Nial's father had proved to be an exceptionally strong king; he was called Criffan Mór (Moor), or Criffan the Great, which enraged his sister, Mongfin, first wife of Nial's father and mother of four of his sons, three of whom rode with Nial. Brian, the fourth, was no doubt skulking somewhere in the shadow of his mother's tongue, swollen with an ambition that far outstretched his ability, and festering in envy of his uncle, the king. For it was

Mongfin who threw her influence behind Criffan when Ochy died and caused him to be elected, intending only that he remain regent-king until Brian came of age. But Brian had been of age for five years now, and Mongfin's heart simmered.

Five great thoroughfares led to Tara: the Slee-Asail from the West; the Slee-Meeluachra from the North; the Slee-Cualann from the South; and across the Liffey at Baile-Atha-Cliath or the town of the hurdle-ford which is a kind of bridge, the Slee-Dawla and the Slee-Moor from the South and South-West. All of these, as well as the many smaller roads and thoroughfares, were thronged with people and animals. Vehicles of every kind jostled one another, and some of those who could not find a place in the city and were prepared to face the twin hazards of robbers and the king's soldiers had erected booths at the roadside for miles outside the city. Nial and his companions, Corc, Fiachra, Aillil and Fergal, made their way with considerable difficulty.

'My God,' said Corc (then quickly made the Christian sign with his thumb against his forehead and glanced sideways at Nial, who winked at him, getting a smile in response) 'there must be half a million.'

'Not so many,' laughed Fiachra from behind, 'you'd only get that many in Munster.' They all laughed, aware of the great efforts and inducements of Corc's father, King of Munster, to make the *aonach* at Cashel the biggest outside Tara.

'Well,' said Corc, 'there's two hundred thousand anyhow, or three. How many in the city normally?'

'Oh – eight, maybe ten thousand, but three thousand of those are troops. There's always one standing battalion here.'

'I don't see why they want them now,' said Aillil, 'the Romans are no threat any more.'

'The danger may not be from outside,' murmured Nial to himself, but loud enough to be heard.

Before they reached the first, outer, wall of the three surrounding the city they were forced to dismount and lead their horses through narrow streets between thatched and wattled houses, blinding in their new coats of lime wash. Some of the streets were paved with stone slabs, some with wicker, some with half-timbers, but most were unsurfaced and all of them bore parallel ruts from the passage of multitudinous wheels over many years, now obscured by the babbling, shoving, gesticulating people who made further progress on horseback out of the question.

It was a cheerful throng through which they pressed, for the prohibition against ill will or rancour which was promulgated one thousand years or so before was still rigorously enforced. Cormac Mac Art, Nial's great-great-grandfather, and the greatest king, so it was said, the land had ever known, had codified traditional criminal law, including those relating to fairs, into one of three books of learning and scholarship compiled in his retirement (occasioned by a facial wound which obliged him to abdicate in accordance with tradition). His book of statutes is called *The Book of Acaill*, from the place where it was written. And as Nial, with smiles and acknowledgements, forced his way through the jostling crowds, the opening words of that great book, as he had first seen them written in his ancestor's own hand in the library of Torna at Cashel, returned to him: 'The place of this book is Acaill near Tara and it was written in the kingship of Carbery Liffey, son of Cormac, the author, who was blinded by Angus Gawbwee . . . '

As if his very thoughts walked visibly beside him, a high, professional voice rang out from one of the booths close by. At the sound some among the crowd turned, first to the booth where a thin man dressed all in brown stared intensely towards Nial, and then, as the man's words became clear, towards the young prince himself. Though there was no room the people seemed to draw back a little and clear a space between the brown man and the youth leading his horse.

The voice of the thin, brown man was astonishingly strong for one so slight. He had an inner strength, like that of tempered metal, which drew attention. And the words he declaimed were the first words of Cormac's *Teagasc an Riogh*, Instructions of a King:

Do not deride the elderly, although you are young;
Nor the poor, though you are wealthy;
Nor the lame, though you are swift;
Nor the blind, though you have sight;
Nor the sick, though you are strong;
Nor the dull, though you are clever;
Nor the foolish, though you are wise.

Be not too wise, be not too foolish;
Be not too conceited, be not too diffident;
Be not too haughty, be not too humble;
Be not too talkative, be not too silent;
Be not too harsh, be not too feeble.

If you are too wise, they will over expect from you;
If you are too foolish, you will be deceived;
If you are too conceited, you will be thought insufferable;
If you are too humble, you will be without honour;
If you are too talkative, you will not be heeded;
If you are too silent, you will not be regarded;
If you are too harsh, you will be broken;
If you are too feeble, you will be crushed!

At first the crowd around and about cheered as the brown man made each pronouncement and the cheering attracted those further off who joined in so that it swelled as he chanted each line. But then the cheering died. Something of the thin man's intensity communicated itself to the throng who now, instead of cheering, looked from one face to the other in silence each time the *dawlee* spoke – for that was what he was; one who had not yet reached the full eminence of being an *ollamh*, a judge or law-giver, but who, nevertheless, had eleven or twelve years of study behind him and was an accomplished advocate and lawyer.

'Why do you quote these words at me?' asked Nial.

'They are the words of a great king!'

'I know that.'

'They are the words of your grandfather's grandfather.'

'I know that too.'

'They are the words of a king.'

'Tell me something I do not know, *dawlee*.'

'They are addressed to a king.'

'I asked you to tell me something I do not know.' Nial smiled and looked around. 'Everyone knows they were addressed to a king.'

The crowd roared with laughter at this sally. The *dawlee* waited until the sound died and then raised one hand. Without taking his eyes off Nial, he said: 'I did not say they were addressed to a king. I said they *are* addressed to a king.'

There was a momentary pause. Then Nial flushed to his hair, and went immediately pale. He turned and walked swiftly away, his short, scarlet cloak billowing with the suddenness of his movement. The crowd parted to let him pass. He turned back and looked full at the *dawlee*, whose eyes were still fastened on him.

'What is your name, *dawlee*?'

'Ibar Mac Sitchenn.'

Nial said nothing for a moment. His eyes were locked with those of the brown man. The tension between them was almost tangible.

'I see,' said Nial. 'I knew your father, the druid.' The brown man inclined his hawk-like face very slightly. 'I will remember you, Ibar!'

The brown man stared back at him silently and Nial could feel rage beginning to boil inside himself. He remembered the past and the promises; he knew himself, both his power and his duty, and frustration put the fill to his anger and he spat at Ibar: 'You spoke treason.'

'My testimony lies before us, like nightfall.'

Nial turned away, the smile gone from his face, and shouldered through the crowd, tugging at the bridle of his startled mount. Corc and the others followed and all were soon swallowed by the crowds, their slow progress marked only by the occasional nervous tossing of their horses' heads. They reached the battlemented gate of the outer ditch, its high walls so broad that a chariot might be driven along the top. The gate was guarded by men of the king's troop. They crossed the *dricked*, the bridge spanning the ditch and leading to the massive gates and the tunnel under the wall, and passed through unchallenged. Inside, between this and the second wall, the houses were more substantial, generally with one or more storeys or adjacent quarters, and further apart. This was where the *feine*, freemen, and their families lived. The district of the petty chiefs, the *arra-dessa* and *bo-aire*, lay between the second wall and the final wall around the royal city of Tara itself. The crowds were less and more orderly, and buyers and sellers - save of precious metals, stones and horses - were forbidden inside the walls proper. But there were plenty for all that.

Nial and the others passed through each of the defences until they reached the old city and the king's *rath*, fortified house, itself, to enter which they were required to prove their identity. Once inside they mounted and trotted past the royal households of Criffan and the provincial kings, and the houses of the nobles. As they rode by the great public buildings, Nial noted again with pride and admiration the splendour of the Tyock Meecuarta, the Mead Banqueting House, rebuilt by Cormac; while it may not have been the largest building at Tara, it was certainly one of the finest. More than eight hundred feet long and ninety feet across, its fourteen doors - six to a side and one at either end - were of enamelled bronze. It had two hundred windows, and carved and painted pillars which rose more than fifty feet to support the mighty roof trusses. Within, there were three levels at each end, and balconies encircled the banqueting hall itself, which could seat more than one thousand nobles according to their station.

A *fled imdell* - or banquet - in the Tyock Meecuarta at Tara differed from those elsewhere in that it was often the custom (perhaps because of the maleness of Tara, who knows?) for women not to sit at banquets with the men, but to banquet in their own hall, which meant, of course, that they were not obliged to wear the *fethal*, face covering, and sit apart. Men were permitted in the women's banqueting hall at Tara only by invitation.

As to the royal banquet proper, three classes of nobles attended. Kings and lords of territories, commanders of the permanent troops including the commander of the king's troops at Tara, and the chief druids and men of learning.

Tables were arranged on both sides of the long hall. Each chief and noble was attended by his shield-bearer, and on the wall behind and above the tables were hooks on which the shields were hung. Protocol was rigid: the right side of the hall, more dignified than the left, was for kings and territorial lords; the left was for the military commanders; the south end facing north was for the largest and most inferior group, dependent chieftains. The king sat among the *ollamhes* and learned men at the northern end where he could face to the south. It was the duty of the chief historian, the *ollamhe* Shan-a-key, to maintain two scrolls bearing the names of the guests in proper precedence, according to which they were seated. Before the beginning of a banquet, after the mead had circled no more than three times, everyone left the hall except the *ollamhe* Shan-a-key, a marshal, and a trumpeter who would sound his instrument three times. On the first fanfare the shield-bearers entered with their lords' shields which they gave to the marshal who hung them on the hooks as the Shan-a-key directed. Each shield bore the emblem or device of its owner. On the second fanfare the guests entered and took their places beneath their shields. Only one side of each table, that facing across the hall, was occupied, and no man sat facing another. At the third fanfare the King himself entered and took his place, with members of his bodyguard behind him.

Once in the city, Nial rode straight across the chariot course towards Rath Grainne, Grainne's Mansion, which glittered in the sun because of the coloured glass that decorated the wall of its *grianaan*, solarium. This was one of the oldest mansions in the king's care and it was here that Nial expected to find his mother Cartan who had preceded him from the south by four-wheeled chariot. Mongfin would not like their being there, but they had the right. The king had summoned the *aonach* which they must attend and Mongfin would not defy her brother, the king, who had welcomed Nial and Cartan, or risk death by provoking them in breach of the Aon Cairde Aonig (*ayon cairde ayonig*), the one universal fair-truce. Nial dismounted before the *grianaan* of Rath Grainne, threw the reins to a weather-beaten warrior who had the stamp of the sea about him, and struck the bronze gong to announce himself.

While he waited for the steward he turned and saw that the man who held his horse was staring at him. The look was neither shifty nor arrogant, neither resentful nor over-humble; it was cool and appraising. Nial, still disturbed by his encounter with the *dawlee*, felt truculent.

'Well?' he snapped.

The man didn't respond. He was fiftyish; clean-shaven, like a Roman, and had deep ridges - one a scar, clearly a sword cut - lining his face which was square and strong. His hair, speckled grey, was also shorn the Roman way, and his shoulders were very broad. He wasn't tall, but he looked strong. A faded green and blue cloak hung from his left shoulder. A sacramasax, the short, Roman sword, hung from his left side.

'You'll know me the next time,' said Nial when the man didn't answer. 'Can't you speak?'

'Well enough,' came the answer, 'and I know you now, Nial. And I'll hold your horse for you - since you asked.'

Before Nial could retort, the steward arrived and, not wishing to create a disturbance in his presence, Nial went with him, merely throwing over his shoulder the insult: 'Don't you know, *leath-Románach*, half-Roman, that old Theodosius hangs men for wearing their swords on the wrong side?'

His mother was a handsome woman still, with the delicate rose and alabaster complexion of many of her race, though faint, thread-like wrinkles were evident close to; like an autumn flower, she had reached the point where her beauty was in transition from one stage to another. In spite of the privations and indignities she suffered at the hands of Mongfin, she retained a bearing and dignity consistent with her lineage.

Cartan was the daughter of a British king, Teyrnon, and in spite of her protests had been married to Nial's father, Ochy Moyvane, as his second wife, even though she was a Christian. Although it was a political marriage, Ochy came to love her more than Mongfin his first wife. Mongfin, a bitter, jealous and ambitious woman, had also been opposed to the marriage but for very different reasons to Cartan, and her husband's growing and obvious preference for his newer and younger wife turned that jealousy into obsessive hatred. Whenever Ochy was absent from Tara, Mongfin had Cartan treated as a menial at court; to the embarrassment of many, she was obliged to fetch and carry water with which to wash the feet and hands of the king's guests, a function normally reserved for the youngest or lowliest member of the household. As it chanced, both women became pregnant within months of one another and in the year 335 both gave birth to boys - Mongfin first, for whom it was her fourth son, Brian. In Ochy's absence, Mongfin had Cartan's son exposed to die outside the city. How she did it or expected to succeed without being detected is uncertain. What is certain is that the infant was found by Torna, poet and *ollave* to Fiach, King of Munster, and brought to Cashel, the king's second seat, where he was reared as a foster child under Torna's protection, together with Corc, Fiach's son. That was twenty-five years earlier and what happened meantime laid the foundations for what was about to take place.

Ochy died in 366 when Nial and Brian were both eleven years

old. By that time Torna had reintroduced Nial to royal Tara in circumstances not dissimilar to those of his illustrious ancestor, Cormac, who was once also banished because of his blood. Ironically, Ochy came to regard Nial as his nominee successor.

In her attempts to secure the Kingship for Brian, Mongfin supported the candidature of her brother, Criffan, at the time of Ochy's death, assuming he would then favour Brian when he came of age. It was a measure of her blind ambition that she believed she might succeed in the face not only of the law, but of her brother too. For Criffan was a leader who grasped hold of opportunity. He extended his authority into Britain and Alban, ruling from the western ocean where the sun sinks to the Ictian Sea between Britain and Gaul. His armies fought many battles with those of the Roman General Theodosius; he subdued the Picts and took tribute and hostages from the Saxons who were raiding across the Ictian Sea to the east of Britain. He even had a Christian church built at Glastonbury which ever since has been known as Glastonbury of the Gael. So, when Nial was brought to his mother through the mansion to the *grianann*, these things were in his mind, because Criffan had let it be known that the time had come for him to nominate a Tanist, successor. 'Who should,' muttered Nial, 'by rights be me.'

Even then he sensed his destiny and as he passed into the sun-filled bower where his mother reclined with some other women, his heart cried out: 'By the three natures of the gods let it be me; by that of the other world, by that of this world and by the god of my soul, let it be me.' But he displayed none of this intensity as his mother rose to welcome him and he in turn greeted her with three kisses.

She stood with her hands on his shoulders looking up at him, and her blue eyes searched his own darker ones, probing for – she knew not what. Some sign of weakness, cause for unease, assessing, perhaps, the accumulation of experience that was the son who stood before her? After a moment or two she seemed satisfied. Her questing eyes relaxed.

'You are well?'

He nodded. 'And you?'

'As well as I can be, here,' she laughed. 'That woman will be the death of me.'

Nial hastily made the sign and turned away. 'Don't say it, Cartan,' he said. 'She would wish for nothing more.'

'I'm sorry,' she said, 'I forgot . . . ' she hesitated. She had been going to add 'how seriously you take such things'. But she thought better of it. 'In any case there is something more she would wish for.' They both knew what she meant. Nial's death would be the finest piece of news Mongfin could have, excepting only the news that her son Brian had been named Tanist. Nial nodded briefly and grunted an agreement. They exchanged a sober look for another moment. Then she laid her delicate, slender hand on his sleeve and led him to a couch on which were arranged cushions of fine doeskin, sheltered from the sun by a canopy of bright feathers. She clapped her hands, asked one of the young women to bring food and turned back to him.

While they ate he told her about his encounter with the *dawlee* and how it had unsettled him. When he finished, her face was grave. She raised her right hand and made the Christian sign before his face.

'I do not know what it might mean, or if it means anything,' she said. 'Strange things do happen and strange happenings mark great events. You were your father's choice. I must ask you to let me give you my blessing. Though you are not a Christian you know that I have always been one and my faith has always been my greatest comfort and source of strength in all the troubles I experience as a stranger, and often an unwelcome and unwanted one, in a strange land. It comes from my heart. My prayers and hopes go with you, my son.'

He was moved by her sincerity and too wise to be impatient with her Christian ways. He knew the strength of her belief, having seen her pray on many occasions, sometimes with tears in her eyes which he found hard to understand, putting it down to the weakness of a woman, or of the faith itself. But although he neither sympathised with nor understood the solitary god of the Christians (and the Romans), he could not fail to recognise power when he saw it and recognise, too, that he needed help from whatever quarter. So he smiled and thanked her. Then he rose.

'We must pay our respects to the king.'

Cartan followed him and they left the *grianaan* for the King's palace. Outside, the grizzled warrior still held Nial's horse as casually as if it were his own. He handed the reins to Nial without deference and with a little smile on his lips. Impressed by his patience and bearing, Nial nodded and asked: 'What is your name?'

'Fergus, lord, Mac Ceil.'

'Well, Fergus, son of the freeman, I will remember you.'

'I hope so, Nial, and I will not forget you.'

They stared at one another on that borderline of acquaintanceship that, by a look or the colour of an eye, can fall as readily into friendship as into hostility. Then with a nod Nial followed his mother's small, four-wheeled chariot with the blue awning, which was already moving towards the palace, a beautifully constructed building of ornamented timbers with a shingle roof of red cedar, which Cormac had also built.

Mongfin and Brian were both already in the audience chamber when Nial and Cartan were ushered in. The king ceremonially raised his knee to them and Nian went forward, bowed, and put his head on the king's breast. His mother, following, did likewise. As he stood up Nial found Mongfin's eyes on him and he was startled by the clear madness there, a glitter of triumphant hatred she took no trouble to conceal. Surprisingly, she stood behind her brother and to his left, and Brian stood behind her, where a gilly usually stood.

'The proper place for him,' thought Nial ignoring the bulky young man, a few months older than himself, for whom Mongfin had risked so much and who, thought Nial, wouldn't make a decent *arra-dessa*, the merest petty noble with but ten tenants.

Having saluted the king they stood back. Criffan then waved his hand towards his sister.

'Come before me, Mongfin - and Brian. What I have to say concerns us all.'

The supercilious smile was still on her lips as Mongfin came round with her son to stand with Nial and Cartan facing the king. Behind Criffan stood his champion, Oscar, a grandson of that other Oscar, son of Ossian, son of Finn Mac Cool, the most distinguished leader the great standing army of Ireland, the Fianna Erin, ever had. It was raised in the time of Cormac's grandson, Con, called Con Kayed-Cath, the Hundred Fighter, because of his success in that number of battles, to defend the nation from the threat of Roman invasion. It had a permanent strength of three battalions each of three thousand men which in time of war was increased to seven battalions. These permanent troops were, of course, just the hard professional core of the available forces. But after Con's death they became overpowerful and arrogant, giving their prime allegiance to their commander rather than the king. Con's successor and Nial's great-grandfather, Carbery, was forced to disband them, which was only achieved in battle between his forces and the Fianna at Gabhra in Meath. The Fianna were defeated, but Carbery was killed in the battle.

Criffan was imposing to behold. He looked about fifty-five years old. He was tall and his oval face was well shaped, a broad brow above a slender, aristocratic jaw. His skin was fair and his hands slender and well kept with the beautifully formed and well-maintained nails of nobility. His long hair, once red-gold, was now pale as the moon. He sat on a low, carved chair with cushions of silk and doeskin, raised up on a dais. On his head he wore the most beautiful royal crown in the known world, a golden *minn*, the exquisite diadem of Tara. An inner cap of purple velvet sewn with gold and silver thread was surmounted by bands and twisted wires of filigree gold that circled his head and sprang out from it in great splendour like the rays of the sun. Beside his chair and his scarlet shield, engraved with gold and silver, rested against a magnificent pair of crossed spears with golden sockets, bronze rivets glittering along their shafts. Had he been standing, the purple cloak about his shoulders would have fallen in five folds behind him. It was fastened with a gold clasp that stretched across his shoulders; on his breast lay a gem-studded sun disc and round his neck he wore a golden torque over a white shirt embroidered with the same precious metal. His belt, too, was made of gold plates and the very sandals on his feet were of embroidered gold, fastened with golden buckles. He had done great things in the thirteen years he had been King of All Ireland, Alban and Western Britain. His great enemy and rival was the Roman General Theodosius who was sent by Emperor Valentinian of Britain to harness what resources he could against Criffan as early as 367. They fought many great land battles, and then Theodosius built a fleet and attacked Criffan at sea.

Now he raised his right hand and immediately his steward, who stood behind Oscar, rang the *crave sheeda* the branch of peace, for silence, so that the tinkling of its little bells became the only sound in the great chamber.

With Pictish and Saxon allies and vassals Criffan had cleared Valentinian's troops from much of Britain and persuaded, or frightened, the frontier troops – the so-called militia, or *limitanei* – into co-operating with him, so that among those who fell before him were the Count of the Saxon Shore, Nectaridus, and the Duke of Britain, Fullofaudes, both killed at their posts, although the death of the latter, who would have fetched a great ransom from the Empire, had put Criffan into a rage.

'I have reached a good age,' he began, 'and have done great things. The Romans withdraw from our lands in Britain and Alban and the Empire is divided and besieged by yellow men from the east. The Goths have destroyed them at Adrianople.

Maximus, the new general, is treacherous. I have recently learned that the scourge of our armies in Britain, the General Theodosius, is dead. The Empire is crumbling. We are the only free, civilised people to have escaped both persecution by Rome and the present persecution of Rome. And I must name my Tanist.'

His voice was deep, measured and slow as befitted a great king, and silence followed his speech. He let his eyes move impassively across the faces of the assembly.

'I know,' he went on, 'that my predecessor intended that Nial, his son by his British wife, should be his Tanist. That did not happen. I became High King.'

'Thanks be to the benevolence of an all-knowing providence,' came the ritualistic intoning of one of the druids, and everyone shouted: '*An Ri Abú, Criffan Abú* – praise the king, praise Criffan.'

Criffan raised his right forearm to his shoulder palm outwards, and the cheering instantly stopped.

'I have in mind what Ochy Moyvane desired,' he said, 'and I have in mind other matters besides. A Tanist must rule if required. A Tanist must have the capacity to be the King. I ask the question: should a Tanist also be an heir? I ask the question: should there be continuity? I ask the question: how shall we best preserve our strength?'

His words caused a sort of silent gasp to rustle in the chamber. What was the King saying? Was he promoting primogeniture? If so the result would be chaos not solidarity. He could not mean that. Or could he? There was still his obligation – if such it was – to Mongfin to be fulfilled.

The King continued: 'I will select the Tanist I consider fittest to rule after me. Whether he is then chosen is a matter for the council.'

These words brought a relief almost as audible and tangible as the silent gasp of a moment earlier. Criffan did not intend anything openly radical. Yet he had deliberately raised the question of new methods. What did he have in mind? Nial felt exposed and humiliated. He was certain the enigmatic manner of the king had to do with his debt to Mongfin. But in what way? From the corner of his eye, Nial saw a smile on her lips as she looked at her brother, whose eyes rested on her for a moment in acknowledgement.

'I shall make my decision known tonight,' said Criffan. Then he raised his hand in dismissal and there was an immediate shuffling as all but the *ollaves* and druids turned to leave.

'Mongfin,' called the King, 'I want to speak with you.'

Nial halted and turned to watch the smirking Mongfin saunter towards the King. Nial glanced at Cartan and they both saw Brian look at his mother and uncle, hesitate a moment as if wondering if he should wait too, and then swagger confidently from the chamber, thrusting aside anyone who was in his path.

As they came out into the sunlight of the courtyard Nial said: 'Well, that's that.'

'It seems like it,' replied his mother. 'What will you do?'

'Just now,' he said, 'I'm going to ride – fast!' Before she had time to reply he walked quickly to where his gilly watched his horse. He snatched the reins, leaped to the *dillat*, the saddle cloth, with a yell to which the spunky chestnut responded with an instant lunge, and galloped through the portal of the palace.

Straight through the city he rode, sometimes shouting at people to clear the way, mostly indifferent to both the danger he was causing and the angry looks and shouts that followed his progress. Once clear of the packed city and its environs he left the road, steering his stretching mount between the temporary shelters and booths, to gallop over the green plain in the warm sunlight. The breeze gentled his flowing hair; the sound of the hooves was soft behind him; he joined with the animal in one motion, sitting high and leaning back, legs clasping her flanks like a girth strap. And all sounds, except their own, faded. They were one purpose. He rode until the city was an indistinguishable darkness mounting from the sunlit plain. Then he slid from her back and threw himself on the grass at the edge of the forest, and looked at the sky. His lathered mount stood a moment, quieting her breathing, and then with stretched and lowered neck walked a pace or two and began to crop the sweet grass. Was he a fugitive? He did not know. He could, he knew, be accused of having broken the *ayon cairde ayonig*. He must have done so, riding through the populace like that, scattering people every which way. Surely someone had been injured, if not killed. Uneasiness began to master his anger. He shook his head to clear it of self-doubt. He was right. He was the rightful Tanist. No! By the gods, that wasn't it. That was not the source of his blind rage. Criffan not withstanding, he was the rightful King! He knew it. He felt and believed it.

'Let them come,' he swore silently of those who might pursue him.

He saw once more the satisfaction on Mongfin's face and he swore again. He remembered why it was she hated him and how it began; the threat he was to her and her plans. It was after his father died, when he was eleven years old - fourteen, nearly fifteen years ago - the year of Our Lord 366 as his mother always said. Nial's mouth twisted in a wry smile. His father was no sooner decently buried, standing in full armour facing east towards the sea and his enemies as was the custom - than Mongfin - even as she schemed and plotted to have her brother Criffan chosen to be King - had her four sons and Nial put to a test of kingship by the seer and mystic, the *gabhann* (smith) Sitchenn.

Nial recalled the day well. It was raining. That particular, heavy rain of large drops which falls in continuous flood to swell the streams into raging torrents and soak the world and all in it so that dryness clings only to a small, yellow space around a fire. They were sent by four-wheeled chariot through the rain and the mud to Sitchenn's *rath*, which housed one hundred people or more. The forge, cérdhcha (Kayrdka), the place of iron, was separated from the other buildings by an inner palisade beyond which women and children might not - except in special circumstances - pass. Their chariot drove straight through the *rath*, past the dwelling houses, the barns and storehouses, beyond the inner palisade and drew up before the smithy, from where even through the pouring rain the force of light and heat from within reached out to them.

Sitchenn came to the door when he heard them arrive and stood there with his hands on his hips, silhouetted against the brilliantly lit interior. He was a big man, not huge like some warriors or foreign slaves, but big: round. He had round shoulders and a round belly and his buttocks were round, as was the bald head that sprouted from a neck that had all but vanished. His nose was round and his blue, blue eyes were round also. The only thing about him that did not suggest roundness was the huge, square black beard that hung to his chest. He looked more like a *bo-aire*, or head freeman, than a great seer. But Nial remembered feeling instinctively wary, although they had not - or at least, *he* had not - been told the reason for this strange journey in the rain, that its purpose was to be of great importance to him. The figure in the doorway called and they dashed through the rain, past his stiff and stainless buckskin apron. And it was that, thought Nial in recollection, that had strengthened his suspicions. Surely a smith's buckskin apron would be dirty and burned? But this one was spotless and stiff and smelt richly of fresh leather as he brushed past.

The forge itself was circular, with but one entrance. Its foundation was a knee-high stone wall upon which the wall pillars were fixed in pairs so that the heavy double wattling could be laced securely and the space between filled with clay. The walls were finished with a mud and dung plaster, whitewashed without and within. There was a hole in the thick thatch above the clay furnace to carry off the smoke and much of the remainder of the space was taken up with implements, fuel, ore and ingots of different metals, and finished products in iron and gleaming steel and bronze. There was so much to see it was hard to take it all in. A huge water trough, *umar*, stood beside the anvil, *ineone*, that itself stood in *cep i mbai an ineoin* – on the block on which the anvil is set. Two apprentices worked a pair of double-bellows with their feet, which was the reason for the great blaze. The heat was intense.

When the five boys were inside, Sitchenn shouted: 'Egan, Ibar – out!'

Nial started. His wandering mind had flicked a memory out of the past and he tried to put the intense face of the morning's *dawlee* on the shoulders of one of the two men who leaped from the bellows-stone at their father's command and strode past him into the rain that day, fourteen years before.

No sooner were they gone than Sitchenn himself turned and followed them, shutting the door behind him. The five boys – the oldest seventeen – looked around and at one another.

'What's happening?' asked Fergal, the oldest, wandering over to the forge where the flame had already mellowed and ceased to roar for lack of provocation from the stertorous bellows. Aillil shrugged. The others wandered here and there.

'Look at this – and this, by the gods! Some blade . . . '

Nial stood in the centre of the building and gazed about him. He walked purposefully to the furnace and examined it, noting the shards of discarded and burnt-out furnaces close by. He inspected the anvil and the tongs, *tenchoir*, and the boxes full of rivets arranged according to size. While he was inspecting these there was a cry from Fiachra.

'Look!'

'What?'

'The roof – it's on fire!'

They rushed to the door, but it was locked. For a split second they looked at each other, and Nial could still recall the four white, wide-eyed faces of the others; the scene was engraved in his memory. As one they turned to the door and pounded on it.

'Help! Fire! *Help*. Let us out!'

But there was no answer. They could hear nothing from

outside, and within only the ominous crackle of the burning thatch. Smoke billowed down, driven by the wind and the rain, and suddenly they were coughing and choking. The fearsome glow overhead began to spread rapidly.

'Help, somebody help.'

Suddenly the door was flung open. Sitchenn stood there, the rain streaming behind him. They surged forward but the huge arms of the smith swung out and blocked the exit.

'No!' he said. 'Save my goods.'

'But the fire - we'll die.' They struggled to get past, but he was immovable.

'Sitchenn - you'll pay for this!'

'Nobody leaves,' he said, 'without saving something from my forge!'

By now half the roof was alight and blazing clumps of thatch were falling everywhere.

'But — ' began Aillil.

'Save!' said Sitchenn.

Aillil turned and looked at the holocaust behind him, then turned again to the immovable Sitchenn. By this time Nial was already moving. What spirit guided him he did not know, perhaps that of his recently dead father. Scarcely thinking, he dashed through the tumbling thatch, some of which glanced from his shoulder, under the blazing roof timbers, and grabbed the anvil by the heel and the snout. It was already warm to the touch and a great weight for a boy his size, but he lifted it clear out of its socket in the block and staggered to the door with it, past Sitchenn, to dump it - and himself, he remembered wryly - outside in the rain and the mud. The others stumbled past with different items: Aillil a shield and sword, Fiachra the sledges, Brian the bellows, and Fergal with nothing but a bundle of firewood.

Nial remembered the occasion well. Sitchenn called it his rebirth.

'Your concern,' he had said to Nial after they had been

properly washed and clothed, 'was for the soul of the forge, which you saved, as your concern in the future will be for the soul of Erin, which you will rule.'

When Mongfin heard the seer's predictions she was furious and sent the five boys twice more to be tested, but on each occasion the prophetic omens guided the smith to the same conclusion.

How long Nial lay there remembering the past he wasn't sure; as long as two points, half an hour? He had no idea. He was roused by the sound of hoofs and, looking up, saw a rider approaching at full gallop. He was still too far away for Nial to make him out but as he drew closer he could see it was Corc, who was flogging his horse with his *echlach*, riding staff, as if he would beat the animal's flanks raw.

Nial sat up. It was unlike Corc to thrash his horse. Nial looked beyond to see if Corc was being pursued. Had he too transgressed the law of fairs in some way? Perhaps quarrelled or somehow provoked an incident (possibly over me, he thought) which at any other time would be a trivial matter, but was a capital offence at an *aonach*? But there was no sign of pursuit and Corc came on as desperately as ever. Nial stood up. As he did so he heard Corc shouting: 'Nial, Nial!'

Nial wondered if Corc was bringing him some sort of warning. He reached for his horse's reins, drawing them over the animal's head so that she jerked up. He put his hand on her muzzle.

'Nial . . . for God's sake . . . the king . . . ' was all Nial could hear, but Corc's reference to his Christian God confirmed that this was no ordinary matter. He was outlawed for sure. Or . . .

'The old bastard has named Brian!' Nial thought. Slowly he mounted and walked forward. He waved to Corc, who reined in his horse, leaning back and hauling on the reins so that the animal skidded to a halt three, four hundred paces away.

Using his hands as a trumpet Corc shouted, 'Quick. Ride. You haven't a moment. The King is dead! Criffan is murdered.'

Before he finished, Nial's horse leaped forward at the touch of his *echlach* and bore down on Corc, who wheeled his own mount and waited for Nial to catch up.

'How?'

Corc paced Nial long enough to give him the facts. Then Nial lashed his horse to full stretch and left Corc behind as he raced for Tara and destiny.

'Mongfin,' Corc had gasped. 'Poison!'

Nial looked at him in disbelief. The King's sister? But the only tension in Corc's face was from the effort of his hard ride. He was in deadly earnest.

'What happened?'

'When we left she stayed . . . remember? I don't know why . . . but the king . . . sent Oscar out too,' Corc gasped. 'Obviously he wasn't . . . afraid of her. But . . . she had wine . . . brought it with her. Poisoned. I suppose . . . she meant to kill Criffan and usurp . . . the throne there and then if he wouldn't make Brian Tanist. There was panic . . . I went after you immediately.'

Nial gave him a look to show how greatly he appreciated that.

'First thing was, Mongfin fell through the door, choking. I was outside with your mother. Then the steward shouted that Criffan was murdered. We rushed in past her; he was dying, sprawled on the floor, a broken bottle beside him. The steward and Mongfin offered wine from the bottle. He accepted. The steward said he pointed out that Oscar was not there to taste. Mongfin laughed, and the King laughed, said his sister wouldn't poison him, said to prove it she could taste the goblet first. And she . . . she did, knowing it was poisoned. Must have been mad. She must have taken only a small sip; it worked on him much quicker, but . . . '

But Nial was gone. Giving his mare her head he touched her with the *echlach* and raced for the city, whence he could already hear the sounds of turmoil. Behind him Corc's voice fell away as he shouted: 'Go, go, go . . . '

Chapter 3

BRITAIN, 389: the Vandal Stilicho, general, ambassador, legate, and nephew-in-law of the Emperor Theodosius, and would-be *magistir militum*, was irritable. His thirtieth birthday and instead of enjoying it in Rome or in the luxury of his own embassy in Constantinople with his wife Serena, where was he? In the most remote province of the western Empire, fortifying this miserable outpost Verulanium in order to protect and defend that decrepit *oppidum*, Londonium, against the combined forces of the barbarian Scots and their Pictish and Saxon allies. (Fortunately, as he knew, the Saxons had their hands full with the Franks just now.) To add injury to insult, forgetting where he was, he'd jumped out of bed this morning in the dark, slipped in the inferior *toral* which was the best in bedside rugs the military headquarters could provide, and had fallen and cracked his hip on his *arca miles*, the chest containing his personal valuables. Cursing, he pulled on two tunics against the cold, smiling in spite of himself while he did so as he remembered what Suetonius wrote two hundred and fifty years earlier about the great Augustus: that, for the same reason, he habitually wore no less than four tunics.

'What's all right for the god Augustus,' he said to himself, 'must be all right for me. But Augustus never came to this benighted corner of the Empire,' he growled aloud.

He rinsed his mouth with water from a goblet, swallowed and then, on the grounds that he was a Vandal first, by birth and upbringing, and a Roman by acquisition, decided that he would breakfast more substantially than on just the mere Roman goblet of water.

'Salthus,' he bellowed.

Instantly his clerk appeared beside one of the pillars of his study-cum-bedroom.

'How do you always manage to do that?' growled Stilicho.

'Do what, lord?'

'Appear whenever I need you. Do you ever miss?'

'No oftener than you, lord.'

Stilicho laughed. He was reputed to be the best bowman in the legions of the west, though privately he doubted if it were true. He was good. No doubt about that. But some of his fellow Vandals, those in the Legio Vandali for example, could give him a run for his money, to say nothing of the Gaulish and German legions of the north. And there were others. The Primi Scotti, for instance. Stilicho's brow darkened when he thought of the Scots and their king, Nial. The invasions and ravages they had made on the province in the past decade - and under his uncle in the previous one. What was his name? Criffan? 'Criffan the Great!' Stilicho snorted. As if, like Constantine, he received the accolade from the Christian Pope of Rome. He took another mouthful of water. That Scot king had plagued the General Theodosius, the emperor's father, just as Nial was affronting him. And the emperor had sent him from the comforts of his Persian embassy to deal with the threat. Not that he minded a bit of action after the enervating life of Constantinople, but this cold, damp British garrison town - and with no more than *one* of the sadly reduced legions and instructions to rely on the local militia, the *limitanei* (he spat the water on the tiled floor in anger) to drive Nial and his Scots back to their own west Britain and Alban colonies! And although Nial and his uncle before him had from time to time broken the Pact of Peace they had made with the Empire, Stilicho was forbidden to engage the Scot at sea or to pursue him west to his homeland, Ierne, sometimes called Scotia from those who lived there or, more properly nowadays, Hibernia.

'You might not return,' he was warned, 'and we cannot afford that risk. Moreover they are themselves useful allies against the Picts at times and have taken the pressure off the Limes Hadrianus. Nor have we any wish to anger them by breaking the Pact ourselves when they may stand as a bulwark in the middle province against the Saxons.' It was a far cry from the great days of the Empire under Trajan and Hadrian and their magnificent legions - the world shook when they stamped - or even Diocletian, Stilicho thought, and his New Army. Where was that army now? Or its grandsons? He shook his head. None of his submissions had persuaded the Consistorium to change its collective mind on that stated piece of tactical folly. 'There are superior stragetic considerations,' he was informed. As a Vandal born and bred, Stilicho could see and feel, almost with his skin, that this policy was ludicrous. And his instinct was backed by reports from his spies. He knew that from the west, Nial, and from the east the Saxons and other Germans would not stop until they carved the Roman province of Britain among themselves. There was one way and one way only to prevent that. Decisive victory now, first over the Scot and then over the Saxon; and strong, permanent, garrisons . . .

He shrugged. Not only was he denied the opportunity, never mind the wherewithal, to win victory, even if he did succeed, permanent garrison troops were out of the question. *Limitanei*! His mouth curled in disgust. There *were* no Roman legions any more, else would he be where he was? He allowed his tabular mind to flicker over the legions now available to the western Empire. They were mainly *foederati*: alien troops made up of fighting men who had sought - what, exactly? Sanctuary was, today, hardly the correct word, where once it might have been. Opportunity? Perhaps. Yes, opportunity within the Empire, to defend it against their own. But opportunity for what? He had little doubt. To exploit the chance as best they could for themselves. Besides the Vandals – of which cultured race he thanked his gods he was one, neither decadent like the Romans he served, nor savage like those he opposed – there were Goths, Scots, Alemanni, Franks, Brettani and others; and in the east there were the Isaurians. Hardly a Roman among them, he thought. May Mithras be praised. What prizes were there for the bold. Stilicho's deep-set eyes gleamed in his dark features. Then narrowed. With a start of surprise at the striking nonsequitur, he reflected how the great rites of Mithraism were about all that bound all these disparate forces of Rome into a body corporate called an army with some kind of allegiance, for there was little else to do so, except the high expectancy and personal rights of being a citizen.

Stilicho was a soldier and no philosopher, but he was hugely ambitious. The thought had already crossed his mind that the vast sums expended in keeping people idle and sapping morale and public spirit, on welfare and public support and the ever-increasing levels of expectancy and right which resulted – 'much more for far less', as one of his angry, dynamic friends put it – was going to lead to ultimate collapse. 'Unless,' he smiled, 'barbarians such as myself can prevent it.' Civilisation was rotting, floundering in liberal and economic confusion. How, he had asked, is it possible to mix an economic system of public welfare and benefaction with a democratic political system? Non posse! Votes were bought and sold. Promises became larger. Corruption consumed the fabric, and the relentless forces of destruction manipulated this situation from outside, and from within – he grinned – to conquer and reap the spoils. He shook his head even as he smiled. He was wandering. The smile that curled the corner of his mouth had a touch of realism. Fatalism too. The Empire was bankrupt. In the circumstances, the defence of Britain was a moral rather than a practical consideration, inspired almost exclusively by the desperate appeals of her citizens for help and the insistence of the emperor and the Pope that Christianity must be preserved against the assaults not only of the pagans, but from the heresies that threatened the centre of the world. Stilicho shrugged again. His allegiance was to Mithras and that was enough for him.

'Bring me food,' he told Salthus, 'and let me see the reports that came during the night.'

Salthus crossed to the table and laid some sheets of parchment, already unrolled and flattened, before him. Stilicho's glance was approving. The man was a reward in himself; he anticipated everything. He would grant him manumission now and slip the gold ring on his finger, but neither of them could yet afford it. Not that it made any difference. The way things were, Salthus was better off with him than as an impoverished freeman. Stilicho sighed slightly. If only his commanders were as prescient as Salthus . . .

'There is something else, lord.'

'What?'

Salthus placed another, smaller and still curling parchment in front of him. It was covered in clear, but unknown, handwriting: small, precise, Greek hexameters. Stilicho picked it up.

'What is it?'

'A poem, lord . . . rather, a fragment. A future poem, I should say!'

'A poem? To me?' Stilicho snorted derisively.

'I think you should hear it.'

'Read it then. Who is it from?'

'Never heard of him. Claudius Claudianus of Alexandria.'

'What does he say?'

Salthus took up the parchment. Like many of his rank Stilicho did not usually bother to read himself and not at all unless it was Latin, and then slowly. There was only one exception to this general rule; he read situation reports assiduously and carried maps in his head as if they were favourite works of art, which was what, indeed, he made of them.

'It is an extract, lord.'

'Read!'

'It is addressed to you, lord. Britannia speaks . . . '

'What did you say his name was?'

'Claudius Claudianus.'

'An Alexandrian? Proceed!'

'Britannia says, "By him - that is you, lord - By him I was protected when the Scot, Nial, moved all Ierne against me and the ocean foamed with their hostile oars . . . " '

'My lord!'

The door crashed open. Stilicho was on his feet. Festus, Pirimpilaris, and two centurions burst in, their battle-worn faces strained and urgent.

'What?'

'The Scots, lord, are west of us . . . '

Stilicho swung back to the table and, gesturing to the reports, snapped at Salthus: 'Bring these. My armour?' Stilicho was striding to the door as he asked.

'Ready, lord.'

The eyes of the three soldiers, who had not, as Stilicho expected, moved to let him pass and then follow, were fixed on him, and something in them stopped him short.

'What?'

'There is more, lord.'

'In the name of Mithras, what? Don't waste time.'

'A great Saxon force has landed behind us at Dubris (Dover) and is marching on Londinium . . . '

At first Stilicho had been alarmed at the news. A new army in his rear was about the worst thing that could befall him at this juncture. If Londinium fell, then he fell with it and all was lost. But a Saxon landing in force? His spies reported that it wasn't possible. Had Festus checked? he wondered. The man said he had, but there was something shifty about him. And he tended to panic. Stilicho took a gamble and, as so often in his career, luck was with him. His own information proved correct. It was not a great Saxon force that had landed, but a small raiding party of not more than one hundred men in two ships. As he had been informed, the Saxons were too heavily engaged with the Franks to mount an assault on Britain just now.

The fact was that the present Saxon force, which had penetrated the river by night, merely presaged those marauding settlers of whom the trembling monk, Gildas, wrote nearly one hundred years later: 'Every colony is levelled to the ground by the stroke of the battering ram. The inhabitants are slaughtered along with the guardians of their churches, priests and people alike, while the sword gleamed on every side and the flames cracked around. How horrible to see in the streets the tops of towers torn from their lofty places, the rubble of high walls, holy altars, mutilated corpses, all covered with darkening blood as if they had all been crushed together in some ghastly wine-press. Some flee, only to be captured and slain in heaps; some, from starvation, surrender to become slaves for ever to the enemy, or to be carried overseas . . . ' What a great irony that Gildas was a Christian descendant - as were many of those whom he described as being dead and enslaved - of the very enemy Stilicho turned to face: the Scots of Ireland, whose kings and colonists were settled between the River Severn and the sea.

Stilicho rapidly scanned his own reports and listened to the accounts of Festus and the other commanders. Then, with that genius and decisiveness which was to carry him to the highest possible level in the contorted Empire, he despatched a force of 250 additional *limitanei* in support of those already facing the Saxons, and with his own legion of 1,000 men and a *vexillum* of cavalry, about another 500, marched against the combined Scots and Picts. Not for nothing did he become known as the 'Protector' under whose patronage the emperor ruled - until Stilicho was felled by an assassin.

Before setting off, Stilicho personally supervised the execution of Festus for dereliction of duty in the face of the enemy and as both a warning and a stimulant to the others. He made the necessary promotions and moved out into the wet morning, his red cloak slapping unpleasantly in the rising wind.

Stilicho ordered his cavalry to make a fast sweep north and scatter the Picts, who ran as the horsemen bore down out of the mist. He himself marched west towards Camulodunum and the Scot. While they were a more formidable foe than the Picts they still lacked the precision of his own regular troops, rather as the standing army of a generation or so ago lacked the precision of the legions of their time. He thanked the gods he wasn't faced with such a force now.

The Scot order of battle was similar to that of the Romans, with one vital difference. On first scouting contact with the enemy, Stilicho formed his troops in line of battle as if he had one of the old legions of up to 6,000 men, using his *limitanei* as *velites*, or light troops, but where Domitian's legions had 10 cohorts each of 300 regular troops and 120 *velites*, plus of course a squadron of 30 horses, Stilicho was forced to reverse and reduce the proportions. His cavalry was further north, scattering the Picts. Nevertheless, although outnumbered, Stilicho was better armed in some ways and this might compensate for inadequate training and discipline. Besides the sword, spear and round shields of the *velites*, his *limitanei* carried a variety of other weapons which, on his personal orders, included a second throwing spear with points so slender that, once thrown, they bent and were useless to the enemy. This extra fire-power provided cover for his heavy troops to move quickly to close quarters with the sword. The heavy troops of *hastati*, *principes* and *triarii* were ordered in depth, similar to the Scot, with the youngest in front and the veterans, the *triarii*, in the rear, behind the *principes*. Stilicho stationed his troops in companies three lines deep and staggered, so that the second division covered the gaps in the first, and the third those in the second. Then he waited for the Scot to attack.

The tremendous fire-power achieved by the light throwing spears of the *velites* did much damage. Although Stilicho suffered many casualties himself in the first encounter, he had the advantage of being able to turn the enemy's darts round and use them in retaliation. After the first shock there was a slight pause while the Scot withdrew to regroup. Stilicho tightened his defences and filled the gaps created by casualties. The second shock was heavier and more prolonged as, without wasting time, the general ordered his swordsmen through the ranks in a quick follow-up to the javelin fire. His second rank immediately marched through the first and engaged the enemy while the first rank fell to the rear and the third moved up to become the second. Now the battle was at its height and concentrated on Stilicho's front and centre.

He glanced at the sun. Any time now. With the extraordinary luck that favoured him in battle all his life, and as if co-ordinated by some unseen and omniscient hand, at that moment there came a shout from his right flank as his cavalry burst into view, bearing down on the Scots' open left. Instantly Stilicho ordered his second rank forward and the third to a flanking attack on the Scots' right, while regrouping those who had been taking the brunt of the fighting in the centre.

When the cavalry burst upon them from the forest, the Scots' left first scattered and then tried to turn to face them, but the Roman cavalry cut through and behind the Scots' front before sweeping west and north, to re-form for another attack. This left the Scots' front and left wing in leaderless confusion. Chieftains could be seen gesticulating as they simultaneously shouted contradictory orders. At this moment Stilicho's left wing charged the Scots' right. It was no overwhelming assault – nor could it have been – but it was enough to draw the enemy's attention to the south and when the cavalry and the rest of Stilicho's troops bore in again, it was in that direction, towards Curetio (Marlborough) and Sulis (Bath), that the Scots began to retreat. And Stilicho knew their ships lay northwards near Deva (Chester) and that to reach them they would want to pass north of Glevum (Gloucester). He hoped to prevent this and pick them off as they straggled up the Severn valley.

But, as the day wore on, the Scot army seemed to melt away in the old campaigning country and the Scot kingdoms in the west, where many of the local troops dispersed. Stilicho fumed and cursed even as he sent small squadrons of cavalry to harry the departing barbarians. If only he had a private army; an army such as Rome fielded one hundred, eighty, years ago. Even a legion, one regular legion! He cursed and kicked the ground with his booted foot.

'Salthus,' he shouted, 'wine! And a woman. Find me a woman!'

Chapter 4

On the morning of the fifth day after the battle, the priest Potitus bent reverently before his small altar in the village church of Bennavem Taburniae. The miraculous moment of compassion and belief, when he would transform the bread and wine into the living body and blood of the Saviour, approached. Making no effort to comprehend the mystery, he offered himself as a totally unworthy agent of the power of the Lord in making the sacrifice. The congregation, standing and kneeling behind him in the little church, was mostly women. The men were already in the fields or at whatever work they did. In any case, he found that church-going was more generally a daily ritual for women whereas, inexplicably, the torments of faith seemed to weigh more heavily on the men. But such thoughts belonged to another time and place and were far from his mind that morning. Outside a hen clucked as it scratched earth, softened a little by the heavy dew and the mist that still clung to these lowland parts even this late in the day.

Potitus's concentration was broken by a disturbance at the door. He swung round. A man stood framed there and even as he saw the figure he recognised the voice of his son, Calpurnius the Decurion - and a deacon of this church, Potitus thought indignantly - raised and shouting.

'Run! Scatter! The Scots. The men . . . to me!'

Without hesitation Potitus raised his right hand: '*In nomine patris, et Filii et Spiritus Sancti . . .* '

By the time he had finished the blessing the church was already nearly empty and those still in it were crowding through the door that Calpurnius held open. A few men stood hesitating outside.

'Where?'

'The other end of the village already . . . '

Potitus could in fact hear the noise, and he hurried, fear rising in him, but not on his own account.

'Sucatus?' asked Calpurnius anxiously.

Potitus felt the fear grab his chest. Only that morning he had forbidden his grandson to accompany him as a punishment for some triviality or other. 'At the farm . . . '

Calpurnius's face tightened. His eyes were suddenly wide and his knuckles went white against the edge of the door.

'I'll get him . . . ' Potitus started forward but his son's hand stopped him. Calpurnius shook his head.

'It's too late!' He tugged his father's arm. 'There's no time.' His voice was hard. His duty was to those he could save. Potitus looked into his son's eyes, and saw the bleakness there, the grimness. Calpurnius saw his father's eyes, pleading and tearful. What could he do? As gently as he could he said: 'It's too late. They are between us and the farms. We must hurry. You men, follow me.'

Even as they left the church on the high ground at one end of the village, smoke began to spiral from a house at the other end. By the time they were down the slope and running for the forest it had thickened and they could hear the crackle of the flaming thatch. By God's grace the Scots were more interested in slaves and booty than pillage, and the remainder of the village was spared, though the miller's house, barns and outhouses were destroyed. He had foolishly tried to defend his family when the Scots first appeared in his compound and, together with his sons, had died for his trouble. Of the miller's family they spared only the old and the very young, taking the healthy and able-bodied with them as slaves. They took slaves from several other families in the village also and plundered whatever valuables they could find. Then they moved on towards the coast like a plague of locusts, leaving Bennavem Taburniae desolated.

Sucatus was discontented. It wasn't his fault that the piglets had burrowed through a weak corner of the wattle fence and made for the woods and the thick hazel-mast on the ground. It particularly wasn't his fault that it took so much time and effort to round them up and catch them, most of which he did himself. His grandfather, Potitus, blamed him nevertheless, and had made him stay on the farm that morning instead of accompanying him to the village to serve Mass. Sucatus supposed he shouldn't feel annoyed at not being allowed to go to Mass: anger was a sin. At the same time, his desire to attend Mass was very strong. It was one of the things he best liked about each day. But then there was the question of obedience. Did the end justify the means? If it did, he should have gone to Mass. That might have calmed his anger. But it would have been disobedient and defiant and it would certainly have angered Potitus. At the same time he was missing Mass . . .

He kicked moodily at a ball of rags. He decided that his grandfather was wrong in forbidding him to go to Mass and that he would be wrong to go. He was pleased with this resolution. The ball sailed up, was caught by a gust of wind that swept through the mist, and landed, muddily, on a clean sheet his grandmother had draped over a bush to air.

'Oh!' groaned Sucatus. And went over to inspect the damage. A long muddy streak ran down the centre of the sheet. 'Oh well,' he thought, 'it would have had to be washed again anyway because of the mist!' He gathered the sheet into a ball and turned towards the farmhouse. At that precise moment one of the servants saw two Scot fighting men coming through the back door and shrieked. Sucatus dropped the sheet and ran towards the house; stopped, knowing something was wrong, and turned to go round the back. Three armed warriors blocked his way. He turned round. Two more. He backed off. One man snapped an order in a foreign tongue and two of them started quickly towards him. Instantly Sucatus turned and ran. He had taken only a few steps when something seemed to explode at the back of his skull and there was only darkness.

He was conscious of light before he opened his eyes, then of voices and then of a pain in his skull, which throbbed with every sound. He opened his eyes and struggled to sit up. The light hurt, causing him to squint, but he could see well enough. He was bound hand and foot, his hands behind his back. He lay in the farmyard, now crowded with whispering people. Some, like himself, were lying trussed on the ground, but most were standing. Above the whispering he could hear loud, guttural shouts and the conversation of confident men in some strange tongue. He guessed what had happened. You couldn't live in West Britain without the constant fear of Scots raiders now that Rome had apparently abandoned them.

Sucatus had just passed his sixteenth birthday. He was a strong stocky youth and had the large head and broad back of one whose ancestors had been workers and warriors for generations. His hair was fair and had been fairer. In time it would grow darker still. His eyes were sometimes blue, sometimes green, changing mood like the ocean; sometimes they were a flat grey, like the cold sea beneath cloud. Even at that age his mouth was severe in repose, though he smiled easily. But he was to be a serious man, not given to humour. As he struggled to sit he bumped against the legs of those nearby.

'Quiet!' hissed a woman's voice. 'You'll bring them on us again with their whips.'

'It's all right,' came a man's voice. 'Do you want to stand?'

Sucatus nodded and the man bent and caught him under the elbows.

Sucatus recognised a neighbouring farmer from a couple of miles away. As the man propped him up Sucatus asked a question with his eyes. 'The Scots! We're captured. We're for the slave market at the Boyne, I shouldn't wonder.'

'No! No . . . ' Sucatus began to struggle. The man hastily clapped a hand over his mouth.

'Shish! It's better than a spear in your belly. Is that what you want?'

Sucatus stared wide-eyed.

His hand still across Sucatus's mouth, the neighbour asked: 'Will you be quiet?' Sucatus nodded. The hand was removed to his shoulder. 'That's better. Keep quiet and you'll be all right. But remember, they'll kill you as soon as look at you if you cause trouble. They haven't time for that. Just stay quiet and do as they say, and you'll be all right.'

'But . . . '

'No buts. Nothing. Just behave.'

Sucatus knew that his father and grandfather were in the village and might get away to safety. But what of his mother and sisters? Frantically Sucatus searched the throng, here, there . . . Gradually, his insistence sank and a better realisation of the position took its place. He looked again at the farmer who was still holding him by the shoulder.

'What will they do . . . ?'

The other shrugged. 'Who knows? Take us with them when they go!'

'And there's nothing we can do?'

The man raised one eyebrow and shook his head.

'But,' Sucatus glanced about, 'there's only ten of them! There are at least sixty or seventy of us. We could . . . '

'What?' hissed the farmer, gripping his shoulder impatiently. 'Don't be stupid. Sixty or seventy women and boys and a few men against fully-armed warriors. If you want blood-letting and murder that's the way to get it. They'd slaughter us all.'

'What then?'

'Sucatus, you are the grandson of the priest, Potitus, aren't you?'

'Yes, of course!'

'And you ask me what to do?' Sucatus said nothing. 'I'll tell you what to do. Do what your grandfather would do. Pray, boy. Pray like hell.'

Soon after that the guards began to move among the prisoners, roughly jostling them, cutting the leg bonds of some and manacling them together with chains taken from a cart that had pulled into the yard. One man, tall and clean-shaven, with dark hair and brown eyes, walked towards Sucatus. Not until he was quite close did Sucatus realise how big he was, standing more than a full head over him. An iron helmet, with a nose-piece projecting to his mouth, made him seem taller. And he was very broad besides. His clothing, although battle-worn, was clean and neat and his armour shone even in the dull light of that morning. In his hand he carried, drawn, a long, leaf-shaped sword. Sucatus thought his last moment had come. He close his eyes and prayed.

'*Pater Noster* . . . ' he began as the man raised the sword. Around him he heard cries and shouts, the one from the people, the other from the soldiers. He was able to distinguish the words '*Moo*' and '*Mooee*' from the latter. (Later he learned they were the singular and plural forms of the word for slave.)

Nothing happened except a slight tug at his ankles. He opened his eyes. The warrior stood in front of him pointing, and roaring with laughter at his distress. Angrily, yet sheepishly, Sucatus looked down. The ropes that had bound his ankles lay, severed, on his shoes. Still laughing, the warrior turned away as another came and shackled him to the farmer. The prisoners were separated into groups of men, women and children, and they were marched quickly to the west in that order.

Because of the drizzle Sucatus saw the sea before the smell of it reached him. They turned north along the coast until nightfall, by which time they had been joined by other bands so that they numbered several hundred when they stopped. They bivouacked in the open, lighting fires against the cold and drizzle. They were given nothing to eat. By morning they were cold, stiff and wet, in great misery, and it was only with much shouting and cursing and many blows that the dispirited and groaning captives were forced to resume the journey. After some hours they saw with a collective shock the first of the ships that clustered like black sea slugs along the shoreline for three or four miles. In the distance they could see lines of people streaming across the sands and grass like ants. Some of these were columns of guarded captives, like their own, plodding towards whatever awaited them at the other end of the sea journey those black ships would shortly make. Sucatus saw that a majority of the captives were, like himself, young people, and of both sexes. Able-bodied men were few and many of those were bandaged where they had been wounded during capture. Sucatus calculated there were perhaps two thousand prisoners and what seemed like four or five thousand warriors darkening the white sands.

The ships were much larger than anything he had expected and far bigger than the one in which he had gone to Gaul in the previous year to visit his mother's relatives. Above them seagulls swooped screaming and fighting for the offal and detritus being thrown overboard as the army returned. Some of the ships were planked and decked, with fixed masts and high sterns and stems, capable of carrying two or three hundred people with ease. Some were smaller, of hides and frames, but were still large enough to carry up to fifty men. At least seventy ships lay at the water's edge, and Sucatus guessed there might be other beaches like this further north.

From his companions on the march he had heard of the battle between Nial and Stilicho, and that Stilicho had been victorious but had not conquered. Nial and his army had turned south, then north again and west to where the fleet lay beached, raiding for slaves and booty as they went.

'So much for Stilicho,' said Sucatus. 'Here we are - and no doubt he'll claim a great victory!'

'No doubt,' said his companion. 'That is war. Those who have nothing to do with it suffer most!'

They were driven across the springy, cliff-top turf that seemed to stretch for ever, then down by a narrow path to the sandy floor of the beach beneath low overhanging cliffs of mud. They were divided into groups and prodded and hustled towards the boats. Sucatus was one of a group of young people, perhaps one hundred all told. Together with two other groups of similar size they were harried towards a cluster of ten boats, their sterns just beginning to be lapped by the incoming tide.

A strong, sturdy man of about sixty with curly grey hair, his stomach still flat in spite of his years, stood in front of the boats eyeing the prisoners as they came towards him. He wore a grey-green short cloak and an air of confident authority. Before they reached him he turned away and barked orders to someone on board one of the boats.

It was some time before they sailed and they were fed while they waited. They had had nothing except water in the past twenty-four hours. Now they were given oat cakes and stirabout, ladled from a great pot – one for each ship, he learned – that hung over smouldering fires on the beach. The stirabout was lukewarm and was ladled into any container they could find, or into their hands direct if they found none. The oat cakes were rock-hard and had to be pounded with stones and mixed with water to make them edible. But it was food, and most of the prisoners gulped it down greedily.

At last they were ordered to the ships and, in a mixture of Irish, Latin and British (which many of the Scots spoke casually if not correctly) they were told to push the ships into deeper water. Then prisoners and soldiers clambered on board and the ships turned westward to the accompaniment of brazen notes from huge, curved trumpets and the rhythmic thudding of drums. The men's voices took up the rhythm in song, and as they cleared the bay under oars, which many of the prisoners were forced to man, their drums and trumpets were answered from many more ships swarming over the surface of the glassy sea. Later they raised sail as an offshore breeze swept up the channel, carrying them before it north-west to the Boyne and the slave market.

In all that had happened, one incident, itself trivial, for some reason lodged in Sucatus's mind as a bizarre symbol of so much that was shattering and terrible. It occurred while they waited to board, having eaten and drunk from the water-pitchers handed round. He was sitting on the outskirts of his manacled group, while the others huddled together in a sodden, steaming cluster seeking imaginary shelter. The man he had noticed earlier strutted up and started to talk with one of those who, leaning on a spear, was nominally guarding the prisoners – although it was now clear that there was no escape unless a miracle occurred. Sucatus did not understand their conversation, but their gestures and actions were clear enough and he guessed that the older man was asking the younger about the campaign and the battle, and the other was telling him with much gesturing and laughter. They both laughed a lot. Sucatus could not see what there was to laugh at in what could be nothing but a tale of woe and destruction for many innocent people. He was fascinated by the two men. The young one bent and drew in the sand with the bronze butt of his spear, the older one leaning over and watching intently. Now they were serious. The young one looked up, over his shoulder, as he drew, and the old one nodded in understanding. Then they both straightened and the older man laughed again and clapped the young one on the shoulder.

'And what did you bring me out of it all, Colman?' asked Fergus. 'Have you nothing for a poor beached old warrior who saved your miserable hide more than once when we stood together and who taught you all you know?'

Colman laughed. 'Poor and old, is it? I pity the man comes against you yet. Indeed and I did not forget you, Fergus,' he said, unwinding a knotted scarf at his waist. 'Look at this.'

He took something from the scarf and threw it in the air, where, in spite of the dullness of the day, it glittered before falling towards the outstretched hand of Fergus, who caught it neatly.

'Well,' he said, looking it over and holding it up the better to see, 'that's some brooch. For me?' He looked at Colman, one eyebrow raised.

Colman laughed and, in his turn, clapped Fergus on the shoulder. 'For you, old warhorse. 'Tis the least I owe you. Bring us a flagon now, and we'll call it quits.'

Fergus laughed in reply and fixed the new brooch in his cloak beside the small bronze pin that held it at the left shoulder. He looked down in admiration for a moment, smiled at Colman and went off to get a flagon. Although Sucatus did not understand this exchange, the meaning was clear enough and he was struck by the beauty of the gold annular brooch with a pin head shaped like a dog, and rubies for eyes. To him it seemed to symbolise both the terror of those from whom it had been taken - some unfortunate man, perhaps, spitted defending his family or wife on whom his bloody corpse had fallen - and the haughty rapacity of those who took it. Sucatus turned away from the sight of those victorious warriors swaggering about the beach and their ships, but only to see the huddled misery of the prisoners in the drizzle.

'At least,' he thought, 'we are alive, *Deo gratias*.'

After a smooth journey through a sea that remained untroubled all the rest of that day, throughout the night and for most of the following day - an event so unusual that it was the cause of comment among their captors - they reached the wide mouth of a broad river. The mist and drizzle cleared during the night and as they sailed north and west Sucatus had seen, at first in the distance and then closer to, the mountains of Ireland begin to gleam as the fingers of dawn passed high above his head and touched their peaks. The purple tips slipped behind and gave way to hills, themselves descending to what must have been a great plain, for he could see nothing beyond a low coastline. There was a large bay at the foot of these hills. Its northern side was formed by a long spit of land stretching out from the plain behind and suddenly rearing into a solitary, high rocky bastion that formed a powerful headland. They rounded it and the two islands beyond, and made way steadily until they reached the river mouth. As they passed the headland trumpets blared from the ships and an answer echoed from the headland.

'Ben Eadir,' nodded one of their captors, 'Howth.' Sucatus later discovered that it was one of several continuously manned look-out posts along the east coast, from where the sea as far north as the mountains of Mourne and as far south as Bray Head and the mountains of Wicklow could be scanned.

When they reached the Boyne the ships berthed at a wooden quay and the prisoners were herded ashore along planks and taken to the slave market at Brugh where they would be sold, singly or in batches, to chieftains and prosperous freemen who might either keep them for themselves or re-sell them inland for profit. Most of the warriors disdained the use of the planks and leaped from the ship to the quay where they were greeted by a substantial throng who had gathered to watch the fun. The crowd was mostly women, colourfully dressed and, like practically any other crowd of its kind at any other time, loud, laughing, jeering and ribald, with the occasional truculent individual or edge to it. As Sucatus stepped off one of the planks and turned left to follow the others, a figure leaped from the side of the ship to the quay. But he misjudged the distance and landed badly on one leg so that instead of going forward to a secure footing, his ankle turned and he teetered backwards towards the space between the ship and the quay, in which he could be crushed. Without thinking, Sucatus's strong arm flashed out and grabbed a fistful of the warrior's clothing, stopping his fall. Sucatus steadied him and helped him forward to safety. Then he saw it was the elderly man who had received the brooch. Fergus looked at him and for a moment their eyes met. Brushing aside the youth's arm he stalked off without a word.

'The bastard,' whispered a voice in Sucatus's ear, 'you should have let him fall.'

'Move!' came the order, followed by a thump from a spear shaft.

The sales took a long time. They were held in the open, each ship selling for itself in a large area behind the quays, and the crowds moved among them, watching in amusement. Only the buyers and sellers were serious and indifferent to the captives' tears, pleading and wretchedness all of which entertained the crowds, especially when a prisoner tried to take his or her grief and fury out on the unsympathetic captors. This was the excitement that added spice to the spectacle.

Sucatus was eventually sold, after some haggling, to a petty chief - Mweelcu - for two handsome bronze cauldrons, each fit to be presented to a king. There were murmurs of surprise when the price went so high, but Mweelcu was determined to have the young man and seemed satisfied. The soldiers too were content. The cauldrons would sell for a great deal. Sucatus was taken north by cart, with some other slaves, to Mweelcu's territory at the foot of Slieve Mish.

Chapter 5

WITH a start Fergus opened his eyes and recollected himself. Leaning back as far as he was able he stretched his arms above his head and yawned. Then he stood, placed his hands on his hips and thrust his shoulders back and his belly out.

'Oh-oh-oh,' he groaned as some of the stiffness left him. More relaxed in body, if not in mind, he clambered on deck again to see if there was any sign of his crew. Nothing, except a man, or it might have been a woman for he couldn't tell at that distance, walking a horse laden with panniers towards the beach to collect sand or seaweed. There was more light and a little more colour now, but the day was still drab and cold. The water was noticeably closer than when he last looked. He cursed and began to fuss at preparations for loading, most of which had been done already. He ran additional planks to the pier so the dogs could be boarded easily – his cargo was wolf-hounds and wool – and checked the bulkhead between the dogs' compound and the space for the wool in the forward part of the ship. Finally he went ashore and walked, slowly, in the direction of the settlement, avoiding the figure with the horse who seemed just as content to avoid him. Fergus tried to appear casual. He didn't want to seem anxious in case the crew appeared. But he was fuming inside. Not because he thought that they'd let him down when the time came, but because he was there and they were not.

'Typical!' he thought. 'What else can you expect from these

young people?' His irritation was not really with his two-man crew, aged thirty-five and twenty-seven, but with his son Aidan and, indeed, himself.

He was generally disgruntled. Partly it was because he resented what age had done to him, pushing him out of the centre of things, the action, to the quiet backwaters of life. But like an old warhorse put out to grass he couldn't savour its sweetness for want of the flavour of smoke and battle. But there was more than that gnawing at his vitals. Something he could not articulate, but could sense; a sickness in the land. He found it expressed in an attitude – in many attitudes, especially among young people – that he could not understand: a dissatisfaction, unease and restlessness; a rejection of established ways of doing things, merely, it seemed to him, for the sake of rejection, without replacing them with any other order. And to make matters worse the young people seemed to think the fault lay with him and his generation, which made no sense at all. 'There's no respect?' he fumed. 'No values any more.' And yet . . . it wasn't that simple. If values and respect were diminished, who was responsible?

'Druids,' he muttered, 'and those Christians.' He scowled in the direction of the settlement, debated with himself whether to go there or not, and finally turned back. He saw his ship in the distance, a little canted to one side, dark and solid, as if permanently settled on the sand. He watched the creeping tide, each wave receding in a curve, only for the next to sweep nearer. He imagined his ship afloat; how graceful she was then, riding the water like a bird, proud in her element, not lying, inert and black, sideways upon the sands, as now.

'Like me,' he thought.

As he returned, confused thoughts about the country and what had happened in it since Criffan's death sixteen years before troubled him. He shook his head. His thoughts were not very profound, but insofar as they were those of an active and percipient man shaken by events outside himself as much as by those that were personal, they had validity. 'I don't know,' he said aloud as if someone were listening. 'I don't know at all.'

It surprised him that he was disturbed more by the reactions of others than by his own reactions. He was a warrior, had been a soldier all his life, accustomed to having others do much of his thinking for him. He knew and accepted that times change. But what had happened in the last twenty years seemed to go much deeper than that. Some sort of collective unrest had afflicted the people like a plague, a pestilence of the body, only this was of the mind and ideas. Could there be poisonous ideas, he wondered, as there were poisonous foods and substances? He thought of Aidan, and sucked his lips in perplexity.

Aidan was typical. Given every opportunity to grow up in reasonable content, he was a rebel through and through. He challenged every established idea and dismissed or rejected things merely because they were established. 'That can't be right,' thought Fergus. When Aidan said the druids had too much power, Fergus was inclined to agree. But he also said that the king was wrong. How could that be? He himself had supported and aided Nial as he expanded his authority into Britain, into Caledonia where the Scots were already well established and paying tribute, even into Gaul . . .

'Yes,' said Aidan, 'no better than the barbarian Goths and Vandals with neither king nor nation. Is that what we are coming to be? Barbarians without learning?'

'But it's conquest,' protested the uncomprehending Fergus.

'It's barbaric,' said Aidan, 'snapping the heels of fallen Rome like mongrel foxes, when we should be replacing the learning that is dying with them in the west.'

'I'll never understand you, boy,' said Fergus angrily, 'you don't know when you're well off.'

'There's no sense in it,' said Aidan. 'Just what is Nial doing, wasting the lives of our best men on long and expensive war excursions all over the world?'

'Bringing back slaves and booty, winning territories . . . '

'Slaves and booty!'

'Yes!'

'Winning territories!'

'Yes. Don't annoy me, Aidan.'

'I'm sorry, father. I don't mean to annoy you. But tell me this. What does he leave behind? Lives, father. How long can that go on? How long can we depend for our survival on wars and slaves and booty? Is that what life is about? If that is all, then our ancestors – including Cormac who devoted his life to learning – were wrong. What use are conquered territories that we cannot hold for more than a few years? If these were the days of Cormac, if we had the Fianna itself, and the country was united, and there was the vision of Cormac behind it, then perhaps we might have something to offer besides the sword, but now . . . '

'Don't talk to me about it, boy, I don't want to hear . . . '

'That's exactly the problem, father. No one wants to hear. No one will stand up and face Nial and say look at what you are destroying . . . '

'Don't talk nonsense.'

'It's not nonsense, father. What has been happening here while Nial is abroad "conquering"? You know as well as I do. The nobles fight among themselves. Connacht against Ulster, Munster against Leinster; all against the King, if the truth were known. And the power of the druids strengthening because of it all. It suits them well. Crom Cruach is worshipped again, as you know, and the schools of learning are neglected. What future is there for young people? What do they hope for? Let me tell you, father, they see only wars and destruction and the tyranny of the druids, and they have a right to more than that, according to the traditions you are so proud of.'

'The glory . . . '

'Don't, father. Nial is burying the good of the past as well as the present to suit his own vanity.'

That fiery speech from his son troubled Fergus. He had served

Nial well, none better, without question or thought of what they were doing. Now Aidan touched a truth buried within himself. In spite of what he might say to Aidan, he saw clearly enough that Nial - of the Nine Hostages, as he was called, because he held hostages from the five provinces of Ireland as well as from Gaul, Britain, Scotland and Saxonia - while successful in war, did nothing towards securing peace and prosperity at home, as had the great Cormac. People did not thrive and prosper on war, or glory. Their whole tradition was based on law and justice and honour. Their wars in the past had been different. Those had a purpose which was to create a peaceful and stable climate in which to prosper in mind and body. Every child knew that. But Aidan was right, Nial's wars were different. To begin with they were extra-territorial, and their purpose - at least beyond West Britain and Caledonia - was neither colonisation nor civilisation. It was, as none knew better than he, simply plunder. Pure, unadulterated barbarism. It upset him to think about it like that, but now that Aidan had started it he couldn't stop himself. Scavenging the corpse of the Empire like the barbarians of Europe. What good was that for their people?

He was conscious of the part he himself had played. He had seen the effects of Roman civilisation on Britain and Gaul, on the dignity of a peaceful life, where the tranquillity of the homesteads matched the best at home. He recalled the clear and abundant evidence of a better way of life, the astonishing luxury of the great villas and towns that he and his companions shattered and put to the sword. What he did hadn't troubled him then. But it did now. The truth in what Aidan said was connected with the sickness of the soul that he sensed all around him. He knew that Aidan's attitude, which he found so hard to accept, was also connected with it, just as he knew that everything that Aidan said wasn't all right. But, more and more, Fergus understood that his reasons for saying it were right.

It was true that the country was not what it once had been.

The king was all-powerful, but there was no stable authority; no sense of peace, of achievement. No tranquillity, no confidence in the future. Instead, the tyranny of the druids matched the ambition of the king, who sought to win the allegiance of the people with his triumphs and the spoils of war rather than with the achievements of peace and prosperity - with death instead of life, Fergus thought.

His feet had carried him most of the way back to his ship and he stepped onto the corduroy road with a firm tread, surprising a small group of curlew who were grazing at the grassy bank. As one they took wing, the soulful double note of their call bleating far out over the reaching tide as they rose and swiftly fled. The incident reminded him of a meeting with an unusual man, one of his first passengers many years ago when he was still a young man and not a trader. He was to pick up this passenger by the order of Criffan and take him to Britain. His ship was late in reaching the appointed place and when it did there was no one to see. The tide was against him and he anchored, coming ashore in a small boat, disturbing just such a flight of curlew as he landed.

His unusual passenger eventually turned up with a large bale on a packhorse driven by a gilly. He was a stern man with a perpetual look of disapproval and his name was Aethius. At their first meeting, although he was brusque to the point of rudeness, some quality about him so fascinated Fergus that he completely ignored an attitude that, in another man, would have led to blows or worse. Aethius 'of Istria', the man said with emphasis - a peninsula, Fergus discovered, somewhere beyond Italy. He had come from Spain to study the libraries and books of Ireland and collect some for the great new library of Alexandria, since destroyed again. Surprisingly, after their first encounter, he and Fergus got on together very well.

Aethius was tall and thin, aged about forty at that time, more than forty years ago. He and Fergus were dissimilar in every way, but Aethius made a great impression on the young warrior in spite of his obvious eccentricities. The cold, sardonic, learned magus was much given to intellectual puzzles which he understood and which made others look inferior and thus fed Aethius's contempt for mankind – except himself – in general. He was also hard to please and very censorious. But he formed an unexpected bond with Fergus even though they were together no more than two days. It may be that in some way, without need of explanation, each perceived that the other was master of his trade (in spite of any shortcomings or imperfections) and that there was no need for pretence.

On the way to Britain Aethius mentioned to Fergus that he had stayed in Ireland longer than he originally intended as he had found considerably more material there than expected and had spent several weeks travelling from one city to another examining books and archives. He used a Greek phrase when speaking of these volumes and the men who compiled them, '*ideo histas*', that is 'uncultivated teachers', and went on, in his condescending manner, to say (in Latin) how impressed he was by the 'volumina' of the Irish.

Fergus felt sad remembering this; more and more, he experienced sadness when thinking of things past. A sudden irritation thickened his blood. For the life of him he couldn't understand what the country was coming to, or why.

A hail from behind checked his thoughts. He turned and saw his two-man crew running towards him.

'What took you so long?' he enquired as they came up, looking at their dishevelled and grinning faces. 'Or need I ask?'

'No need.'

'Drink and women,' he said with what genuine disgust he could muster.

'Huh,' said the older, Eoghan by name, 'you sound like one of the Christian priests beyond.'

'Pity you don't pay more attention to them, then,' snapped Fergus.

'Well, I'm glad the Christian young ones don't pay that much attention to them,' laughed Con. Fergus grunted and together they walked to the ship, arguing amiably.

'Any sign of Aidan?' asked Fergus.

'Isn't he with you?'

'If he was with me, would I be asking where he is?' growled Fergus.

'He could be any place so,' said Con.

'The mother take him,' snapped Fergus, quickly making the protective sign just in case the mother might have heard him. 'Where did he get to?'

'Went off with some fellow, last night. I thought they were like ourselves, drinking and who . . . '

'Aidan doesn't do that,' snorted Fergus. The other two looked at each other, wondering whether to laugh or not. They well knew how Fergus had spent his night. Hadn't they given the doxy the flagon of wine to bring to the boat with the money he gave them? But Con said nothing.

'No,' said Eoghan. Fergus grunted.

'But where is he?'

'He'll be here before the tide and not a bother on him,' said Eoghan.

'When what's to be done is done. Well, come on. Standing here won't get us loaded.'

They had barely reached the end of the pier when several carts trundled round the bend and on to the corduroy road. They heard the rumble of the wheels, and the sudden barking of the startled hounds. Two hours later a faint suggestion of warmth had dissipated the pallor of the day somewhat, much of the frost had thawed, and the ship was loaded with her cargo. The incoming tide lapped purposefully about her keel and lower timbers. At any moment the men expected to feel the tilted deck move beneath their feet as the ship began to float. The wool was stored forward and the huge, hungry, vicious and frightened dogs had been carefully brought on board, one at a time between two men, and tethered in the pen, where they immediately set up a continuous barking and howling.

'Feed the brutes,' Fergus snapped and one of the handlers shouted to a companion to help him. They brought offal in stinking cloths and tossed it to the dogs which began to growl and tear at the bundles.

'Give them plenty water,' said the handler. 'There's herbs in that'll keep 'em quiet for a while, but they'll be fierce thirsty. Plenty more food for 'em here!' He and his companion brought a pole from the cart from which animal heads, hare, and other items were suspended. 'This'll do 'em until you get to Gaul.'

Fergus paid them little attention. With one eye on the tide he glared towards the settlement for a sign of Aidan.

At last two figures - one of whom was Aidan - sauntered round the bend and came casually on. Fergus turned his back and waited.

''Lo father. All ready?'

'No thanks to you. What kept you?'

'Sorry. Didn't think you'd mind. Knew there was nothing much to load. Look, can we give my friend a passage? To Gaul.'

Fergus turned to the other man. He saw a broad-shouldered, broad-featured man in his early twenties with short, light brown hair. He was not tall and stood with his feet apart as if he grew from the ground. He wore simple clothing of the cheapest kind. But his eyes were dominant, strange; grey at the moment, they gave the impression of depth and changeability, like the sky even on a dull day.

'Who is he?'

'Sucatus, father. A friend of mine - a Christian . . . '

'Roman?'

The other nodded. Aidan looked from his father to his friend, smiling and anxious, and back.

'Where from?'

'Bri-tain . . . orig-inally.' He spoke with the slight accent that he was never to lose.

'And you want to go to Gaul?'

'Yes.'

'Hmm,' Fergus mused, looking the young man over. There was something wrong here. 'You're young. What are you doing here? How long is it since you saw your family?'

Sucatus didn't answer. He had recognised Fergus immediately from his brooch, and would have known him even without it. He was surprised and yet not startled, and preferred not to let the recognition show, only saying inwardly, 'Into thy hand I commit my spirit; thou hast redeemed me O Lord, faithful God.'

Fergus obviously did not know him. 'Have you any money?'

Sucatus shook his head.

'Anything to pay your fare with?'

Again Sucatus shook his head.

'He could look after the dogs. He's good with dogs, aren't you, Sucatus?'

Sucatus again said nothing; exchanged looks with Fergus.

'A slave, aren't you? Runaway.'

'Father, he needs help . . .'

'Well, he won't get it from me. Or you! I thought you had more sense. Helping a runaway slave. Don't you know the trouble that could get us into?'

'That's not the point . . . '

'That *is* the point, and you'd better not forget it either on my ship.'

'But he's not even from around here. He's from the north. He travelled for six days until yesterday he reached the Christian settlement beyond.'

'He's a Christian. Let them help him. We have our own problems.'

'But, father, what'll happen if he's left here?'

'I don't know what'll happen if he's left here and I don't care. I want no more of it. I won't take him and that's it.'

'He's my friend . . . '

'Friend? You only met him last night. Where were ye last night anyway? With women, I suppose, drinking.'

Neither Aidan nor Sucatus answered him and Fergus knew his accusation was unjust. He glared at them.

'You're wasting time talking. He's not going.' Fergus turned away.

'Then neither am I.'

The instant response that sprang to Fergus's lips was 'Suit yourself'. But he checked it. He turned and looked squarely at his son. Then transferred his gaze to the man beside him.

Something in the way that Aidan spoke rather than what he said made Fergus hesitate. He realised that this was not mere petulance or momentary anger. Aidan meant it. He studied this man who, in so short a time, had managed so greatly to influence his only son. Sucatus looked levelly back with his deep, grey eyes. Fergus found his look vaguely disturbing, but before he discovered the reason Sucatus turned to his son.

'No, Aidan. Thank you, but there is no reason for you to stay. If I do not go with you I will get to Gaul some other way. You must not allow me to come between you and your father. Go with him. I will be all right.'

'But, Sucatus, I . . . '

'There is not point in staying. I will go soon anyway.'

'After all we talked about and said . . . '

Fergus's eyes narrowed. 'What was that?'

Aidan turned to him, his face serious. 'I don't know how you're going to take this, father, but whether I go with you now or not, I intend to become a Christian.'

For a moment Fergus looked at him in perplexity. Then he threw back his head and laughed.

'A Christian, is it?' he exclaimed. He turned to Sucatus, still laughing. 'I suppose this is your doing?' Then back to Aidan. 'From the way you said it I thought it was going to be something serious. Well, you can be anything you like, son, as far as I'm concerned, so long as there's some bit of sense to it, and I suppose being a Christian is as good as following Lugh, or Mithras or, or – what is it that fellow in Cork is who's trying to steal our trade?'

'A Jew.'

'Yes. A Jew. Be a Christian, what's the difference? Everyone has notions at your age.'

'And what about Sucatus? He can come?'

'No!'

Sucatus smiled and put his hand on Aidan's arm. 'It's all right, Aidan. Leave it. You go with your father.' He looked at Fergus and nodded.

'I appreciate what you say,' said Fergus. Then with an excusing wave of his hand added: 'You appreciate my position? An escaped slave . . . ' He shrugged.

Sucatus nodded. 'I understand, Fergus.'

Something in his level gaze, about his general demeanour, again troubled Fergus. As if he saw it, Aidan broke in.

'He's good with wolf-hounds, father. He could keep them quiet.'

For a second Fergus felt like giving in. Then he shook his head. 'No. It's too risky. Sorry.' He turned away. 'Time to go, Aidan, the tide has turned.' And they could clearly see the swirling and eddies on the surface indicating that this was so. The ship now floated free, tethered to the pier by mooring ropes, ready to swim on the surface and ride the waves.

Aidan looked at Sucatus. 'I wish . . . '

'I'll be all right,' said Sucatus.

'Take care of yourself.'

'You too.' They clasped one another for a moment and then Aidan turned and jumped for the rail of the ship. He landed awkwardly and slipped backwards, but his father, standing just in front of him, turned as he cried out, shot out a hand to grab a fistful of his clothing and pulled him to safety.

'Careful,' he said, pulling Aidan to the deck. As he did so his eyes lifted beyond his son and found those of Sucatus. Instantly

Fergus remembered. He stood for a moment, his fingers still locked in his son's shirt, looking at the young man on the pier as the ship began to move out, pushed by a strong leg at the bow. Hardly realising what he was doing, over the shoulder of his son he jerked his head at Sucatus, who responded instantly and leaped for the deck where he landed lightly. Fergus released his hold on his son's shirt and turned away. Aidan turned towards Sucatus, beaming.

'I told you it would be all right,' he said. '*Deo gratias*,' smiled Sucatus, and they went and sat in the lee of the stern rail as the ship slipped down with the tide and the brown sail rose, creaking, on the mast, with little wind to fill it.

That night, when they had eaten and a lantern had been fixed to the swaying masthead, three of them were in the cabin. Con was asleep. Fergus and Eoghan were on deck, steering and keeping watch.

'Sucatus,' whispered Aidan.

'Yes?'

'You were a slave for six years?'

'That's right.'

'Herding on Slieve Mish for some chief.'

'Mweelcu. Yes.'

'Why did you decide all of a sudden to escape?'

Sucatus laughed. 'I didn't decide all of a sudden. I always intended to escape. But I had to wait . . . ' he paused.

'For what?'

'Well . . . you'll think this very strange. Perhaps romantic . . . '

'What?'

'I had to wait until God told me it was time to go.'

'You mean the Christian God?'

'Aidan,' asked Sucatus gently, 'have you forgotten so soon what I told you last night? There is only one God.'

'Yes, yes, I know. You mean he came and told you when to escape?'

Aidan heard Sucatus chuckle. 'Not exactly, no! But one day I knew that he wanted me to go. I knew the direction to go, and I knew I'd find a ship to take me to Gaul when I got there.'

'You *knew*?'

'I knew.'

'You left Slieve Mish and went nearly two hundred miles in six days without knowing the country and you *knew* there would be a ship going to Gaul?'

'Am I not here?'

'Yes, but . . . How could you know?'

'Did I not meet you?'

Aidan didn't reply. A moment later he asked another question. 'But what actually *made* you? I mean, there must have been *something*. And Gaul! Why Gaul? I thought your people came from Britain.'

'Hmmm. Wa-al, I tell you,' came the deep slow, accented voice. 'What you say is true. Something did happen. I learned something. I learned three things.'

'What? What did you learn?' Aidan could sense the other smile.

'First, I learned to talk to God. There on the mountains, every day for six years, summer and winter, springtime and autumn. Every day I spoke to God, in the snow and in the sunshine. And then, one day, God spoke to me. Like I told you.'

'What else did you learn?' Aidan felt cheated and couldn't keep disappointment from his voice. He expected more than an account of his friend's spiritual experiences, profound though they may have been; moreover, he suspected that Sucatus was teasing him saying these things, knowing what he wanted to hear.

'Wa-al,' Sucatus drew the word out, 'I also learned that my family had left Britain and gone back to Gaul, which is a good reason for wanting to go to Gaul instead of Britain.' Aidan laughed.

'Will you be able to find them?'

'Oh yes. I will go to my uncle. He will know. He is bishop at Tours . . . '

'A bishop!'

'Yes. You didn't know I was so well connected, did you? And also . . . I will tell you a story. A thing that happened that lit a fire inside me that would not go out when I heard about it.'

'Yes.'

'Did you know that, in the last year, the Emperor Theodosius had the great idol of Jupiter Serapis at Alexandria overthrown and destroyed. Can you imagine? After hundreds, perhaps thousands of years' idolatry . . . one great gesture, and the idol topples in the dust by the hand of a Christian prince in the greatest city in the world. Well, not by his hand, but one of his soldiers.'

'I thought Rome was the greatest city in the world.'

'Rome? No! Alexandria, the capital of Egypt. There is the greatest city of the world, where darkness and light battled recently, and light was victorious.'

'How? I mean what happened? Do you know?'

'In Egypt there is a mighty river, the Nile . . . '

'Like the Shannon?'

'A hundred, a thousand, Shannons. Each year it floods, inundates and makes fertile the desert.'

'So does the Shannon.'

'It is not the same. If the Nile did not flood all Egypt would starve, utterly. This flooding happens each year as it has since the world began and the Eygptians believed it was caused by Jupiter Serapis, so they built a huge temple at Alexandria in his honour.'

'Like . . . '

'Like nothing you or I have ever seen. A hundred steps, I was told, led up to it, and it was surrounded by many courtyards and colonnaded sanctuaries. In the centre of all sat the great statue of Jupiter Serapis, distinguished from the Roman Jupiter by the basket on his head and by the three-headed, three-tailed monster carried in its right hand. Wa-al, the Bishop Theophilus of Alexandria destroyed the temple after the pagans barricaded it against the Christians, killing and torturing many whom they had captured. When the Roman Christian victors came to the statue all were afraid to touch it because of the superstition that if anyone dared violate it the Nile would cease to flood and heaven and earth would instantly return to original chaos. Even though they were Christian they were afraid. Then one brave soldier of Rome, carrying a battle-axe, climbed a ladder while the silent crowds watched from below. He climbed until he reached the shoulder of the idol. Standing there he looked down at the fearful crowd. Then, strong in his faith, he spat on his hands and swung the great axe against the idol's cheek. It fell. There was no retribution from the heavens. The soldier struck again and more idol fell. Now the crowd cheered him and the great idol was broken to pieces and dragged through the streets of the city.'

Sucatus paused. His account was as vivid as if he had been there himself.

'And then?' asked Aidan.

'Then? Then, it happened! The Nile did not flood at its accustomed time and the people were terrified. But suddenly it rose to an even greater level than usual and flooded a greater area ensuring more fertility than ever for the year.'

'Who told you all this?'

For a moment there was no reply. Then Sucatus said: 'Would you believe me if I told you it was the very soldier who struck that first blow? So grateful is the Empire today to its faithful servants that he was shortly after sent to Britain and left behind when the last troopship departed. To save himself, for the remaining Romans were hunted down like hares by the Saxons, he escaped to Ireland like many more and I met him by chance with a troop of Nial's in the mountains where we were both glad to speak Latin again.'

'What will you do when you get to Gaul.'

'Find my family. Visit my uncle . . . '

'The bishop?'

'Yes. I have heard of men I would like to meet. One a priest in

Hippo, in Africa, called Aurelius Augustinus that I heard of, and others.'

'But what will you do, Sucatus?'

'Do?' Sucatus sounded surprised. 'But I thought you knew. I am driven . . . the fire, I told you. I shall, with God's help, be one of his priests.'

'And me? What about me?'

'You, Aidan?' said Sucatus gently. 'You must do what your conscience tells you. You say you want to be a Christian. It is a first step and may God bless the road you take.'

'And will we ever see each other again?'

Again Aidan could almost see Sucatus's smile. The quiet smile of a strong man who knew who he was and where he was going.

'Who knows? Perhaps we will try to keep in touch?'

'Do you think that you will ever come back to Ireland again?'

'Ireland?' Sucatus's voice grew suddenly hard. 'What has Ireland done for me that I should ever go there again? Broken up my family, destroyed my home, made me a slave for six years! I should be anxious to return to the people who did these things? I mean no offence and nothing personal, Aidan, but no. I doubt if I will come back to Ireland,' said Sucatus, who, before he eventually returned some thirty-seven years later was to become the priest Patricius, or Patrick.

Chapter 6

ITALIA 432: A film of snow decorated Rome, and the city on hills astraddle the muddy Tiber, gleamed under a blue sky. From the window of his study, Celestine surveyed all of which he was bishop and successor to Peter. He stood with his hands clasped behind his back, a tall, ascetic-looking man over sixty. He had been Pope for ten of the most troublesome years since, twenty years before his birth, Julian the Apostate reigned for three terrible years during which he tried to supplant the Church of Christ with the bloody paganism of the Mithraic bull. The Empire was attacked on all its borders, as well as from within, and reduced by warring hordes; the Church was even now assailed by the obscene Mithraic paganism of Julian and the revival of Egyptian belief at the *serapeum* in Alexandria. Christian belief was besieged by one powerful heresy after another: Arianism teaching that the Christ was inferior to the Father; the Manichean heresy claiming that all things 'human and divine' were capable of resolution; the Donatists; and, most subtle and insidious of all, the Pelagians. Celestine's mouth tightened. Those 'enemies of Grace' the Scot heresiarch Pelagius and his equally gifted and misguided disciple Celestius, long since banished from Rome and Africa thanks to the Bishop of Hippo, Aurelius Augustinus, had reappeared in disrupted Britain, where their wealth and eloquence fell on fruitful ground. Enormous crowds flocked to hear their pernicious doctrine exalting free will and denying both original sin and God's divine and sanctifying grace as the means of salvation; and there was no Augustine to protect them from the error.

A vestigial smile twitched the corner of Celestine's disciplined mouth as he recalled the thunderous condemnation of Pelagianism by that old, fiery and most human of bishops who had so sadly died in the year just gone. His death had occurred in the third month of the siege of his city of Hippo by Genseric's Vandals, under whom Arianism once more flourished in Carthage. Perhaps it was fitting that Hippo lay close to Carthage where, as Celestine recalled, Augustinus himself had flirted first with Manicheeism and then with the mother of his son, who had also adopted Christ. The bishop's condemnation of Pelagianism had been vehemently endorsed '*apostolici vigoris auctoritate*' by Celestine's predecessor Innocent. The rictus that passed for his smile was replaced by a frown as Celestine remembered not just the words of that condemnation, but their present irony: 'The case is finished: may Heaven will that once and for all the error ceases.'

But the case was not finished. Heaven had not so willed. Pelagius and his heresy thrived again on the Christian fringe of the known world, and were a burgeoning threat to it.

Just as fifty years earlier the Roman Britons had been afraid when the cohorts withdrew after Stilicho's abortive victories and had appealed to the emperor for aid (to be told that they must rely on their own resources), so now the British bishops were alarmed by Pelagius's successes and had appealed to the bishops of Gaul (with which jurisdiction they had a special affinity) for help. Even if the province were lost to the barbarians they wished to prevent it being also abandoned to heresy.

Standing at the window of his study in that year of Our Lord four hundred and thirty-two, dressed in a simple white robe, Celestine pondered the consequences of that delegation's visit: He stretched out a finger and on the glass, misted from his warm breath, drew the stylised and superimposed Greek characters 'Chi-Roh' which made the Saviour's name and had superseded the fish to become the symbol of Christianity: ☧. And he prayed for the grace and the wisdom to act correctly and in the faith of God under what had also been the standard of the Great Constantine.

The Deacon Palladius of Auxerre, who had been directed by the bishops of Gaul to seek from himself an authority to meet and challenge the heresiarch in Britain, was much in Celestine's mind and he recalled the analytical wisdom of that gentle man: 'Your grace, Pelagius and his disciple are both Scots, and Celestius in particular has an eloquent and persuasive tongue. As your grace well knows, the Scots have long mingled both their bread and their blood with the Britons . . . even claiming kingship over them. When the forces of the Empire withdrew, the relationships deepened. One might justly say that for good or ill the Britons know the Scots better than anyone else and have been accustomed to being led by them. How, then, will they not respond to the preaching of a Scot bishop, heretic though he may be? Will they know that? Who in Britain will successfully oppose such as Pelagius and Celestius? Your grace knows better than I the assaults of body and mind with which the Church is threatened; the damage upon us. Should the soul of Britain be lost to the Church of Christ as her soul is lost to the Empire, then neither Roman justice nor Roman creed are likely again to live there, and the corruption may penetrate south to Gaul and meet response from Vandal and Goth, already influenced by heresy, to say nothing of the Visigoths and those Asiatic demons, the Huns. We must abort this canker before it takes root.'

Palladius's quiet voice and direct logic rendered what he said the more horrifying. Celestine's response had been as direct. The Bishops Lupus of Troyes and Germanicus of Palladius's own city of Auxerre led a mission to Britain to confront the heretics. All Britain had heard, and interest was enormous. Remembering, Celestine slightly shook his head. 'My Christ,' he murmured, 'what if they had not been stopped among a race so educated and intelligent!'

Multitudes attended the debates, which became a series. Pelagius and Celestius presented themselves in great splendour and evidence of material wealth with which the poverty and lack of ostentation of the orthodox bishops made a striking contrast and one which Pelagius expected would work in his favour. But the opposite was the case. The contrasts were too great: the ease of life and ease of faith suggested a spiritual poverty which dismayed the Britons, abandoned by the similarly sybaritic Empire, and the austerity of Christ's faith and poverty won a resounding victory. Palladius later told Celestine: 'In my opinion, your grace, it was this remarkable contrast showing an abundance of wealth and spiritual poverty in the incorrect and unsustainable order, as much as the learned eloquence and humility of my lords bishops, that verified the truth to the eager Britons - a more intellectually curious people it would be hard to find.'

Because of the narrowly averted threat to the Faith in Britain and prescinding from that to the role and influence of the Scots there, as well as the fact that Pelagius and Celestius were both Scots, Celestine had initiated a further step. Ierne, Hibernia or, as the Scots themselves called it, Erin, lay to the west of Britain. Since it had never formed part of the Roman dominion, information about it was scanty and unreliable, seldom first-hand and usually the more dramatic rather than factual accounts of traders, captured or exiled Scots, or the occasional limited information from a civil or military peace mission. As far as he understood, it was an island somewhat smaller than Britain, possessing geographic advantages which might be envied anywhere and, in spite of the fact that the people were pagan, barbarous and cruel, certain social advantages as well. Firstly they were an homogeneous people speaking one language and their diverse ruling system had a limited democratic base of the Greek variety. They also possessed a legal codex of some kind, he was informed, and set great store by learning and erudition.

Celestine turned away from the window and crossed to his

writing table from which he picked up a rolled parchment. For some minutes his unhurried eye traversed the narrow columns that divided the large page and his thin lips moved as he read. Then he lowered the page and, lifting his head, repeated aloud the words he'd just read: '*Ergo agnis ovibusque Dei est haec sola voluntas et bona libertas, evdare torva cruenti ora lupi, vitaque frui perpascua Christi*' – 'Therefore the lamb and sheep of God have this one wish and good freedom; to escape the threatening jaws of the devouring wolf and to enjoy life in the pastures of Christ.'

His eye returned to the page and a single line seemed to leap towards it from the careful script: '*Ignotos oculis viderunt lumine cordis*' – 'Blinded by ignorance, yet they knew Him with their percipient hearts.'

Celestine laid the parchment on the table and turned back to the window, looking out at the clear sky without noticing it. It was still not too late. He could reverse his intention. He had insufficient information to make a decision.

The parchment he had been reading was a remarkable and, in its own way, disturbing document; an epic which only that year had reached him from Athens where it had caused a sensation. It was written by one Sedulius who once had lived and taught in Rome – Celestine vaguely remembered him – before accepting Christ and going to Athens. There he established a school of poetry and literature at which he taught a tight metre form, strict with hidden rhythms and assonance which, it seemed, was characteristic of the poetry of Hibernia. But the real and immense wonder was that this recent Christian with an unpronounceable barbarian name, spelt Saidheal, had written this glorious poem; the first epic of Christendom. In beautiful and sonorous verse it told the story of the coming and redemption of Christ's life, of his death and resurrection; and more, with impeccable insight and untainted by any vestige of the heresies that flourished about him, Sedulius retold the message of the Redeemer who was the Christ.

'And he too,' Celestine muttered, 'is one of these barbarian Scots!'

The previous year - when the epic was first penned and the Council of Ephesus was summoned to try the heretic Bishop Nestorius - Celestine decided to send a bishop to Hibernia where he was aware that some scattered Christians lived among the Scots, even that there was a settlement or two on the south-east coast. His action was prompted by the possibility that Pelagius and Celestius would return to their own country and arouse there a religious fervour in support of their heresy. It was too great a risk to ignore. The gentle deacon, Palladius, was an obvious choice for the mission. He was well thought of and was supported by the bishops of Gaul. He understood the importance of the mission and was familiar with Pelagius, and with his heresy. Moreover, Palladius had the advantage of long association with a fellow deacon from Auxerre who, as a young man, had lived among the Scots (as their prisoner and slave, Celestine later learned). Accordingly, Palladius was consecrated and despatched - but cautiously and with instructions first to secure the colonial Scots of Caledonia. They had established a new kingdom there and were already in contact with Christian Britons to the south where the remarkable Bishop Ninian was doing such great work from Whitehorn.

Celestine sighed. Within months of his consecration and departure the gentle Palladius was dead, having achieved little in his brief episcopate, and the problems not only remained unresolved, they had multiplied. Now Celestine was considering a bold and unpopular stroke, and he was by no means sure he was right. Two men were waiting in separate rooms to see him. One of them was there to help him decide; over the other rested a question mark, and the more Celestine considered it the more doubtful he became. He shook his head and lifted a small hand bell from the table. The door opened quickly and silently in response to his ring and a deacon stood there.

'Ask the Bishop of Auxerre to come in,' said Constantine. 'I want to speak to him alone. Allow me a quarter of an hour by the water clock before interrupting.'

The priest nodded and withdrew. A moment later the ex-soldier Bishop Germanus who, three years before, so successfully opposed Pelagius at the behest of the British bishops, came in. The two men greeted each other formally in Latin, which was gradually becoming more the language of the Universal Church than that of the shrivelling Empire.

'Your grace.' Germanus crossed the room towards Celestine, arms outstretched. The Pope clasped him ritually. As he was tall and thin, and Germanus – or Germanicus as the Pope would call him – was short and round, it was an awkward formality which in any case was not in accord with Celestine's austere demeanour.

'My lord.' Celestine turned to the table and indicated that Germanus should sit. 'May I first of all congratulate you on your success in Britain.' Germanus half-raised a deprecatory hand. 'It is well-deserved,' went on Celestine. 'First you defeat the heretic. Not content with that, you go on to defeat the Saxons and the Picts in battle at – what did they call it? The Alleluia Victory, was it not?'

Not sure if he was being reprimanded or praised, Germanus murmured, 'Yes, your grace.'

'The Alleluia Victory! It has an appropriate ring to it, my lord, and on the Field of Germanicus, if I am not mistaken?'

Germanus had had enough. Blunt and forthright, he both disliked and suspected the indirect way. What, after all, was Celestine, but a bishop like himself in all material things? The question of papal supremacy was still very much an issue and Germanus, able and skilful, had no intention of being the subject of effete condescension from any quarter.

'Your grace is not mistaken,' he said shortly. 'Maes Garmon, they called it, Germanus's Field in the Brettonic, after our victory. But your grace must realise that it was the Christian

Britons who were victorious over the heathens, not I.'

'But it was you who led them, Germanicus, and for that you have our thanks and the thanks of all Christendom.'

Germanus relaxed. The Pope was not reprimanding, much less ridiculing him. It was just his way.

'I did what was required, your grace.'

'And did it well, my lord.' In his own way Celestine also preferred the direct way. Now that the niceties were more or less satisfactorily over, he said: 'But a problem remains.'

Germanus waited.

'You know to what I refer?'

'I think so, your grace. I regret that I did not come to Rome before now, but . . . '

It was Celestine's turn to gesture dismissively. 'How could you come to Rome, my lord? What you had to do in Britain was far more important.'

Angrily Germanus glanced at him, but saw that Celestine was quite sincere. 'My God,' he thought, 'that's the trouble with talking to such ascetic people, they're so honest they always say what they mean.' Which was disconcerting. For Germanus it meant he had to think thrice, instead of the normal twice: first hearing what was said and then translating it into what was meant. With Celestine he had to translate back again because what was heard was also what was meant, as if one were talking to a hyper-informed child, he thought, as he made the necessary adjustments. But he could not bring himself to relax completely, which made it much harder work for him than if his companion had been devious. Surprised by the thought, it suddenly occurred to Germanus that Celestine too might be finding the convers-sation difficult, but for different reasons, and he decided to make it easier for him.

'It was sad about the Bishop Palladius,' he said.

It was as if a barrier blocking communication between them vanished. Celestine's stern face enlivened, although his sorrow was no less than that of Germanus.

'It was so sad,' he said. 'You knew him well, of course.'

Germanus nodded, thinking of the little Italian deacon who, so many years ago, had come to him at Auxerre and with a wit and intelligence of penetrating and gentle accuracy had brightened his solitary life in a way that no one else had ever done.

'Yes, your grace. I knew him.'

'I also. As you know, it was on his recommendation that I . . . approved . . . the mission of the Bishop Lupus and yourself to Britain to deal with Pelagius.'

Germanus nodded.

'It was because of his remarkable power of analysis that I despatched him to Hibernia to secure it against the heresiarch.'

Germanus needed little telling. He had been appalled when he first heard the news. Palladius! A scholar, an adviser and analyst of the highest calibre, sent out with no more than a papal exhortation to secure, develop and consolidate the establishment of Christianity in the remote west; Ultima Thule as it was aptly called by the ancients, where the Empire itself had never penetrated. He recalled his immediate response when he heard of Celestine's decision: 'Is the man mad?' Palladius had no experience of administration or of preaching to the unconverted, and knew nothing of those to whom he was sent. Involuntarily Germanus shook his head. He remembered the remorse he had felt afterwards for his lack of charity towards Celestine, and the pity that had followed his anger at the waste, after Palladius's sudden and untimely death.

'His death was a great blow to us,' Celestine said. Germanus merely nodded. 'And there remains the complication of the heretic. Pelagius is himself a Scot . . . ' Again Germanus nodded. 'If he should take it into his head . . . '

Germanus knew all this better than Celestine. He knew what the Pope was going to say before he spoke.

'You take my point? We must do something. I have given this much thought, which is why I asked you to visit me.'

Germanus appreciated the tact with which Celestine referred to the papal summons he had received.

'Pelagius is already there, your grace.'

'What?'

'At least, that was my most recent information about him when I left last week in response to . . . to come here.'

The Pope crossed himself and muttered a prayer.

'You must send someone else, your grace.'

The Pope nodded in silence. For a moment Germanus was silent too. Then a thought struck him.

'It wasn't your intention that I . . . ?'

Celestine shook his head, and lowered his eyes to conceal his disappointment. Not that he had intended to send Germanus. But the vanity which prompted his response . . . 'Yet are not all men of influence unconsciously vain,' he thought, 'otherwise would they be men of influence? And is it my own vanity to be blind to it in myself?' He looked at Germanus. 'No, my lord, but I do seek your advice.'

'And will willingly have it, your grace. If you commanded me, of course, I should . . . I would . . . '

'It does not arise, my friend . . . if I may . . . ' Germanus smiled. 'I had not intended to ask you. What you are doing in Gaul is vitally important. We could not risk weakening the position there by removing – by asking you to relinquish it.' He paused. 'I need your advice on whom to send.'

Germanus leaned back. This was a different matter. He had been singled out for his advice on a matter of geographic and, perhaps, doctrinal, importance to the Church.

'Of course,' he said.

'The doctrine of Christ and the Trinity must be protected against onslaught, must spread to all the peoples of the world for their salvation and everlasting glory. They must be protected against false doctrines having the appearance of the truth. It seems to me that the Church of Christ has now an opportunity to take a great step forward in the far west just as it did in this very city a hundred years ago when the great Constantine recognised it, and at the same time to secure a new stronghold for the Lord and Saviour of mankind.'

'I agree, your grace.'

'The news you bring makes this all the more urgent. And there are other factors. Visigoths have already once laid waste this city of ours. The Huns gather to leap at our throats. You do not need me to tell you the Empire is decaying and facing destruction. When that occurs, my lord, what will then happen to the Church?'

'The Church will survive, your grace. It must. Look at what we have achieved . . . '

'My lord Germanicus, what we have achieved we have been able to do only because the light of education and understanding was there before us, borne on the marching shoulders of the Empire. When the Empire lies in the dust and is no more beneath barbarian boots of mail, when the light is extinguished by godless heathens, when civilisation is overthrown by slaughtering, war-loving and illiterate nomads, what then, my lord?'

'What are you saying, your grace? It cannot happen. In Hippo, the library was preserved by Alaric . . . '

'Alaric is neither Hun nor Goth. He is a Vandal. Although Arian, he accepts Christ. Vandals are at least half civilised. You do not compare like with like.'

'But, your grace, the picture you paint is unthinkable . . . '

'Like it or not, my lord, we must think on it.'

Horrified, Germanus stared at him. To make it worse he knew that the sense of horror did not spring from what Celestine had said but rather from a realisation that he was expressing a possibility so obvious and awful that he, Germanus, had deliberately shut his mind to it. He looked at the cold, gaunt man before him with a new respect.

'The man we select,' went on Celestine, 'must be capable of planting the Faith firmly in Hibernia and of securing it so that it will not wither under the blight of heresy – as you, my dear friend, have thwarted the blight in Britain.' He paused. 'I understand that the Scots are not complete savages and that they already respect learning,' he smiled his faint smile, 'rather like your Vandals. If this misguided disciple of misfortune Pelagius, who was once our bishop, and his eloquent fellow-Scot disciple are already in their native land, they could lead the entire nation into the arms of heresy. And after that . . . ' Celestine spread his hands and shrugged expressively.

'Your grace, I may be wrong,' Germanus said, 'but I believe that Pelagius is no longer driven by a genuine belief. He is older now – over sixty – and bitter at his failures. He grew accustomed to adulation and to the trappings of power, but during my encounters with him in Britain I came to believe that the fire of conviction had died in him.'

'It could hardly be otherwise, my lord, when he did not speak with Christ. And I well understand that he cannot bring himself to recant now. But what is your point?'

'I think he has gone to Hibernia, to his own people, to lick his wounds and get what acclaim he can, rather than rouse the race with a religious fervour which they – and he – must by now know is proclaimed heretical throughout the world. One of our strengths must surely be that if the people are to be won to Christ, they will choose the right way rather than one known to be outlawed.'

'Well said, my lord. Nevertheless,' insisted the Pope, 'the danger is great. He must not suborn Hibernia.' Germanus assented and Celestine went on: 'As we may anticipate, even from there may yet be called to return the Light of the World, if it be extinguished for a time, again to illuminate all Europe. It shall be our reservoir,' he ended and looked at Germanus. 'The question is who shall fill it?'

'Perhaps one of the British bishops . . . ?' began Germanus, but Celestine shook his head impatiently.

'One of those who were so insecure that they sent for you to deal with Pelagius? One of them will fill this reservoir?'

A new thought occurred to Germanus: 'Your grace, Palladius's mission was to the Scots in Caledonia. Is your intention now to send a bishop directly to Hibernia?'

'Yes,' said Celestine, 'and no. Palladius was sent to the Scots colony in Caledonia only because they were more accessible - or,' the Pope smiled in recollection of what had, in fact, happened, 'because we thought they were more accessible, both physically and spiritually. As you know, through them we hoped the Faith would be carried back to Hibernia.'

'I see,' Germanus acknowledged. 'In fact I did not know. Since Bishop Palladius went first to Hibernia and then to Caledonia, I naturally believed that such was your grace's intention.'

Celestine paused a moment before replying. There was confusion of motive and design which he must clarify, but it had to be done tactfully if he was to fulfil his intention. It was Germanicus who had recommended sending a mission to the Scots in Caledonia, though he had not known beforehand that Palladius was the choice and, Celestine suspected, it was a choice he had disapproved of.

'We both know,' he said, 'that the confrontations of Bishop Lupus and yourself with the heretics in Britain were not important to the faith alone, they had grave political significance as well. The bond between the British diocese and the See of Gaul is of great consequence and will be even more important as new rulers supplant the old.'

Germanus nodded. He appreciated blunt speaking. 'That is clear.'

'Your recommendations to send a mission to the Scot colonies in Caledonia we believed - and still believe - to have been wise and correct. Whitehorn is nearby and Bishop Ninian has extended his influence substantially. Your proposal to consolidate that influence by a further extension into the bordering Scots colonies impressed us.'

Germanus nodded in acknowledgement. He was obviously being flattered for a purpose, but what?

'Which is why we adopted your proposal and despatched Palladius as bishop to the Scot Christians.'

For a moment they exchanged looks which were as eloquent as the words left unsaid, each of them, in his own way, thinking of Palladius.

'You do not need me to tell you what happened,' Celestine went on. 'It is my belief that the divine hand of the Almighty Providence was manifest in the misunderstanding which first took Palladius to the Scot homeland. For even though it may have precipitated his untimely death, the mistake emphasised that aspect of the question which we have just discussed. We *must* send a bishop to the Scot homeland.'

'But your grace . . . '

'Hear me out, my lord Germanicus. I have given this much thought.'

Germanus's mind, faster than the other's, had quickly understood the validity of the proposal. He wished to avoid a mere repetition of what he had heard already. But for him, also, there was the need to be tactful. He listened until Celestine had finished. Then he said: 'I fully agree with your grace's outline. I have two observations, the first of which your grace has already accepted in principle and the second of which you have done me the honour of consulting me about. Firstly, I believe the mission to Hibernia would be greatly encouraged and made easier if it percolated from the north which is adjacent to their Caledonian colony . . . '

'But the Christian settlements are in the south-east.'

'Precisely, my point, your grace. And it was for that reason that Palladius went there instead of to Caledonia. Those settlements are very much *with* but not *of* the people. They are not representative and are considered alien. The people are made suspicious and are turned against them by their pagan priests – the *dlee*, similar to Gaulish druids but with more authority. On the other hand Christianity is known to the Scots in Caledonia. They intermarry and intermingle with Christians day by day and they are also in constant communication with their homeland, but especially the northern part from which the colonists mainly come. Your grace, we are concerned to a very large extent with attitudes and if we can operate from a base of acceptance rather than one of alienation, I believe success will be surer and speedier.'

'Well said, my lord. It parallels my own thinking. I thought to instruct our bishop to proceed to the northern part of Hibernia . . . '

'Not the colony?'

'I shall explain my reasons in a moment.'

'Your grace . . . '

'Which brings us to your second point.'

'Yes.' Germanus was pleased that the Pope agreed with his general thesis; worried because of the modification. But then he did not possess all the facts. 'Who shall be sent?'

Apparently Celestine did not hear him. 'When you and Bishop Lupus were in Britain, who accompanied you?'

'Hmm? Oh, nobody in particular. The usual servants. Palladius for a while, the deacon Patricius . . . '.

'Patricius!'

'He is also here in Rome as your grace commanded . . . ' Realisation suddenly struck Germanus. 'Your grace is surely not thinking of Patricius?' He spread his hands in helplessness. And in his momentary surprise, uncharacteristically expressed his feelings. 'Ohhh! This whole thing . . . You know who he is, of course?'

'His uncle was Bishop Martin of Tours, was he not? The eremite?'

'Indeed,' said Germanus drily, 'and Patricius - for all his virtues, and they are many - has inherited much of the family disposition. Do not misunderstand me, your grace,' he added quickly as Celestine's face seemed to become even colder and more withdrawn, 'I am not criticising Patricius capriciously. But he seems to arouse a precisely similar resentment, and for similar reasons, among his fellow clerics as his uncle did before him. He is considered unsophisticated, your grace, unlettered, rude, untutored and insufficiently acquainted with doctrinal and theological studies.'

'Similar shortcomings did not prevent the holy Bishop of Tours from being markedly successful, as I recall, and such criticisms, in the long run, reflect less on the saintly Martin than on his critics.'

Celestine spoke a little more sharply than he might normally have done, but here was raised one of the current - and bitter - controversies that flourished throughout his domain. The open feud between those in the Church who believed it should be simple and direct and complained that many bishops were proud and worldly and too involved with power and matters of state. And those same worldly prelates who ruled their sees according to the circumstances and resented interference from those whom they would unquestionably dismiss as being '*voces et praeterea nihil*'. But, in a troubled world, the Pope was required to accommodate both points of view. Germanus was nonplussed. He had placed himself in the position of criticising Patricius, when he did not intend to and, as an envious man, when his concern had nothing to do with himself. He tried to correct matters by changing his approach.

'Your grace, strong-willed men who rely on their own resources and inner convictions are often calumniated by weaker and envious mortals . . . '

Celestine allowed a glint of humour to appear fractionally in the corner of his eyes as he asked in a dry voice: 'Are you preaching at me, my lord?'

Startled, Germanus looked at him for a moment, his mouth open in his wide face; then he lifted his chin and laughed. Celestine smiled. A curious understanding had been established between these dissimilar men and Germanus promptly thought to take advantage of it.

'Your grace . . . ' he paused. While this sudden warmth was helpful he did not want to wrong-foot himself with the Pope a second time, yet what he wished to say was riddled with dangerous pitfalls. Nevertheless, it was so central to the present problem that there was no way he could avoid it. He swallowed and swore to himself to be tactful; and immediately did the opposite.

'As you know, the bishops - of Gaul, of Spain, even Italy - were jeal- not in favour of the Bishop of Tours?'

Celestine nodded. Who knew it better?

'He was not one of them, he was not an aristocrat educated in the finest academies and skilled in philosophy, languages and doctrine. I feel I can speak freely, your grace, being of them myself.' Celestine acknowledged this imperceptibly and Germanus continued: 'Martin was a soldier, no less, virtually lacking education as the bishops understand it and I understand their attitude even if I do not share it. I was a soldier myself.'

Celestine nodded. 'So was Saul, was he not, my lord?'

'Of course, your grace, I appreciate the established precedents, but that was nearly four hundred years ago. Today we are dealing with a worldwide organisation of Faith and on our bishops rests the onus of trying to maintain - often from their private means, as your grace well knows - the Latin culture and some semblance of order in our disturbed society, besides administering the affairs of the Church. How can they do it without power, without influence, without means and education? All this calls for a very special kind of person, your grace. In a word, an aristocrat. Our bishops must be lay judges and administrators; they negotiate and deal with invading barbarians; they are forced to be proud and powerful. These men of authority are essential to the Church. How can we expect them to take kindly to rude individuals like Martin and Patricius who do not belong to their caste and educational background? In spite of his success, your grace, they closed ranks against Martin and they will do the same thing to Patricius.'

'I have already been informed, my lord, that Patricius is not acceptable as a bishop and I have no doubt that he will not be "acceptable" as my emissary to Hibernia either.'

'So you know?'

Celestine looked at him a moment before replying. 'How,' he asked himself, 'could the man think I would not know? Is it more arrogance?' He inclined his head. 'It was made quite clear to me.'

'Then I am wasting my breath.'

'The point, my lord, is am I wasting mine? What do you advise?'

Germanus stuck out his lower jaw and sucked his upper lip between his teeth. Obviously Celestine had already consulted other bishops about Patricius, but not, it seemed, about sending him to Hibernia. Why himself? There was nothing he could tell the Pope who, he began to suspect, had already made his decision. He spoke with uncustomary caution.

'All other things being equal, my advice, your grace, is not to send a man who would give concern to the bishops.'

'And if all other things are not equal?'

'Then, your grace must do what your grace is there to do, reach a decision that is in the best interests of Christ's Holy Church.'

Celestine slowly rose to his full height without answering, crossed to his spot by the window and looked out at the city. Germanus waited for him to speak. At last, his eyes still directed beyond the window, Celestine replied.

'It seems to come to this, then,' he said quietly. 'For some reason beyond our capacity to determine, the Almighty Father has decreed that this remote and heathen island shall be a haven. But for what?' He turned back to Germanus. 'The heresy of its countryman, or the one True Faith?' Celestine smiled wryly. 'And to add to our troubles we are afflicted not only with heresies from within and pagan armies from without, but the bishops and curia of our own Church are jealous of whom we might send.' He lifted his hands and massaged his eyes for a moment with his fingertips, as if he were praying. And so he was. Germanus lowered his eyes to the table and added a heartfelt prayer of his own to strengthen this remote man to whom he was unexpectedly drawn.

Suddenly Celestine dropped his hands and gave a short, barking laugh. 'And why are they jealous of him?' he asked. 'Not because he's not the best man for the job, for they neither know nor care, but because he does not resemble them.'

'Your grace . . . '

'Forgive me, my lord. I sometimes feel a little tired. You have been much help.'

'You have made a decision?'

'First I will see Patricius.'

'You may find him . . . difficult.'

'I anticipate it.'

'He is very strong-willed.'

'He will have need of it. He is not disobedient?'

Germanus shook his head. 'No, your grace. His mind focuses on a narrow beam.'

'Then it will be more concentrated.'

'He is not tactful.'

'Then he will be direct.'

'He is no longer young.'

'He knows the Scots and speaks their language.'

'He is not an administrator.'

'What need is there of an administrator in a land where the very idea of central administration is foreign? And if he is strong in Faith . . . '

'Finally, your grace, he does not wish to go.'

'Oh!' exclaimed Celestine. 'How do you know that?'

'He told me.'

'But how? You did not know my intention until now.'

'It had nothing to do with that, your grace. He has a friend from Ireland – a merchant – who is also a Christian. For years he has asked Patricius to go back, saying they need him, and – apart from the question of authority – Patricius has constantly refused to return to the land where he was enslaved. At different times they each came to me about it, but with different motives, of course. And,' he admitted, looking steadily at Celestine, 'I'm afraid I gave Patricius the assurance he sought.'

'What was that?' Celestine's voice was uninflexioned.

'That I could see no possibility of an unwilling and unskilled deacon receiving such a mission.'

'I see.'

'Patricius has always been adamant in his refusal. I'm afraid he is not the man for the job,' Germanus finished lamely.

'On the contrary,' Celestine's contradiction was gentle, 'what you tell me merely serves to strengthen my faith in him. He sounds exactly right to me.'

'Then may the hand of Christ guide your grace.'

'Thank you, my lord.'

Germanus rose to take his leave. 'There is one more thing, your grace.'

'Yes?'

'Patricius was with me in Britain. He went to the west, where his family had farmed, and administered there for a while.'

'Yes?'

'He was not particularly successful.'

'I see. Why do you tell me this?'

Germanus pursed his mouth. 'I have no particular reason. Perhaps old associations were too much for him. I thought you ought to know.'

'Thank you, my lord.'

'What will your grace do about the opposition to Patricius's consecration?'

The Pope paused a moment. Then a smile broke his narrow, severe features, bringing a sudden gaiety to eyes that were unexpectedly mischievous: 'I shall be a more devious political bishop than all the other political bishops, my lord, and my left hand shall not know what my right hand doeth.'

Germanus smiled back. 'I wish your grace every blessing and success,' he said as Celestine accompanied him to the door.

When he was gone Celestine stared at the closed door for a moment before turning to his table, picking up the bell and ringing it. His deacon appeared quickly and, his back towards him, still gazing through the window, Celestine said: 'Ask the deacon Patricius to come in, father.'

The deacon withdrew and Celestine bent his head for a moment to ask Almighty God to guide him towards the decision which was truly His purpose. He heard the door open and close behind him and turned to greet the deacon Patricius.

Celestine knew that the man who stood inside the door was nearer fifty-five than fifty, but he could not have guessed from his appearance. Of average height, Patricius was broad and muscular; in fact broadness was characteristic - Celestine corrected himself - at least, a physical characteristic, of the man. His head was large and had a broad forehead and jaw with, between them, broad cheekbones. Sharp, blue eyes with tiny pupils roved steadily, almost calculatingly, from place to place. When he smiled the eyes also smiled, but this happened seldom. The quality of his smile now was even rarer: it was a smile of deference.

Arms outstretched, Celestine crossed the marble floor to greet his visitor.

'Your grace does me honour.' Even in Latin Patricius's accent was still noticeable.

'Patricius,' said the Pope, embracing and turning him in one movement. His arm about the other's shoulders, they went towards the table and chairs. He indicated that the deacon should sit.

'Do you know why I sent for you?'

Even to one as accustomed to extreme reactions as Celestine, the effect of his words on Patricius was startling. The deacon's face hardened. The high cheekbones whitened and the blue eyes became chips from a frozen sky. His wide thin-lipped mouth became a straight line before he rasped, 'I think I can guess, your grace, but . . . '

The Pope held up one hand to stop him. He must not go too far so soon. Patricius glowered.

'Do not, I beg you, hear me with a closed mind, Patricius.'

Patricius stared at him, his great jaw set and, in spite of the Pope's admonition and before he could continue, Patricius blurted: 'You, too, want me to go back there. Why am I being pursued?' he demanded, but not of the Pope alone.

'How do you know what I want you to do?' Celestine was both intrigued and angered. How had Patricius learned of his intention? Who had been so impertinent as to tell him? It could only have been one of the bishops he had consulted, but even they could only have guessed, at best.

'How should I not know, your grace? Again and again I am driven towards these pitiful Irish sinners and pagans, as you would drive a herded sheep.'

'You still have not told me . . . '

Patrick lifted a hand in a gesture reminiscent of the Pope's own when he had interrupted Germanus and, surprising himself, Celestine paused.

'Why should I go back to a people from whom I barely escaped, your grace? What can I, a mere deacon, do for them? But that is the path to which I am being directed.' He looked at Celestine with hard, penetrating eyes and spoke in his deep accented voice: 'And you would have me do it also. That is why you brought me here, is it not?'

In spite of Germanus's warning, the other man's bluntness surprised Celestine.

'I must ask who told you.'

Patricius's expression did not alter: 'No man told me. I know . . . from Jesus Christ our Lord.'

Celestine wondered if he had mistaken his man. Was Patricius after all another mere emotional fanatic with mind and judgement warped by years of over-anxiety and the powerful words of the Gospels operating on an unbridled imagination?

'Your grace, I have feared and avoided this moment. Why should I welcome it when I know that it brings the cross I must bear the rest of my life? Am I not a man, your grace? Not even a priest, like my grandfather. Barely permitted to be a deacon. And yet I am summoned as surely as you summoned me. For years I fled from the voice of Christ which has pursued me, and from the messages and letters He caused to be sent to me.' He withdrew a folded parchment from his tunic and handed it to Celestine. 'See for yourself, your grace. It was brought to me less than a month ago by a Vandal, Victoric, who captains one of the ships of a friend of mine in Ireland, a merchant.'

'You have friends in Ireland?' asked Celestine, taking the letter and unfolding it, but keeping his eyes firmly on Patricius.

'He helped me to escape more than thirty years ago.'

'And you have kept in touch?'

'We write, as your grace can see.'

Celestine opened the letter and glanced briefly at the short, clumsily written Latin phrases: 'I am your friend, Aidicus, and, once again, I write to you, Sucatus Patricius, with the voice of the Irish, and we ask you to come again among us as when you were a boy, for we have need of you. We do indeed have need of you, Patricius. Write to me and I will, myself, captain the ship to bring you home . . . '

'To bring you home, Patricius?' The Pope laid the letter on the table beside him, ignoring Patricius's outstretched hand.

With great vehemence Patricius said: 'Your grace, the Scots *destroyed* my home.'

Before replying, Celestine observed the strong, impetuous man for a moment. Strength emanated from him like an ocean swell. It was obvious why the bishops opposed him; at any other time, for any other purpose, he himself would probably oppose Patricius. But he could visualise that strength and the patent intellectual honesty of the man winning the admiration of half-educated, aspiring barbarians who respected themselves enough to confine their heroic traditions of honour within the framework of written law. He thought of the magnificent epic lying on the table and for a moment his eye wandered to it. Then a vague recollection inspired him.

'I'm told, Patricius, that you were a slave in Hibernia for several years?'

Patricius nodded. 'Six.'

'And you escaped when a voice instructed you to do so?'

'The voice of God, your grace, which came to me in a dream. I remember it well.'

'And is it the same voice, Patricius, you hear now telling you to go back?'

Patricius's face went suddenly white, the eyes blazing more fiercely than they had before. For a long moment he stared at the pontiff. Celestine sensed the struggle taking place in the other as some power of the Spirit in him contended with his mortality. Patricius lowered his head and clenched strong fists on his knees. When he raised his head again a few moments later his face had become extraordinarily haggard and drawn and his eyes were pitiful in their deep sockets. When he spoke he sounded hoarse! 'It is the same voice . . . '

Thus was begun the singular mission which, in a single generation, converted the pagan and warlike people of Ireland to the way of Christ to which they have been devoted ever since; and within another generation so inspired them that shortly after Patrick's death great schools of learning flowered. Passionate and dedicated missionaries in their hundreds carried the Faith along the paths their fathers and grandsires had bloodied with the sword, to begin the remarkable work of returning to the Continent, whence Patrick had brought it, the Faith of the universal Church of Rome.

That the bishops – those of the curia and those of Gaul and Britain who might, with just reason, have expected the papal legate to have been chosen from among themselves – might not be excessively offended, Patrick was consecrated in secret and admonished by the Pope not to reveal the fact until it became necessary to do so or until such time as the need for concealment no longer existed. And Patrick was as faithful to his mission as he was to the encouragement of the Almighty Word that guided him. Moreover, at that historic meeting in Rome the Pope added: 'You will be my trusted legate in that ultimate place, Patricius. And while there you will be alone in great measure. You will be surrounded by enemies. You will leave powerful enemies behind who will wish to see you fail. But remember, when you speak you do not speak as the ambassador of the Pope, but as the ambassador of Christ our God and with His authority. Do this and you have my support in all that you do.'

Chapter 7

On a still evening some two months later, which would have made it towards the middle of March in the year of Our Lord 432, a ship glided into a bay in western Gaul. The water was oily smooth with a slight rolling swell, enough to swing the mast in an arc as she moved slowly towards the shore under the power of four gigantic sweeps, each manned by two men.

There were no lights to be seen in the town, but this far north there was still enough from the vanished sun to enable the ship to work to an offshore anchorage. Aidan dropped a stern anchor and nosed forward another hundred feet or so before dropping two from the bows. He knew what changing tide or weather conditions might do, to say nothing of both together. Because of the calm, he was late, but he knew his passenger would wait. He gazed shorewards. He had waited for this moment for over thirty years and now it had arrived his feelings were mixed. He was far from being excited, as might have been expected, or as he might have been ten years ago. He wondered why Patrick had suddenly changed his mind and, yet again, reached for the short and unexpected letter that he had received four weeks earlier. But he didn't take it from his pouch; he knew it by heart. 'I, Patrick, your friend in Christ, greet you. I am commanded to return to the land of my youthful captivity and bring the pagan barbarians to the love and understanding of Christ, our Lord. I hear your voice and do as you ask. If you will, as you have said, I would wish to make the journey with you rather than another. I shall be at Bayonne in eight weeks. I am yours in Christ and in the

Trinity of the Holy Name, Magonus Sucatus Patricius, priest.'

The joy this letter should have brought to Aidan was not there. Instead it raised worry and doubts as if, throughout the years – perhaps not the earlier ones, but the later ones, surely – he had requested Patrick to return without really believing that he would do so. Worse, he suspected that he would have continued to make the requests long after he knew they were futile merely for his own sake, that he might be seen as constant. He wondered if he were, indeed, a hypocrite.

He turned from the shoreline and the darker hills behind and looked over the placid evening sea towards a greenish sky that spanned the heavens above the hidden resting place of the sun. 'It doesn't matter,' he thought. 'What difference does it make now? It has begun.' He saw the evening star appear, then took a small boat and went ashore to meet the friend he helped escape from captivity so long ago.

Aidan went first to the inn where he enquired after the agent of a Gaulish merchant with whom he frequently traded. He also asked where the local priest lived, for there, he knew, was where he would find Patrick. Unloading and disposing of his cargo – for he was far too practical a merchant to have sailed light, even on a voyage as important as this – could wait until morning. Aidan was several inches taller than his father had been; from the gangling youth who pleaded with Fergus to take Patrick on that fateful voyage to Gaul he had developed into a broad-shouldered, deep-chested man, still lithe and quick of movement in spite of being in his mid-fifties. He had not let his accumulated wealth trap him into a life of too much rich food and drink and too little exercise; he frequently captained one of his many ships himself. He ate sparingly, and when he was forced to travel by land preferred to ride or walk rather than take a chariot or public cart. As he strode through the narrow, smelly streets of Bayonne towards the church in which the priest lived beneath the squat belfry, he wondered about Patrick. What sort of man was he after all this time? What sort of man had he himself become? He had seen intense youthful friendships die instantly on renewed acquaintance after a separation of a few years. 'A man grows as life directs him,' he thought. He knew that he had changed. Patrick too must have changed. He was concerned that the passage of time might have so altered each of them that the cherished friendship, so potent in youth, was in reality merely a fragment of time held in suspense, enduring only in the mind and in certain effects resulting from it. He need not have worried.

Before he could knock a second time the misshapen church door, of worn and irregular weather-beaten planks, swung open and a square figure was framed in the faint candlelight from beyond.

'Aidan? I guessed it was you.'

It was the same voice, deeper and richer, but vibrant and strong as ever, lacking only the hint of humour Aidan thought he remembered.

They talked into the night until the old priest, whose room Patrick shared, grumbled gently, reminding them that at his age he found it hard enough to rise without their making it more difficult by disturbing his rest. They continued their talk much of the following day, which began when Aidan went to Patrick's morning Mass and received the great Sacrament from the hands of his old friend, and they talked the day after that as Aidan's ship, with a cargo of silk and wine, lurched through the chop on the suddenly boisterous sea between Gaul and Ireland.

They explored and explained the past so that the bonds between them were renewed and strong. Aidan told Patrick of his early exploits: his years abroad fighting with the soldiers of Gaul and Ireland and Britain and others of the Celtic hegemony against the Visigoths and the Romans; how his father, old Fergus (long dead), had with extra taxes purchased his freedom from military service when he grew too old to look after the family shipping and herding interests; of how he had married and - like his father - sired several daughters and one son, another Fergus; and of how he built the trading activities of his father, based as they were on the one old ship that Patrick had escaped in, into an enterprise of seventeen vessels trading with the Empire as far as Alexandria and Antioch, and with the Saxons and Franks in northern Europe.

Patrick remained silent for most of this recital, but the manner of his doing so displayed his vibrant and concentrated interest. He wanted to know everything and when Aidan paused or slowed or hesitated in recollection Patrick nodded energetically for him to continue, looking at him with his compelling eyes, and Aidan proceeded with the telling.

In turn, Patrick gave his account to the merchant, beginning with a phrase he was to use again and again in circumstances which emphasised with enormous power the strength of his feelings in this regard.

'Aidan, my friend, I never had any reason except the Gospel and its promises why I should ever return to the people from whom once before I barely escaped. I know I must forgive my enemies, but in my heart . . . ' he stopped. He turned to Aidan full face and, with that commanding presence that so often bound his own forthright goodness to the sense of justice and truth in many of those he was henceforth to meet, he said: 'My uncle, Martin of Tours, about whom I think I told you when we first met – I remember how impressed you were . . . ' Patrick produced one of his rare smiles. 'He was a great and simple man, who died soon after you helped me escape. By then he had left his bishopric and had become a hermit, living in a cave and working only for the poor of the district. It was his belief that the Church should return to the simple ways of the early days . . . '

'You believe that too?'

Patrick did not immediately reply to his friend's question. Then, slowly, he said, 'No. We cannot go back; but neither should we go forward too quickly. And I think that is our present weakness. We must not try to force an institutionalised Church on those who are not institutional. Nor can we permit the institution, even in the name of obedience, to usurp the authority of the Word. That too is a heresy . . . And I have no doubt that you will quickly see the converse heresy, the denial of the Church as the universal instrument of the Word because of the necessity for internal obedience. But Christ did not give us an institution, He gave us the way to salvation. The Almighty God in His infinite mercy gave to us His only son and He gave to us His Church; we developed the institution and it must not be allowed to become more important than the Church. Neither can we refuse to see that if it is one and apostolic it must also be organised as it extends. If the law of God is in conflict with the law of the Church, then by definition it is no contest. No. I do not entirely agree with my uncle, but I do not entirely disagree with him either.'

He paused again and his eyes roamed across the deck to the restless sea before he resumed. 'A short while later I met another remarkable man, also, alas, on the point of death. He was a priest and had suffered at the hands of the institutionalists just as Martin had. His name was John and they called him golden-mouthed, Chrysostomos, because of his remarkable eloquence. Indeed he was held to be the greatest orator of the Church and became Bishop of Constantinople. But this great gift also brought about his downfall at the hands of the dissolute Empress Eudoxia who had him banished. When I met him at a place called Comana he was dying, but his will and spirit still burned with a great pure flame. He, too, believed in the simple Word of God and he told me of others: the famous Antony who, a hundred or more years ago, gave away all he possessed and chose to live in the desert where he strove to find Christ in himself. He rejected the hierarchical empire that we are creating. For, Aidan, make no mistake, the Church is taking over where the Empire is leaving off. Her methods, her administration and structures, her operations are patterned completely on those of the Empire; the very language we have chosen for our rituals is neither the Greek nor the Semitic of the early fathers, but the Latin of the Empire which once persecuted us.

'I also heard of a saintly man, Simeon, who for the past three years has lived on, and daily preached from, the top of a pillar outside Antioch, living only on what food is placed in a basket he raises on a rope and by the Word of God. But of them all, perhaps the one who, after the great father of priests, Saul, impressed me most was the late Bishop of Hippo who died last year, Aurelius Augustinus, whose writings have nailed the nature of the true Faith to the fabric of this world in letters of fire. Such are the people who, at different times, have moulded me and my thinking.'

Patrick went on to tell Aidan about his struggles in the religious life, at first as a lay associate of the very lowest rank; about his travels from one religious community to another in Europe; about his family and their return to Britain, and about their distress and anxiety over his own restless inability to stay with them for very long because he was pursued from within.

'You,' he smiled, 'were part of that pursuit. And now, paradoxically, when I am returning whence I fled, to where I have no wish to go and to those who persecuted me - now, after so many years, I am at peace; I am no longer pursued.'

Aidan's response was as direct as his gaze: 'We need you,' he said simply.

Again Patrick scanned the grey sea. Suddenly he was aware of the continuous slapla-slapla-slapla of the chop against the canted hull and he caught sight of a drifting seagull hanging for a long moment above the mast before weaving away on motionless and disappointed wings when no offal was tossed overboard.

'Then you must tell me all you can, Aidan,' he said, 'for I have much to learn and little time in which to do it.'

Aidan paused, and when he spoke what he said was highly important.

'Palladius's mission didn't fail just because he died,' he said. 'I don't think it would have succeeded even if he had lived.'

'Explain.'

'I have noticed that you always refer to yourself as ''priest''.

You say you were ordained by the Pope himself. But you have not said that you are a bishop.' He looked at Patrick. 'That is so, isn't it?'

'What you say is correct.'

'So I conclude that, whatever the reason, you are not coming as a bishop.'

'Go on.'

'As I said, I don't know the reasons for such a decision, but I am sure it is right.'

This so startled Patrick that it almost showed but he controlled his surprise.

'Why do you say so, Aidan? It is very interesting.'

'Because the fact that Palladius was known to be a bishop hindered rather than helped him.'

'And you think it would be the same for me?'

'I'm sure of it.'

Aidan explained that Palladius was welcomed joyfully by the Irish Christians; became, in effect, their visible and institutionalised head, and this worked against him.

'A moment ago you pointed out some of the problems of institutionalisation. What happened in Palladius's case was that those he most wanted to reach, the pagan Irish, became more suspicious than ever of the Christians when they saw they had a new leader. As you well know, Christians in Ireland are often slaves, or secret Christians - like an important woman I'll tell you about in a moment - and are usually believed to be Roman sympathisers, sometimes with good cause. When a recognised leader came among them from Rome . . . Well, in my opinion it was a fatal mistake. Moreover, Palladius spent all his time here - I mean in Ireland - preaching to the converted. I know this is important, but like I said the converted are suspect anyway. There are exceptions, of course, like the woman I'm going to tell you about . . . '

'And yourself . . . '

Aidan smiled. 'Yes, and me.'

'Who is this important woman you mentioned?'

'Scath. She's married to Felim, King of Trim near the Boyne, son of the Ri-Eireann (King of Ireland), Laoire. More importantly, like yourself, she is both a Christian and a Briton . . . '

With uncharacteristic force Patrick interrupted, a rare occurrence when someone was speaking to him: 'I am a Roman citizen.'

'Have you not heard what I said?' asked Aidan. 'Better you be a Briton, old friend, and I'll tell you why.'

'Go on.'

'Scath is devout. Extremely devout. Her son, Forten, and my own Fergus are good friends, and she is anxious for Forten to be a Christian.'

'I see.'

'Do you? Convert him and you have converted the grandson of the Ri-Eireann. With his approval you may win, without it your mission must be limited and could fail. Don't make the mistake Palladius made. He never won the approval and protection of kings and nobles, much less that of Laoire who succeeded his cousin, Daithi, or Daffyd as you would call him . . . '

'Daithi? Then Laoire did not succeed . . . Nial?'

Even so many years later it was quite an effort for Patrick to utter the name that, above all else, reminded him of the days of his enslavement, the persecution and disruption of his family.

'No. Although he is Nial's son he did not succeed him. That is not our system, which is by election from among those who are eligible. At that time, Daithi was preferred to Laoire, and became king after Nial. When Daithi was killed – and that's a remarkable story . . . ' Aidan's eyes looked into space as if drawing visions from it. 'He was killed in the Alps fighting the Romans, by lightning, when he destroyed the hovel of a hermit . . . '

'Aidan!'

'Hm? Yes?'

'What has this got to do with Daithi's death?'

'Eh? Oh! Well, I just thought you'd be interested.'

'I am, but some other time, please.'

'Well, when Daithi was killed, Laoire was elected. In fact, the genealogy is something you *must* understand. If you don't you could make very serious mistakes.' Aidan prepared to tell Patrick of the nascent struggle between the Ui Neills of the North and the Ui Neills of the South, both of them descended from three brothers who defied their father, Nial, and established dynasties which were to become rivals for the Kingship of Ireland for five hundred years. But Patrick stopped him and surprised him with a question which, temporarily, diverted his intention.

'How did Nial die? May he rest in peace!' he added.

Then Aidan told Patrick the great story of Nial's assassination on a foreign field, when he was performing a strange, ancient and kingly function at the request and for the benefit of women.

'Moreover,' said Aidan, 'believe it or not the reason for his murder goes back more than three hundred years.'

The scepticism was plain in the corner of Patrick's eye, but Aidan was undeterred.

'True,' he went on. 'The cause was a woeful and enormous tribute laid in perpetuity on the kingdom of Leinster. It is due on alternate years and is called the *boru*, or battle, tribute. And it is truly formidable: five thousand cattle; five thousand hogs; five thousand bronze or brass cooking vessels; and five thousand ounces of silver.'

Patrick was impressed: 'You mean this is actually paid?'

'It often has to be fought for; usually the King wins and it is paid, but it has caused tremendous bitterness and bloodshed for twenty generations for although it is unlawful it is just.'

'And how did this cause the death of Nial?'

'Do you not want to know why it is imposed?'

Patrick smiled. 'I would not dream of spoiling your story.'

Aidan was serious. 'Don't treat this lightly, my friend. A great deal will depend on your ability to appreciate and understand such matters as the boru tribute and what it has brought about.'

Patrick nodded.

'More than three hundred years ago the High King was Tual the Legitimate, father of Felim the Lawgiver . . . '

'I thought Cormac Mac Art was the great lawmaker.'

'Yes, he wrote and codified the law, but many of them were pronounced by Felim, what you might call a *lex talionis*.'

'An eye for an eye.'

'Some of the Christ's words are harsh.' Aidan paused, then went on with his story. 'Tual had two daughters, Dairine and Fihil, and Dairine married Ochy, the King of Leinster - Ochy is a family name among them - and this Ochy was a lecher.' Patrick's brow darkened slightly, but Aidan didn't notice. 'After they had been married for a while Ochy grew tired of her, coveting the younger sister, Fihil. So he imprisoned Dairine in a tower in his castle and gave it out that she died in a plague. He went mourning to Tara where he was received with sympathy, and Tual offered him Fihil as a new wife to console him.'

Patrick shook his head, but remained silent.

'Ochy brought Fihil back to his castle at Naas and kept her there. After a while she penetrated the tower where her sister was confined and discovered the truth.'

'But tell me,' asked Patrick in genuine curiosity, 'since, regrettably, it is still the custom, isn't it, for a noble to have more than one woman, why did he not just ask for the second sister?'

Aidan looked at him in horror.

'They were king's daughters,' he protested, 'sisters. The law would not permit, and the sept could not allow, two king's daughters to the one man.'

'I see,' said Patrick. 'I'm sorry I interrupted, old friend. Please go on.'

Aidan took a deep breath. Educating Patrick was not going to be easy.

'Overcome with shame, the sisters - and please, Patrick, we

are not talking about Christian morality; they had been outraged within the recognised and established virtues and customs of their tradition.'

Patrick replied: 'I know, I know. Please go on,' and returned his gaze to the grey sea.

Aidan felt he was being laughed at, but shrugged it off and proceeded with a little less enthusiasm than before. But soon the sense of drama overtook him again and his voice became stronger and more confident.

'As I said, the sisters, overcome by their shameful predicament, made a pact and committed suicide rather than face the shame of the world . . . ' He became absorbed in the telling, reliving, in his mind's eye, the story which was part of the oral history that fashioned the outlook of the people Patrick moved steadily towards as the black ship ploughed the turbulent sea crests at the direction of its great sail.

'When Tual heard what had happened he marched into Leinster, burning and destroying all before him. The kingdom was only saved by Ochy pledging the tribute I mentioned, for ever, every second year. That is how it started. In law, however, no one can require tribute from the King of Leinster, for he is king of a province, one of the Pentarchy. As to the death of Nial, ironically that was accomplished by yet another Ochy, himself son of the King of Leinster, Enna Kinsella, and the cause was payment - or, if you like - nonpayment, of the boru tribute. This is what happened.'

Patrick leaned back, settled more comfortably against the rail of the ship and a coil of rope and closed his eyes as Aidan began what was clearly going to be quite a yarn. Without opening his eyes he asked: 'You don't mind if I ask a question from time to time?'

Aidan started, turned back for a moment from his wandering into the past, and said, 'Mind? No-o, no. Ask anything you like.' Then, looking at the grey sky, he went on as if there had been no interruption.

'Ochy Mac Enna, only the son of the King of Leinster, resented the tribute so much that when Nial was absent on an expedition . . . '

'To Britain, no doubt,' commented Patrick drily.

'As a matter of fact it was,' said Aidan, not noticing the irony in Patrick's voice. 'While he was away, Ochy attacked Tara, would you believe it, but of course was driven off. When Nial returned he ravaged Leinster in revenge and captured Ochy, but he later escaped. And that's where the final tragedy – ' he did not see Patrick's eyes jerk open at that ' – began. On his way home after escaping, Ochy tried to force the poet Ladcen to give him sanctuary – and more, I'm told, for he had a beautiful wife – in his home beside the Liffey. When the poet refused, Ochy flew into a rage and killed Ladcen's son. Bad blood seems to run in that family! Now, for violating a poet, not all the power of Leinster could protect him and he fled to his cousin, Gowran, king of the Dalriadan colony in Caledonia.'

'How does Nial's death come into it?' asked Patrick, whose tolerance was brief when it came to the involved and convoluted accounts of events so beloved by those he was going to meet.

'Patience,' said Aidan. 'Can't you listen? A few years later when Nial planned a large expedition against the Franks in Gaul he ordered Gowran to provide a contingent for the army. This was Ochy's chance. Still burning with hatred he travelled with the colonials solely, it seems, in the hope of getting an opportunity to murder Nial. The chance came when the army was camped on the banks of the River Loire – do you know it?'

Patrick nodded.

'It is our – I mean an Irish – tradition that the King marries the earth and fructifies it.' Hurriedly Aidan held up his hand as Patrick scowled. 'I know, I know. I'm not defending such pagan practices . . . '

'Idolatry,' muttered Patrick.

'All I'm saying is that it is the tradition and, in their ignorance, the people believe in it . . . '

'Heathens,' growled Patrick and Aidan stopped. There was silence for a few moments between the two friends, one angry, the other offended. Suddenly Patrick's scowl vanished, to be replaced by a dazzling smile. With all his formidable charm he asked: 'Aren't you going to continue?'

But Aidan was also determined. 'I don't mind being interrupted, Patrick; I don't even mind that you only half listen to the understanding behind what I'm telling you; if you refuse to understand the hearts and minds of the people to whom you are going that's your own affair. But I see no reason at all why you should be angry with me for telling you the facts.'

Patrick stretched out his hand and touched Aidan's arm. He realised that his own sense of outrage at pagan abominations had, unwittingly, hurt Aidan who was only doing what he himself had requested.

'You must forgive me, Aidan,' he said, his accent a little thicker than normal, 'you are right, of course. I cannot conquer in Christ's name, in Christ's cause, in the way of Christ, unless I am fully informed. *Mea culpa.* Please go on.'

Slowly Aidan began again. 'The King marries the earth-mother, which is why, as long as he remains powerful and virile, the land is fruitful. And because the King lives at Tara it is a masculine place, whereas all - or most - other places are not. Moreover, in some respects the King belongs to all the people and in some respects he belongs only to women . . . '

'I have heard of these abominations.'

'Abominations they may be, Patrick, some of them, but morality and rectitude are not the same thing and it is perfectly possible for a man or a woman or a whole people to be mistakenly immoral and yet right in heart. Is that not so?'

Very quietly Patrick said: 'Aidan, I need you. Please go on.'

'Women have the right, particularly - but not exclusively - women who are barren, or who are afraid that they no longer interest their husbands, to see the shape of the king. That is a powerful remedy for such afflictions, and when requested by five or more women the king is obliged to comply. The greater the king the greater the potency. The Ri-Eireann's seeing is most potent of all.'

'What do you mean? See the shape of the king.'

'They see him naked with an erect member.'

'And do you believe such primitive and revolting superstitious customs have merit, O great defender of your traditions?' Patrick found it difficult to keep the sarcasm from his voice.

With considerable dignity Aidan replied: 'I am a good Christian, Patrick, as you well know, who plagued you to return to the pagans you scorn so much, that you might lead them to the arms of Christ. I do not believe in idols or in heathen worship, but neither do I pretend to understand all the workings of the Almighty God through the instrument of the universal Church, known or unknown. And I know that women, barren for many years, have conceived after such an audience; that women whose husbands had strayed found themselves cherished again. What the cause may be I leave for better men than I to determine.'

'For a Christian you sound perilously like a heretic.'

'All my life, until I met you, I was worse than a heretic, Patrick. Now you tell me something: while the Church of Christ clearly has a monopoly of divine truth . . . ' Patrick nodded in confirmation, ' . . . are the shades of meaning all quite clear? Does God not move in a mysterious way and are we to shut our eyes and say He is wrong when it is we who do not understand?'

'Continue my friend. You bring me what I need most.'

'What is that?'

'Knowledge and humility.'

For a moment Aidan said nothing because of the sudden tears that sprang in his eyes. Then he went on: 'It happened that in the army camp there were many women, wives and followers of the men, and some of these, seeing the king walking by the river, appealed to him to turn aside and show them his shape, which he agreed to do. So, sending his retinue away - for this was for women only - he removed all but his cloak and turned to stand before them. They completed the rite . . . '

'Which is?'

'They must lie upon the ground.'

'God in Heaven! To adore such a thing?'

'No! Please try to understand. To identify with the union between king and earth.'

'Mmmm.'

'Ochy, watching his chance, was hidden on the opposite bank. As the king stood there in the full majesty of all he represented, he let loose a foul arrow which pierced the king's heart and killed him where he stood.'

'You sound regretful?'

For a moment they looked one another in the eye.

'As a matter of fact,' said Aidan, 'I am regretful.'

Chapter 8

FOR the rest of the voyage there were many periods of discussion when each man spoke and listened with concentration. These were interspersed with long and easy, companionable silences. At times Patrick prayed by himself or sat alone, doing nothing, looking at the sea while Aidan attended to one shipboard duty or another; at times, as when they ate in the cabin, they exchanged general ideas as men do. On the fourth afternoon after they sailed, when the south-east coast of Ireland appeared as a blue, irregular edge above the horizon, Patrick, sitting in the lee of the ship's rail, took from his pouch a precious piece of parchment. He studied it, almost reluctantly, for a moment and then called Aidan and asked him if he had ink, and a pen.

'Black?' asked Aidan. 'Of course. Just a moment.' He disappeared through the hatch to the cabin. While he was gone, Patrick put his leather purse on his knees and waited. A moment later Aidan returned with an *ayarkeen*, part of a cow's horn stopped with a wooden plug, in which he kept a supply of carbon ink, blacker than the blackest night, for recording transactions. In the same hand he also held a short, strong, swan's quill.

'You're all right for a knife? You have your own?' Aidan teased.

Patrick smiled and nodded and took the proffered pen and ink. Aidan stood for a moment, uncertain if he should sit with his friend, but when he saw that Patrick was absorbed in what he was doing he returned to the steering oar and watched for the sandy islands that marked treacherous sandbanks lying off this coast.

With the small knife he kept principally for the purpose, Patrick sharpened and split the quill. He wedged the *ayarkeen* securely in a handy coil of rope, dipped the quill and poised it above the parchment which lay on his pouch on his knees. A long moment he remained thus, apparently undecided, in reality shaping words in his mind. Suddenly his eyes sharpened and lost their faraway look. Quickly and decisively he started to write:

I arise today through a mighty strength, the
Invocation of the Trinity;
Through belief in the Threeness,
Through Confession of the Oneness
Of the Creator of Creation . . .

His pen hovered a moment above the words he had written, then plunged towards the paper with renewed energy as if the words could not be written quickly enough to keep pace with the mind directing them. Patrick frowned in concentration as the script flowed onto the parchment in black letters that would live for two thousand years and more:

Christ shield me today
Against poison, against burning,
Against drowning, against wounding,
That I may receive abundance of reward.
Christ with me, Christ before me, Christ behind me,
Christ in me, Christ beneath me, Christ above me,
Christ on my right hand, Christ on my left,
Christ where I lie, Christ where I sit, Christ where I arise,
Christ in the heart of every man who thinks of me,
Christ in the mouth of every man who speaks to me,
Christ in every eye that sees me . . '

He paused. 'Christ in every ear that hears me,' he murmured, his lips moving over words which were to follow his name through centuries and acquire the title *Breastplate of Saint Patrick.*

'Through belief in the Threeness . . . ' From habit the twisted, arthritic finger moved slowly and unnecessarily below each well-remembered word as his old lips formed the melodic and sonorous syllables. He was obstinately proud of the fact that in this, the first of his labours among the Irish, there was no hint of assonance or any other native influence which might be detected in a good deal of what he had written afterwards.

'Even,' he mused, 'in my last testament!' He glanced at the small pile of vellum on the table at his elbow, which contained the testament he had just completed. 'But what will I call you?' he wondered aloud, as if the prayer itself might provide the answer even as he went on reading and the gnarled finger continued its unsteady trace. 'Through belief in the Threeness . . . ' It was strange how, ever since he had first written the original draft, he kept returning to this prayer, changing it, adding to it, taking away again. It was as if, in his bones, he knew it was still incomplete, still not the full declaration of Spirit that he wanted to make, even though he knew that what was there was correct as far as it went.

Without warning, a memory filled his mind, enveloped him like a war-cloak, and he shivered. For he recalled his first meeting with Laoire, the then Ri-Eireann, and the grave significance the phrase 'Through belief in the Threeness' had had on that occasion. Images from the past began storming through his mind, clamouring for attention and bringing confusion with them. For a moment he was unable to order his thoughts and, for one of the few occasions in his life, he felt frightened. '*Domine Jesu Christe, exaudi me in die qua invocaverimo te,*' he cried in momentary anguish, and immediately felt calmer. His thoughts became more orderly. He recalled the ancient words of Amergin, the first poet of Ireland, which he had learned from the poet Duach, who was the first of Laoire's household to pay him respect:

I am the wind of the Sea,
I am the Wave of the Ocean,
I am the roar of the Tide . . .

Hardly realising he did so, and motivated by some unfathomable inconsistency, he picked up his quill, dipped it in his *ayarkeen* and began to write. Allowing the full accumulation of his teaching and of his learning, of the marriage of two cultures which he had brought about, to mingle with his impassioned memories, infuse his blood and inform his spirit, he added the following to the prayer he had begun over thirty years earlier on the day when he first sighted the coast of Ireland from the deck of Aidan's reaching ship:

I arise today, through the strength of heaven;
Light of Sun,
Radiance of Moon,
Splendour of Fire,
Speed of Lightning,
Swiftness of Wind,
Depth of Sea,
Stability of Earth,
Firmness of Rock.
I arise through God's strength to pilot me.
God's might to uphold me;
God's Wisdom to lead me;
God's eye to look before me;
God's ear to hear me;
God's word to speak for me;
God's hand to guard me;
God's way to lie before me;
God's shield to protect me
God's host to defend me . . .

Patrick stopped. His hand dropped to the vellum resting on the writing board on his knees. He raised his head so that the light struck his eyes which were still changeable, but clouded now. His look went out through the open doorway of his house past the other buildings of this small - and recent - monastic foundation lying on the slope of a hill between the settlement of Dubhlinn and the wicker bridge at B'lath Cliath. The view wavered and misted before he could distinguish details of the sunlit headland in the distance across the bay or discern the glittering of the speckled sea beyond. But he had seen it all before, and listened to the compelling music of the colours, the shapes, the natural wonders about him. An awareness of their beauty, like an awareness of the people he served, had entered into his unwilling and reluctant being. And how he had fought both! Painfully he reached an arm for the first page of his testament which he laid before him. He lifted the *flesc fille*, poet's rod, of white yew and gripped one end of it in his left hand so that it lay across the page to steady his right hand as he inscribed. He grunted with pain at the effort. He dipped his quill in the *ayarkeen*, and slowly and carefully, in large letters, wrote at the top: CONFESSIO. Having done so he leaned back and yet again read what he had earlier written: 'I am Patrick, a sinner, most unlearned, the least of all the faithful and utterly despised by many . . . ' He paused a moment, wondering if he ought to delete the last five words; then remembered why he had written them and clenched his jaw, forgetting, until it reminded him, the painful tooth remaining at the back. 'My father,' he read, 'was Calpurnius, deacon, son of Potitus, priest, of the village of Bennavem Taburniae; he had a farm nearby where I was captured . . . ' More calmly than ever before he recalled, again, details of his capture more than sixty years ago, but with as much bitterness as ever. And as always he criticised himself just as bitterly for his lack of charity. It was only in private and at moments like these that he was thus assailed. But it had become more frequent as the years passed. Helplessly he shook his head. He had fought this stiff-necked obstinacy all his life and the best he could do was offer it to God as something he was ashamed of.

Deliberately he moved his thoughts forward. For some reason - perhaps because of his *Confessio* - he was prepared to indulge this mood for reflection; 'Or perhaps,' and he smiled wryly, 'it is because I am near the end.' He gave his recollection free rein to wander where it would over what had happened since his first landing in Ireland as a missionary. Certain things stood out, not only because they were themselves important, but because in some cases they also had significance for himself personally.

Of all the incidents leading to the widespread conversion and baptism that took place under his hand, followed in turn by the startling growth of voluntary dedication to the Almighty God by the young intelligentsia, none was so full of consequence as his first meeting with the King Laoire. It took place about three months after his arrival, and two significant events had occurred in the meantime, one being the baptism of the king's grandson, Forten, which Aidan had persuaded a surprised Patrick not to perform himself.

'Why not?' he had asked when Aidan first advised against it.

'Because it's not fitting,' was the reply.

'What do you mean, not fitting? He's the king's grandson. You yourself told me how important it was. If it wasn't for you I'd never have known about it.'

'Then listen to me now,' said Aidan. 'You got good advice before and you'll get the same again. If you're going to talk with kings, you must think like a king yourself, behave like one.'

'But I . . . ' protested Patrick.

Aidan raised his palm and stopped him with a smile. 'I know,' he said, 'you're going to say that you're not a king and you don't want to be a king.'

'Correct,' Patrick drily agreed.

'But that's not the point,' Aidan went on. 'The point is that kings will ignore you if you don't impress them, if they don't think you are somebody of consequence; important,' he hurried on before Patrick's anger could bridle, 'and on their terms. Surely that is clear?' he ended.

Patrick looked at him enigmatically for a moment and then jerked his head slightly, a mannerism which was the outward expression of an inward shrug. 'Very good, Aidan. Now, tell me why my *not* baptising Forten is more impressive than my *doing* it.'

'Because he is the king's grandson and you have not yet met the king. I think it is important you demonstrate that you have held yourself in reserve for that. Whether you like it or not your mission has political and social implications as well as the obvious religious ones, and our kings and nobles are much more aware of this than you appear to be. You must take into account that, for us, religion at present . . . '

'You mean idolatry!'

'Call it whatever you like. It's religion to the people who believe it.'

'Tchah!'

'Patrick, don't be like that. For us religion is so . . . so intricate a part of life that to change the web of it means changing the woof also.'

'I don't understand you. Speak plainly.'

'Religious beliefs - rather, practices - are so bound up with everyday life, with law, for example, and social order, sowing and harvesting, fertility in cattle - that anything you do to change them is bound to affect the fabric of social and political life.'

'Naturally. It happens everywhere; it happened in Rome itself.

'That was different. Constantine made Christianity the official religion of the Empire. It's not like that here. Here belief comes into the daily lives of the people in a way - in a way not entirely different to the way that Christianity does, even if the expression of it is . . . '

'Patrick, please listen to me with your mind and your heart as well as with your ears and your faith. I'm telling you what you need to know. You must try to understand. The fruit on this tree of ours is ripe and ready to fall. But who is going to catch it? You or someone else - Pelagius? If it is going to be you, you must be ready. And, old friend, you won't succeed unless you see the fruit for what it is - very rewarding, but easily bruised - and stand beneath it with gentle hands to receive it.'

'Are you telling me I don't see clearly. Is that it?'

'In a way I suppose I am,' said Aidan. 'You see everything that is not Christian as idolatrous or pagan. In the strict sense of the word you are right, of course. But, Patrick, people are people, they may arrive at like beliefs by different roads.'

'You said something very similar to me on the ship.'

'Possibly. You make it very clear that you don't sympathise with the idea very much.'

'Nobody,' said Patrick with a touch of the defiant obdurateness that often made him so unyielding when to bend would achieve more, 'can arrive at the truth without the grace of God, or do you deny that too? Are you already a Pelagian?'

'Old friend, don't be angry. There is no question of finding truth without the grace of God or the intervention of the divine saviour, but will you sit there and tell me that you know all the mysterious ways in which divine providence achieves this miracle . . . every time?'

Patrick set his jaw and said nothing. He was irritated at this repeated reproof from Aidan.

Anxiously Aidan went on, by no means sure that he was being understood or even that he wasn't making matters worse. But he felt he had no choice.

'Patrick, all I'm trying to say is that I think the Irish belief that gods have three natures or aspects is not dissimilar entirely to . . . '

'What's that you say?'

'I'm talking about the three natures of, well, god, as the Irish understand it . . . ' Patrick's mouth was open. 'There's the aspect of the soul or spirit, the aspect of creation, and the aspect of learning or enlightenment, all in one . . . ' But Patrick had collapsed to his knees. Tears ran down his upturned cheeks. His hands were clasped and raised to the sky.

'*Deo gratias*,' he cried, '*in nomine Patris, et Filii, et Spiritus Sancti* . . . '

Aidan looked at him in amazement. 'You mean you didn't know?' he asked.

From his kneeling position Patrick shook his head. He was shattered by this extraordinary revelation; his sense of humility before the power of the Almighty overwhelmed him. After a while, he regained his composure and Aidan helped him to his feet. Patrick turned and clasped both Aidan's hands in his own.

'My dear brother, how foolish and arrogant I have been! On your ship I asked you to teach me but, even as I asked, I was unwilling to listen to your wisdom. I beg your forgiveness and I ask you once again to teach me and,' he added, totally unable to restrain the glint of mischievousness that in spite of himself crept into his eyes, 'this time I promise I will learn.'

Aidan smiled, then laughed outright when he saw Patrick smile too. He shook Patrick's hands.

'Old friend. It will be hard for you.' Aidan looked away a moment and then met Patrick's eye squarely. 'Was it not the great Saul who said, "If there is anything you want, pray for it, asking God . . . '

' . . . with prayer and thanksgiving,' Patrick took up, 'and that peace of God which is so much greater than we can understand will guard your hearts and your thoughts, in Christ Jesus . . . " '

Both men were suddenly silent. Then Patrick asked, 'How is it that you know that scripture so well?'

Aidan's face was serious as he answered. 'In the absence of proper guidance, I had to make my own way in the Faith. I found Saul a good guide.'

Patrick put his hand on his friend's arm. 'Truly, I will listen,' he said.

Accordingly, Forten was not baptised by Patrick, but by his nephew, Loman, a British priest, who came to join him soon after he arrived. Later, when he came to meet Laoire, Patrick was glad he had listened to Aidan's wisdom.

Patrick arrived in Ireland while the festival of Imbolc, devoted to the goddess Brigit, was being celebrated. Brigit was the daughter of the god Dagda, fabulous king of the Tuatha de Danaan, the People of Annan, who were the first civilised people to colonise Ireland. She was worshipped in her three aspects: that of fertility, wisdom, and poetic inspiration. Her rites had once been a powerful influence in the community, but with the passage of time her ritual observances centred increasingly on seeking her protection for a good lambing season. Since shepherding was exclusively work for *fudirs*, or other social outcasts and slaves - especially young females when it came to lambing time - it was a festival that had become peculiarly their own and was neglected or given only token recognition by the middle and upper classes. By Patrick's time it was the slaves' annual festival and two days after his landing he strayed into just such a fair. Because it was a slave gathering, the *dlee* (druids) ignored it, and its solemn religious aspect had long since been dissipated. It was, by now, essentially a holiday occasion for slaves and *fudirs*. They ran foot races, performed feats of strength and held competitions of one kind or another. A great deal of beer was consumed followed by dancing and love- and merry-making.

For centuries *fudirs* and slaves had cared for in-lamb ewes and for the lambs themselves for the first ten weeks. As time passed they acquired skills and techniques of breeding and rearing which were of inestimable economic importance, as the entire wool trade ultimately depended on the supply of lambs and on their welfare. Thus the upper class's tolerance - even reluctant encouragement - of the festival which helped keep slaves and *fudirs* content was more a grudging recognition of their fundamental economic importance than any concern for their leisure activities.

The fair was taking place near an oak wood in what was later to become the kingdom of Kildare - Cill Dara, the oaken church. As Patrick and his small group of friends and disciples, Aidan, Loman and a local giant called MacCartan among them, approached, they were jostled and chaffed by happy, laughing and shouting people on the road. Patrick was entranced and enormously enjoyed the effervescent - if vulgar - atmosphere. He smiled from ear to ear and Aidan, uncomfortable and self-conscious surrounded by such people in his own country (as he would never have been in similar circumstances abroad) saw him in an entirely new light. Aidan would much rather have been away somewhere else among members of his own class, but he hid his discomfiture as well as he could. Even MacCartan, who had appointed himself Patrick's protector and bodyguard, towering head and shoulders above most other men on the road, looked anxious from time to time as he tried, quite unsuccessfully, to keep his bulk between Patrick and the carefree mob.

MacCartan's fussiness, which was almost matronly and might have been comical in so large and formidable-looking a man were it not graciously encased in gentleness and concern, was extremely convenient when it came to swollen rivers, for example. In the manner of the country, he hoisted the Roman priest on his back and waded with him to the far side; a service for which Patrick was particularly grateful as arthritis - the 'wounds of Christ' which were to cripple his hands and feet in old age - even then afflicted him painfully.

'Hey,' roared a large, rough, red-headed man, 'who cut yer hair?' He slapped Patrick on the shoulder before MacCartan could stop him and turned for appreciation to his three companions - a bald-headed, rotund man of middle age, a fat woman wrapped in a huge cloak in spite of the heat of the day, and a tall, thin woman whom he was clearly out to impress. And with some success, for she threw back her head and gave vent to a strident, high-pitched laugh, like a jay, when he looked at her for approval.

'You one a them foreigners?' asked the fat woman jovially but with an interested glint in her eye, 'a Vandal, maybe?' Vandals often had money.

Patrick, smiling, shook his head.

'Naw,' guffawed the red-headed giant, 'he's a Christian. An' a druid what's more. I've seen your sort before. Am I right, mister?'

Patrick nodded.

'There y'are,' said the red-head to the thin woman, who was clearly impressed with his knowledge. Satisfied he turned back to Patrick, ignoring MacCartan's glower. 'Come far?'

Patrick looked at Aidan. 'Where?' he asked.

'Wexford,' said Aidan shortly, acutely embarrassed by being thus engaged in conversation as an equal by an obvious *fudir*, who equally obviously realised his embarrassment and was enjoying it thoroughly.

'Ah!' he said. 'There's Christians there.'

'I knew a Christian once,' said the fat woman suddenly and they all looked at her. She was taken by surprise, as much at herself for speaking as by the attention she got, and laughed. 'She-eh-she was a quare wan,' she went on. 'Didn't seem to enjoy herself very much, if you know what I mean. She was a foreigner too. British! Wouldn't – ' she glanced around quickly and then, with a saucy defiance, ' – wouldn't screw with anyone only the master, and then only because she couldn't stop him!'

She was obviously being deliberately coarse and expected Patrick to be shocked. But he only smiled at her and said: 'She must have been a fine girl. Perhaps she had other things on her mind besides pleasures. Was she a slave, I wonder?'

'Well . . . '

'Did you know her well?' he went on, before she could say yes.

'Well, I suppose I did. Worked alongside of me at the lambs and in the dairy, she did. Always laughing, she was, when she wasn't serious.'

'Seems like strange behaviour for one who didn't enjoy herself much,' said Patrick catching her eye, and for a moment, her mouth fell open. Then she laughed.

'Ah, you're too cute. Sure I only said that to take a rise out of you. Don't I know from her what all you'se Christians are like? Tell us, do you never get 'ere an oul' tumble from a girl yourself?'

This question was so unexpected and outrageous that, for a moment, no one reacted to it and the fat woman looked in silence at Patrick, who remained smiling. Then Aidan and MacCartan exploded simultaneously.

'What do you mean . . . ?'

'Who do you think you're talking to?' MacCartan made a grab for her, but the red-headed giant came between them and the two big men glared at each other in the middle of the road.

'No, no, it's all right,' said Patrick. 'It was a perfectly natural question even if, perhaps, rather strangely expressed. But I'm sure it was prompted by a perfectly normal curiosity. And the answer . . . '

Aidan heard MacCartan draw in a shocked breath.

' . . . is no! Now would you two please stand back from each other. You're blocking the road and these good people can't get by.'

Slowly the two big men backed off and stationed themselves one on either side of Patrick who continued on his way, talking to the fat woman across the great chest of the red-headed man.

'I'm sure you already know the Christian attitude to promiscuity,' he said.

'Sure of course I do,' said the fat woman. 'It's not that I don't understand. Between ourselves they're pretty narrow here too . . . '

'Never stopped you,' growled the rotund man, who was her husband and on whom she bestowed a complacent smile.

'It's that I don't understand not having anything to do with it at all,' she went on to Patrick. 'I mean there's nothing like a good – ' she hesitated and looked around; what she saw made her decide to amend the wording she had intended to use – ' – a good oul' roll to, you know, loosen you up and release the tensions and the like of that; make life a bit easier, if you know what I mean.'

'Certainly,' said Patrick, to the horror of his companions, 'but it is a privilege that is confined to marriage only.'

The fat woman threw back her head and laughed. 'You better tell that to him, then,' she roared, digging the rotund man in the ribs with an enormous elbow. 'Sure he's so confined he hasn't seen what he has this past twelve months, and then he didn't know what to do with it.'

'That's enough now,' roared MacCartan.

'It's all right,' said Patrick, 'there's no harm being done.'

'You're a strange kind of a Christian,' said the fat woman. 'Any Christians I ever met before pretended to be shocked by the like of that. I didn't think you'd be so open.'

'I don't think I was being particularly broad-minded,' said Patrick. 'You didn't say anything I basically disagree with.'

'Tell us,' she enquired, 'what makes ye Christians at all?'

'Love,' began Patrick.

'Well, by Ishtar,' said the rotund man sourly, 'there's no doubt but you're talking to the right one so, there's nothing you'd want to know about love that one wouldn't be able to teach you.'

'Ah will you shut up,' she said affectionately, nudging him in the ribs with her massive elbow again. 'Don't I keep us happy?' And to Patrick, 'What sort of love?'

'The love of Jesus, the Christ, our Lord,' he replied. Then a strange thing happened. The teasing smile that had been on her lips faded and a frown appeared momentarily between her brows.

Her eyes looked puzzled, then brightened to interest, and she turned towards him.

'Tell me!' she commanded, coming round the red-headed man to walk beside Patrick.

When they reached the *cloonayna*, or fair field, an hour later, the fat woman had promised Patrick to become a Christian – 'tomorrow!' He smiled and spoke to Loman whom he was leaving behind in the area and he undertook to baptise her. She looked slightly taken aback at this, but nonetheless agreed; and so it turned out, and the fat lady never – well, seldom – again went rioting with every man she fancied.

As Patrick and his companions walked onto the thronged field with its notable lack of well-dressed men and women and horses and chariots, there was a commotion in front and a tall, well-dressed, dark young man of about twenty – obviously one of the landed class – burst, laughing, from a group of peasants, who half-heartedly attempted to impede him. Behind him he pulled a girl who seemed unwilling, but more because of the attention they attracted than from the fact that he was taking her with him. The youth had an air of self-confidence and authority, some might call it arrogance, that came from knowing he had power over those around him. The girl too was different. She was very beautiful and as fair as he was dark, small where he was tall and lithe, humbly and neatly dressed where he was expensively and carelessly clothed. He was laughing and thrusting people aside while she blushed and hung back. There were mutterings behind them as they passed. By chance they made straight for where Patrick had stopped when he noticed the commotion. And when the young man thrust through the crowd nearby, Patrick's face went white and he seemed to fall back a step. But he faced the newcomer who, still laughing, stopped in front of him, as if it had been a prearranged meeting.

'What is your name?' asked Patrick.

'Duach,' cried the young man loudly, 'and do you like my lady?'

'She is charming,' said Patrick drily.

'She has just been married,' laughed Duach.

'To you?' asked Patrick, looking at him straight in the eye.

The smile went from Duach's face to be replaced by a scowl and those around Patrick were silent. They knew very well what the tall young man meant and why he was there. At that moment another man, smaller and sturdy and wearing the single colour of a *fudir*, appeared behind the couple, his face furious and his eyes blazing with suppressed rage. Duach stared at Patrick a moment, then laughed loudly.

'To me?' he cried. 'Of course not. Would I marry a slave?' He looked round laughingly and received a few scattered and nervous plaudits in reply, but there was mostly silence.

'Then whom has she married?' Patrick queried.

Still holding the girl by the wrist Duach looked round without concern.

'That fellow!' he cried, indicating the angry-looking man. 'You there. Come here!' The other shouldered his way through the crowd and stood on the other side of the girl, who looked at him appealingly, but in such a way it was evident that she enjoyed the situation and did not, in spite of her blushes, seem entirely averse at the prospect of Duach's intent.

'Did you marry this woman?' asked Patrick.

'Aye, sir.'

'Then why,' Patrick asked Duach, 'are you taking her off?'

'Not that it's any of your business,' came the reply, 'but because she is my slave and I have the right of the first night. Everybody knows that.'

'I see,' said Patrick. He turned to the girl. 'And what do you say?'

'I must do as my master orders,' she muttered, looking down.

'So – !' said Duach, starting off, his hand still round the girl's wrist.

'Just a moment,' said Patrick. He looked at the newly-wed

man. 'There's something I have to say to you first. Are you a Christian?'

'No, sir.'

'Perhaps you will be!' Duach snorted derisively.

'Duach,' Patrick went on, turning to the handsome young man, 'I have seen you before.'

'Me? Where? I never saw you before.'

'Not in the flesh. In a dream.'

There was a gasp from the crowd, and those nearby moved back and cleared a circle round them. Duach himself paled.

'You are a *dlee*?'

'Not such as you mean. I am a Christian priest. And I am here to save your soul for Christ.'

'There's nothing wrong with my soul.'

'It is in mortal danger.'

'From what?'

'From the enemy within you.'

'Bah,' cried Duach, 'there's no enemy . . . '

'Are you sure?' asked Patrick, his compelling eyes locking with the other's. 'Listen to me a moment, Duach. You do not have the right to do wrong. You know in your heart that what you intend is wrong. You are merely perpetuating and taking advantage of an abuse of privilege.'

'It is privilege! I have the right. They do not. The law permits it . . . '

Quickly Aidan stepped forward and whispered in Patrick's ear. Patrick listened for a moment, his face still turned towards Duach, who had halted in mid-sentence.

'I'm told,' said Patrick, 'that the law tolerates it, but recognises it as an abuse.'

'They have no rights,' muttered Duach sullenly, looking at the glowering bridegroom.

'Are they not human? Have they no souls?' Patrick demanded.

'They're not equal.'

'They are equal in the sight of God. And before God I tell you that you know what you propose is wrong.'

Duach let the girl go and took a step towards Patrick. MacCartan moved forwards, but Patrick put out an arm to restrain him.

His face very close to that of the smaller Roman, slightly stooped in order to do so, Duach hissed: 'Where did you say you saw me? In a dream?'

'Yes.'

'What was your dream?'

'You will believe me?'

'First tell me your dream. If it is true I'll know.'

'Not only you will believe me, Duach, but before we leave here I'll baptise you and you will become a Christian.'

At this Duach straightened. He looked about and laughed, but no one else laughed, and he turned back to Patrick.

'What do you say? You're mad.'

'Two nights ago I saw your face as clearly as I see it now. I recognised you when I saw you today.'

'How? What was I doing in your dream?'

'I was pouring the water of holiness on your forehead and marking you with holy chrism.'

Duach drew back and, involuntarily, made the sign against evil. 'The gods protect me.'

Patrick smiled. 'Don't be afraid. The God I bring you to is the only God. And he is a gentle God.'

'What does he want from me?'

'Your love.'

Duach looked sceptical.

'There is nothing He cannot or will not protect you against if you only come to him with love in your heart.'

'Is that all?'

Patrick spread his arms and stood there saying nothing.

'Tell me about your dream.'

'You will sin again.'

'What do you mean, sin?'

'Be patient with me, Duach, God is demanding and I am merely His ambassador.'

'What does he demand? Ask me and I will get it for you.'

'You! That is what He wants.'

'Then he wants too much. I have affairs of my own to attend to . . . '

'God will not interfere with your affairs if you carry them out honestly and in justice.'

'Then what?' Duach muttered.

'It is not this life that matters, Duach, but the next . . . '

'This one is enough for me.'

'You don't care what happens to you in the next life?'

'I care about now. Reality! Not fairy tales about mysterious lands . . . '

'Duach, you have a destiny. Twenty years from now, you, by then a Christian nobleman, will have a daughter . . . '

Duach laughed. 'I haven't even got a wife . . . '

'This child's mother will be a slave - you won't change all that much - hence your sin.'

Duach made an angry gesture.

'That's enough wizardry. You're making it up!'

'I wish I were. It is no pleasure to me to have these things happen in my sleep. I spent most of my life running away from them, and they, and God, pursued me until I came here.'

'Your God pursued you?'

'Not *my* God, Duach, *our* God.'

'Well, whatever. Why did he pursue you?'

'I don't know.'

Duach looked at him calculatingly. 'Your god is the greatest god of all?'

'The *only* God.'

'And he pursued you?'

'Yes.'

'Then you must be very important.'

'Indeed I am not. I am humble and tormented and I have a job to do. You can help me.'

For a moment the young man said nothing. Then he said: 'If I can I will. But first you must tell me your dream.'

'Your daughter, who you will call Brigit after the gentle tradition the name has among the people of the earth, the slaves and the *fudirs*, will be for ever known as the Queen of the Irish.'

'The Queen of the Irish!' Duach laughed. 'How can that be?'

Patrick shook his head. 'I don't know how it can be. I only know it will be.'

They talked together all day, the priest and the young nobleman who until then had been thoughtless and heartless, during the course of the day Patrick first baptised and later married the young couple in the Christian fashion. He baptised and prayed with many other Christians, new and old, many of whom shed tears when they met him as he was the first priest they had seen in their years of captivity. In the evening Duach brought the priest and his companions back to his *rath* where he provided them with food and shelter, and before the candles and rushes were extinguished he himself was baptised.

The fair, which continued next day, gave Patrick an opportunity to get to know some of the common and landless people. As he quickly discovered on the first day, Aidan was correct: many slaves were Christians, principally foreigners who had been captured abroad, and their children. He and his companions were in great demand during the two days of the fair, baptising, counselling and offering the Holy Sacrament. And it was here that he first established the practice which came to be for ever associated with him, of setting himself up near a well. Wells were the women's meeting places where they gathered and gossiped as they came for water, and it was at wells that Patrick won the women of Ireland to the Faith, even the daughters of kings.

Duach was so highly impressed that he swore to Patrick before he left on the third day that if he ever did have a daughter, she would be the lawful daughter of a properly wedded wife. Patrick smiled at him and gave him his blessing.

During the next three months Patrick and his small company travelled considerably and met and baptised many people, some of them important. On Aidan's advice he made a point of meeting local nobles and trying to obtain from them two things, firstly safe conduct and secondly the right to preach and to baptise in their territory. Sometimes, but not always, he converted the noble and much of his household. But he usually managed to get the safe conduct. Moreover, when he was moving from the territory of one overlord to that of the next, he also sought safe conduct from one to the other. At this time Patrick experienced few of the problems that arose in places later on. But there was one painful exception. He went out of his way to visit his former master, Mweelcu, now old and unbalanced and over seventy. They were halted at the borders of Mweelcu's lands - he had become suspicious and a recluse in his dotage - and were asked the usual questions, who they were, where they came from, why, and so on. Filled with a joyful expectancy at the prospect of meeting the man whose slave he had once been and of baptising him, Patrick sent Benin ahead under an armed guard to tell Mweelcu that Sucatus was returning after all these years as a messenger of hope with the gift of true Faith, the greatest he could bring.

Benin was the son of a chief, Sescna, with whom Patrick and his followers stayed on their journeyings. Patrick baptised Sescna and his family and had his permission to baptise anyone in his territory who was willing - provided Patrick did not exercise undue pressure. So for four days they travelled and worked, talking, meeting people, visiting settlements, being threatened and vilified by *dlee* and, especially at night, enjoying the challenge of argument and debate with the *ollamhs.*

On the fourth day Patrick fell asleep in the afternoon sun in the *grianaan* of Sescna's *rath*. While he was sleeping Benin, then eleven years old and already a knight, came with some wild flowers that he had idly gathered and, seeing Patrick asleep, was at first tempted to drop them on his face and wake him. He stole across the cropped grass to do so. But, as he held them above the face of the sleeping man, he suddenly and for no reason he could explain changed his mind and instead gently laid them on his breast as if they were a covering. At that instant Sescna appeared. 'What are you doing? Stop that!' he said angrily, but in a low voice, to his son. 'You'll wake the poor man.' But it was his voice that wakened Patrick who realised what had happened when he noticed the flowers.

He smiled and said to Sescna, 'Don't reproach Benin. He was being kind to me.'

So great became the bond between the ageing man and the boy that when Patrick and his followers were leaving, Benin pleaded to be allowed to go with him and this was agreed.

When they reached a small rise above the glen in which Mweelcu's *rath* stood, they were alarmed to see smoke and flames roaring up from the main dwelling. They ran to help but it was hopeless; worse, Mweelcu and some of his family perished.

'But what happened?' asked the aghast Patrick of Benin. The boy was ashen-faced and in a state of shock.

'I – I – I told him you were coming,' he stuttered. 'I . . . '

Patrick took him gently aside, but his own people and curious and aggressive followers of Mweelcu's crowded round to listen. So intent was everyone that the majority missed the sound of galloping hooves.

The ring of jostling figures was becoming hostile when a small, authoratitive man strode through the muttering crowd, elbowing them aside as he came.

'Come with me!' His voice was loud, but in a quieter tone he added, 'For your own sakes.' Then, turning back the way he had come he put his hand on Patrick's arm. 'Stand back,' he cried. 'I want to talk to this man.'

He was Mweelcu's grandson Fiac who had been hunting and just returned. His lathered horse stood where he had dropped the reins. He and Patrick learned from the house servants and Benin what had taken place.

'When he understood who you were and what you wanted he went into a frenzy,' said Benin. 'I never saw anything like it. I . . . ' he stopped. 'I mean . . . '

Patrick smiled and nodded. 'Go on, my son.'

He ordered the servants to shut and bar all the doors and windows of the house from the outside. He barred them from the inside himself. There was no one there but his women and some children.

'Then he set it alight. I saw it all. Over the noise of the flames we could hear him shouting that he'd never receive any - any runaway slave in his own house, much less receive his gifts. I saw him at a crack in the shuttered window screaming that he'd die before he'd let you near him again. He said he wouldn't lose face like that and all those with him would die too. And - and - they did . . . '

'We couldn't do anything. We tried to break in, but it was impossible. We tried to beat out the flames, but the fire had started on the inside and we couldn't do that either. We could hear them screaming . . . and then they stopped, one by one. And over all, the old man's voice shouting and cursing . . . '

'He was mad,' said his grandson flatly, who didn't quite know, at first, whether to give his attention to the young boy, obviously a nobleman, or the erstwhile slave who seemed to be in authority. But he soon realised Patrick was a foreigner, a Christian and of some importance, and spoke to him with understanding.

'Something like this was bound to happen sooner or later,' he said. 'He was getting impossible. The tragedy is that the whole family seems to have gone except myself.'

But the entire family had not perished. As Mweelcu barricaded the door and windows against Patrick, his youngest son Erc and his two young sisters were playing by a small lake with a flotilla of sticks and bits of wood which was an invasion fleet in some foreign sea. They did not return until the fire had burnt itself out. Patrick baptised them and left them in the care of their nephew, Fiac, who swore to look after them.

'Now,' Patrick said to Aidan and Loman, his own nephew, 'it is time to visit Laoire. The glorious week of Easter is upon us and it is then, with the risen Christ at my right hand, that I would like to meet the king.'

'That is a good time,' said Aidan. 'And it coincides with the feast of Bealtaine, when the cattle and all fruitful things are dedicated by the king, and fire is brought to life again.'

'Ah yes,' said Patrick, 'I had forgotten. Remind me.'

So Aidan proceeded to do one of the things he did best, tell a story. He told of the feast of Bealtaine and its importance and how it first was celebrated so many countless generations in the past that it was older than the people of Annan themselves. He told how Mide, druid of the first Tuatha de Danaan king in Ireland, Nemed, celebrated Bealtaine on the Hill of Usna where even older ceremonies had been performed before.

'Bealtaine is the feast,' he said, 'for a bountiful year, when the fruits of each year are burgeoning. The fires of the land are extinguished and two sacred flames are lighted and cattle are symbolically driven between them for protection against disease. That is the first fire and light and it is made by the king, from which every other fire in the country draws flame, with a small bow and a stick and tinder.'

'I see,' said Patrick. 'Let us go and see this festival.'

Aidan looked at him aghast. 'Us?' he asked.

Patrick smiled. 'Why not? Is that not where the king will be? Is that not where the most important people in Ireland will be? And is it not therefore the place for us to be also?'

'But, Patrick,' protested Aidan, 'it was near there, at Usna, like I told you, that Mide lit the first Bealtaine fire in Ireland; that's where he cut out the tongues of the false dr– I mean the druids who were there before him – and buried them so that they could not challenge him . . . '

Patrick had drawn himself up and stood with his chin raised so that, although he was not very tall, he was impressive. He did not look at Aidan. He looked south over the hills and drumlins of this northern land, and his strange eyes seemed to see vast distances.

'Then that is where I shall light the Fire of the World,' he said, 'and silence the tongues of today's druids with the word of Jesus, the Christ, and faith in the Redeemer in the name of the most holy Trinity, by the grace of God.' And he walked in the direction he faced, leaving those of his companions who were with him to come or stay with Loman, as they pleased. Aidan and MacCartan moved with one accord and fell into step on either side of the older man.

'Patrick . . . ' began Aidan but, glancing at the other's face, held his peace. 'The chariots are over here,' he ended lamely, and was rewarded with a smile that lit Patrick's face with simple happiness as he changed direction and went to where the cumbersome four-wheeled chariots they had acquired – each drawn by two hardy ponies – stood under a flowering thorn tree. Aidan looked at MacCartan and shrugged and the two men followed.

Chapter 9

REMEMBERING, the old man smiled to himself. Then, as rememberance brought with it a whiff of atmosphere, his smile faded as he recollected again the doubts and worries that assailed him during those four days of Holy Week while they went towards Usna to meet Laoire. Even though he concealed it from his companions he was very nervous during the journey. But he placed his trust in God, offering the devotions of Easter in an appeal for the success of his mission. In the silences of night, with little to hear as the owl circled silently but the occasional sharp bark of a fox and howl of a prowling wolf in the forest and the rustle of unseen creatures in the foliage and overhead, Patrick went beneath the stars and prayed until the dome of heaven lightened, when he slipped back to his tent for some rest before beginning the new day.

The old man shook his head at the memory and turned to his *Confessio* for the comfort and security of words which correctly reflected his feelings at the time, and which began with a quotation from scripture: '"By the tongue will be discovered the wise man, and understanding, and knowledge, and the teaching of truth." But of what help is an excuse, however true, especially if combined with presumption, since now, in my old age, I strive for something that I did not acquire in my youth?' He raised his head from the page and gazed, without observation, through the door. Then read on again: 'It was my sins that prevented me from fixing in my mind what before I had barely read through . . . As a youth, nay, almost as a boy, not able to speak, I was taken captive, before I knew what to pursue and what to avoid. Hence today I blush and fear exceedingly to reveal my lack of education; for I am unable to tell my story to those versed in the art of concise writing – in such a way, I mean, as my spirit and mind long to do, and so that the sense of the words expresses what I feel.'

Patrick paused and lifted a twisted hand to his eyes to rub them. Was he being fair and just? To himself no less than to others? He had done his best. He opened his eyes again and held the sheet a little closer to them.

'But if it had been given to me as it was given to others, then I would not be silent because of my desire of thanksgiving, and if perhaps some people think me arrogant for doing so in spite of my lack of knowledge and my slow tongue, it is, after all, written: "The stammering tongues shall quickly learn to speak peace." . . .

'Wherefore, then, be astonished, ye great and little that fear God, and you men of letters on your estates, listen and pore over this. Who was it that roused me up, the fool that I am, from the midst of those who in the eyes of men are wise, and expert in law, and powerful in word and in everything? And He inspired me – me, the outcast of this world – before others to be the man (if only I could) who, without fear and reverence and without blame, should faithfully serve the people to whom the love of Christ conveyed and gave me for the duration of my life, if I should be worthy; yes, indeed, to serve them humbly and sincerely.'

The vibrancy of his own words once again excited Patrick's sense of mission.

'In the light, therefore, of our faith in the Trinity I must make this choice, regardless of the danger I must make known the gift of God and everlasting consolation, without fear, and frankly I must spread everywhere the name of God so that after my death I may leave a bequest to my brethren and sons – so many thousands of people . . . ' The old man's eye slipped down the page, caught the phrases that meant most to him until, near the end, he came to the following remarkable statement: 'This sun which we see rises daily for us because He commands it so, but it will never reign, nor will its splendour last; what is more, those wretches who adore it will be miserably punished. Not so we, who believe in, and worship, the true sun - Christ - who will never perish, nor will he who doeth His will; but he will abide for ever as Christ abideth for ever, who reigns with God the Father Almighty and the Holy Spirit before time, and now, and in all eternity. Amen.'

Outside his small house a wayward cloud brought an unexpected drift of misty rain pattering across the dry ground on its way to the bay and the sea beyond. A shadow moved with it across the landscape and he was struck by the contrast between the sussuous greyness now about his settlement, and the bright reflected sunlight in the bay and on the headland of Howth beyond. As his dim eyes registered the image a splendid rainbow sprang and arched across the sky, shining like a diadem on the world.

Patrick leaned back watching the rain-locked shadow drift away from him. The rich smell of fresh dampened earth drifted in through the open door. The shadow advanced on the bay, staining the water in one area only, changing the texture of the waves. Then it went as suddenly as it had come. But the rainbow remained, spanning what he could see until it too gently faded or was absorbed by the bright scene beyond. It was on such a day that they journeyed to Slane, a few miles from Tara, to meet King Laoire thirty-three years before. They arrived as the sun settled in the west with the lingering decline of a clear, spring evening on Easter Saturday, four hundred and thirty two years after the crucifixion of Christ. He remembered clearly how, as they approached from the north, the small hill of Slane - known to the Irish as the sepulchre of Fiach, because a retainer of that name had interred the dead in trenches there after a battle with Munstermen - rose above the otherwise flat landscape close to the Brugh of the Boyne, some of the monument's ancient white stones still glimmering in the evening light. Below them the tranquil river proceeded towards the Western or Irish Sea that separated him from his homeland. In the distance they could see, against the fading light, the great white ramparts and battlements of Tara crowning a hill similar to the one they stood on and about ten miles distant, so that it was truly called 'white-sided Tara' by the poet. Between themselves and the mysterious Brugh which the *dlee* claimed to be the sacred home of the sun god - and which was now largely overgrown - stood some scattered houses, little more than huts of the most rudimentary sort. These were the homes of outcasts and other untouchables who were willing to live within the shadow of the strange otherworld that surrounded the Brugh for the sake of the sanctuary it provided, and eke out whatever existence they could foraging and poaching. A group of these scavengers and outcasts followed Patrick and his people to the top of the hill when they saw that they were neither noblemen nor troops and began to beg, looking about the while to see what they could steal. Ignoring the protests of Aidan, Patrick offered them a little food from their own meagre resources and some clothing, with which they were far from satisfied. Then he celebrated the miracle of the risen Christ under the twilight sky between the two four-wheeled chariots.

He spoke this prayer for Holy Saturday: 'Holy Lord, Father Almighty, eternal God; work with us who bless this fire in thy name and in that of your only begotten son Jesus Christ, our God and Lord, and of the Holy Spirit; and help us against the fiery darts of the enemy, and enlighten us with heavenly grace: Who lives and reigns in the Trinity with the same only begotten son of thine, and with the Holy Spirit, God, world without end . . . ' Then he lit a small flame in tinder with flint and steel.

Turning to Aidan he asked, 'You say that tonight also happens to be the night before the pagan festival, all fires are extinguished and the king lights one from which all others are rekindled?'

'That's right,' answered Aidan.

'Then I shall light a fire that will kindle a flame such as has never been seen in Ireland before and, with God's grace, will last to eternity. Gather kindling and firewood.'

All the power in Ireland is focused and concentrated in the triangle embraced by Usna, royal Tara and dark Tlachtga of the sorcerers, bounded by the Brugh na Boinne (the ancestral womb of the world) and joyous Taillte. Here the power of the symbols of the world converge and concentrate and make a contact with that other world. Who does not know that fire is the proclamation of supremacy? And that the more potent the kindler the more potent the fire? Mead's fire blazed for seven years, shedding its fierceness over the four quarters of Ireland. In this knowledge the mighty assemblies of Usna, Tara and Tlachtga have been the mysterious conclaves of the people of Ireland since before time. Their rituals are gateways between the seen and the unseen; bridges enabling the power of the invisible to pass over and illuminate the visible with strength and acknowledgements, to return the powers of the kings, the recondite ones of the *dlee* and those of the multitude. The fires were lighted by the King before the solemn banquet, the Feis of Tara, at which his espousal of the reborn realm was celebrated. Following the initial ceremony of death and birth, the Feis of Tara was performed but once every three years, or as the king ordained it. But the reunions, or *aonigh*, of Usna and Tlachtga were another matter. Here, at each half year, were extinguished and kindled the cycle of fire that ensured continuance of prosperity and fruitfulness under benign and potent authority. The fire of Bealtaine, spring, was lit up on the central fire-altar at Usna; as the nights grew dark the fire of Tlachtga to guard against the onset of winter was lit at the assembly of druids at Samhain. Of the two assemblies Tlachtga was the more awesome while Usna was the more communally significant. For it was at this time of year that the lighting of the new fire on the hearth of every home in the land became a matter of the greatest significence, full of danger. Each domestic fire had to be kindled from a flame or an ember from the fire of Usna, itself kindled with bow and drill by the King while the *dlee* chant spells and incantations to preserve the cattle from disease through the coming year, or from a sympathetic ritual fire. Symbolic beasts of every domestic sort were driven between the fires at Usna - for there were two - and then driven to the east where they would remain between the fire of Usna and the fire of Tlachtga, which occurred at Samhain.

The spring fire was kindled on the five-ridged pillarstone at Usna, which marks the navel and centre of Ireland and stands above the tongues of the old druids silenced by Mead. About these fires was a round hearth of great size, showing that they were the fires of men. The hearth at Tlachtga, to the east, was square, indicating that it was the fire of the hidden world. The two are linked as night and day are linked, and as the light and dark seasons follow one another. Women played an important part in the spring rituals. In the morning, before dawn, they would wash themselves in dew and gather wild flowers and budding green stuff with which to decorate themselves and their houses. The sombre autumn festival of the witch goddess Tlachtga was attended by men.

Laoire, Ri-Eireann and King of Albyn and West Britain, had spent a good deal of the day with his queen, Blaheen, Little Flower, preparing for the evening's celebrations. His great palace, Rath Laoire, had recently been completed, and hummed with activity throughout the day as fresh rushes were strewn in every room, perfumed water was sprinkled on them, wine and mead were stocked and enormous quantities of food were prepared and cooked. The banquet would be cold, to begin with at all events, as every fire would be extinguished before the sun set on the king's feast.

When the first *cadar* - quarter of a day - was less than an hour old everyone of importance had assembled at Tara to prepare for the journey to Usna and the ceremonies due to take place there in full darkness. The five kings of the provinces had arrived with their queens and retinues as well as the three other classes of king, down to the *ur-ree*, under-king, of a *tuath*, which was the smallest territory whose ruler could be called a king.

In ancient times a *tuath*, as the name signifies, was a tribe or clan of one family, the smallest political and legal administrative community. In time the term came to represent the land occupied by the community. Originally the king of a *tuath* could muster not less than seven hundred warriors, but as the term came to mean a minimal territory, that criterion too altered, and many large *tuaithe* were capable of providing substantial armies. The minimal territorial requirement of a *tuath* was called a *tricha-kayd*, that is thirty hundreds, consisting of not less than thirty *ballys*, or townlands, each containing twelve *sesrachs* or ploughlands. A ploughland was as much as a single plough could turn up in a year. A townland sustained four herds of seventy-five cows, three hundred cows in all, and at that time one cow required thirty acres. A *tuath* was about one hundred and seventy-seven square miles, say thirteen miles by fourteen. And sometimes three, four or more *tuaithe* formed one territory ruled by an under-king. There were eighteen *tuaths* in the Province of Meath; thirty one in the Province of Leinster; thirty five in Ulster; thirty in Connacht; and seventy in the two Munsters. The kings of the five provinces, the Pentarchy, ruled constitutionally in accordance with the law and immemorial custom. Over all was the Ri-Eireann, King of Ireland.

As the Bealtaine night crept across the sea towards Tara from the east, an anticipatory hush seemed to envelop the land. The Tyock Meecuarta, grey and sombre in the twilight, was thronged with nobles who spoke in hushed tones that matched the rustling rushes underfoot. The doorkeepers, *doresid*, and the nines of the king's bodyguard, the *comaytid*, were particularly vigilant because of the absence of lights. But this was unnecessary on such an occasion (although it was commendable and comforting for the King). Tonight of all nights the king was safe from assassin or sudden rage because of the awesome night it was. Following the murder of his father, Nial, in Gaul and the death of Daithi likewise, a *geasa* was put on him that he would never go abroad, a prohibition given additional force since it was foretold that he himself would find death between Albyn and Gaul. So he remained in Erin. Laoire was anyway a domestic king, a king of good government, whose mind and concern were on Ireland, not on aggrandisement and glory overseas like his father and grandfather, Nial and Criffan.

As the west faded to an impression of umbral light on the horizon, Durrach, the king's major-domo or *taoiseach-teglig*, stood casually beside one of the huge windows of the hall. His staff of office (a huge black beam 'like a mill shaft', as Patrick later described it) was in his hand, and he wore his fleece-lined cloak of office in spite of the warmth within and the coloured glass, some of it Roman and Egyptian, that kept out the night chill. He glanced out - and suddenly stiffened. He bent closer to the window, peering through one of the mottled panes. Then swiftly he turned and strode to the nearest door, thrusting aside anyone in his way. A strange hush, like a ship's wake, followed him, and heads turned after him. He wrenched open the mighty door, holding the frame in one huge hand, and stared into the diminishing evening. Then he turned and cried to the hall, 'Sacrilege!'

An immediate and total silence fell.

'Sacrilege,' he cried again. 'Fire! On Slane.'

The sudden quiet at his first cry gave way now to instant commotion. Kings, queens, lords, nobles turned towards Laoire, who was reclining on his couch, or *lepad*. Laoire sat up straight and then stood on the luxurious coverings in order to see over the distressed heads of his nobles to where Durrach stood by the door.

'What?' he cried. 'Fire?' He could hardly believe it.

'Beyond,' confirmed Durrach, 'on Slane, by the Brugh.'

Laoire stepped down from his couch and crossed swiftly to the door beside Durrach, a path clearing for him as he did so. There was no doubt. In the distance a pinpoint of light danced and winked at the darkness. Fire beyond doubt. Deliberate fire.

'So!' whispered the king.

The druids Lochru and Lucht Maol, Servants of the Light (meaning the sun in this case), began to shriek, lament and foretell disaster. In particular Lochru, dark, sallow, and thin-visaged, with deep-set eyes and a mouth set in the continual sneer of a man dissatisfied and insecure - in spite of all his power - tried to take control of the situation and dramatise it. Behind the histrionic exterior burned a cold mind avid for power. For some time his rage had been directed against foreign influence of any kind, but particularly against things Roman and Christian, which - with some justification - he felt challenged and undermined his own position and that of the other *dlee.* He became the moving force of a campaign to revive the long-abandoned custom of offering to the idol, Crom Cruach, the first-born of the nobility instead of merely the first fruits of cattle and crops which for many generations had come to be acceptable substitutes. He had some support, particularly from the septs which came to prominence in the wars of Criffan, Nial and Daithi, and now sought respectability. Except for a few traditional fanatics, the established septs and nobles and the younger nobility gave him little or no support. Cause for a real sacrifice could secure his authority in these volatile times and this might be just the opportunity he sought. Lucht Maol, the second chief druid, was of two minds; undecided between loyalty to his calling and what he plainly saw as the only reasonable - indeed inevitable - road ahead, he gave Lochru tacit support. Since a good deal of opposition came from percolated Christian thinking, Lochru might also use this opportunity, if such it was, to exterminate the Christians once and for all. In this Lucht Maol would support Lochru, since here, he knew, lay a profound threat to what he represented.

So, ignorant of the real purpose of the fire on Slane or of the challenge it presented, Lochru threw himself into an ecstasy of fuming passion and screamed denunciation and retribution to the shocked assembly.

Laoire understood precisely what Lochru was doing and was as determined to prevent the incident - whatever lay behind it - becoming the opportunity he sought. He allowed Lochru to continue until he had generated a common reaction, then he stopped him.

He stood by the door and raised his arms, wide, above his head and remained so until the hubbub died down. Then he nodded to Durrach who immediately shook the *crave shida*, branch of peace, so that the sound of its many bells rang and tinkled through the hall, bringing immediate silence.

'We must know who has lit this sacrilegious fire, and why,' he announced. 'It is some great omen . . . '

'Evil power,' began Lochru, 'evil omen of evil gods . . . ' but Laoire stopped him with a glance.

'This has been done by someone who knew what he was doing, knew the consequences of his act. There can be no doubt about that. It is deliberately done for us to see.'

This self-evident observation, made calmly and with full regal authority, reasserted just enough control at just the right moment. Laoire smiled inwardly at Lochru, who was so easy to manipulate. He had allowed Lochru to whip the people together - why not? - and then, when they were of a single mind, had taken them from him at a firmer level. Lochru was dangerous because he was a fanatic, but he would never learn.

'But what are we to understand from it?' Laoire asked. He looked about him. All attention was on him. At the far side of the hall the people were climbing on tables to see and hear, and there were irritated cries of 'Sh-sh!' and 'Quiet' at the noise being made. He felt satisfaction. He had control.

'A challenge, Laoire,' roared a voice he recognised as Cruhoor of Connacht, and he smiled without showing it. Of course it was a challenge. But to what or whom? Was it to his advantage or not? That fire purposely and purposefully stated defiance of custom, no doubt about it. But was that necessarily threatening? Whom did the challenged custom most benefit and revere? The *dlee*. Laoire was well aware of the theological convulsions wrestling for truth in the minds of men. He himself believed in the old ways, but his wife was Christian and had familiarised him with wider and more compassionate horizons, teaching that each individual's soul had in it knowledge of an almighty god.

He knew also of the recent activities of Christian missionaries: Palladius (who had died in his kingdom); Pelagius the magniloquent, himself Irish; the recent arrival, Patricius; and the others. The strength of their convictions, as he knew from Blaheen, could produce such defiance. Just as he knew that his Christian wife made him suspect and vulnerable to the reactionaries. But he was King and must act as King.

'Go!' he said. 'Find them and bring them here. Let nine chariots be yoked together, according to the tradition of the gods, and bring them to me.'

There were murmurs of approval when he invoked the mystic number nine. Immediately men of the bodyguard (with Durrach ahead of them) clattered from the hall to where the ever ready harnessed chariots of the guard stood outside. Some of the horses reared and tossed their heads nervously, stamping and neighing, as the men burst shouting from the doors, but were quickly calmed as they were led through the triple gates of the ramparts and yoked together. The men, chariots and horses, eighteen abreast, swept across the plain with a tremendous crash of wheels and thunder of hooves, sods of earth and lumps of grass flying into the dark sky like a flock of night birds.

When they reached the bare hill of Slane with the fire blazing from its breast-like summit and saw before them only Patrick and his unarmed companions, the horses were slowed to a startled walk, then reined in. Behind the chariots the troops on foot and in single chariots crowded in, until on one side of the summit a powerful host had gathered, dressed for a king's banquet, armed and ready for battle. On the other side were Patrick and his disciples, simply dressed, standing between their wagons where they had been interrupted in their prayers, all illuminated by the flickering glare from the large fire between them. The scavengers had fled as soon as they heard the challenging thunder of approaching chariots.

The moment of surprise passed. From his chariot Durrach, who had taken in the situation quickly, pointed his *echlach* at Patrick and shouted: 'Seize them!'

Unceremoniously, Patrick and the others were seized, bound and marched towards Tara, their protests and concern over their belongings ignored. On the way Durrach was surprised and worried when lights unexpectedly gleamed from the direction of Tara, shining through the night for all the world to see.

Chapter 10

IN the midst of recollection the old man's eyes half focused on his *Confessio*; unconnected phrases, of their own accord, registered with him: '"I have set Thee as a light among the Gentiles, that Thou mayest be as a salvation unto the utmost part of the earth." . . . So, now, I commend my soul to my faithful God, for whom I am an ambassador in all my wretchedness; but God accepteth no person, and chose me for this office - to be, although among his least, one of his ministers.'

How unyielding and stone-like was the weight of unknowing in his heart as Patrick was brought, once again the prisoner of Irish soldiers, to Tara that Bealtaine night. He was not afraid of the consequences, but he prayed he might be given the grace to survive and open the gateway to salvation for the multitudes of lost souls populating Ireland. He already knew that the acceptance of Christianity was only a matter of time - and, perhaps, even bloodshed. But what of the interim? What if the foul heresy of free will and sinless birth of the apostate Pelagius gained approval and thwarted the advent of the true Faith? What if the people now rejected the Almighty Himself? Was he, Patrick, destined to vanish into the maw of some hideous pagan ritual even as the people hovered on the brink of the world of light? He could not believe it. His given purpose was too compelling, too clear and specific.

He was brought to the Tyock Meecuarta, now ablaze with

light, and hustled through the glittering and hostile throng to where, surrounded by his intimates, Laoire reclined on his couch, as Patrick himself later recorded: '*manducandibus illis et bibentibus vinum in palatio*.' The King looked at him expressionlessly, without greeting. When the gasping herald had brought news of who was coming, Laoire had told the company that no greeting or any other mark of respect due to strangers visiting Tara was to be offered to Patrick. Whatever his intentions, this Christian druid must answer for his crime, and Laoire intended to dominate from the start. He had thwarted Lochru by declaring that since sacrilege had been committed and the perpetrator arrested nothing more significant could be done either to offend or placate the gods than to see justice done. The ceremony at Usna might therefore be performed on this occasion with a minimum of ceremony, with whatever necessary subsequent rituals performed by the druids, while he supervised the more serious matter of the offenders. Accordingly, together with only a small guard and a handful of his confidants, Laoire had raced on horseback to Usna, lit the sacred fire and carried back the burning brands while Patrick was being brought to Tara. Hence the unexpected efflorescence of lights in the darkness ahead that Durrach had seen when returning with his captive.

When the foreign priest was brought before Laoire an incident occurred for which no one could later account. Behind Laoire stood his full bodyguard in two broad wings. On either side of him sat the chief men and women of the realm; on his right the chief *ollamh*, or lawmaker and magus; on his left Lochru, sharp and cunning. Shields of bronze, silver, gold and enamel glittered from their places on the walls above their respective owners; jewellery and fine clothing glowed from one end of the mighty hall to the other, and from the balconies music sweetened the atmosphere, which was heavy with heat and smoke. Patrick, in his early fifties, short, muscular, strongly built with a squareness about him and strange eyes of remarkable intensity and changing colour, stood before the king. They looked silently at one another and then calmly Patrick looked at those sitting near the king, his eyes resting on each for a moment (*a bratha*, or the twinkling of an eye) before returning to Laoire. But his look and personal dignity produced such an effect on Duach, chief poet of the realm, that, in spite of Laoire's admonition, he stood out of respect and was joined slowly and compulsively, by the King's nephew, Erc. Laoire's face darkened with anger at the extraordinary insolence of his chief poet and his nephew. Without glancing at them he gestured to them to sit. At the same time, he himself reluctantly raised one knee to Patrick in a moderate gesture of civility. There was a rattle and rustle throughout the great hall as the hundreds of seated notables awkwardly followed his example.

Hesitantly Duach and Erc resumed their seats and each received a grave acknowledgement, an inclination of the head, from Patrick. Then he lowered his head to the king.

'Who are you?' Laoire's question was not what he had intended to say. He already knew who Patrick was. His intention was to establish his guilt before the assembly and then execute him.

'I am Patrick. A sinner and priest of Christ, the Lord my God.'

'You committed sacrilege with fire!'

Laoire's accusation struck anger in Patrick like a lightning flash striking a hay barn: his wrath exploded. Raising an unconsciously dramatic arm he levelled a finger at Laoire, then swung it to include the whole assembly.

'It is not I but you who are sacrilegious,' he cried. 'Sinners before God and the world to whom, in my ignorance, I bring the Faith, the instrument of the Lord God. In the words of our Lord, Jesus Christ himself: "I have come to bring fire . . . and how I wish it were blazing already!" ' He stood for a moment before lowering his arm, and then Laoire's queen, Blaheen, rose to her feet.

She was a very striking woman. Tall, with red-gold hair –

now flecked with grey – she still possessed the lissome, wide-hipped body that had captivated the wild imagination of many a man and the heart of Laoire more than thirty years before. She was his second wife, daughter of a lesser king from Wicklow who had married a daughter of one of the British colonisers, from whom Blaheen had received the Christianity to which, like several of her noble sisters, she clung in very difficult circumstances, sharing her faith with slaves and outcasts. Only the wisdom of Laoire enabled her to retain it at all, for he recognised Christianity for the global influence it was . . . But for Ireland, not yet!

Now tears, both of recognition and appeal, overspilled her eyes as in the past they had involuntarily filled with tears of regret at Laoire's contradictory refusal to respond to her faith. She saw Patrick through a blur and cried: 'Patrick! Priest of Christ! Roman! Do not condemn the High King and I promise you Laoire will come to you and worship our God.'

A gasp rustled down the hall, and Laoire, shocked that his queen had so far forgotten herself, was forced to raised his hand and have the *crave shida* rung until the chattering bells restored order.

'You are a Christian?' asked Patrick when quiet returned.

Blaheen had time to nod before Laoire cried, 'Enough! I will never be a Christian for I cannot under *geasa* to my great father, Nial, and even if I could I would not!' He glared defiantly from his wife to Patrick, who all but blenched. Nial again!

'You will risk your immortal soul?' he asked.

'My life has been spent risking my mortal one,' was the reply, 'I won't change now for the word of a – a Roman priest.' He spat the words. Already Laoire could see he must either be deprived of the execution he relied on or of the trust of his wife. He had not foreseen such a dilemma, though he understood it clearly.

'Why are you so hostile,' asked Patrick, 'when what I bring you is eternal light and life?'

Lochru sat close, crouched forward and listening to every word, ready to pounce on anything which might give an opportunity to further his reactionary designs.

But Laoire had had enough. He stood and with a great rustle the assembly followed suit. He locked eyes with Patrick. They were much of an age, Laoire being perhaps a year or two older; each saw that the other would not give way, and they saw something more in each other.

In Patrick Laoire recognised a man who was obdurate, would not bend on principle; whose forthrightness was such that he would break uncompromisingly rather than philander with expediency. Laoire saw in this an advantage for himself in dealing with this man, who extraordinarily and unexpectedly, had become suddenly important.

Patrick saw an opposite force in Laoire: a strong, just man whose life had been spent balancing forces so as to hold on to power that he might preserve an equilibrium in the state. He also saw a man of some refinement, intelligence and even culture, barbaric though it was.

'Come!' said Laoire, and stalked off.

'Laoire,' shrieked Lochru, stepping in front of him. 'the sacrilege . . . '

The King brushed him aside with his arm without breaking his stride. He well knew the risk he ran in publicly rebuffing the *dlee*, but he could not permit Lochru to take control.

In his private apartments in Rath Laoire the king nodded to a chair and grunted to Patrick, 'Sit!' Patrick did so and the two men studied one another by the powerful light from three *ree-innlis*, or king's candles, each of beeswax and thicker than a man's body, that illuminated the room.

'What am I going to do with you?'

'Listen to me, my lord.'

'Why should I do that?'

'Because I bring . . . '

'Don't start all that again. You bring me nothing I don't already know about.'

'Then you know Christ?'

'Do you take me for a fool? Of course I know about the one called Christ. Who doesn't? What good is it to me?'

'What good? *In nomine Deum!* You're talking about your eternal life, your immortal soul.'

'Now you listen to me, Patrick. I have no doubt you are a very good, very sincere man. And I have no doubt your new Christianity is a better religion than our old ones. But while you are making Christians out of my people, I still have a country to run . . . and not everyone in it is on my side. There are those beyond . . . ' he nodded towards the Tyock Meecuarta from where the rumble of voices still came ' . . . who would like nothing better than to see us both disposed of.'

'I'm talking about souls . . . '

'And I'm talking about my people!' snapped Laoire impatiently. 'What good is it to them if I or a handful of my people get eternal life? Our own gods promise us that already, if one is to believe the *dlee*.'

'And do you believe them?'

'I don't know. The question is, why should I believe you?'

'Laoire, I haven't come with revolution. I'm no threat to you, or yours. I will only threaten, and destroy . . . ' he paused, but Laoire did not interrupt him ' . . . the idols and heathen abominations that you worship, and under which your people suffer.'

'Not so much . . . '

'They suffer in mind, body and soul. How can you deny it?'

Laoire didn't bother to try. 'Then your threat is to the *dlee*, to our traditions, and so to me!'

'No!' said Patrick. 'Christianity can – does – co-exist with every sort of tradition, as long as it is not evil or blasphemous. Christianity flourishes in Greece, Syria, Egypt, Africa, Rome, Britain, Gaul . . . nowhere have the traditions of the people been rejected or destroyed except when they were evil. Why should

Ireland be different? Do you,' he added, 'find it so impossible to distinguish between what is good and what is evil?'

But Laoire ignored or chose not to notice the sarcasm.

'Hmm,' he said. 'But yours is the religion of Rome and Rome is dying, nearly dead. Why should we exchange beliefs we have held for thousands of years for something merely a few generations old and already dying?'

'Do not confuse Christianity with Rome, Laoire. Christianity is the Church of God, Rome is merely an empire.'

'The greatest empire the world has ever seen!'

Patrick shook his head several times and continued as if there had been no interruption.

'When the Empire is gone, Christianity will survive and continue to the end of time. Its message of truth is self-evident. Yours – although it is thousands of years old – is not the way of life, but the way of death.'

Laoire was silent for a moment. He was far from ignorant of the political and religious issues convulsing the known world and, in fact, derived satisfaction from the fact that his *geasa* enabled him to adopt an isolationist policy that protected him from the political upheavals in Europe and elsewhere, and from doctrinal and theological schisms and confrontations that divided whole peoples no less violently and bitterly. But he clearly realised the impossibility of remaining aloof indefinitely. Trade and commerce alone would see to that and, as it was, the spread of Christianity, through external associations of all sorts was already a positive factor that could not be ignored. Its appeal to youth, noble youth, was phenomenal. In his own youth he had been receptive to new ideas. He had become aware of Neo-Platonism through one of his tutors, a student of Plotinus, and had been much taken with the concept of pure intelligence cognizable by intellect alone. Later, through various Roman military associates, he became aware of Mithraism, the recondite idea of a sun god possessed of three aspects – of which Christianity was the implacable foe. Now, through Blaheen, he had come to a sufficient understanding of Christianity to feel some sympathy for such noble teaching. For himself he knew that his forces were strong enough to contain and isolate most invading armies; of that he was satisfied. In any case, he could not see the Empire - or any other European power - sending a substantial fleet to attack him on his powerful and united home base, with inevitable heavy losses and probable destruction. There were so many easier and richer spoils available for much less effort, as Genseric and more recently the Hun Ruas and his nephews Bleda and Attila were effectively demonstrating. Yet now, here in front of him and in spite of his deliberate withdrawal from Europe, was personified one of the very problems he had hoped to avoid.

But, he thought, perhaps it wasn't after all such a bad thing. The time might be ripe. Isolationism also had drawbacks, the power of the *dlee* being one of them. Long since, Laoire had concluded that there were six main sources of power in society; military, political, economic, legal, administrative, and spiritual. And he did not really look on the law as a source of power so much as its executive instrument. Ideally, he believed, they should all be vested in one able authority - such as himself. But, since it was far from being an ideal world, that was not the case and one learned to live with imperfections.

In his view there were three main sources of power: military, political, and spiritual. And, he suspected, of those three spiritual power was the strongest. That it provided an unprecedented power base in any community he understood clearly; and more. He realised how the carefully balanced forces in a well-regulated system could be more easily upset by an alignment between the source of spiritual power and one of the others than by any alignment which did not include it. Certainly spiritual power in the hands of others had at times dominated kings and kingdoms mercilessly. But in this modern and enlightened age this was no longer the case - and he was determined to keep it that way.

Yet the mind of man was a mysterious instrument, to be

manipulated – as well he knew – by the adept, and there were none more adept than the *dlee.* He had long felt the need for some way of distracting and dissipating their resurgent power. Perhaps Christianity was the way. Once the strength of the *dlee* was satisfactorily offset, he could deal with Christianity in his own good time. He still held the reins politically and militarily, by and large. As far as economic and administrative powers were concerned, they were all very fine in theory (although he knew conditions were different under the Empire), but he could never see such conditions developing in Ireland where personal independence and free enterprise were so highly esteemed.

He was conscious, too, of growing impatience and restlessness in the young nobility, that firm skeleton of the community upon which the muscle and sinew of society hung. From his informants and his own skilled observation he could see that they were instinctively aware of being stultified in a society that had reached the apogee of development from its own resources, and were avid for a new intellectual impulse; in danger of toppling into decadence without it. To see and understand this was one thing. To be able to do something about it was quite another. He looked coldly at Patrick.

'I ask you again,' he said, 'what use is it to the majority of my people if a few initiates are saved for eternity?'

It was a significant question. He wanted to learn if Patrick's answer would be the same as Blaheen's. It was. He made the same claim, and this was of great importance to Laoire.

'Jesus Christ, our Lord, the Divine Saviour,' replied Patrick, 'won for all mankind the glorious privilege of life after death before the throne of God, and not for initiates alone.' This was the startling and novel idea Blaheen had also tried to convince him of. And he had heard it elsewhere. Eternal life was on offer not for just the few elect, but for everyone, even the most humble. No wonder the slaves supported it. The wonder was that kings and queens were willing to share it with them.

'This is the truth?'

'Let me tell you what Augustine of Carthage said in his book *The City of God*,' said Patrick, 'and you will know it is not just I who say this, but some of the greatest minds in the world. Besides Augustinus, there were Jerome, Ambrose of Milan . . . '

'What did Augustinus write?'

'I'll summarise it as best I can. He said: "There is the City of the World and there is the City of God." Christ Himself said on one occasion something similar - render unto Caesar what is Caesar's and unto God what is God's. Augustinus elaborates. "Earthly cities are plentiful. They are ephemeral. In this sense the Empire itself is a city. They come and go and have significance only as part of the divine plan. Man, all men, are citizens of the City of God simply by the fact of being men. The kingdoms of the world will pass, but the kingdom of God in Heaven will last for ever." '

Laoire considered a moment. 'And you say that this teaching will not reject our traditions?'

'Why should it, except the evil of idolatry? There is no monopoly of mundane truth.'

'You know I should have you burned, don't you?'

Patrick looked at the king. 'But you're not going to, are you?'

'I don't know,' said Laoire, half believing it. 'Is there any real reason why I should not?'

'Because,' replied Patrick, 'in your heart you know I speak the truth.'

'The truth!' Laoire's tone was caustic. 'Tell me what that is, Roman priest, and I will *give* you your life.'

Patrick looked at Laoire, who was openly smiling, but did not smile back. He simply said: 'Truth is the Word of God.'

Laoire's smile faded and his hand moved, involuntarily, to his chin.

'Indeed,' he said. 'If there is one god above all, then this must be so. But tell me,' he went on, 'is it not true that there are many Christianities?'

'No . . .'

' . . . the Arians that I hear of from my friend Genseric the Vandal, and the Greek – what? – Gnostics? What of the Bishop Nestorius and his followers? And our own Pelagius teaches something else again – all Christians.'

Patrick was taken aback by the extent of Laoire's information, though he knew he should not have been. He was a powerful ruler, after all, wise and shrewd. When he asked the question which had to follow, Patrick could only deal with it simply.

'Why should I listen to you above them?'

'Because I preach the truth.'

'The Word of God?'

'Yes.'

'Is not that what they all say?'

On a table beside Patrick stood a beautiful Egyptian basin in which grew an abundance of plants and flowers as if they were in a garden. And indeed that is what it was, a miniature garden, carefully tended and brought to and from the sunlight by skilled gardeners, so that it flourished indoors to give pleasure and delight to the king. Patrick leaned forward and plucked a simple trefoil hanging from a cluster on the rim of the bowl, and held it up.

'I know that you accept the mystery of a triune being,' he said. 'It is a concept you already possess. Three in one – "Through belief in the Threeness",' he quoted from the prayer he had recently composed on Aidan's ship. Laoire nodded. Patrick continued with words he was to use at the beginning of his *Confessio* many, many years later and which have remained the kernel of the belief he was communicating.

'There is no other God, nor ever was, nor will be, than God the Father unbegotten, without beginning, from whom is all beginning, the Lord of the universe . . . and His son Jesus Christ, whom we declare to have always been with the Father, spiritually and ineffably begotten by the Father before the beginning of the World, before all beginning; and by Him are made all things visible and invisible. He was made Man and, having defeated death, was received into heaven by the Father, and He hath given Him all power over all names in heaven, on earth, and under the earth, and every tongue shall confess to Him that Jesus Christ is Lord and God, in whom we believe, and whose advent we expect . . . '

Laoire did not interrupt. He was intent on the man in front of him and the conviction that filled him. Patrick's words were the pillarstone of his belief and from this expression of faith, in later years, were to radiate his giant humility before the grace of God, his dedication to the Holy Trinity and his thunderous denunciations of the enemies of both.

Patrick continued, ' . . . whose advent we expect to judge of the living and of the dead, who will render to every man according to his deeds; and He has poured forth upon us abundantly the Holy Spirit, the gift and pledge of immortality, who makes those who believe and obey sons of God and joint heirs with Christ; and Him do we confess and adore, one God in the Trinity of the Holy Name . . . '

Chapter 11

His old eyes, misted a little by emotion, scanned the words as he recollected the events of that night with the king, dead these two years, who had both given and lost so much. For Laoire had accepted Patrick and given him far more than permission to baptise and convert, he gave him protection throughout the realm - a protection violated in only a few isolated instances, and then by banditry rather than anything else. More, he permitted his family to be baptised, in particular and dramatically his daughters Eithne Bawn, the Fair, and Fedelema Roe, the Russet, who suffered from the wasting sickness and died shortly thereafter. But Laoire was resolute in his own refusal to accept the cleansing water and the holy oil that would enable his entry to the Kingdom of God, and it was the memory of this, the loss of such a strong and noble soul to everlasting Limbo, that brought tears to Patrick's eyes. For Laoire had also, eventually, given him friendship - even if it was the hesitant and qualified friendship of a king.

Laoire had been killed, ironically between two hills in Leinster called Albyn and Gaul, when struck by lightning after violating a most sacred oath to 'the sun and moon, water and air, day and night, sea and land', for which the pagans claimed, the elements passed a doom of death on him: the earth to swallow him, the sun to burn him and the wind to depart from him.

'Old customs die hard,' Patrick thought, though Lochru had long since died and with him the attempt to revive the past. It was with sadness that Patrick recalled the old king's injunction before a battle that never was – a battle of greed and revenge, it would have been, motivated, perhaps, by a mind no longer in full possession of its youthful faculties. The cause went, yet again, back to the boru tribute on the head of which Laoire's father, Nial, was murdered in France by Ochy, son of the old King of Leinster and uncle of the present sneering king, Dulaing. Some years before Laoire's death the Leinstermen again refused the tribute and the king, with an inadequate army, marched to claim it and was defeated; worse, he himself was captured and held to ransom. The Leinstermen demanded that he swear the elemental oath never again to demand the tribute. Having done so he was released. But when the unpaid tribute became due on the third successive occasion, Laoire, compelled by some passion of age to demonstrate his authority, and brooding on his humiliation at the hands of the Leinstermen six years earlier and on the death of his father at the hands of Ochy, was driven to revenge and to breaking his mighty oath, against the advice and wishes of everyone. He knew himself what a fatal compulsion drove him, but he could not, or would not, withdraw and said only to Patrick, who was by now his respected friend: 'Nial, my father, would not permit me to believe, but commanded that I be interred on the ramparts of Tara, standing facing the enemy as for battle, as we have been accustomed to do, armed and ready, and in which manner we shall remain until the Judgement Day.'

And at this concession of recognition Patrick was moved to add 'Amen!'

But Laoire was not killed in the battle, nor yet after it; he was killed before ever the battle occurred, between the two hills so inaptly named, by a bolt of lightning, and it was held to be because he was in breach of his oath . . .

A flash on far-off Ben Eadir, Howth, penetrating the mists of age and time, settled on the old priest's eyes and, with a sigh, he recollected himself. The flash, he thought, was probably no more than the glint of sunlight on a polished shield or blade. Perhaps they were changing the guard on the coast watch. Patrick relaxed again, his restless eye still scanning the vellum at random.

'Wherefore may God never permit it to happen to me that I should lose His people which He purchased in the utmost parts of the world . . . '

The words brought back the memory of a most bitter and dramatic moment.

Following his acceptance by Laoire, Patrick travelled throughout the east and centre of Ireland winning enormous popularity, with mass conversions and baptisms. In particular he attracted the younger nobles who brought with them power, authority and leadership, to which they added enthusiasm and energy. Through them and their influence, backed by the good will of Laoire, Patrick not only made many converts, he established churches and religious settlements which were administered through an amalgam of adapted native and Roman systems.

All this was possible because of the respect and friendship that grew between Laoire and himself in the days and weeks following his lighting of the forbidden fire on the hill of Slane.

'Tell me,' said Laoire irrelevantly (they were in the midst of a discussion on law), 'you did know what you were doing when you lit that fire, didn't you?'

'I had a pretty good idea.'

'You really believed you were safe?'

Patrick recalled an early conversation with Aidan as he escaped from captivity, and gave one of his rare smiles.

'I'm here, am I not?'

'Mmmm.'

'My safety depended on the man I was to meet,' went on Patrick. 'It is no flattery for me to say that no king worthy of the name could be indifferent to the Christian faith, backed by the great power of Rome – ' he shrugged ' – even if it is on the wane. It is obvious that the message of Jesus, the Christ our Lord, is spreading throughout the world and is being accepted by every great monarch. Would you be so different?'

'You are a shrewd priest.'

'I am a fool, guided only by my own faith.'

'If all men were as honest as you the world would be a difficult place indeed.'

'Intolerable,' agreed Patrick, 'but then they would have no need to persuade great kings to learn the Word of God, for they would know it already.'

Laoire grunted. Then smiled. 'As I said, shrewd! Personally I do not reject the words you bring. It seems to me that Christianity has much to offer. But then so have other religions.'

'This is the true faith.'

'Are they not all – to those who believe in them?'

'Don't play the fool with me, Laoire.'

'Very well. But remember, Patrick, if I wanted the Roman legions here for any reason, you would be a priest of Mithras sitting there.'

'God forbid, I am not fool enough to believe that you permitted me to live and, with God's help, to do much besides, simply because you succumbed to *my* words. God has touched you, Laoire, whether you know it or not.' Laoire shrugged and smiled, and Patrick continued, 'Certainly, it may be that He made political necessity the instrument of His purpose. What of it? If you find it expedient to accommodate Christianity and ally yourself with powerful kings elsewhere . . . ' Laoire gave no indication of what he was thinking. 'Your own colonial tributary kings – how many of them are Christian? Do you think I don't know that the authority of the druids is falling in ashes everywhere but here? And do you think I don't know that you know it and that they are ready and willing to sacrifice anything, even you, to preserve their power? Of course you recognise the political value of Christianity; its social value. My prayer is that of your wife, that before your death you will also come to recognise its spiritual importance.'

But in this Patrick was to be disappointed. Nonetheless these two pragmatic leaders understood one another well and Patrick had another, immensely valuable set of gifts for Laoire: an understanding of Roman law, which was enhanced by his common sense and a willingness to place this knowledge at Laoire's disposal.

'What do I need Roman law for? We have our own law, which is more comprehensive and more just.'

'It is not written and regulated.'

'True.'

'That would be a great achievement.'

Laoire looked at the priest calculatingly for a moment, then changed the subject. But the king was to return to this again and again, so that discussions on legislation, procedure, and political as distinct from administrative strategy became commonplace between them. For the moment each left the question of administration in abeyance hanging, as it were, somewhere in the narrowing gap that still divided them.

With the permission and protection he needed to proselytise Laoire's kingdoms, Patrick founded churches in an expanding circle about Tara and then, as the circle grew and it became impractical to operate in this fashion, he made direct forays into a district. When he arrived somewhere which had some spiritual meaning for the people of the district, perhaps where a venerated monolith had been erected in ancient times and where animals were slaughtered and sacrificed, Patrick made a point of accepting the old beliefs and customs and adapting them to Christian use. In such places he built a church, established a priest and, having blessed and consecrated the standing stone to cleanse it, carved - often with his own hands - the Cross of Christ or the symbol Chi-Rho on it. He did not try to abolish local festivals either, but endeavoured to persuade the people to dedicate them to holy martyrs whose relics were in the churches he built.

One of his journeys took him northwards through the lake country, where he converted many people, baptised them and built churches as he went, the last at a place that in later times came to be called Granard. Here, to his wrath, he learned that the so-called *ri-idal na hErin*, the king-idol of Ireland, Crom Cruach, was situated less than twenty miles away in Magh Slecht, the Plain of Prostrations.

Crom Cruach of Magh Slecht was made of gold and there were twelve stone idols around him, set in four rows of three. Until the coming of Patrick, says the ancient tradition, Crom Cruach was god to every people that occupied Ireland. It was to him they used to offer the first-born of every stock and the first-born of every family. To him without glory they would kill their piteous, wretched offspring with much wailing and peril, to pour their blood around Crom Cruach. Milk and honey they would ask from him speedily, in return for one-third of their healthy issue. Great was the horror and the terror of him. To him noble Gaels would prostrate themselves. From the worship of him with many slaughters the plain is called Magh Slecht.

The origin of the worship went so far back that none then remembered it, but the *dlee* ensured that animal sacrifice still continued. What roused Patrick's anger at Granard was the shamefaced whisper that reached him with much shaking of heads and sadness that at least one local chief – by name Faillge Berroyde – had forced his people to prepare for a resumption of the older worship and the slaughter of their own first-born.

It was the second autumn of his arrival in Ireland and though the days were fine, and amber and gold burnished the forests, the plain, when Patrick reached it, lay glowering beneath a low covering of misshapen grey cloud.

A local noble, now baptised and servant of the church at Granard of which he was to become a deacon, pointed the way and presently Patrick discerned the infernal idol, covered in gold sheeting, glinting evilly through the dusk. He shuddered at the sense of malignancy that reached out from Crom Cruach and the twelve, squat, stone idols that surrounded it in an oppressive circle. With malevolent offensiveness the *dlee* who were guardians of the place suddenly appeared and accosted Patrick and his followers.

'What is your business in this holy place, Taillken?'

Taillken was the druidical name given to Patrick. It derived from a prophecy which expressed the druids' fear at the possible spread and establishment of Christianity in the country and was used to frighten the idol-bound natives into resistance:

The Taillken will come over the furious sea.
His cloak pierced for his head,
His staff with a crooked head,
His platter in the east of his house
And all his household will cry Amen.

And it is a fact that all the churches built by Patrick were aligned east to west with the entrance at the western end and the altar at the eastern.

'Holy place!' roared Patrick advancing on the *dlee*, so that they fell back - for they were not of the stuff of Lochru and Lucht Maol - 'cess-pit of abomination; filth and corruption!' Brandishing his staff he strode angrily past them and into the circle of idols. There he stopped, not because of the twittering *dlee* behind him but because he did not know what to do next. These monstrosities were of great stone, sunk deep in the ground, emerging out of it like rooted Cimmerian giants of perpetual darkness, and, in the case of Crom Cruach, towering twelve feet or more. This was the one to destroy. But how?

Behind him his friends and disciples hurried past the *dlee*, who ran off to fetch help, and now stood irresolutely behind him. Suddenly Patrick recalled how nearly forty years before he had heard of the destruction of the Jupiter Serapis at Alexandria by the brave Roman soldier he had met in the mountains and how the story had fired his determination to escape.

Raising his iron-shod staff in both hands as if it were a heavy spear he ran at the idol and rammed it in the joint of one of the sheets of gold plating. He wrenched, and wrenched again. Tugging out the staff he jammed it in again where the plating had buckled, this time a little higher, and again wrenched. Gold rivets popped and the plate ripped outwards revealing a dark triangle beneath, which was stone. A rank smell which might have been blood, a vast accumulation of gore, emanated from the exposed stone but that only added to Patrick's fury. From behind him in the distance came a shriek as the *dlee* saw what he was doing, but it was drowned in a shout of joy that welled from the throats of his followers who with staffs, sticks and staves descended on the pillarstone and ripped the golden covering from it. Patrick stood back when they started and watched. A curious calm replaced his passionate near-frenzy of loathing. He discovered that he had lost his *graif*, the stylus he used for writing on waxed slates or boards. As the stone of Crom Cruach was laid bare by his fellows he took a pitch-soaked torch and carefully searched in the heather until he found it glinting among the stalks and replaced it under the flap in his sleeve where he habitually carried it.

When his followers had finished and the stone pillar stood black as the night, divested of its golden sheath, they turned to him in triumph.

'We are not finished yet,' he said. 'It must be destroyed completely.'

They looked back at his strong figure. Even his strength could not do that.

'But how?' they cried. 'It's impossible. Look at it.'

But Patrick, recalling what he knew of Egypt and what he had heard of stone monuments elsewhere in Ireland and Britain, knew the answer.

'You,' he cried, pointing to Benin, 'and you Cormac, all of you there, gather brushwood – as much of it as you can get! Pile it around the base of that – that monstrous profanity. You, Fiacra and Nial, and you others,' he went on to most of those who remained, 'fetch water, lots of cold water.'

For a moment they looked at him blankly, exchanging looks with one another for explanation.

'Quickly!' he cried. 'Quickly!' and they ran to do what he asked.

'What are you at, at all?' asked MacCartan who remained behind, his eyes on the shadows beyond where the *dlee* might lurk. 'Do you think to burn it, or what? You won't be able, you know.'

'I think I might,' said Patrick. 'Leave it to me.'

'Indeed'n I will,' said MacCartan, 'and the Lord give you sense and me patience. Unless, of course,' he added hopefully, 'you're going to do a miracle.'

Patrick nodded gravely. 'Perhaps I am,' he said, 'perhaps I am.'

'Well now,' said MacCartan, leaning back on his heels with a satisfied expression of anticipation on his face, 'is that a fact? Well, well, well! A miracle, by God.'

'By God, indeed,' replied Patrick fervently.

It took a little time to gather, pile and arrange the wood, but when it was stacked around the pillar to his satisfaction, Patrick stood for a moment in prayer and then lifting his head and his arms to the dark clouds cried: 'O Lord Jesus; Almighty God, Father and Holy Spirit, guide me and direct me that I may cast out and destroy this evil and conduct and cherish this land and its people in the true Faith through the power of Thy Holy Grace.' And every voice there joined him in the final 'Amen'. Then he lit the cone of timber surrounding the tall idol. Quickly the flames spread, and began to roar loudly, racing up the incarnadined sides of the pillar and sucking clean air in at the bottom of the pyramid to gather a white heat around the base. It was an extraordinary scene. In the centre of the ancient druidical circle of malevolent stones the great idol was being, as it were, cleansed by fire before its destruction, while Christian priests and acolytes stood around in the illumination praying with their leader. The power of the light pushed back the darkness of the night and shut out the druids from their most solemn place.

When the fire had almost died and slender burnt branches of

the cone arched crookedly and unsupported above the glowing embers beneath, Patrick ordered that the cold water which had been brought in troughs and containers should be dashed against the white-hot base of the pillar from all sides. At the first touch of the water a cloud of thick, white steam, writhing and convulsing like a living thing, billowed up towards the sky with a fearful hissing that sounded like a malediction. One or two drew back; eyed one another. But Benin and others persisted. Again! Three times: And through the hissing and steam that obscured the pillar the sound of a mighty cracking seemed to split the night. With it came a lurching, twisting movement within the obscurity. Some there later swore they felt the very ground heave under their feet. They ran back in fear. It was said that the motion and noise were caused by the spirit of Crom Cruach in flight before the power of Patrick. When they turned again to look, they could see nothing. The fire was dead, steam and smoke, now silent, rose thickly into the night from blackened embers. MacCartan held a rush. Then another appeared and another, converging towards the centre where Crom Cruach had reigned for more than one thousand years. A wayward gust of wind dropped upon the cloud of steam and smoke, flattening it and sending it low across the circle. The watchers gasped. Crom Cruach was no longer tall and straight; it was cracked and warped, twisted to one side, the west, and it declined towards the ground on which so much blood had been poured for its sake and into which it would shortly vanish for ever.

As confidence and trust grew between them, Laoire began to question Patrick closely on matters of law: on legislative and judicial processes elsewhere; on the responsibilities of individuals to the law; of their rights before it; of penalties and reforms.

'You know,' he announced one day about five years after they had first met, 'by and large I think our system is better than any other.'

'Mmm,' said Patrick cautiously. 'The true fathers of all their peoples lead them in the spirit of Christ which is love and solicitude for all.'

'And am I not just?'

'Your laws are excellent, Laoire. But . . . '

'But what?'

'You still cling to the *lex talionis* - the law of revenge.'

'Does not your own teaching declare this law, an eye for an eye?'

'The Old Testament of the Jews. Do not pretend with me, Laoire.'

'I was only testing you,' muttered Laoire gruffly, feeling foolish. He felt that he was being impelled on a certain course, and that was what he resisted. He was not used to compulsion.

'There are deeper reasons and stronger laws to which men, kings and nations are subject. It is for us to discern these reasons and in their light to become, before Christ, spokesmen for justice and the moral order which is superior to force and violence. In it is expressed all the dignity of men and nations.'

'You speak with great power.'

'Because I know that in your heart you are a believer in justice and truth and a true Christian.'

'I have not seen - nor have you shown me - that there are laws superior to our own.'

'I did not say that there were. But it is true that the laws here have become diffuse and complex . . . in particular with regard to the penalties.'

'I have the same thought.' Laoire hesitated. Then, looking directly at Patrick, he went on: 'It has been in my mind for a long time. Since before I met you. But the task is so great . . . there was no one I could rely on, no new dynamic. Now there is you.'

'What is it you want to do?'

'I want to revise and codify our laws to become the finest body of corporate law in the world.'

'Complete reform?'
'If necessary, yes.'
'How would you set about it?'
'With your help.'
Patrick sat back and contemplated the king, whose fine aristocratic features were taut and marked with concentration. He knew that Laoire was deeply concerned with the rule of law, but this! Had the king any idea of the degree to which helping in such codification would allow Patrick to influence the whole future development of the Irish nation? As if he heard the unspoken question Laoire interrupted his thoughts.

'I realise what this could mean to you . . . ' He paused. There was yet another reason for what Laoire had in mind. His brothers Eoghan and Conal had gone north, against their father's wishes, to found new kingdoms in Ulster where the power of the once mighty Emrin Maeha-Armagh, seat of the one-time invincible Red Branch Knights, was in decline. This had been the case ever since the balance of national power centred on Tara in Meath and Cashel in Munster. The rise of the Fianna, the standing army of the Rí-Eireann, had had a domestic purpose besides that of opposing any possible threat from the Empire, and it had been instrumental in the deterioration of Ulster. The province was now unruly and decentralised. It was into this situation that Eoghan and Conal marched to found kingdoms of their own, henceforward known as Tir Eoghan and Tir Conal – the Territory of Eoghan and the Territory of Conal. They remained, however, true sons of Nial. All three brothers agreed that they would for ever be known as the people of Nial: the Northern Ui Neill and the Southern Ui Neill. Moreover they decided that they would, as of right, lay claim to the Kingship of Ireland for their family alone, in violation of the rights of other royal lines. This was unprecedented and unlawful. Laoire himself proposed that the province of Meath should be subsumed into the Kingship, which would automatically assume a new titular authority, King of Tara, though Tara was not a royal but a sacred place. Now

Laoire wanted to enshrine these innovations in the corporate law of Ireland so that even if his family could not achieve the absolute authority of primogeniture, the power would be kept in the family. But if his plans became known he ran the risk of assassination. He must move cautiously, deviously and apparently constitutionally, as that wily old warrior, his father Nial, had advised. The fierce opposition of the established nobility to what Conal and Eoghan had done in creating new kingdoms was evidence enough of this need.

'Do you realise the authority it would vest in me?'

Laoire replied without hesitation. 'I realise that of all men none that I know will exercise that authority with such devotion to what is right and just.'

'And Christian.'

'So be it,' said Laoire.

'Amen,' replied Patrick and they smiled.

Laoire appointed a royal commission of nine composed of three kings - himself, Corc, the Christian King of Munster, and Daire, King of Ulster; three bishops - Patrick, Coyrnuch, and Benignus; and three *ollaves* - Duach, Rossa and Fergus. The commission was to examine, review, revise and encode the thirty-five volumes and tracts of civil law, the Faynachus. The great work was to take three years' deliberation, and was completed in 441.

The laws of Ireland were traditional and very complicated and were intended to legislate for all ranks of society in all circumstances. They were based on justice and on the concept that much is expected from those to whom much is given.

The law forbade a noble to demand excessive service or rent from a poor man, or for a poor man to provide them. The king himself was bound to do justice to his humblest subject, for the law, while acknowledging his rights, also enumerated his duties. The law stipulated that among those who could be degraded were 'a false-judging king, a stumbling bishop, a fraudulent poet and an unworthy chieftain or neglectful *ollave*'.

The *log-aynach*, honour price, was an instrument of great potency, graduated in scale according to rank. The higher the rank of the offender, the greater the honour price which was payable in addition to legal penalty or *eric.* This had another powerful effect on men of rank, which was that if a nobleman was found guilty of an act against a commoner, he suffered the indignity and loss of face of having his honour price reduced to that of a person of lower rank.

One legal penalty was the embarrassment fine which was imposed on those found guilty of insulting behaviour. It was payable to people of all ranks, with a few notable exceptions deemed to be uninsultable: ne'er-do-wells, squanderers, idlers, misers, satirists and clowns. Lawyers, however, had no rights before the courts against insults because it was said that 'a man who is paid to abuse others is not entitled to claim damages when abused himself'.

Foreigners, too, benefited from the laws. Any alien coming into the country to pursue a suit against a native was entitled by law, to his choice of Irish advocate to prosecute his case.

What was, perhaps, most remarkable about these laws was that enforcement depended simply on public acceptance of morality.

In some cases distress was avoided if a plaintiff 'fasted against' a recalcitrant defendant and this was always necessary where the defendant was a noble and the plaintiff was not. The plaintiff, having served due notice, sat before the door of the defendant's house without food, and the defendant was bound to fast as long as the complainant fasted. This was an appalling disgrace for the defendant, and worse censure befell him if he did not submit to it, for 'He that does not give a pledge to fasting is an evader of all,' maintained the law. He became an outcast if the plaintiff died.

The laws were, however, cumbersome and vexed in precedent, and the commission set out to give them a new order. The three great achievements of Patrick in this regard – second only to the achievement which enabled him to be selected for the commission in the first place – were to cause the law of compensation to be substituted for the *lex talionis*, to preserve the old traditions in Law (as in much else), and to provide bishops with status, dignity and rank equal before the law to that of kings, *ollaves* and poets. The revised code was called the Senchus Moore or, as it became more popularly known, Cáin Phadraig, (Coin Fawding) Patrick's Law.

Indicative of Patrick's approach to his work are these words in the introduction to the five books of the Patrick's Law: 'What did not clash with the word of God in written law and in the New Testament, and with the consciences of the believers, was confirmed in the laws of the *brehons* by Patrick and by the ecclesiastics and the chieftains of Ireland: and this is the Senchus Moore.' It was to remain the principal volume of Irish statute law for hundreds of years. And Patrick wrote into it the following Rial Phadraig, Rule of Patrick: 'Here is what the testament of Patrick contains for the souls of the men of Ireland: every *tuath* will have a chief bishop to ordain its clergy, to consecrate its churches, to give direction to its chiefs and nobles and to sanctify and bless their children after baptism.'

Patrick had long since disclosed his status and, on so doing, had encountered opposition to his being 'first bishop' of Ireland from four bishops from the south-east, whence they had come from the Irish colonies in Britain: Ibar, who was the most obstinate and last to yield; Declan; Ciaran; and Ailbe. But such problems were well behind him by the time the great legal work was completed.

The whole of the cáin and the laws from which it derived rested on the sanctity of the verbal contract, 'for the world would be in confusion if verbal contracts were not binding', according to Duach. It also, of course, depended on the moral force of public opinion.

The commission also helped the final codifying of the criminal law and law of personal injury embodied in *The Book of Acaill* which the great Cormac Mac Art had compiled in his retirement some two hundred years earlier. When asked what was the worst sort of pleading before a *brehon*, Cormac replied: 'Contending against knowledge; Contending without proofs; Taking refuge in bad language; A stiff delivery; A muttering speech; Hair-splitting; Uncertain proofs; Despising books; Turning against custom; Shifting one's pleading; Inciting the mob; Blowing one's own trumpet; Blustering.'

In spite of the clear-sightedness and common sense that promoted this recital from Cormac, the practice - endemic in certain professions, including the law - of dazzling and excluding the laity with abstruse brilliance by wrapping the discipline in a mystique, in an obscure language that none but the initiated could understand, prevailed. Notwithstanding his reforms, and simplification, and the later reforms by Laoire's committee that resulted in the Patrick's Law, jargon was reintroduced and the exclusivity - and implied superiority - of the advocates was thus preserved.

Chapter 12

HE leaned back in his chair in the settlement above the bridge at B'lath Cliath and closed his eyes. Fatigue overcame him these days with increasing frequency and his body was no longer fully commanded by his will, or his mind by the desire to work. Without intending it he dozed. Disconnected images performed a slow masque behind his eyelids to a pattern that seemed purposeful, but made no sense. The board on his knee slipped and the movement penetrated his dream. He opened his eyes with a start and a feeling of time lost. He sighed. The afternoon sunlight was still bright. Only the distant shadows were a little bluer.

He leaned forward to replace his writing board and the fallen sheets of vellum and arranged them as before, or so he thought. Then he glanced at the sheet in front of him and saw that it was no longer his *Confessio.* The writing had no title, and began: 'With my own hand I have written and composed these words to be given, delivered, and sent to the soldiers of Coroticus; I do not say to my fellow citizens, or to fellow citizens of the holy Romans, but to fellow citizens of the demons, because of their evil works . . . '

Patrick's jaw set and his brows drew together. A spasm of hatred and nausea gripped him and he closed his eyes to control his feelings and offer a silent and intense prayer . . .

A thin sea mist, humid rather than wetting, laid a veil upon the coastline. But the strong light of the sun penetrated it and at times the filtered blue sky might briefly be seen. The warm mist had a redolence peculiar to itself, as if it drew from the ground the odour of its riches. Some three hundred people, the majority newly-baptised Christians, were happily assembled on the sward in front of a little church, known as the *dertuch* or oak-house because it was built of oak planks. The church was one of the most recent in the *tuath* which lay on the Wicklow coast roughly half way between the bridge of B'lath Cliath and the place from which Patrick first escaped. Behind and west rose the mountains and in front lay the sea beyond which was West Britain, though none of these things could be seen that day because of the mist. The little church itself was only recently consecrated by the bishop of the region, Aidan, who because of illness was not able to be present on this important occasion.

Earlier, shortly after dawn, about a hundred of those present, men, women, mostly children, had been baptised by priests and deacons and holy women who devoted their lives to the service of God and lived together in celibacy in simple huts and shelters around the church. Friends and relatives also came to celebrate and the new Christians were distinguishable in their white garments and, in some cases, by the holy oil that still glistened on their foreheads.

After the baptisms the Holy Sacrifice had been offered and then the cheerful people mingled; a group of musicians sang to the accompaniment of harps and the gathering ate casual food, nuts, berries, and cheese, and drank milk and *metheglin*, mead, flavoured with hazelnuts. They were a noisy, chattering, carefree group when the renegades fell upon them.

Coroticus was a Briton who once had been a decurion of the Tenth Legion. But some ten years earlier he had deserted, made his way back to Britain, and become a renegade, gathering around him a swarm of blood- and loot-hungry savages who lived by the sword: Picts, Saxons, Britons like himself, and dissident Scots from the colonies in Alban and West Britain. Just as had the warriors of Criffan and Nial, Britain and Gaul - albeit on a grander and more political scene - Coroticus's pirates ravaged the same coasts, but included Ireland, for slaves and booty. Indeed, if Coroticus showed any prejudice it was in favour of raiding Ireland now that it was largely Christian and the great fleets were laid up, for here was the traditional enemy he could hate with a clear conscience. That he, too, had been baptised a Christian, and that Saxon, British and Irish kings were of one mind in seeking his destruction, meant nothing. The great and bloody swords of Ireland had almost all been sheathed and exchanged for the Cross of Christ, and Coroticus, the pirate could reap unchallenged. There were no Roman troops in Britain; he sneered at the *limitanei* (or what was left of them), and avoided the armies of kings.

Aidan's grandchildren, two girls and a boy, had been baptised that morning and he, his wife and his daughter-in-law were all there to see. Fergus, his son, was at sea with a convoy of three ships, heading for Poitou in Gaul with hides to exchange for wine. They were with some friends, eating honey cakes and drinking milk and *metheglin* when Aidan heard his wife gasp. He glanced at her and saw that she was looking over his shoulder, her expression awestruck. He turned in time to see a warrior in full Roman battle dress, a sword in his hand, emerge from the mist, followed by twenty or thirty more. Not all were dressed like the first, some were wild and shaggy whom he immediately identified as Picts, some were Celts, clean and tidy, and some wore mail and armour like the Goths and Franks. He instantly knew them for what they were. Before he could shout, a sword sliced through the neck and arm of one of the priests who had turned, smiling, to greet whoever it was that approached him from behind. Aidan pushed his terrified wife and some of the others and shouted 'Run, run' as a column of blood spouted from the priest's torso. The throng screamed and began to scatter, children streaking for cover or standing helpless as was their nature. The pirates rushed among them, cutting to right and left. The first to die were the unarmed men and older women.

The last thing Aidan saw before a thick, broad-bladed Pictish spear transfixed him from behind was his daughter-in-law, Failve, rushing her children away and looking back at him with agonised features. He plainly noted before he died that she wore the brooch his own father had given him. Before the incongruity of the thought was complete he fell dead, the weight of the heavy spear rolling his lifeless body slightly to one side upon the ground. The Pict who had killed him placed a foot in the small of his back and tugged at the spear until it came free, bringing with it a large wedge of Aidan's flesh and much blood.

Of those who were not killed the majority were captured and carried off to be sold as slaves. Failve and one of her daughters, Orla, who lay for a half day in a hollow under a fallen tree not three hundred paces off, survived. But Aidan's wife was slaughtered after a multiple rape, and his grandson and other grand-daughter, Aiofe, were taken, the holy chrism still glistening on their pale foreheads above their terrible tears. Aoife was so badly shocked that she never again spoke and as best he could her brother cared for her. But to no avail, for three days later she was knocked on the head with a club by one of Coroticus's soldiers because of her infirmity. He had wanted to abuse the child.

The carnage and desecration Patrick saw when he reached the scene on the afternoon of that same day was something that stirred his soul with lasting anger; he would never forget the sight. He had some idea what to expect before he reached there; shaken messengers had met him on the way. As Odran, his charioteer, lashed the ponies to a fast run, the messengers held the sides of the chariot with one hand and ran alongside.

First they saw the smoke, a smudged pool against the sky, filling from a thin stream of darker smoke still rising from the remains of the thatched roof of the church. Then they saw the desolate church itself and, as the noise of their approach reached them, the rising and flapping of birds, black and white. Finally they came upon the sorrowing people whose wailing mingled with the harsh cries of the birds.

The dead had been carried to the open space before the church and were laid out in nine rows, nine bodies in each. They had been covered with leafy branches and linen cloth through which a multitude of stains showed where they had been struck down. In every direction the sward was marked with gore and flesh, and it was on this residue that the pertinacious gulls and black carrion birds, in spite of the sporadic efforts of the mourners to keep them away, had been feeding. Even as Patrick's chariot halted, a couple of venturesome ravens fluttered, one behind the other, to the edge of a bloodied patch and walked stiffly towards it, bright-eyed heads cocked and heavy beaks dipping swiftly. Overhead the white gulls swooped and burdened the atmosphere with their raucous cries.

The victims were solemnly interred with dignity and grace and immense mourning. The sorrow was not relieved by the common knowledge that more among the captured must surely die and that the fate of the remainder would, if anything, be worse. Of the three hundred or so people who had gathered that morning, eighty-one were buried, forty-nine escaped and the remainder, about one hundred and seventy, mostly children but some older, were taken by the pirates. There was a brief moment of joy in this great sorrow when Aidan's daughter-in-law, Failve, and little Orla were discovered safe. The extent of his personal loss in the death of Aidan, his first close friend among the Irish, struck Patrick anew and, even as he comforted Failve, his own tears swelled with rage.

When the funeral ceremonies were over and he had commiserated with the sorrowing people, Patrick went to an empty cell which had been occupied by one of the young noblewomen dedicated to Christ, who had been taken. In a cold and passionate fury he began a letter to Coroticus who was well known to him by reputation. This is part of what he later recalled having written:

'The day after the newly baptised, anointed with chrism, in white garments, had been slain – the fragrance was still on their foreheads when they were butchered and slaughtered by the soldiers of Coroticus – I sent a letter with a holy presbyter (a nephew of Aidan's called Fiach) whom I taught from his childhood, clerics accompanying him, asking them to let us have some of the baptised they had made captives. They only jeered at them . . .

' . . . hence I know not what to lament more: those who have been slain, or those whom they have taken captive, or those whom the devil has mightily ensnared. Together with him they will be slaves in hell in eternal punishment; for who committeth sin is a slave and will be called a son of the devil . . .

' . . . wherefore let every God-fearing man know that they are enemies of men and of Christ my God, for whom I am an ambassador. Parricide! Fratricide! Ravening wolves that eat the people of the Lord as they eat bread! As I said, the wicked, O Lord, have destroyed Thy Law, which but recently He had excellently and kindly planted in Ireland, and which had established itself by the grace of God.'

When Patrick thought of the fact that Coroticus, like himself, was a Briton, despair almost overwhelmed him.

' . . . And if my own people do not know me, a prophet hath no honour in his own country. Perhaps we are not of the same fold and have not one and the same God as father . . . It is not right that one destroyeth, another buildeth up . . .

' . . . What shall I do, Lord, I am most despised . . . Look. Thy sheep around me are torn to pieces and driven away, and that by those robbers, by the order of the hostile-minded Coroticus. Far from the love of God is a man who hands over Christians to the Picts and Scots. Ravening wolves have devoured the flock of the Lord, which in Ireland was indeed growing splendidly with the greatest care; and the sons and daughters of kings were monks and virgins of Christ – I cannot count their number. Wherefore be not pleased with the wrong done to the just; even to hell it shall not please.'

Patrick drew a comparison between the behaviour of the pagan Franks and the so-called Christian soldiers of Coroticus.

'. . . This is the custom of the Roman Christians of Gaul: they send holy and able men to the Franks and other heathen with so many thousand *solidi* to ransom baptised captives. You prefer to kill them and sell them to a foreign nation that has no knowledge of God. You betray the members of Christ as it were into a brothel. What hope have you in God, or anyone who thinks as you do, or converses with you in words of flattery? God will judge. For scripture says: Not only they that do evil are worthy to be condemned, but they also that consent to them.

'. . . O you fair and beloved brethren and sons whom I have begotten in Christ, countless in number, what can I do for you? . . . Perhaps they do not believe that we have received one and the same baptism, or have one and the same God as father. For them it is a disgrace that we are Irish. Have ye not, as is written, one God? Have ye not, every one of you, forsaken his neighbour?

'. . . where then will Coroticus with his criminals, rebels against Christ, where will they see themselves, they who distribute baptised women as prizes . . .

'. . . I ask earnestly that whoever is a willing servant of God be a carrier of this letter, so that on no account it be suppressed or hidden by anyone, but rather be read before all the people and in the presence of Coroticus himself. May God inspire them some time to recover their senses for God, repenting, however late their heinous deeds – murderers of the brethren of the Lord! – and to set free the baptised women whom they took captive, in order that they may deserve to live to God, and be made whole, here and in eternity. Be peace to the Father, and to the Son, and to the Holy Spirit. Amen.'

Chapter 13

WHEN Aidan's grand-daughter Orla came to bring him to supper, Patrick was asleep, the writing board and sheets of vellum fallen to the floor. He sat facing the door, the evening sun flooding the room from a window behind him, so that she did not at first notice that he was sleeping. When she did she paused and smiled gently with the tenderness and great affection which was a single example of the feelings of everyone in Ireland by now when they saw or heard of Patrick.

She softly wakened him and because of the crippling pains in his joints helped him to his feet. And he leaned on her as they went to the refectory.

After supper she and her family - for her husband and young baby were with her, as well as her beloved mother who had saved her from Coroticus's pirates - made Patrick comfortable on a *lepad*, couch, for they had prepared a surprise for him. This was a *rackera*, a poet and storyteller, who would entertain them with the lore and ancient literature of Ireland, which Patrick dearly loved to hear. Indeed, he enjoyed it so much that he had sometimes felt guilty for indulging himself. But he was aware of the value of the old tales as the living culture of the people and caused them to be written down so that, in all their wisdom and delight, they might be preserved for the benefit of future generations.

That was his last night of such enjoyment. The next week he set out for his seat at Ard Mhacha, Armagh. As the acknowledged Primate of Ireland, his principal church was there. First he proposed to visit the little church at Saul in Down, which was the first he built in Ireland before lighting the celebrated fire on the hill of Slane. His journey took him north along the coast, over the wicker bridge at B'lath Cliath, and thence, still northwards, by the plain of Muirhemne, territory of the celebrated pagan hero of four centuries earlier, Cuchulain, before reaching Saul, north again of the blue shoulder of the Mourne mountains.

The journey took six days, for now he travelled slowly and everywhere was greeted by crowds who wanted him to stay with them. Each time he gently and smilingly refused, saying over and over, in a voice full of love and still accented even after all these years: 'Dear brothers and sisters, in the name of the Lord I exhort you to preserve the great treasure of your fidelity to Jesus Christ and to his Church and, as is said in the Acts of the Apostles, be ''faithful to the teaching of the Apostles, to the brotherhood, to the breaking of bread and to the prayers''.'

He pressed on through the early springtime, with definite purpose. The festival of Imbolc, of the slaves and lambing, was a month or more gone by, and the country was showing that pellucid light, green and crystal, which is the manifestation of the new. Near Dun Dealgan, the castle of Cuchulain, now in ruins outside the settlement, he spent the night at a church and primitive monastery.

They hadn't intended to stay there, but because he was tired they stopped early. There was still activity in the monastery, so he rested in a sheltered spot which caught the sun, and began to pray by himself. But soon, as word of his presence spread, people gathered. At first the young monks, former princes, tried to keep them away, but Patrick told them to let the people come to him. Among them was a middle-aged man carrying a little girl in his arms, who promptly fell asleep when he laid her on a heap of straw while he listened to Patrick. The man remained at the back of the crowd and bent his head, covering his eyes with the palm of one hand, elbow resting on knee. He was heavyset and richly dressed, but the lithe grace of an active youth was vestigially evident when he moved. After a while the mouth of the sleeping child fell open and she began to snore, then to talk in her sleep – nothing sensible, agitated mutterings, such as children do. But the cries were loud and clear above the words of Patrick.

'Sh-sh,' went her father, for such he was, and the child moaned and turned over. But it happened again a few minutes later.

'Sh-sh,' he whispered again, urgently.

Patrick looked towards them. 'Never mind,' he called. 'Let her sleep. She does not disturb us . . . '

The man raised his head for a moment when Patrick called out, turning towards him.

'Duach!' Patrick tried to stand up – for he had been sitting addressing the small company – but found it difficult. 'It . . . it is Duach, isn't it? Are my eyes deceiving me again?'

The man stood, shamefaced, hands clasped before him.

'Your eyes do not deceive you, Patrick,' he said. 'You are right. It is I, Duach, a sinner.'

'Come!' called Patrick, smiling with joy at this reunion. 'Come here where I can see you.'

Duach hesitated.

'Come!' called Patrick again, beckoning. Duach moved slowly through the throng, his reluctance plain.

'G-' He paused.

'What?' asked Patrick as Duach came up to him, his strange eyes resting calmly on the other man.

'Give – ' again Duach paused and Patrick nodded at him to continue. Duach went on with a rush, 'I ask your blessings.'

By way of reply Patrick turned to where the child still slept.

'Is this your daughter?' Duach nodded. 'And she is called Brigit?' Again Duach nodded, but did not reply.

'Hmm,' continued Patrick. 'And was it as I said?'

Duach turned his bent head a little to one side as if he were looking for some way to escape answering the question. Then he looked first down at the ground and then at Patrick. A third time he nodded.

'Let her sleep,' said Patrick raising his hand to bless the now quiet child, 'and be content. In your own way you have fulfilled God's divine and mysterious purpose. I bless you both and everyone here, and all my people in this land now and for ever more . . . *in nomine Patris et Filii, et Spiritus Sancti* . . . '

Next day, the fifteenth day of March 461, with the year beginning in great clarity, he entered Saul where he had built his first church. And he was content. He never left it. On the seventeenth day he died and all Ireland descended into the Laíthi na Caoínte (*Leehi na Cweenta*), the Days of Lamentation, which lasted for twelve nights, while the nation whom he had brought to Christ bewailed the most mournful loss it had ever known.

Among those who travelled to Saul and thence to Armagh for the period of great mourning was a grandson of Nial Niallach, whose warriors captured the young Patrick and first brought him to Ireland as a slave almost seventy years before. With him from Donegal this minor king brought his five-year-old son, Phelim, to mourn the passing of so great a man.

Chapter 14

THE Emperor Justinian wrested Africa again from the Vandals; the Anglo-Saxon conquest of Britain proceeded, but, for the first time in centuries, the war fleets of Ireland were still, rotted on the beaches or under the tide for want of use. This corner of the world, in the autumn of Anno Domini 536, was at peace.

From all the land drifted the drowsy sounds of summer, chief among them the echoed croak of the hidden corncrake. Phelim, under-king, *ur-ree*, of this north-western *tuath* lying between the small, oval Lough Gartan which gave his *tuath* its name and the great bite of the northern ocean that was Lough Swilly, dozed comfortably in the afternoon sun and snored, as content as any man has a right to be.

Crimthan, his son, was at present satisfactorily fostered nearby with the priest Crownawn (his third fostering and not a bad thing for a contender for the kingship of Ulster and the Pentarchy - even the Rí-Eireannach itself, perhaps!). Phelim's domineering wife Eithne, a daughter of the King of Munster, was away on a visit to her father, and he, too, was at peace. Gently Phelim belched the gaseous remains of lunch (apples, beer and chicken) past half-open lips, and smiled without opening his eyes. From the middle distance percolated activities of the *rath*, performed by other people. He folded his hands loosely above his satisfied stomach, settled himself more comfortably on his *lepad* (in the most sheltered part of the *grianaan*, out of the wind) and drifted . . .

Not far away his cousin Aine (Ann), spoke to her surviving child, Dermot, who was eleven. She was a widow, anxious, earnest and determined; qualities flawed a little perhaps by a compulsive intensity which many found unsettling. Her other children had all died at birth in spite of the best endeavours of midwives; her husband had died in a fatuous blood feud.

She sat on a high Roman stool and Dermot stood in front of her. Her hands were on his shoulders to give additional emphasis and gravity to what she said. 'You are Dermot, son of Aine, daughter of Aidan, son of Orla, daughter of Fergus, son of Aidan.' She looked into his eyes as if she would impress on his mind what she said by force of her will. But he already knew it all, far better than she understood. Something in his calm assurance suddenly made her heart turn within her. She suppressed the feeling. She told herself that it was time Dermot accustomed himself to firmness. But in fact it was she who lacked it, had she known, and her efforts were misdirected. 'The world is not a cushion,' she thought bitterly. Aloud she said: 'Aidan was the son of Fergus who was the first to receive this' – she brought one hand from his shoulder and opened it in front of him – 'in the wars of Britain in the time of Nial Niallach.'

Dermot looked solemnly at the brooch lying in his mother's hand. He had seen it many times before and knew its history intimately, but he listened gravely as she told him, once again, of the murder of Aidan eighty-six years before at the baptism ceremonies in far-away Wicklow; of how it had come to her own father, another Aidan, from Orla who had escaped from the soldiers of Coroticus and had known the saintly Patrick before he died.

He had admired the brooch for as long as he could remember, especially since he knew it would one day be his to wear and keep in trust for a child of his own. They were not wealthy compared with their relatives – of course there had been the *eric* payment (but for manslaughter, not murder) of twenty-one cows, and the honour price of the killer. But as he was only an *ogue-arra*, the lowest grade of non-noble free tenant, his honour price had been merely another three cows. Dermot was determined to restore the wealth and dignity of his family.

Every time his mother had taken the brooch from the box where she kept their few valuables and unwrapped its soft woollen cloth, his heart had beat a little faster with excitement and anticipation - and perhaps impatience too. Now he listened to the tone of her voice rather than to her words. She was very earnest as, with hands become unaccustomedly clumsy, she pinned it to his short tunic; then returned them to his shoulders where he felt her fingers twitch and clutch very slightly. A long moment she looked at him and then she felt tears burning behind her eyes. It seemed as if she was going to kiss him and his fear of it must have shown, for she drew back and turned him round, away from her, instead. She gave him a small push. With mixed feelings of pride and pain she restricted the sob in her throat to a barely audible catch, but she could no longer restrain her tears. Through them she watched as, straight-backed, her son walked away, the brooch on his chest giving him self-importance and dignity. It was a solemn moment for both.

It was also the prelude to one of those moments the texture and sense of which can be recalled completely in later life - perhaps because they are keystones of time in a lifespan, essential to the whole fabric which makes up the individual. At all events, what occurred next was of great importance and greatly affected the lives of Dermot and the youth, Crimthan, who at that very moment was coming towards him from Crownawn's church and into his life in a way which would fix him there, close and influential, for the next sixty-one years. Crimthan, his cousin, the king's son, who was to be neither one of the Pentarchy nor Rí-Eireann, and yet would wield as much power as both; who was to go to war and to God in almost the same movement; who was to bring the Faith, and with it the shaping of the future, to Albyn at the same time that he preserved the past for Ireland; and who was to take the name Colm, or dove, in religion and be called Colm Cille, Colm of the Churches.

Dermot walked from the *rath* along the path that skirted the western shore of the lake and ran past the common land where two teams of boys were playing hurley, the curved broad-bladed ash sticks flashing and clashing about a leather ball as each side strove for a goal. Dermot paused near where some youngsters, about his own age, or a little older, were watching, and became absorbed in the match.

The teams were of boys from the *rath* against boys from the surrounding *tuath*, who regularly clashed in nascent rural-urban rivalry. Naturally Dermot supported the *rath* and when that team lofted the ball in a great arc and pursued it down the field towards the goal line, his spirit rose with the leather ball and a yell of excitement leaped from his throat. But as luck would have it he had stopped beside a group of youths from the surrounding *tuath*. They looked at him - first in silence, then with resentful murmurs. Unaware of their attention, Dermot cheered on his favoured team as one of the *rath* players stretched high with his hurley and hooked the flying ball away from an opponent and into his hand. In one movement he turned away, ball in his left hand, hurley arcing wide in his right. A *tuath* defender tried to hook it so he could not strike, but like a dancer he wheeled again, and bringing his hurley wide and under, caught the ball as he turned, to send it arcing high again towards the opposing goal. It fell short and hurleys clashed in mid-air as four players tried to capture it once more. A *rath* player kicked it back towards another *rath* attacker who gathered the low ball on his stick as he ran and held it level on the blade in front of him as he continued down the pitch. Twice he swerved to avoid defenders, their hurleys striking at his own to dislodge the ball. Then, quickly dropping the blade of his hurley, he struck, low and hard. The ball hurtled towards the opposing goal like a *tathlum* from a sling. But the *tuath* goalkeeper was good. He stretched a hand before him and the ball lodged in it. He struck it back towards the attacking players, seeking a man of his own team who would drive it up the field to safety. But his strike was short and it fell towards one of the *rath* attackers who swung on it as it dropped and doubled it back, low, whence it came. Another *rath* attacker near the opposing goal caught the flying ball on the blade of his hurley and swung with it so that it crashed past the goalkeeper for a score.

Dermot's cheer was loud and unrestrained, until a voice beside him stopped him. He looked round, his excited smile fading to surprise and faint dismay when he saw he was surrounded by four youths, all of them bigger than himself and none of whom he knew except by sight.

'What's up with you?' growled one.

'What do you want here?' demanded another. 'You should be over there.'

And sure enough, Dermot could see that all the *rath* supporters were, indeed, on the other side of the field.

'Oh,' he said, 'yes, well . . . ' He moved to go, but was prevented.

'Hold hard a minute,' said one of the others, placing himself between Dermot and the field so what was happening could not be seen, 'who do you think you are to come here and start shouting like that?'

'Yes,' said another, 'for a rotten flukey goal!'

'That wasn't a fluke . . . ' Instantly Dermot regretted his words, but too late. The youths crowded closer.

'Oh, it wasn't?' said one leaning forward and grabbing him by the front of his tunic. 'Here, what's this? Look at this, lads.'

'Leave that alone,' cried Dermot, held in the grip of the larger youth, fearful that his brooch might be damaged. 'Don't you touch that.'

'Well,' said one youngster, 'a brooch, is it? You're too small for such a brooch. Isn't he lads?'

'Yes! Much too small,' they sneered, crowding still closer.

'Sure a brooch like that is too fine for the likes of him altogether.'

'Leave me alone! Take your hands off me!' Dermot's voice was shriller than intended and, in his anger, he struck out.

'Ah, a little *gaiscah*, brave one,' sneered a boy contemptuously, knocking Dermot's hand aside and grabbing for the brooch.

'Don't touch my brooch,' he cried, fighting and desperate now.

'Don't touch my brooch,' they mimicked, one of them slapping Dermot's face. 'Don't touch my brooch,' he sneered again and grabbed Dermot by the tunic where the brooch was pinned.

'No,' said someone from behind, 'don't touch his brooch!'

They all turned swiftly, the one holding Dermot suddenly letting go of him when he saw who spoke, so that the smaller boy stumbled. For a moment, nobody said anything. The aggressors stared at the newcomer, who looked back easily. He was about their age and size. But he carried himself with a confidence they didn't much care for. Moreover, they knew who he was.

'What's it to you?'

'You heard me,' said Crimthan. 'Leave him alone. Are you all right, Dermot?'

'Yes.' Unmolested, Dermot joined Crimthan and turned to face his tormentors.

'Now,' said Crimthan, 'go.'

'I suppose you'll make us?'

'I will!' said Crimthan. Now his voice had a hard edge.

'You and what army?' said the youth who had grabbed Dermot's brooch.

Crimthan's movement was swift and unexpected. He hurtled forward, left arm swinging in an arc as if to strike his opponent with it. The youth raised his right arm to protect himself; whereupon, still in mid-flight, Crimthan transferred his weight from one foot to the other and hit him hard in the stomach. He doubled up, winded.

'There was no need for that!'

'What call had you to do that?'

The other three were resentful but cautious now. This was more than they had bargained for. They helped their companion to his feet and moved off muttering about what they wouldn't do if he weren't the king's son, and just wait till they got him alone, which they would, never fear; just wait!

'Thanks, Crimthan,' said Dermot with something of the mild hero worship that he retained in a more modified and mature form for the rest of his life.

'Weren't you the little eejit not to look where you were?' said Crimthan impatiently. 'You were dead lucky I was coming home.' Dermot said nothing and fell into step beside Crimthan. 'Where did you get it anyway?'

Pride swelled in Dermot again. 'Aine gave it to me. And it goes way back. To Nial Niallach. Further maybe.'

Crimthan stopped. 'Let me see.' He lifted the material under the brooch on his cousin's tunic and peered at it. 'Mmm. Not bad. You should be more careful of a thing like that and not be wearing it out and around where you might lose it or break it, or have it stolen,' he added with a look that damped Dermot's pride.

'I suppose you're right,' he said disappointed. 'Why are you coming home? I thought you'd be with Crownawn still.'

Crimthan looked at him sidelong. He was fifteen and a head taller than Dermot, strongly built though not tall. His hair was fair and he had fine, curved eyebrows which frowned momentarily before he answered. 'I'm still with Crownawn. That's what brings me home.'

Dermot smiled. 'That's a queer one.'

When Crimthan laughed his expression changed. His face lit up joyfully in a way he never lost. It did so now as his laughter joined Dermot's. Then he became serious again.

'Well,' he said, 'I've decided – I suppose there's no harm in telling you, you'll know soon enough anyway – I've decided to be a priest.'

Dermot halted and gaped at him. 'You! A priest! But . . . '

'I know the buts.' Crimthan swiped slowly at the grass verge with the switch he had picked up as they walked. 'And this is the biggest but: it's what I want!'

'You could be anything; King of Ireland . . . '

Crimthan looked at him strangely, Dermot thought. And then he realised it wasn't strange at all. It was just that it was the look of an adult: distant and deep, with thought in it.

Crimthan transferred his gaze out over the lake. 'Maybe.' He turned suddenly to Dermot and stopped. 'Look, I'm going to face all this when I tell them at home. Don't you start. The long and the short of it is, it's only partly my own decision . . . '

'You mean Crownawn?'

'He knows nothing about it! I mean there's something outside of myself won't leave me alone. I push it away, but it keeps coming back. Over and over! I fight it and try to forget it, but I might as well try to forget I'm alive. If I don't be a priest then I'll be nothing; for God.'

Dermot looked at him with shining eyes.

'That's great,' he said. 'I think that's absolutely marvellous.'

They smiled and went on towards the *rath* where Crimthan knew he faced the first major battle of his life and the one that was to shape it.

Suddenly the grown-up, troubled look vanished from his face. Swiftly bending he grabbed a fistful of mud, straightened and, like lightning, rubbed it on Dermot's cheek, pushing him sideways at the same time so that he stumbled into the long sedge between the road and the lake.

'Come on,' he shouted, 'you eejit, last one home's an Aethiop,' and before Dermot was out of the sedge, laughing and shouting in pursuit, Crimthan was twenty yards down the road, his joyful grin beaming back at his younger cousin.

Chapter 15

Aoife was sixteen in the spring of 544 and ripe for bed. The wonder was that it hadn't already happened, for she was truly beautiful. She possessed long fair hair tinged with gold that cascaded about her back and shoulders like a shimmering garment. And she had green eyes. She was neither too tall nor too short and had a way of moving, so lithe, that at first glance she appeared to be thin though she was in fact well rounded as a woman should be, with firm flesh and taut, honey-coloured skin. All of this made her very desirable at an unusually early age. Since she was twelve she had attracted covetous glances but her self-consciousness, her gentleness and modesty, protected her and she remained unmolested. Not that she was unaware of the opposite sex. Far from it; sometimes unformed yearnings disturbed her and delayed her sleep at night longer than usual. She was the daughter of a *fudir*, an outcast, which made her especially vulnerable and only her indefinable but positive purity of spirit and the patronage and protection of the Abbot Berkan – affectionately known as Mo Bhi, My Being – who employed her father in his small monastery still afforded her protection at her age.

Mo Bhi's monastery was Glasnevin on the banks of the River Tolka where it flowed sluggishly towards the broad estuary of the Liffey just north of the wicker bridge at B'lath Cliath. It was quite different from the great monastic schools such as Finian's at Clonard, Congall's at Bangor or Brendan's at Clonfert. These had a complement of more than three thousand students each and young men and women flocked to them – and to lesser seats of learning also – from all over Europe. Glais Nephin had only fifty monks and was a preparatory institution. The larger monasteries counted the sons and daughters of kings, lords and princes among their hosts of students. Countless servants, tradesmen, hangers-on and others lived with and off them, so that a major monastery was a scholastic nucleus around which grew and developed a huge settlement, sometimes of as many as ten thousand people. The settlement at Glasnevin had hardly fifty families, about three hundred people. There were other small unrelated settlements all about the low heights above the marshy estuary of the Liffey from Dubhlinn in the west close to the old *rath* where Aesold, daughter of King Aengus of the Liffey, had lived (and where there was now a church, Chapel Aesold), northwards and east to those at Feyn Ishka, Cowra, Fionn and beyond Glasnevin at Santry.

Like larger monasteries, Glais Nephin and its surrounding district required administration and public order which meant a certain amount of co-ordination among the settlements north of the Liffey. Administration tended to stem on the one hand from monastic nuclei and on the other from the power of the king's writ. When necessary, troops of the king's standing army were billeted near a monastery, this was rare; the moral force of public opinion normally provided the only sanction required to maintain public order.

The great monasteries were the major universities of Europe when all other advanced educational resources were trodden beneath the inexorable and savage feet of barbarian lords. They were schools of secular as well as ecclesiastical learning where, besides philosophy, scripture and the classics, general literature, science and mathematics also flourished. Most of the students were not intended for the Church, but for ordinary civil or military life. Many future kings studied at Bangor and Clonard.

Foreign students were numerous; part of the city of Armagh (which was the great theological centre of Ireland, and later no one who had not studied there was permitted to give public lectures in theology or scripture) was called Trian-Saxon, the Saxon's Third, because of the large numbers of Saxon students attending there. In a later century seven streets of Kilbally, Churchtown, were entirely occupied by the *gall*, foreigners. By far the greatest number came from Britain - by the 'fleet-load', as Adhelm, Bishop of Sherborne, later expressed it; and Bede remarked the great number of English nobility and lower orders who perished in Ireland in the plague of 664. But there were also many Romans, Gauls, Germans, Greeks and, even, Egyptians - some of them refugees from the persecutions of Justinian.

But Glais Nephin (Glasnevin) was a small monastery, solely devoted to the monastic and spiritual growth of its members and to preparing exceptional students for further study at such places as Clonard. The huts, or cells, of the fifty monks occupied one bank of the River Tolka, with the settlement all round it, and the church was on the other bank, reached by a footbridge.

It was here that Crimthan was sent to prepare for and, it may be, to test his resolve in the monastic life. And it was here that his devotion, which in no way diminished his regal and fiery spirit, became assured. On one notorious occasion he swam the Tolka in winter because the bridge had been swept away and he did not want to miss Vespers. Here, too, Dermot followed him, but Dermot's vocation was less profound.

A part in the practice known as *virgines subintroductae* was required of Aoife from time to time, and she disliked it intensely. It was a severe method of attempting to determine if a novice had the control and detachment expected of a monk. Such asceticism later gave rise to the great austerity of the Culdees, 'companions of God'. *The virgines subintroductae* required that a beautiful girl be brought into the cell of a devout aspirant in order to give him the glory of overcoming the agonies of lust. The girl was not expected to behave lewdly but to demonstrate in one way or another, physical desirability so that the novice was truly tested. Reluctantly Aoife had participated in this practice a number of times, but only when persuaded to do so by her father. It could mean something extra from the abbot, who was quite unaware of her reluctance or the reason for it. He approved using a chaste girl rather than, as in some monasteries, girls who gave the impression of never having been chaste at all. In his innocence he assumed that the ascetic benefit worked both ways. But it was a cause of great distress and remorse to Aoife. So when Bran, her father, told her that once more she was required to enter the cell of a novice about whom there were misgivings, she protested.

'Not again, father. You promised . . . '

'Ah I'm sorry, darlin'. Th'abbot asked specially for you. 'Tis a great honour . . . '

'But I don't like it. It makes me ill. An' - an' I don't think it's right.'

'Dammit, girl, doesn't the abbot know if it's right or not?'

'But it's against nature . . . '

'Sure isn't that the whole point? Them monks aren't a bit natural. Don't you know that as well as I do? Standing for days up to their oxters in winter water because they have natural thoughts. Where's the nature in that, ha?'

'I wasn't thinking of just the novice.'

'What then?'

'There's me.'

'What about you, for God's sake! Sure what's there to think about? All you must do is spend the night in his hut-een and he won't even look at you, let alone lay a finger on you. Where's the harm in that?'

'I know, father, I know! But what about me? What am I to think about the torment any man would feel?'

'But, sure, amn't I telling you? Them people don't feel natural the way the rest of us do at all. They're . . . they're above that sort of thing. Above it altogether. Their minds is on a different class of a plane teetotally, and it doesn't do them wan bit of harm.'

'Then why do I have to do it so?'

'Ah, will you stop asking questions an' do it, that's all. There's a haunch of venison in it for us, the abbot as good as told me. Sure that's meat for a week.'

'And what about me?'

'Holy . . . ! What about you?'

'What about how I feel, upsetting and disturbing, maybe, a young man who wants to devote his life to God – and would, only for me? What about that? I have to live with that, don't I?'

Bran was not an understanding man, but he was not obtuse or indifferent either. He saw, or sensed, his daughter's distress. He changed his tone.

'Ah, now, now, now,' he said patting her like he had when she was a child and had hurt her knee, 'you're making too much of it altogether. Sure didn't I tell you? Them fellas aren't ordinary. They don't feel . . . feel, eh, you know, at all! Sure lookit, couldn't you go in there as bare-assed as the day you were born, an' the spirit'd never move a hair of one of their . . . eh . . . one iotem! Isn't that a fact?'

She couldn't but smile. Yet her doubts remained.

'I'd rather not,' she said, trying to laugh. But in her eyes there were tears. And while Bran was compassionate, he was also practical. He put his arms round her.

'I know, *croidhe*, my heart,' he said, 'but, sure, what else can we do? What rights have we? *Fudirs*! We must live. We must all do what we can, even if we don't like it. And this is what you can do. An' anyway,' he added, 'won't you maybe save some fella from being a bad monk and make a better man out of him? Think of it like that!'

So she tried to think of it like that, but with no great success; yet with enough to give her the determination needed to help her father and do her duty as she saw it. He shook her gently by the shoulders.

'There's my girl,' he said. '*mo geersha.* Listen. I must go. There's a ship in below – ' and he turned her with his hands so she could see it perched against the far end of the long unsteady jetty on the estuary of the Tolka. 'I must help unload her for the abbot. There's something in it,' he said. 'I don't want to miss that.'

'No,' said Aoife. 'Go on.'

'And about the other,' he nodded, 'you'll . . . be all right?'

'Don't worry, father, I'll be all right.'

'That's the girl.' He patted her cheek, turned, and began to trot down the hill towards the waterside with the steady, loping pace of the established *fudir*, anxious to please in order to exist. She looked after his drab, strangely dwarfed figure and felt her heart move with compassion, while she wished it were something more. She knew she had no right to despise him but without understanding her feelings she despised everything he represented and that made her feel very guilty.

Bran trotted down the hill through the bunched houses of the settlement, neither receiving nor giving greeting as he passed people and buildings, until he reached an open space where the jetty began and where a number of bullock carts were drawn up waiting to be loaded. A line of men was already returning from the ship with goods.

'You better hurry up,' said one of the carters, 'you're the last.'

Bran nodded and started along the jetty, a black, rickety structure on stilts, which stretched across the mud flats to the distant sand and the ship. He was immediately put to work unloading wine, early cereals and a variety of goods including some furniture. The ship had come direct from Massilia in the Mediterranean with a mixed cargo, and as Bran went on board a small black rat staggered down a rope and vanished, stumbling, along the causeway in the direction of the settlement.

It was something more than a week later that Aoife was brought to Dermot's cell. She wore just a thin slip of white linen which was modest but clung provocatively to the contours of her body.

Dermot was now nineteen and had followed Crimthan loyally and determinedly since the day eight years before when Crimthan intervened on his behalf over the brooch. He'd gone first to Moville where Crimthan had taken the name Colm and then to Glais Nephin and Mo Bhi, arriving as Colm was preparing himself for the advanced University of Finian of Clonard and his destiny. But the self-doubts and digressions of mind that had for some time assailed and haunted Dermot were now assuming frightening dimensions. It was as if he were pursued – not by God, as he had heard said of Saint Patrick – but by something else; something profane. He was afraid that it was the devil tempting him. More than once he mentioned these struggles of the spirit to Colm, who dismissed them as a passing phase. Desperately Dermot mentioned them to the Abbot Berkan, who listened courteously and with a serious smile. He then suggested that these trials were nothing abnormal in a healthy young man. He should pray and work harder. To all of this Dermot acquiesced, but all the same . . .

He was sitting on his *lepad* – really no more than a slightly raised platform covered in branches and rushes with a *brath*, or cloth, laid over it – trying to memorise the Latin of the Psalms, when something paler hovered on the other side of the *brath* covering the opening to his hut. He could see the opaque glow through the heavy cloth and wondered . . . But not for long. The *brath* was drawn back and Aoife, her head cast down so that her marvellous hair covered her forehead and eyes, was ushered in by Berkan.

Dermot jumped to his feet. Instantly he knew why they were there and with a despairing look at the abbot he fell to his knees and raised his hands to cover his eyes. Before he could order his thoughts Berkan spoke.

'This is Aoife, my son, a beautiful child of God. She is here at my request to help you overcome some of the matters that have lately troubled you. She will not speak to you, nor you to her, and I shall be outside. I give you both my blessing.' And saying no more he left as quietly as he came.

Dermot did not move. He was stunned. He had heard of this trial . . . there were rumours . . . . and he had known certain novices who, after several pale quiet days that had often succeeded periods of visible and sometimes voluble distress, had left the monastery with discreet farewells and with the spent air of exhaustively achieved tranquillity.

Aoife stood a moment and then quietly turned towards the stool and sat on it. When Dermot peered through the gaps in his fingers her feet were in view and he stared in horror for a moment, then closed his eyes. But a few moments later he opened them again; felt his eyelashes brush against the palms of his hands. The small feet were still there; still beautiful. He groaned silently and tried to force himself to concentrate. But a vision of the girl herself, whom he had seen more than once in the settlement, sprang to vivid life in his mind's eye, and he shook his head on a rigid neck. That it should be her, of all people! Here . . . !

He groaned loudly and as he did so turned his head slowly from side to side in great torment. The movement slightly changed his aural focus and he heard a new sound; a sob! He froze. He spread his fingers, looked between them. Aoife sat on the stool, very straight, her head still bowed. But as he looked she raised her face, flaring her nostrils so that the tears flowing down her cheeks would not force her to sniff. Hardly realising he did so, Dermot rose and crossed to her. Her eyes were closed but the tears slid from beneath smooth eyelids like dew forming on a petal, and he put a hand behind her head . . .

The next night, after an unnerving day during which, with great kindliness and in the light of what occurred, he was encouraged to look closely at himself, independently of any comparison with Colm, he tried to explain his weakness to his friend with the following poem, which he sent to him before he saw him.

With her head down they brought her
To me, rigid in my cold place;
At night they softly brought her
To raise torments before my face.

And I bound my wrists with my beads,
I drove hard prayers to my mouth;
Sharp stones pierced my quivering knees;
A fierce sweat rushed out of my blood.

My Christ, I set my mind on Thy Passion
And it raging at the bridle it bore;
Turmoil rose in me like an ocean
And I clung my terrible eyes to the Floor.

Like my purpose the day is now past;
New night; new self! All empty; vast!
- But Lord, Lord, I cannot sleep
For the dreaming of little feet.

Dermot was particularly nervous about meeting Colm. He had modelled himself so closely on his cousin that his own failure seemed almost an affront, certainly disloyal. But he need not have worried. Colm saw him first across the muddy campus and smiled and waved as he walked towards him, ignoring mud and puddles alike. Although it had rained heavily in the early morning, and the river was brown and swollen, the sun now gleamed through gaps in swiftly-moving clouds and, behind Colm, the thatched roofs of the settlement gleamed, yellow above the walls of the huts and houses. Some of the walls were richly decorated in bright colours with the traditional motifs and Christian symbols which monks in similar monasteries were already incorporating in manuscript copies of the Psalms and Gospels. Indeed when he spotted Dermot being quietly conspicuous, Colm was painting the wall of a whitewashed hut with an elaborate Gospel scene. He was particularly talented at it and was in great demand for such work, which was used by the monks and priests to illustrate the story of the Gospels when they preached in public. He still held a brush in his hand as he came towards Dermot.

'Well, Dermot. So you found yourself out at last?'

Colm's greeting was saved from sounding too cynical because it was given with love and affection, and Dermot smiled.

''Fraid so,' he said, and shrugged. Colm placed an arm about his cousin's shoulders.

'Don't be down,' he urged. 'I read your poem . . . '

Dermot was almost more anxious to know what Colm thought of the poem than anything else.

Colm read his feelings accurately enough and continued, 'It is a fine poem. Exactly catching the dilemma of someone drawn by two courses, each different, but both noble and essential in their own way.'

'Did you feel that?'

'Indeed yes. What's more,' he added, giving Dermot a thump with the hand still lying across his shoulders, 'don't be foolish enough to think because you feel more strongly impelled one way rather than another that you have failed in anything. How could you fail by being true to yourself? That's not reasonable.'

'What about God?'

'What about Him?'

'What about being true to God?'

'What about it? One can't be true to God if one isn't true to oneself. There are more ways to reach God than by mortification and rejection of a "normal" life. Denying the world and the flesh isn't denying your own self so much as perfecting a way towards God. But it's not the only way. If everyone followed that path there'd soon be nobody left at all. Better to choose the right way for you than meander dangerously on a path that's wrong for you and could only lead to trouble. I think you've done the right thing.'

'You mean you think that Berkan has done the right thing.'

'Perhaps that too. Anyway you'll be a better, wiser and holier man in the world, I think, than you would be if you were a dissatisfied, disillusioned and frustrated monk.'

'I suppose that's true.'

'Of course it's true. Now come and say a prayer to thank the Lord for being so good to us.'

It was later the same evening that they first learned about the unusual numbers of dead and dying rats all over the settlement. Indeed as Colm himself returned to his hut one came towards him through the doorway. But not quick and scurrying in the normal way, along the wall and avoiding open spaces, but staggering straight at him. He watched and, just outside the door, it turned its head suddenly to one side and fell over, dead, a scarlet drop of blood at the tip of his pointed, unpleasant snout. With a stick – for rats made him feel nauseous – he lifted the small carcase and carried it outside the settlement perimeter where he deposited it in a hole. But every morning from then on the rats were found dead or almost dead in droves. On the third day the carcases were, on Berkan's direction, gathered and burned; but, before evening, there were as many littering the settlement again. And nearly all had a drop of scarlet at the nose and were strangely misshapen and swollen.

The whole settlement became restless and uneasy; some blight, Teidm (*teddim*), hovered over it, of that there was little doubt, but its nature eluded them. They remembered rumours from Europe, before that from Egypt, Greece, of a fearful pestilence that had stalked those places, killing the rats before it killed the people, and they flocked to the church to pray and beseech heaven to confine the demons of pestilence and restrain them from assaulting themselves. They crowded there, hundreds of them, where they felt safe . . . and where the infected fleas all the more easily did their deadly work.

Older people, recalling stories of how the druids could halt the invisible demons of pestilence, persuaded the monks to parade through the settlement with the Host to frighten and overcome the demons. And so in solemn procession Berkan led the monks, followed by many of the people all carrying candles, around the entire settlement singing the Psalms to the accompaniment of two harps, sweetly played by the best harpers there. And as they walked, again and again the shuffling feet of those in the procession kicked or trod on the small, soft bodies of dead or dying rats.

It was the fifth evening that the first victim in Ireland – a child who had been unwell and restless for some days – died from the bubonic plague which swept up Europe from its origin in Eygpt and, riding the scuttling back of the rat from the ship unloaded by Aoife's father, first decimated and then destroyed the monastic school and settlement at Glasnevin. Among other lives it took that of the abbot, Mo Bhi, before marching through the whole island slaughtering many thousands as it went.

At first the child had seemed only dazed and sleepy, perhaps a little flushed. Then, very quickly, he became prostrate with a high fever and burning thirst. The glands of his groin swelled agonisingly like oranges and felt like lumps of fibre under his skin and, like his stomach, became covered with huge red blotches. Even in his delirium he was in intense pain and vomited a great deal. His parents were frantic for he was an only child. They brought him to one of the evening church assemblies, to be blessed by the abbot.

After Berkan had blessed the feverish child his parents took him home and moved his bed to a warm corner near the fire, in spite of his fever. The domestic animals were separated from him by only an unplastered inner wattle wall. His thirst was intense and he could hardly speak through cracked and burning lips. Later the fever abated, but he turned a fearful yellow colour and the glands in his neck and under his arms also swelled, the pain causing him to make sudden and unexpected movements. Then the fever flared again, the red blotches on his abdomen and groin grew brighter, he turned his head quickly to vomit . . . and died, a gush of blood flowing from his mouth. Within hours the glands of the swollen groin ruptured on the corpse and a putrid fluid oozed forth. Soon there were other victims, swollen, yellow and burning with a fever that sometimes temporarily abated as their beleaguered glands rotted and burst in erupting corruption.

Following the early deaths a sort of fearful silence at first descended on the community. The people attended the devotions organised by the monks and, between times, kept to themselves or huddled in silent, watchful groups of two or three, seldom more. They avoided glancing at one another, afraid of what truth they might discover lurking in each other's eyes. But soon they were forced to recognise that a terrible tábh (*tawve*), pestilence, had arrived in their midst. Because of its effect on the victims they called it the *bwee cunnil*, the yellow plague, and the whispers gave way to loud shouts and lamentations.

Through those days Colm and Dermot worked night and day with the other members of the community. But even monks, in spite of great prayer and fasting, were not safe and were struck down along with the rest. Within a week the settlement was ghostlike, its population either dead or gone. Only those few of the monks who still lived remained. Beyond, less than half a mile away, was a mound of fresh earth, a communal grave in which lay many of the community; it matched, some said dejectedly, the place called Tauv Lacht, or Tallaght, plague-grave, which stood on a hill across the bay where one of the early colonies of settlers had been wiped out by another plague in ancient times.

Before the sickness took control of his mind, Berkan called Colm to his bedside.

'You must go, my son,' he said. 'Escape while you can. You above all.'

'I must stay here, father, with you and my brothers.'

'No!' Berkan's voice was sharp in spite of his illness. 'You must go. If you stay here you will die. I order you. There is so much for you to do.'

Colm believed him. He knew there was nothing he could usefully do any more at Glasnevin except watch others die, perhaps die himself.

'Take Dermot with you,' said Mo Bhi, 'and may God keep you safe to do His will.'

He groaned as pain from those appalling glands streaked through him and shuddered in spite of himself, making it worse.

'Try not to move,' said Colm, who had observed that the smallest movement in an afflicted person could bring instant death.

'Go, son,' gasped the abbot. 'You have my blessing . . . Leave me . . . the pestilence might reach out to you from me . . . ' He attempted to lift his hand in blessing, but could not and relapsed into uncontrollable fever and incoherence. For a moment Colm stood at the door of the tiny hut, then stepped into the light and the scene of desolation that was all that remained of the settlement and monastery. Nothing stirred. Even the birds seemed to have gone and the silence had a cold, unpleasant, and heavy atmosphere like death itself. A monk slipped by among the monastery buildings, did not look up, and disappeared again. Colm pressed his fingers to his burning eyeballs and rubbed them. He was extraordinarily tired, but he knew . . . was impelled by . . . the importance of getting away. The hand of death held this place firmly and was tightening. Nothing that remained could expect to survive. He went towards Dermot's cell and found him sitting listlessly outside, his back against the low wall and his legs drawn up, staring between his spread knees. He did not move as Colm approached.

'Are you all right?' Colm's voice was urgent; anxious.

Dermot raised an exhausted arm and, without looking up, said: '*Moriturus te salutamo*.'

'Come on,' snapped Colm. 'Are you all right, I said.'

Dermot raised his head and, seeing the fire in Colm, nodded. 'Yes. I'm tired, but I'm all right . . . I think.'

'You're not sweating?'

Dermot shook his head.

'Well, get up. We're going.'

Dermot looked at him uncomprehendingly. 'Going?'

'Yes. Come on.' Colm reached a hand to catch his cousin's and with surprising strength pulled him to his feet.

'Going?' repeated Dermot. 'Where?'

'Back to Tir Connail, Donegal, for you,' Colm grinned, 'and to Clonard for me.'

'What about the others?' Dermot gestured half-heartedly towards the settlement. Colm's face hardened.

'We *must* leave,' he said. 'The others will also go, or die.'

He turned away, but Dermot did not immediately follow and Colm turned back.

'Come on,' he snapped. Then, seeing his cousin's distress and realising it was the same as his own, added, 'It's the abbot's order. We *must* go.'

'He told you?'

'Yes.'

'But not me . . . ?'

'You too!'

Dermot stared unbelievingly a moment. Then sudden animation illuminated him. A smile of joy – the first for days – lit up his face, and he turned and ran towards the settlement, in the opposite direction to Colm.

'Hey!' shouted Colm. 'This way!'

'Wait,' came back the shout. 'I'll only be a minute.' And Dermot's flying legs carried him round the corner of a building.

A few moments later he returned to view dragging someone, who was obviously protesting considerably, by the hand. At first Colm could not make out who it was, but recognised a *fudir* from the clothing. They came closer and he saw it was a female. She stopped protesting as she was pulled nearer, but hung back sullenly, her head down and silent.

'What's this?' Colm asked impatiently. 'Who's she? Why did you bring her here?'

'She's coming with us.' Dermot sounded unexpectedly authoritative. Colm glanced at the woman. She was dishevelled. Her hair hung untidily over her face, and her clothing was dirty as well as drab. She was entirely pitiable, but he could not understand Dermot . . . Then, as he was about to snort in disdain, something familiar about her caught his eye and he looked closer. Shocked, he stepped back and raised his hand.

'*In nomine Domine*,' he murmured sadly.

'Her father died two days ago,' said Dermot. 'She's eaten nothing since, and . . . '

'Bring her!' said Colm and turned away in case his feelings betrayed him. This was the beautiful Aoife who sang about the settlement. 'My God,' he thought, 'what evil have we done to merit this?'

Dermot put his arm round the girl and she came with them quietly. Colm paused and then shrugged. Who was there to see Dermot being so familiar in public with a *fudir*? Even if there were . . . ? Before starting they went to a sweat-house. They lit the prepared fire outside and when it was thoroughly alight put in the large stones. Then they went inside and poured water on the hot stones, sitting in the steam until the sweat poured from their bodies and soaked their clothing. Then they put on clean clothes and left, taking with them a few personal belongings and some food only.

They took the road north past the settlement and even smaller monastery a few miles away at Santry, and on towards the *bruden*, or public hostel, at Lusk fifteen miles away. Passing Santry they saw no one, the houses were deserted. Behind the village a pathetic mound of fresh-turned earth similar to the one at Glasnevin showed why. As they moved on they met some stragglers on the road, but few, and they kept to themselves. They stopped to rest and eat at a place where a scattering of fine trees marked the curving border of a great sward that, from its colour and texture, clearly rested on sandy soil. It was almost flat and the shimmering light indicated the proximity of the sea.

Colm sat with his back to a tussock and chewed on a piece of cold meat. He looked about him.

'This is a good place,' he said. 'What do they call it?'

'Sórd (Swords), I think,' said Dermot.

'I like it,' said Colm. 'It'd be a good place for a settlement. There is peace here and strength.'

'Maybe you'll found one,' Dermot said.

'Maybe I will,' said Colm. 'Here, pass me a piece of that bread, will you?'

Aoife spoke little. She was still overawed and shocked by all that had happened – her past life, her family, all she knew and all she thought of as the future, gone in a few days. She ate dutifully as she was told, but without tasting. But, little by little as they travelled, she began to recover her sensibilities.

From Swords it was less than seven miles to Lusk and the great *bruden* where they knew they would be welcome. As they approached the town they met more and more people, many, like themselves, refugees from the area near B'lath Cliath, but others with frightening stories of rats elsewhere emerging to die.

Colm's purpose in going to the *bruden* at Lusk rather than one of the smaller *brees*, or public hostels, of which there were ninety-three in Leinster alone, was twofold: firstly, he thought (wrongly as it turned out) that it was sufficiently far away from Glasnevin to be safe from the *bwee cunnil* at least for the moment; secondly, it was one of the six 'chief courts of hospitality in Ireland' and often entertained kings and nobles of the highest class. As a prince of the Ui Neill and a cousin of the King, Tual Melgarve, he and his friends would be well cared for and helped on their way.

The free public hostels were part of the universal standard of hospitality and generosity in the country; they were also places of asylum or sanctuary and, like the private castles of the nobility, were surrounded by a *maigen*, precinct, within which no one must break the peace. Inside a *maigen* a fugitive, no matter what his crime, was safe, together with whatever property he had with him whether it was his own or not. There were regulations governing sanctuary in a nobleman's home. The first requirement was that the owner (who was also frequently a law-giver or magistrate within the *maigen*) or a member of his family legally entitled to act for him should give the fugitive permission to enter the precinct and should claim asylum for him from his pursuers. The second requirement was that the owner should inform the pursuers officially that his home was a *maigen*, and the third was that the owner should guarantee that the pursuer would suffer no loss by the shelter (generally lasting three nights and days) afforded the fugitive, who would not be helped to escape justice. If any of these conditions were broken the fugitive might be arrested in the *maigen*.

There was a vital distinction between the sanctuary of a private residence and that of a public hostel. The sanctuary of a *bruden* was absolute and inviolable, depending on no conditions and no man's will or caprice. The same absolute sanctuary applied to a church. In both places a murderer might claim protection from the immediate vengeance of his victim's friends until he could obtain a fair hearing before a *brehon*. 'Every *bruden*,' proclaims the old law, 'is an asylum of the red hand – the manslayer.' This was the law which came down through the generations from the time of the People of Annan, the Tuatha de Danaan, and some there were who attributed it to the influence of Co'en, friend and adviser of the great King Cian whose people came from the deserts east of Egypt. Christian Irish were astonished to find that the six great sanctuary *brudens* of Ireland were closely reflected in the Old Testament of Jewish people which was explained to them by the monks, and they wondered at the similarity between their own way and the way of the Lord set out in Numbers 35, 6, Deuteronomy 4, 42, and Joshua 20, 2.

Although the most magnificent *bruden* in Ireland had been destroyed four hundred years earlier, it was still alive in tradition and repute. This was Da Derga's hostel, Downach Bruden, Donnybrook, situated on the River Dodder where one of the five great highways from Tara, the Slee Coolin, crossed it. At B'lath Cliath the highway crossed the bridge over the Liffey and ran south for a few miles until it reached the Dodder, before continuing southwards through the district called Coolin, by the settlement of Bree, to Wexford. The famous hostel, capable of seating one thousand people, was burned and destroyed with all inside by Irish and British marauders four hundred years before. The king, Cunnera, was staying there at the time, and he perished in the flames, along with his retinue. Yet the attackers lost more than they gained, for they had not expected to find the king there so well prepared, and they died to the last man.

To the great *bruden* of Lusk, then, founded by the father of Cuchulain's wife, Emer, came Colm and his companions late on the day after they left Mo Bhi's monastery at Glasnevin, which was never again to revive as a monastery. It was during his brief stay at the *bruden* that Colm heard of the death of his cousin the King, Tual Melgarve of the Northern Ui Neill, who died of the pestilence, blood gushing from his mouth. After spending three nights and three days there, as was their right, the travellers continued northwards on their journey.

Colm spent the next three years studying at Clonard under Finian who came to be called the teacher of the missionaries of Ireland. There Colm became a priest, ordained by Bishop Etchen (whom he found ploughing with a pair of oxen when he sought Holy Orders). It was many years before he went to the secluded monastic settlement of Moville, which undertook advanced studies, and which was presided over by the enigmatic figure of the other Finian who was to bring so much sadness into his life.

Chapter 16

COLM's arrival at Clonard was delayed, firstly because he had to return to Donegal with Dermot and Aoife. Secondly, the funeral and mourning of Tual Melgarve, and the election of the new Rí-Eireann and its aftermath all took time; it was several months before Colm returned to the south from the mountains of Donegal, where the heather was already darkening for winter.

Because of the changes that followed the death of Tual Melgarve he was entering what was now unfriendly - if not downright hostile - territory. Even so his journey was uneventful.

The new King, Diarmuid (he scorned the alternative spelling, Dermot) was of the Southern Ui Neill, a matter of grave and distressing consequence for Colm and his people of the Northern Ui Neill.

When, more than one hundred years earlier, Eoghan and Conal, sons of Nial of the Nine Hostages, had established new kingdoms by force in Ulster, they introduced three new political and geographic concepts: they disrupted the old established five provinces of Ireland and substituted four; they instituted and laid claim to the new kingship of sacred Tara, roughly incorporating the province of Meath; and they laid claim to the Kingship as a right of the Ui Neill. From this last arose the intense rivalry between the two branches of the family that sundered the loves and loyalties of a great dynasty which, through one branch or the other, ruled the nation for eight hundred years. But they did more: in continuing to levy the

Boru Tribute on Leinster, whose king was a Pentarch and should not have been required to pay tribute to anyone, they extended the dimensions of their usurpation further. The rivalry between the two branches of the family began in 483 when Lughaid, son of Laoire, became King. He belonged to the Southern branch and was followed by two Kings from the Northern branch. Now the Southern Ui Neill again governed at Tara, and nothing was surer than that they would try to keep the kingship for themselves. This could well mean eliminating main contenders from the Northern branch - of whom Colm was one. Clonard, less than thirty miles south-west of Tara, lay in the heart of Southern Ui Neill territory.

When Colm first saw the settlement sprawling beside the upper reaches of the River Boyne he was astonished by its sheer size. He had come south until he struck the chariot road on the sandy ridge, eiscir riada (*eshkir reeuda*), dividing Ireland from west to east, and followed it to Clonard. The road passed the monastery straight as an arrow, then crossed the Boyne beyond and to one side of the settlement, continuing its way eastward over the plain of Meath. Chariots were banned from within the precincts of the settlement or the chaos would have been unspeakable. As it was, the peripheral stables, paddocks, cattle and other livestock pens almost entirely surrounded the approaches to the place and the constant noise of animals was complemented by the shrill buzz of numerous human voices. The streets were narrow, corduroy or dirt, and impossible to maintain. Colm stabled his horses - he rode one and trailed a pack animal - and went into the settlement proper.

The collegiate town was very like the traditional bardic and law schools on a grander scale. Circumstances had combined to the advantage of such establishments and their growth and development owed as much to the paucity of institutes of higher learning elsewhere in the western world as to the zeal and enthusiasm of missionaries and pedagogues. Where bardic and law schools were usually conducted by *ollaves* with between four and fifty students occupying a small compound, here there were labyrinthine streets and passages connecting numerous small compounds. In both systems instruction, where practicable, was undertaken in the open air; if the weather prevented this it took place in an open-sided roofed enclosure.

As Colm went towards the principal oratory where he expected to locate Finian, he found the overwhelming evidence of intellectual activity on a grand scale stimulating and exciting, and looked about with a smile and with eyes of wonder. At the same time he found the evidence of superficiality and unavoidable self-importance in such a large gathering disturbing - and then he criticised himself for being critical and dismissed his misgivings. He saw groups of boys and girls between the ages of twelve and fifteen, the elementary grades of *ullerra, taman* and *drisac*, under instruction from more senior students who had advanced to the fourth or fifth of the Seven Degrees of Wisdom in the twelve-year course. No distinction was made at the elementary stages between lay and secular instruction, nor any between the degrees and levels of learning at later stages for, as one *ollave* wrote in the time of Patrick: 'The degree of wisdom in the monastic schools corresponds with the degrees of the poets and *ollaves.* Wisdom is the mother of each profession and it is from her hand they drink.' In another compound were advanced students under the direction of professors, themselves belonging to one of the Seven Degrees of Wisdom.

The narrow ways were also full of children and hens, ducks, the occasional young pig tethered outside a hut, servants, traders, teachers and students; everywhere students of both sexes, the swaggering rich and fee-paying with servants and hangers-on to the obviously impoverished free student working his passage as best he could. Seldom had Colm seen such a huge and purposeful peaceful gathering. The noise, the apparent confusion, the smell were forceful to say the least of it. Here and there smoke added murk to the atmosphere. Suddenly he was hailed from behind.

'Hi! Crimthan!'

He turned. A young man of his own age, richly dressed with the five colours of a prince bright in his new tunic, shouldered his way smiling towards him.

'Crimthan! How are you? Remember me? Ge'Olf! Tara, last year, at – ' he dropped his voice and looked round theatrically, but still smiling, ' – at a banquet of the King.'

Colm remembered. Son of a Saxon King of Wessex, Ge'Olf had been a guest at Tara with his father and was one of the group of young men, which included Colm, who had argued the nights away settling the world more to their satisfaction as young men have ever done.

'Ge'Olf!'

'What are you doing here?'

'It is I should ask you that question. And with an Irish prince's tunic . . . ' Colm smiled and fingered the fine woven wool. 'What's wrong with your own?'

'Do you like it?' Ge'Olf looked down and admired himself. 'I've only just had it made. The colours are much better than ours and at least people will know my rank when they see me.' Colm laughed with him. Ge'Olf was an open, fair-haired, blue-eyed young man with a strong jaw and large, clean limbs. Colm had liked him a year ago for his openness and admired him for his evident courage.

'Perfect,' he said. 'An Irish peacock with a Saxon head. But you haven't told me. What are you doing here?'

'My father has decided I need to learn how to be a king,' said Ge'Olf, 'and insists I know such things as writing and Latin, Greek, mathematics, the movement of the heavens, science . . . ' he threw up his hands, 'as well as fighting, poetry and music. I keep telling him I can employ people to read and do sums for me, but I can't convince him!'

'So there's some wisdom in the family,' laughed Colm.

Ge'Olf laughed too and took his friend by the arm. 'But what about you?'

'What is more natural than that I should be here?'

'I'd have thought you'd have gone to that new place in the North, what's it called, Bangor . . . ' he stopped and this time there was no smile on his face as he looked around. Even here one had to be cautious.

Colm nodded. 'I thought about it. But Clonard is the greatest place of learning. Finian has taught everyone who has done anything, including Congall of Bangor. The teacher of the monks of Ireland, they call him. And anyway, Bangor is Dalriada territory.'

'I know!' said Ge'Olf.

'Well, then, that's why I'm here.'

'But – ' began Ge'Olf, and Colm silenced him with a glance. Ge'Olf changed the subject. 'When did you arrive?'

'Thirty minutes ago.'

'Then you haven't seen Finian yet?'

'No.'

'Come on. I'll take you.'

They climbed through the narrow passages between the houses towards the oratory, its high gable roof and the tall, wooden belfry adjoining it visible ahead of them as they shouldered their way through the lively crowds. Eventually they emerged from the encompassing buildings into an open space at the centre of which stood the oratory and the episcopal buildings.

'Well,' said Ge'Olf, 'there you are. I'll see you later.'

'Won't you come with me?'

Ge'Olf shook his head and smiled. 'No thanks. I prefer to familiarise myself with the Lord Abbot from afar – and I certainly prefer him to familiarise himself with me from much further.'

Colm laughed. 'I can imagine,' he said. 'Where will I meet you?'

'The Saxon *bree.* That's in the street of Saxons.' He shrugged. 'Where else? I'll meet you there, say in the first hour of the second *cadar*.'

'Right,' agreed Colm, and they clasped arms.

The oratory was built in what became known as the Hiberno-Romanesque manner and looked like a small church, though in fact it was the focal point of a vast open-air church surrounding it. The building was oriented west to east and the thick walls and corbelled roof were of stone. The iron-bound oak door was under an arch of fine carved sandstone, at the western end. Above the door, inlaid into the sandstone, was a small white cross of marble. There was a small square window in the eastern wall, opposite the door.

Beside the oratory stood a tall pillar that had once been the centrepiece of some old, pagan ritual. Now it had a Greek cross with the Celtic Chi-Roh symbol carved upon it. Beside the oratory, on a great stone slab - also carved with a cross, this a Latin cross with wedge-shaped terminals decorated with spirals - stood a wooden altar beneath a taut canopy supported by four painted poles, its fringes fluttering in the breeze. A low stone wall enclosed a large space around the oratory and altar, and another wall, curving slightly, separated the oratory, the altar and high cross from the people's enclosure. The entire open-air church was protected in bad weather by leather covers now furled to the poles which stood at intervals along the wall and three or four yards inside it. Behind the altar a great display of banners and flags stood forth in the wind, in the centre a great white one of the Holy Cross.

Behind the oratory were the bell-tower and several other buildings. They were also of stone in the traditional circular pattern, less finished than the oratory, but corbelled in much the same way. They were round outside and square within, with built-in cupboard recesses and platforms for bedding. Unlike those in more remote western areas, the permanent monastery buildings at Clonard were not dug out and half-buried for protection from storms and gales, but stood naked on the open hilltop. From where he stood, Colm could see that a wall encompassed the entire monastery, some fifteen feet thick and twelve feet high, through which he had come without realising it in the narrow passages between the houses that stretched about on all sides except the river side.

A small, dark, wiry man wearing the white and unbleached robes of a monk came from the belfry building. As he approached, Colm could see a smile of greeting on the thin, brown face and extraordinary bright eyes that glowed with warmth and intelligence and seemed to encompass one with a look that was bigger than the man himself. On his hand he wore a ring.

'My lord,' said Colm, going on his knees before Finian.

'Get up, get up,' said the abbot, putting a hand under the young man's elbow. 'You must be Colm. I've been waiting for you.'

'You do me great honour,' said Colm standing and - although he was not himself a tall man - looking down at the abbot.

'Nonsense,' said the other who, while still holding Colm's elbow, looked sideways at him - as indeed he seemed to look at all things. It was no impediment, for he saw everything, even what he was not intended to see. Colm later realised that many small, thin men have this curious way of looking at things, as if in some mysterious manner it enhances their vantage point. Finian nodded his head very often as if events and the things he saw - his eyes were for ever on the move - confirmed what he had already inferred. Still holding Colm's elbow he guided him towards the building he had just left.

'You do us honour, Colm,' he said. 'A prince of the Northern Ui Neill . . . ' He waved his hand.

'I wish to be a priest, my lord,' was the reply. 'Where else would I come?'

'Hmm!' Finian's response was noncommittal. Colm's answer might have been either humility or arrogance. It would take time to discover which. What he knew of him was impressive enough, however. Colm was preceded by tributes not only from his native Tir Connail, but also from the lamented Mo Bhi of

Glasnevin who had recommended him to Clonard to complete his final years of study.

Finian took Colm to the monastery refectory and they broke bread and talked as the light faded in the east and, to the west, along the headwaters of the river, the coloured sky painted a bright and shimmering path. When they came out again the western sky was the colour of a duck's egg and stars glimmered faintly. From their position Colm calculated that it was the second hour of the first *cadar*, or the tenth hour of the shiftless – he smiled at the pun; he should say shifting – Roman clock.

'Hmm,' said Finian, a habit of his. ''Tis later than I thought.'

'Where shall I build my hut?' asked Colm.

'Why here,' replied the abbot, 'beside the church. Where else?' And that is what Colm did.

He spent that night with his Saxon friends talking, exchanging news and sharing opinions – some of them, for instance about the new King, by no means safe. But he enjoyed himself. At one stage Ge'Olf, who had drunk a little more beer than he could safely cope with, grabbed Colm by the elbow during an argument in which he was getting the worst of it and stood up, lifting his other hand high to silence the hubbub and attract attention.

'Here, gentlemen,' he cried, 'here is the man who truly imbibes his knowledge.' He was still holding Colm's sleeve. 'Here is a man who flings his knowledge at us, not from his head, but out of his stomach where it lies until he needs it. Did you hear what he did with his first Latin alphabet?'

Colm groaned. 'Sit down, Ge'Olf, you clown,' he said. He knew what was coming.

But Ge'Olf ignored him and just grinned down at him.

'Will I tell you?' he appealed to the others.

'Yes,' they shouted. 'Tell us, tell us, tell us,' they chanted.

'Come on, Ge'Olf, said Colm beginning to be angry as well as feel foolish, 'sit down.'

'Oh no,' grinned the other. 'They're entitled to their story. Aren't you, gentlemen?'

A great roar greeted this. 'Tell us, tell us, tell us,' they chanted.

'Well . . . ' began Ge'Olf and he launched into a lengthy and highly coloured version of the story which seemed to dog Colm's footsteps wherever he went, and was to follow him beyond the grave. It was fostered, irritatingly enough, by his parents who derived huge mirth from it every time they told it, which they loved to do in his presence. It was so well known, and Ge'Olf's telling was so funny, that Colm could not take offence, though he disliked it all the same. He learnt his first Latin alphabet from Crownawn, whom Ge'Olf had never seen but whom he described with hilarious accuracy. One day the old priest had mislaid or run out of slates and wax tablets. As luck had it they were not at Crownawn's but at Rath Gartan, Colm's home. Fresh bread was being made and they were sitting beside the ovens. The priest, to permanently illustrate his lesson, wrote the letters in a lump of dough which was then baked and emerged shortly after with a golden brown crust and the letters of the alphabet inscribed thereon.

'Now,' said Crownawn, 'I'll leave you and when I come back you will have them off by heart.'

'But,' guffawed Ge'Olf, 'he didn't have them off by heart, did you, Colm? After studying them for a while the poor growing boy got hungry and ate the bread, so he got them off by stomach . . . ' Ge'Olf collapsed – along with his friends – in loud semi-drunken laughter, during which Colm was able to make his escape.

Colm stayed three years finishing his studies at Clonard, then five more as a professor in which he condensed the period of time it normally took to achieve the seventh Order of Wisdom, becoming a *drim cli*, a ridge-pole of wisdom, before his fourth year was completed. During that time he was ordained – not by Finian, though there had grown great bonds of affection between them – but by the humble Bishop Etchen of nearby Clonfad, a small monastery reminiscent of Glasnevin, which seemed to both Finian and Colm more appropriate. He wore the Patrician or St John's tonsure, *ab aura ad aurem*, shaved from ear to ear, with the hair long and flowing at the back (known in Britain as the tonsure of Simon Magus).

While he was at Clonard two things of personal importance took place. One was the close and important friendships he made with men who became legends in their own lifetime, such as Ciaran who founded the monastery at Clonmacnoise and Killian his disciple; and Ruadhan who played such a strange part in the drama that was about to develop. The other was his resolute refusal, against all Finian's persuasiveness, that the greatest thing he could do for God was to carry back to Europe the light of Christianity which had been virtually extinguished there.

'My place is here,' retorted Colm, 'among my own people and it is here I can do most good.'

Colm's great love of his country and his people worried Finian, because in it he saw pride, even arrogance, and an unworthy attachment to material things. But when he broached the subject Colm dismissed the idea.

'Not at all,' he said. 'I suppose what you suggest is reasonable enough in some cases, but not in mine. You may take it that my feelings are deep and genuine and concern only what I can do for the people and for God.' Which was an answer that in no way diminished Finian's unease. He was Colm's confessor as well as friend and tried to encourage him to a humbler and more tractable outlook, with little success that he could see. He encouraged him to pray *cros figil*, that is kneeling with his hands stretched out in the form of a cross, so in his prayers his eyes might speak to God by being raised to Him, the knees and legs by kneeling and the hands by *cros figil*. And always he endeavoured to instil in Colm the same response he had found in some of his other 'Twelve Apostles', as his disciples were coming to be called. One of the twelve was already dead, Mo

Bhi, and of the remainder Finian was convinced that Colm had the strength, vision and courage to greatly develop and expand the work already being done by Irish missionaries in Britain and Europe. He was particularly concerned to match the explosion of fervour that had swept Africa and the East thanks to the enlightened and vigorous rule of Justinian in Byzantium and the successes of his generals, Fares and Belisarius. But might not decadent Byzantium fall? And Rome? Yet nothing he could say had any effect on his disciple, who listened calmly whenever Finian broached the subject, and then merely said, 'I know what I must do.' Colm was later to become a close friend of Columbanus at Bangor, a man twenty years younger than himself, who did precisely what Finian had hoped for Colm - who was by then fulfilling both their expectations in the most unexpected manner.

After he left Clonard Colm started out on what he firmly believed was to be his destiny; founding a community of related religious houses throughout the country which would form a local base for the spread and development of religion in the daily lives of the people. His first such foundation was near his own home on the edge of a *doire*, oak wood, and came to be called Doire-Columcille, the oak wood of Colmcille, or Derry for short. He then moved south, back to the area he loved so well, and founded a monastery at Durrow, fifteen miles west of Clonard. He established other houses in the area and then, moved by a letter from Dermot and by some half-remembered and impulsive promise to God after they had escaped the plague at Glasnevin, he went eastward to Swords and established a foundation there. And it was from near there, at Kells, that the great events which ennobled his life beyond the power of kings began.

As he matured, Colm had filled out. He was not tall, but he was well-built and strong. He had square-cut features with large, grey eyes and curly hair that fell in waves from his tonsure to his shoulders. On the road between two of his houses at Kells and

Skreen he was overtaken by a cantering horseman. It was raining and the road was a muddy waste of rivulets and bubbling, foam-flecked pools. He heard the horseman coming behind and stepped aside to let him pass, but instead the animal was reined in beside him, the hot, damp smell of its flanks sharpening the air like ammonia.

'Are you going far, *a vrawhir*, brother?' asked a well-remembered voice. 'Can I . . . '

Colm looked up and smiled.

'Colm! By Jesu! Get up, man, and don't be standing there in the muck.'

Dermot, now a strong nobleman who had succeeded in developing his family fortunes, leaped from his horse and bent his back for Colm to mount. But Colm stopped the gesture of deference.

'No need of that between you and me,' he said. Taking hold of the horse's mane he gave an *ech-laym*, steed-leap, and was in the saddle in an instant. Then he looked down mischievously at Dermot standing in the mud and rain, and with a huge grin on his usually calm features he clapped his heels to the horse's flanks, and was away with a yell through the rain for a hundred and fifty paces, mud flying in all directions. Dermot gaped after him for a moment and then began to run, laughing, his fine clothing becoming spattered with mud under his cloak.

Ahead, Colm pulled the horse back on its haunches and turned the animal across the road.

'Come on!' he called. 'I'll give you a ride.'

Dermot spent three nights at Skreen with Colm before riding on to Tara where he was bound, and a great deal of the time was spent in talk.

'How's Aoife?'

Dermot hesitated. He wasn't sure how much Colm knew or guessed.

'She's fine. I suppose you know that we had - difficulties - with my mother while she was alive?'

'Naturally.' Colm was matter-of-fact. 'What did you expect? You can't really suppose that a noblewoman, especially one like your mother, would be satisfied to see her only child, only son, marry a slave.'

'Colm!' Dermot was shocked.

Colm held up his hand. 'I'm not defending her attitude. I'm merely telling you you shouldn't be surprised by it.'

'Hmm,' said Dermot. 'Well, it was troublesome for a while, but after my mother died – '

'God rest her.'

'Amen. After she died it was different. Through everything Aoife was marvellous.'

'You're very lucky, then.'

'Maybe she was a *fudir*, but to me she's always been a queen.'

Colm laughed. 'It's good to hear a man say that about his own wife after . . . how many years is it? Fifteen? Seventeen?'

'More like twenty!'

'*Deo gratias*,' said Colm, 'twenty! Who'd have thought it. And the children. How are they?'

'Fine . . . '

They caught up with the past and filled the gaps and – both being noblemen of the Northern Ui Neill – discussed Diarmuid's Kingship.

'How much longer can it last?' asked Dermot. 'Apart from anything else,' he burst out indignantly, 'he has two wives!'

Colm laughed and spread his hands. 'Such is the way of kings. One of them is barren, as you know.'

'The other is bald, so they say.'

Colm laughed. 'Hush!' he said, 'even monasteries have ears.'

'Seriously,' went on Dermot, 'we both know that Dermot and his clan plot to keep the Kingship for the Southern Ui Neill. If they have their way it will never come to us again.' He leaned closer. 'I hear they plan to eliminate any of the Northern Ui Neill who might be a threat – they're forming an alliance with Dal Riada.'

‘Colm sat up. ‘What?’

‘True. That’s why I’m here. To learn the details – if I can!’ he grimaced wryly.

The Dal Riada occupied the north-eastern part of Ireland, Antrim and Down, and were related to those who had colonised Albyn and on whom the Ui Neill imposed their authority when Eoghan and Conal took over the crumbling kingdom of Emhain Macha.

‘It will be dangerous for you in Tara.’

‘Perhaps.’ Dermot’s voice was low, but hard. ‘But I don’t think he’ll try anything directly. I come as a herald – ’ he reached into his satchel and produced a herald’s wand, ‘ – and he’s hardly going to commit murder on his own doorstep.’

Colm grunted.

‘But as far as you are concerned,’ Dermot went on, ‘I’m glad we met. I’d have come to see you anyway. You’re too vulnerable here. Tara is only three miles away and you’re the one person of us all he fears most.’

‘Me?’ laughed Colm. ‘I’m a priest.’

Dermot looked at him. ‘Would that stop you if it was a question of the Kingship for us?’

Colm returned his gaze for a long time before he answered, the grey eyes clouded over. He shook his head slightly. ‘I – I don’t honestly know,’ he said.

‘Look,’ said Dermot. ‘Get out of here – even for a while. Go somewhere else. Found another monastery . . . ’

‘I had been thinking of going to Finian of Moville,’ began Colm.

‘Never heard of him. Moville? Near home?’ There was a place called Moville some twenty miles north of Colm’s foundation at Derry.

‘No. This place is at the head of Strangford Lough. Down – Patrick’s territory. You wouldn’t know about Finian, he’s just returned recently from Italy . . . ’

‘Oh him! I know who you mean now. Cousin of Diarmuid’s,

isn't he?' Dermot gave him a steady look. 'And Moville's right in the heart of Dalriada country . . . '

'Well,' said Colm, 'I want to . . . '

'It's better than here, I suppose,' mused Dermot.

' . . . some advanced study,' ended Colm lamely.

It was as a result of this conversation that some weeks later Colm journeyed north again, first to Derry and then to the new, secluded, ascetic monastery of Finian at Moville. This Finian was an eremite, renowned for his learning, who twenty years before had taught in Britain, at Whitehorn in Northumbria which he left in strange circumstances.

Chapter 17

WHITEHORN, 540: Finian the Irishman was a tall, thin, severe-visaged young man who usually wore his cowl because, he said, he was susceptible to the cold; doubly so because of his tonsure. After God, books were his passion. His cold, austere, and generally rather unsympathetic demeanour belied his nature, which was friendly, gentle and tolerant, except when his strict sense of justice felt outraged. Then he could be intractable in a quiet and inexorable fashion. Also in contradiction to his appearance went a quiet but puckish sense of humour which occasionally caused him considerable trouble, as much because it was so unexpected in one seemingly devoid of a sense of fun as because of its nature. When he was a *desgibel*, disciple – that is one of the third order of the Seven Degrees of Wisdom of the academics – in Whitehorn his sense of humour became tangled with his strict sense of justice, with consequences that caused much annoyance to the abbot and his own rather swift and unscheduled departure elsewhere. Significantly, books were also involved.

Whitehorn was a large establishment similar to the Irish teaching monasteries. It had grown and developed since Bishop Ninian's day when, because of the brilliant whitewash he maintained on the walls, it was called Candida Casa. Many of the *ollamhes* were Irish or the products of Irish academies, including the Abbot Mugint who was intent on making Whitehorn as important in North Britain as the great academy of David was in

West Britain. For that reason he extended its influence as far afield as possible attracting the finest students from Northumbria, Pictland, the Irish Dalriadan colony in Albyn, even from as far as Middle England.

The academics were both male and female, and here lay the kernel of the nut on which the austere Finian bit his tongue.

A certain young woman called Drustic, daughter of a minor Northumbrian king, who was there to develop her Latin and mathematics and mingle with young marriageable nobles from adjacent Albyn and Pictland, had shown her lack of fitness for such responsibilities by falling head over heels in love with a common free student from Ireland, called Rioch. Rioch, proud, hardworking and dedicated to his studies, was flattered, but practical. Besides, the lady did not appeal to him. Nothing Drustic could say or do - and she was prepared to say and do a great deal - affected the sensible Rioch, who remained polite and uninvolved.

Drustic attended some of Finian's classes, as did a young Pictish nobleman called Talmuc, and she had become aware of Finian's passionate fondness for books, which he had reason to conceal. Drustic's father, whose forebears had been citizens and guardians of Rome before the collapse of the Empire, owned a substantial library. That he neither did nor could make use of it had not prevented him from keeping it as a relic of what had been and, who knows, what might yet again be.

In order to curry favour with Finian, Drustic wheedled from her father a book - a rolled Roman parchment - and presented it to the overwhelmed monk. His appreciation was so marked that it lodged as exceptional in her devious mind and it later occurred to her that through this weakness - as she saw it - she might yet persuade (or compel) Finian to help her get her way with Rioch. Accordingly one November afternoon, when the world was cold and damp, one of her waiting women came to Finian's hut and announced that her mistress wished to see him. Somewhat to his own surprise Finian followed the slave through the slippery streets of the monastery to where Drustic's standard fluttered outside a group of huts and tents surrounded by a low earthen rampart. The slave beckoned and Finian followed her into the tent. It was his first visit there. Drustic clearly liked and enjoyed her comforts. The tent, and no doubt also the adjoining huts, were lavishly and gaudily furnished in the fashion of the vulgar neo-barbarism then popular in Britain and Europe. Finian looked gravely at the proud young princess who had summoned him.

'Finian,' she said without preamble, 'you already have one book from my father's library.' He nodded. 'What would you say to the entire library of the abbot?'

Finian gasped. 'Mugint's library?'

The library at Whitehorn was notable in Britain for being one of the finest collections of modern works and classical rescensions, Christian and pagan, in the country. The thought that first occurred to the appalled Finian was that Drustic planned somehow to steal the library and wanted his help.

Drustic simply looked at him with large cornelian coloured eyes from under her fair eyebrows. She did not alter her expression.

As one who found it impossible to conceive of anyone parting with one book, much less a whole library, Finian spoke with sharp authority.

'How could you say such a thing?' he snapped. 'The abbot has no intention of parting with his books.'

'What makes you so sure of that?'

'Don't be ridiculous, Drustic. Why would he do such a thing?'

'Whitehorn is as important to Mugint as his library is to you; more perhaps. Mugint needs funds. He has tried to build it up into a place of first importance.' Drustic's manner was offhand, but her statements were decisive. 'He has encouraged all sorts to come here. But now there are too many free students and not enough fee-paying ones. If Whitehorn is to keep going he must have more money and he has already let it be known that the library is for sale.'

Finian's face went white. What she said had the ring of truth about it. He was aware of Mugint's concern for the future of Whitehorn and of his struggles to find funding. But to sell the library, the very cornerstone of knowledge – Finian was appalled.

'How do you know all this?'

Again Drustic looked at him with that enigmatic and infuriatingly superior expression before replying. Then she said: 'Because my father is one of the people Mugint offered it to and he asked me to look into it for him.'

It must be true. The books were for sale, but he was personally penniless. He could probably raise the money from home . . .

As if she'd read his mind Drustic went on: 'And there's no point trying to negotiate something yourself. The word has been spoken,' by which she meant that a verbal contract existed subject only to the final figure.

'Then that's it,' said Finian, trying to control his anger with Mugint for not offering the books to him when he must have known he would be interested. 'How could I get them? How could you offer them to me?'

Drustic smiled. 'I can buy them,' she said, looking at him very directly, 'and I can sell them later to whomsoever I wish for whatever I wish.'

Finian gasped. 'You would do that . . . to your own father?'

Abruptly she leaned forward, her eyes shining as she said what he wanted to hear.

'Listen, Finian, my father has no need of books, and you know it. Hasn't he already sold you one of his own? He cannot read and never – and I mean never – is read to. It bores him. His only interest – and it's through me it's there – is to help the abbot. So, when Mugint offered the books I told my father to buy them and he said yes, of course. Neither of them can back down now. But if I tell my father that I want the books for myself and am willing to pay him back for them in a reasonable time . . . '

'What do you want from me?'

Finian's blunt question interrupted her. It was beautiful, it was plausible, but it was patently devious. There had to be a *quid pro quo* and he already suspected what Drustic was after. What she said next confirmed his fears.

'I want Rioch!'

Finian stood. 'I'm sorry, Drustic,' he said, 'you know as well as I do that I cannot marry you to Rioch, and even if I could it would never be allowed.'

'Who said anything about marriage?' Finian sat down again. 'You send Rioch to me, at night, to my tent here on whatever pretext you like, and you'll have the abbot's library the following day.'

Could she be serious? He looked at her in amazement and saw that she was unsmiling and earnest. He sighed and leaned back. Choosing his words carefully he said: 'Drustic, if you yourself cannot get him by means of your undoubted and lavish charm and loveliness, what good will it do you to trick him and bring him here like that?'

'Let me worry about that!'

'There is surely some other way?'

'He's shy. You know that yourself. If I go to him he'll feel loss of self-respect. But once he feels my arms round him and the warmth of my belly . . . '

Finian held up his hand. He'd heard enough.

'Drustic,' he said, 'you can't coerce the man into loving you.'

Drustic was on her feet before he'd finished. 'Do you want those books or not?'

He looked coldly at her, beautiful and repellent in her fury and desire.

'Yes,' he said, 'but not that much. I understand how you feel, but . . . '

'You understand nothing,' she snapped, her eyes blazing. 'I want him.' Then she turned away, her back quivering with spasms of anger and passion. Finian was shaken by her abandon.

'There is nothing I can do,' he said.

She wheeled on him. 'There is,' she whispered and her voice was so malevolent that involuntarily he shivered. 'You can send him here to me . . . and,' she added desperately with a naive and transparent change, 'you can have the books!'

Something like compassion for this turbulent woman of such profane morality touched Finian, but he stood up and shook his head.

'I cannot,' he said, gently.

'You will!' she hissed. 'If you refuse I will tell the abbot that you forced your way in here tonight and tried to fornicate with me . . . ' She was leaning forward, half crouching. Her face was sharp and angular in the poor light of the tent. Finian raised a hand in involuntary protection and continued the movement to cross himself.

'I'm going,' he said, and turned away.

Before he reached the doorway she spoke again in that whispering voice. 'Remember what I said. If he's not here tomorrow night . . .'

Finian went out into the clean night air before she finished. Outside he breathed deeply and looked at the silent stars in their velvet canopy. He shook his head and returned to his hut, and all through the night the episode plagued him. Next day one of the first people he encountered was Talmuc. The prince was slightly older than most of the other students and Finian had established a closer relationship with him than he had with the younger pupils. Nevertheless, he knew nothing of Talmuc's feeling for Drustic. This morning Finian was overcome with the necessity to tell someone about the extraordinary proposition put to him the previous night. Who more natural to confide in - without, of course, revealing names – than his friend and pupil, Talmuc? He did not notice the strange look on Talmuc's face as he proceeded to unburden himself.

After his initial surprise Talmuc listened impassively. The priest's agitation alone convinced him that this wasn't one of Finian's jokes. Finian ended saying: 'There it is. And, you know, in one way I feel sorry for the poor wretch. But on the other . . . *In nomine Domine*! Talmuc, you should have seen her. I wouldn't have believed it if I hadn't seen it myself. I had no idea, I never knew that women were so . . . so . . . '

Talmuc nodded sagely, and said nothing.

'And I must say,' went on Finian, 'you have no idea how relieved I am that I don't experience reciprocal feelings. I was quite startled by her, how shall I put it, vehemence! Quite startled. I wonder,' he mused, 'if it is simply the nature of women, or just of this particular one . . . '

'It could be,' said Talmuc.

'I can't help feeling that she should be made to see the enormity of what she tried to do,' said Finian. 'Obviously I can't go to the abbot. He would be very upset. On the other hand . . . '

'You should do something.'

'I should,' agreed Finian. 'But what?'

'Supposing she goes to the abbot? Carries out her threat?'

'Oh, I don't think there's much danger of that. That's all it was, a threat. Anyway I doubt if the abbot would believe her.'

Talmuc looked at the earnest, skinny man before him and hid his smile.

'Probably not,' he agreed.

'But I feel, somehow, responsible . . . ' He paused helplessly.

'Would you, ah, leave it to me?' asked Talmuc innocently.

'It ought to be brought home to her,' said Finian.

'Indeed it ought,' agreed Talmuc.

'But it means revealing who was involved,' hesitated Finian.

'Don't let that trouble you,' Talmuc reassured him. 'I think I can guess.'

'How?' Finian was genuinely surprised.

'I have a gift. It was Drustic, wasn't it?'

'How did you know?' gasped Finian.

Talmuc spread his hands. 'Will you let me see what I can do?'

Finian looked at him for a moment before reaching out and squeezing his arm.

'Thank you,' he said.

Thus it was that in the dark that night Drustic entertained a visitor to her complete satisfaction and perhaps surprised herself by vindicating her own forecast as to the results, for her passion for Rioch evaporated and from then on she was to be seen continuously at Talmuc's side, whom she was eventually to marry. But not before an unfounded scandal concerning the part played by Finian in Drustic's somewhat anticipatory pregnancy scuttled ratlike through the settlement of Whitehorn. Mugint was very angry. In particular he did not want to offend Drustic's father who had done so much to help save the monastery not only by purchasing the library, but in insisting that it remain where it was for safe-keeping as long as the monastery should last.

Chapter 18

MOVILLE 561: In the gentle landscape four miles south of Bangor at the head of Strangford Lough, where the Irish or Western Sea ploughs a long, north-running furrow into the land, Finian built an oratory. Twelve huts surrounded the small stone building and in these the monks lived austerely and devoted themselves to study and contemplation. Discipline was harsh, the atmosphere unsympathetic, reflecting the personality of the man Finian had developed into since he left Whitehorn twenty years before. Nonetheless Finian was a gifted teacher possessed of the grace of enormous insight into scripture and with a profound grasp of adventuresome and flexible theology that was nevertheless authentically orthodox. No one knew why he chose Moville since, as a cousin of Rí-Eireann Diarmuid, he might have had a site wherever he pleased. It was speculated that there was some underlying political motive connected with the King's new relationship with the Dal Riada in whose territory Moville lay. But Finian let it be known (and himself half believed) that it was because Moville was polarised by the saintly Patrick's first foundation at Saul at the opposite end of the lake.

Colm and Finian were of an age, but whereas Finian's achievements were international – after leaving Whitehorn he had spent some time in Lucca, Italy (going under the name Fridiano) – all of Colm's work took place at home. At the age of forty, Colm was still restless; in spite of the many monasteries he had founded he was burdened by a sense of failure and looked on the world as still to be conquered; for God, it is true, but conquered nonetheless.

Consistent with his lifelong passion for books, Finian had brought back from Italy a cherished copy of Jerome's translation of the Psalms, and on this book events now turned which were to affect the social and political structure of Ireland and Albyn for hundreds of years to come.

Colm's motives for making the long journey from Derry to Moville were mixed. Partly he was prompted by what Dermot had told him and what he had learned since his return to the north; he was anxious to discover at first hand what the situation was between the Dal Riada and Diarmuid and what, if anything, Finian had to do with it. But he also wanted to study with a teacher as fine as Finian; he had an idea, as yet not fully formed, of co-operation between them which, if they jointly worked to contribute to the welfare of the whole community, might somehow help resolve political tensions. Since his own establishments were essentially pastoral, though monastic in structure, and Finian's were contemplative and academic, Colm thought there might be room for joint undertakings (an idea successfully developed by Congall at Bangor a few years later). He was to be surprised by the inflexibility of Finian's opposition. A third motive was more philanthropic and yet it was the cause of terrible troubles. Colm was acknowledged as one of the finest scribes in Ireland. For that alone, quite apart from his eminence as a noble and churchman, he was held in great esteem. At a time when all books were handwritten, a scribe's skill was highly valued, and a great deal of his time was devoted to making copies, of the scriptures in particular. Knowing Finian's love of books, Colm generously thought to offer his services to him for the duration of his stay at Moville. Besides being an excellent calligrapher Colm was also a sensitive artist.

The monastery at Derry was on a small island in Lough Foyle. The morning he set off for Moville, accompanied by Dermot, was one of those strange days when the sky is hidden behind a continuous grey sheet of rumpled cloud, with darker patches here and there, but when clarity and visibility are exceptional. They had climbed the hill overlooking the island and below them, heading south-west, they could see an impressive and colourful procession. Colm's jaw set. There were at least twenty-five people, as far as he could judge, and numerous animals, chariots and wagons. Banners fluttered from poles attached to the leading vehicles and even at that distance he could make out the haughty figure of a man, alone but for the charioteer, sitting at the right side of the lead chariot, which had a canopy of dyed bird-feathers over it.

'Look,' he said bitterly, 'a visiting poet.'

Dermot nodded. 'Parasites!' he snorted. 'They're storing up trouble for themselves.'

'They seem to be heading for Rath Phelim.'

Dermot squinted. 'Looks like it.'

'Small good it will do them,' Colm continued, 'my father is away at Cruachan and no one is there but the steward. They'll be disappointed,' he added with satisfaction. 'Won't waste too much time, thank God.'

'Something'll have to be done,' growled Dermot, who had recently suffered at the hands of a *fochloch*, a lesser poet.

For longer than could be remembered, way before the time of Patrick, the Aes Dána (*awce dawna*), Men of Endowment, were considered the most important element in Irish society. In particular the file (*fille*) the highest order of poets, sometimes also called *éicas*, were held in regard. They were men of wisdom who had spent twelve years at one or more of the classical schools where they had acquired the Seven Degrees and the Seven Orders of Wisdom. It is important to distinguish between a file and a mere bard or versifier, who did not have any of the seven degrees of poetry and was said to be 'without lawful learning except his own intellect'. The highest order – like the highest order of any discipline – was *ollamhe, ollamhe* file, doctor of poetry. The following six orders of poets were *anruth, clee, cana, doss, firmid* and *fochloch.* Each had an established retinue which could accompany him on *coowirt*, the circuit of visiting. An *ollave* had a retinue of twenty-four pupils or disciples, an *anruth* sixteen, and so on to the *fochloch* who had two. But all were entitled to go from king to king, noble to noble, one after another, with their retinues and be lavishly maintained for as long as they chose to stay. On their departure they were presented with a gift of no mean value in return for their poetry - particularly for a poem written in the noble's honour. In law, poets were the co-equals of kings and had the same rights of hospitality in a *bruden*. Occasionally a poet was too lazy or preoccupied to go on doowirt himself and instead sent a disciple, with an appropriate retinue, to bring back the rewards. The custom was seldom broken since it was an appalling disgrace to refuse a poet his entitlement. It was further secured by the most powerful weapon available to the poets in a society where honour and loss of face were twin cornerstones of law and public morality: satire. The satire of the Irish poets was no mere lampooning; it was the most baleful ridicule ever developed and was universally believed to be capable of raising mental and physical blemishes on the afflicted. Authentic accounts exist of poets composing An Áer *(awyrs)*, satires, that blighted crops and cattle and raised ulcers and blisters of shame on the face of the person against whom they were directed. Indeed the name of the poets, *fillee*, derives from *fih*, poisoning with satire, and *lee,* splendorous praise. Among their distinguishing marks of dress and accoutrement every poet had a small cauldron of gold or silver, weighing twelve ounces, which hung from his spearhead. Into this nobles placed their donation. Not surprisingly it became known as 'the cauldron of greed'. Hence Colm's satisfaction in knowing that his father was not at his *rath* to offer the *ollamhe* poet hospitality.

He and Dermot reached Moville three days later. The first meeting between Colm and Finian was uncomfortable and stilted, both men feeling the tension and attraction of opposites. One was an open, dominant man of action; the other academic, withdrawn, suspicious, almost self-effacing; they were linked by their lineage, by their commitment to work for God and by their common love of knowledge and in particular of books. But Finian loved books acquisitively, as a source of knowledge for himself; Colm so that he could pass on knowledge, illuminated and beautified by his calligraphy. When, as a great privilege, Finian showed him his copy of the St Jerome Psalter which hung in a leather satchel on the wall of the oratory, Colm gasped with delight and astonishment and Finian immediately wished he hadn't been so impulsive.

'Did you make the copy yourself?' Colm asked.

Finian's face hardened. He wondered if perhaps Colm was taunting him. Worse, seeking an opportunity to do so.

'In Italy,' he said shortly, 'these things are done by lay deacons and the like,' a retort which was as petty as it was inaccurate.

Colm hardly heard as he admired the book's beauty, his eyes roving the thick, four-folded pages. 'I see,' he said. Then he looked up. 'May I – do you think I could read it while I am here?'

Finian hesitated. He would have liked to refuse, yet how could he? Practical considerations apart, it would be improper to refuse. But . . . he breathed deeply through his long nose.

'If you can find the time,' he said, 'you can study it here in the oratory.'

'Of course. It will be a privilege.'

Dermot did not remain with Colm. He had taken an instant dislike to Finian. He felt Finian was not only austere but supercilious as well, and had difficulty in suppressing the irrational anger that this provoked in him. In fact Dermot was unjust. While overly suspicious in some respects, Finian was far from feelings of superior condescension. It was, perhaps, his directness and infrequency of speech that gave the impression of haughtiness. And there was no doubt that he conspicuously lacked the courtesies and graces normal in civilised society. So when Dermot said that he would be leaving the following morning Finian accepted this as a statement of fact and said nothing, making no courteous attempt to dissuade him.

Next morning was instrumental in more ways than one. As abbot of several monastic houses Colm had established a set of rules which were observed in all. As time passed these rules were strengthened or modified as circumstances and devotion required. His views on food were flexible - until that first morning at Moville when Dermot came to him after the sacrament had been offered in the oratory before dawn.

'Do you know what?' Dermot demanded.

'What?'

'There's nothing to eat until the night.'

Colm smiled at his indignation, but was surprised. In most monasteries the presence of a visitor - except in Lent and Advent - meant a relaxation of the regulations, even on Wednesdays and Fridays, and this was Tuesday. When, on Dermot's behalf, he mentioned it to Finian a little later the reply he received was decisive for himself no less than for Finian: 'That is the rule. Like everyone else here he must abide by it as long as he is here.'

When Colm spoke to Dermot again he was yoking his chariot.

'I'm going,' he said. 'If I didn't happen to have some fruit and salt pork with me I'd starve,' he added indignantly. Then he turned to face Colm. 'Do you know what they do eat - all you're going to get as long as you're here? Once - ' and to emphasise the point he tapped Colm in the chest with a vertical forefinger, 'once, mind you, a day?'

Colm shook his head.

'I'll tell you. I've been making enquiries. Cabbage *or* beans, flour and water, and maybe a biscuit and a bit of fish if you're lucky.' He stared at Colm, looking for signs of dismay and outrage. But Colm only smiled.

'We all eat too much anyway,' he said.

Dermot returned to his harnessing with a derisive snort.

'Well, it's not for me. Best thing ever happened to me . . . '

'I know,' said Colm. 'It was Aoife.'

Dermot frowned. Then laughed with Colm. 'You know me too well, old friend. And you're right, of course. But I can't stay here anyway.' He pulled a face. 'I'd better go and pay my respect to Finian. I'll see you before I go.'

Colm wandered towards the oratory and, as he went, decided that in the monasteries under his control there would henceforth be two meals a day with a varied diet except on Wednesdays and Fridays and during Lent and Advent, or when visiting *peregrini*, or guests, justified something more.

In the oratory he began to read the Psalter of Jerome of Bethlehem. Earlier Finian had reluctantly removed it from its satchel and set it on a table for Colm. He was overwhelmed by the beauty of the simple and uncompromising language. As he read he was moved by a profound desire to proliferate the Word of God as best he could by making a copy of the manuscript. Ordinarily he would have foreseen no difficulty. But with Finian . . . Colm did not want to risk refusal. Before he had completed reading the first page he hurried out again to intercept Dermot.

'Do something for me.'

'Of course. If I can.'

'In Derry there are five sheets of vellum in my teog leabhalr (*tyog lyower*), book satchel. I was keeping them for some special copying I wanted to do. Will you have them sent to me?'

Dermot frowned. 'What for?'

'I want to make a copy of that Psalter of Finian's.'

Dermot drew back in surprise. 'Are you mad? That man won't allow you to copy it. Sure the whole world knows about him and his books.'

'That's why I won't tell him until it's finished.'

Dermot's jaw dropped. 'You are mad . . . '

Colm hurried on. 'Look! Where's the fault? With him or me? He has the Psalter. I am a scribe. He ought to – it's his duty

– to spread it. I only want to help by making a copy . . . '

'You rationalise it well,' said Dermot. 'But that's not the point, is it? Think about what's going to happen when he finds out?'

Colm spread his hands. 'What can happen? I am a scribe; it is *my* duty to make copies.'

Slowly Dermot grinned. 'He'll go through the roof, that's what.'

Colm returned the grin. 'Then he'll be wrong, won't he? And in any case no harm will be done. I'll make a beautiful transcription. I'd feel wrong if I didn't. Now will you send me the vellum?'

Dermot nodded. 'Give me seven nights. I'll send it by horseman.'

Colm smiled. 'And quills and my *ayarkeen*,' he said. 'And by the way, I want the good vellum, the five sheets of calfskin. Tell Cairbre. He'll know the ones. Not that goatskin.'

Dermot nodded and they embraced in farewell.

Seven nights later, as promised, a horseman cantered into the monastery and handed Colm his satchel. Inside were five beautiful, thin sheets of pristine vellum. It was characteristic of Irish books of that time that the vellum and parchment of which they were made was folded in sheets of five in the Eastern manner rather than in sheets of four according to the Roman way, one more legacy of the enduring intellectual influence of Africa and Byzantium to add to the monasticism that had begun to make the Church in Ireland distinctive.

That night, by the light of a shielded candle, Colm inscribed the first curving capital which swept down the page to a depth of eighteen lines and swirled gloriously upon the margin; then in small, neat, square letters he blocked in the everlasting words. He did not notice at the door behind him the thin visage of Finian directed expressionlessly towards his back. So it continued for twelve nights.

As dawn filtered across the lough on the twelfth night and the flame of the candle bent and fluttered in the morning breeze, Colm laid down his last pen with a sigh. His work was finished, the final page concluding with a scroll in three colours. He sat back and lifted the vellum in both hands, letting the pages fall with the fitness and cohesion which is a vital property of vellum. Slowly he turned each page, looking over what he had written, and was satisfied. He picked up Finian's copy of St Jerome's Psalter and returned it to its leather case. He stood up to hang it in its place, turned, and came face to face with Finian who was framed in the pale light that filled the open doorway behind him.

'Your work is done, then, Colm?' he asked drily, holding out his hand. 'I shall be pleased to add it to my teach (*tyock screptra*), bookhouse.'

Colm looked at him uncomprehendingly. 'I beg your pardon?'

Finian's hand remained outstretched and Colm made to hand him the leather case containing the original Psalter, but the abbot ignored his gesture and kept his hand as it was, stretched towards the table where Colm's new manuscript lay.

'I'll take that, if you don't mind.'

'You mean my copy?'

'I mean *my* copy.'

Realisation dawned on Colm. He felt exasperated, yet was tempted to laugh at the pomposity of the other man.

'Oh, come on, Finian,' he said, his voice perhaps a little too peremptory, 'you can't be serious.'

'I am extremely serious. Why do you think I made no protest about your nocturnal activity? It is obvious that since you believed what you were doing was in secret, you also realised I would not approve.'

'So you knew all along?'

'Certainly. And I may say I am surprised a man of your standing should betray hospitality in such a manner.'

Colm felt the blood drain from his face and his lips tightened.

'Control your tongue, Finian. You do not have the right to speak to me like that.'

'The same right you had surreptiously to steal a copy of my book.'

'Surrep . . . steal . . . ' Colm stuttered a moment and stopped. He looked silently at Finian for perhaps a minute, his eyes locking with the other man's until he felt calm. It was clear that Finian believed himself to be in the right or he would not adopt so ludicrous an attitude.

Eventually he said: 'Finian, I am merely doing the work expected of me: spreading the Gospel. That is why I made the copy.'

'You did it in secret. Why was that necessary? Could you not, as a mere courtesy,' and the contempt in his voice was offensive, 'have asked my permission?'

Again Colm hesitated. The truth, that he believed Finian would have refused permission, would be no help. But what else could he say?

'Finian, you know as well as I the terrible shortage of such books - especially such a marvellous one - and all credit to you for bringing it back . . . '

'You do me too much honour!' Finian was caustic, and genuinely aggrieved.

Colm restrained his impatience and tried again. 'You can't keep this entirely to yourself.'

'I do not. It is for my monastery.'

'I mean, you cannot refuse to allow copies to be made.'

'I refused no one!'

Colm's jaw clenched. Clearly, Finian was going to hold fast to his moral superiority.

'Such a book, by one of the most learned and eloquent of the Church fathers . . . '

Finian interrupted, his cold sarcastic voice like a frost in the room. 'It is illuminating to know that you regard so highly one who denounced the great Augustinus.'

‘Finian! You know better than I the importance of Jerome. Yet you want to deny to me this copy for those in my care.’

‘You had no right to duplicate my property by stealth at night. There is no honour in that.’

Only considerable self-control and the knowledge that he believed Finian’s unreasonableness to be obsessional and therefore uncontrollable prevented Colm from thrusting the other man aside and storming headlong out into the morning.

‘Give it to me.’ Finian’s voice was as level as his outstretched hand. Righteousness glowed firmly in his eyes, matching twin red spots high on each sallow cheek.

Colm was as calm. ‘I will not!’

Finian slowly let fall his hand and drew back; a tall, thin, bitter man.

Before he could say or do anything to provoke irreversible consequences, Colm said: ‘I’ll tell you what I will do. I am willing to submit the matter to the king for arbitration.’

‘The Rí-Eireann?’

Colm had meant one of his cousins, Donal or Fergus Mac Murray, joint kings of the Northern Ui Neill, but from the tone of his question it was evident that Finian, who was of the Southern Ui Neill, would not accept them. The alternatives were to nominate Laib, King of the Dal Riada, in whose territory they were, or to accept the High King and rely on his regal impartiality. Quickly Colm realised that to nominate the Dal Riada, already in ‘secret’ negotiation with the King, would be to invite disaster. On the other hand, in spite of his assumed impartiality in judgements, the King was not well disposed to anyone of the Northern Ui Neill. But what other choice was there? Colm was beginning to wish he’d followed his instinct and just brushed past Finian with his book. He shook his head. Impetuosity would achieve nothing. He looked grimly at Finian.

‘Very well,’ he said.

Finian drew himself up and again stretched out his hand.

Colm thrust Finian's leather satchel into it, put his freshly written vellum pages into his own teog leabhar and strode past Finian saying: 'I'll keep the manuscript until the case is heard.' He walked out into a close, grey morning with cloud lying low over the land. He did not look back to see Finian's sallow features suffuse with red.

Although it was a private and ecclesiastical matter, word went round and the Forrad, the judgement hall of Tara, was crowded when the King entered to hear the case.

Nobles, especially those of the Southern Ui Neill, and ecclesiastics predominated. Nobles of the Northern Ui Neill were fearful of treachery, even within the precincts of the Courts of Justice, because of the conflicting feelings they believed the King to have, and few were present. They argued that while Diarmuid might be expected to give a fair judgement, and might even wish to do so, the temptation to consolidate his position and that of the Southern Ui Neill by a stroke could not be overlooked. The King of Munster and his principal *dawlee*, advocate, kept a watching brief for the absent Northern Ui Neill leaders.

Rí-Eireann Diarmuid entered the Forrad through a private door from the royal apartments in the adjoining Teach Cormac. It was more secure than any of the other royal palaces - such as Rath Laoire - at Tara. Both the Forrad and Teach Cormac were within the Rath na Ree, the Fort of the Kings, which roughly conformed to the walls of the ancient Crimson City, or Caher Crofinn. According to historians it was built by the first Celtic people in Ireland, the Tuatha de Danaan, People of Annan; or, as some said, by an even earlier race. In any case it was where Diarmuid felt secure and he had moved the royal household back within its ancient stone walls and ramparts. Now he showed no emotion as, from his seat on the dais, he looked round the assembly with his expressionless eyes and saw what he already knew: the Northern Ui Neill were thin on the ground. He considered this an insult; that, at all events, was his first satisfaction of the day, and it was to build.

Finian, the complainant, was to give evidence first. He was succinct and his advocate remained seated. When he finished the King thanked him and turned to Colm, who was a 'tongueless person', that is he conducted his own case, and asked if he had any questions. At first Colm was tempted to say no. But looking at the lean figure on the raised *cos-na-dala*, witness stand, he thought of the trouble he was causing over nothing but what was a duty, and his discretion was vanquished.

'Thank you, *a Rí*, my King. Yes, I have something to ask.' Turning to Finian he looked at him for a considerable moment and saw steadfast conviction in his eyes, which unsettled him slightly. His own conviction was so overwhelming he could not understand how anyone, let alone Finian, could disagree with it. He had assumed that Finian's stand was simply petty-mindedness, and that Finian knew it. Now, suddenly, Colm realised his mistake.

'You knew from the start that I was making a copy of the Psalter?' he asked the cold-faced man in the witness stand.

'I did. I suspected it when you first showed an interest in reading it.'

Colm smiled so that the King could see. 'Then you knew before I knew myself.'

'Perhaps I know you better than you know yourself.' Colm's smile vanished. 'In any case I did not say I knew it then, but that I suspected it then.'

'If you knew what I was doing why did you not try to stop me or speak to me about it sooner?'

Finian looked at him expressionlessly. 'Why should I? Another copy, by the distinguished scribe Colm, would be a welcome addition to my library.'

'You did not believe that was *my* purpose?'

Finian looked back at him and then turned slightly away. 'No, I did not.'

'What did you think my purpose was?'

'To make a copy for yourself.'

'To proliferate the word of God and make it available to my own flock.'

'I repeat, for yourself; for your own library.'

Unable to contain himself Colm burst out: 'But it was more than that!'

'So you now say. You did not come to me and say so before you began the copy secretly in the night.'

Colm saw he was getting nowhere. He tried to retrieve the deteriorating situation. 'Do you still believe that I want this copy merely for myself?'

Finian was unmoved. 'I do not know what to believe.'

Colm turned to the king. 'I have no more questions,' he said.

The king nodded and looked at Finian. 'You may step down.'

The thin man bowed and left the *cos-na-dála*.

'Do you wish to offer evidence, Colm of Derry?' asked Diarmuid.

Colm nodded his assent and moved to the witness stand. He noted that the King referred to him as Colm of Derry in the heartland of the Northern Ui Neill, in spite of the fact that he had three monasteries nearby, one of them at Kells no more than three miles away.

His evidence differed only slightly from Finian's. When he was finished Finian's advocate stood up.

'I have only one question to ask, my King,' he said and, without waiting, turned to Colm. 'Why did you make this copy surreptitiously without seeking permission first – as any normal,' and he put the slightest stress on the word, 'person would have done?' He waited, a smug, self-satisfied expression, not uncommon to his profession, on his chubby cheeks. Colm hesitated and the advocate, with the theatricality of his calling, threw back his head ostentatiously and looked at the high ceiling, the picture of patience before lesser mortals.

'Well, *a ollamhe*, my doctor, will you answer?' he asked, dropping his gaze and looking directly at Colm.

In a firm voice Colm did so. 'Because,' he said, 'I did not think I would be given permission.' A slight gasp came from the body of the crowded Forrad.

'I have no more questions,' said the dawlee, and sat down.

The King nodded at Colm. 'You may sit,' he said. He turned immediately to the *ollamhe brehon*, doctor of law, who sat beside him. Judicial wisdom in a king was of the highest importance and Diarmuid understood this well. He had here an opportunity to give a judgement which would illustrate his kingly inspiration and, simultaneously, inflict on the Northern Ui Neill a moral defeat more powerful than a pitched battle. Inexplicably, Colm had played into his hands. He remembered from childhood the story of his ancestor - indeed, an ancestor of the protagonist also - Cormac Mac Art. When Cormac was a child he lived at Tara in disguise because the throne was occupied by a usurper, Mac Con, and Cormac dared not reveal his identity in case he was killed. Near Tara at that time there was a large *bruden* run by a woman called Benned, some of whose sheep broke into a field belonging to the queen and ate a crop of woad to be used for wool dyeing. The queen took proceedings against Benned and the matter came before Mac Con who decided that the sheep should be forfeit in payment for the woad. This judgement was given at the Festival of Tara sessions and Cormac was present. Moved by his inspired sense of justice he jumped to his feet and shouted: 'That is not a correct judgement. The cropping of the sheep should be sufficient for the cropping of the woad; the wool for the woad. Both will grow again.' That was immediately seen to be a true judgement and Cormac was recognised as the true king. Shortly thereafter Mac Con was deposed and Cormac was placed on the throne.

Having consulted with the *brehon*, Diarmuid spent some time going over his notes, making additions now and again with a quill in a golden holder that, from time to time, he dipped in a gold *ayarkeen.* Then he laid down his pen and leaned back, letting his eyes rove over the throng before he spoke.

'I have listened to the evidence with interest,' he began. 'It has profound implications. The spread and development of literacy and education, even among the lower orders, is accelerating at a pace never before experienced in the history of man. Clearly the demand and requirement for copies and for scribes to make them is, and will continue to be, unprecedented.' He paused to consult his notes and Colm felt a little more confident. 'If literacy and education are to continue there must be books and copies of books. Thus the questions of ownership and of rights vested in written matter will inevitably arise, as they have done in the case before us, for that is what is here at issue. We have heard arguments pertaining to the use and benefit this particular copy might or might not be put to; we have heard that such use is a proper – indeed it has been argued that it is the only – use to which such a work should be put. And we have heard it argued that this requirement, because of its character, supercedes all other considerations, including the right of ownership.'

Colm realised then that he had lost. The question was to what extent.

Diarmuid again consulted his notes and then went on: 'I have put these considerations aside in reaching a judgement on this case. I will not comment on them other than to say that this court has no reason to suppose that the use and benefit to which the defendant might put the book would in any way be superior to the use and benefit to which the plaintiff might put it. They are both eminent men in their calling; they are both distinguished ecclesiastics and they are both men of honour. I may say that I feel I would be failing in my duty if I forbore to observe how sad it is that two such men find it necessary to have recourse to this court to resolve their difficulties for them.' Again the High King paused. 'The judgement of this court is as follows: *Leh goch bowin a bohineen; leh goch lyower a lyowereen* – to each cow its calf, to each book its reproduction.'

There was immediate uproar. The ushers called in vain for silence. The King stood to leave by the door to the royal apartments in the Teach Cormac and as he did so he caught Colm's eye. If he saw the anger and frustration there he gave no sign.

Chapter 19

LIFE at Tara proceeded normally. The King was ever alert and watchful for danger and any opportunity to strengthen his position and that of the Southern Ui Neill against the claims of the Northern branch of the family. Out of the blue another opportunity arose within three nights of his giving judgement against Colm.

Besides the Forrad and the Tyock Cormac there were several other state buildings within the great white walls of Caher Crofinn. Among them was a strong timber two-storey building where the king's hostages lived, some comfortably, some less so. It was known as Dúma na nGíal (*Dooma nuh Nngeeal*), the Mound of the Hostages, for it stood on a raised bank which was twice the height of a man, fifty feet in diameter on top and more than seventy at the bottom.

Among the hostages was Curnan, son of Aodh (Hugh) King of Connacht. Aodh was an aspirant to the Kingship and bitterly resentful of the usurpation – as he saw it – of that office by the Ui Neill and of their disregard for tradition. For political reasons he was nevertheless an ally of the Northern Ui Neill. As a result Curnan was carefully watched, though he was not confined and fettered as were some hostages from lesser or more doubtful kings and nobles. A king's son had the right to be fettered with gold and Curnan wore a symbolic chain of golden links on his leg. It so happened that the hostages of Dúma na nGíal had been challenged by the youths of the king's household to a hurling match on the *magh-mon*, sports plain, immediately outside Rath na Ree beside the *cet* or chariot course. Curnan, a stocky youth with a head of curly black hair and sky-blue eyes, was a skilled player and was given the honoured post of cúl báire (*cool boyra*), rear guard, to protect the goal. The first team to score a goal won the match. Like his fellows he spent the preceding night cleaning both himself and his equipment, especially his two *camaín credumna*, bronze-mounted hurleys, ringed with brass, which were among his proudest possessions and proper only to the son of a king.

The day was still and windless with a high, even blanket of light cloud drawn across the sky. Beneath it the air was warm and humid and even the birdsong seemed desultory and more muted than usual, although swallows flashed in loops and circles all about the hill of Tara and the outskirts of the city. The hurling match was not a great event and didn't attract a large crowd, but when the teams took the field there was a respectable number of onlookers – supporters, soldiers, idlers and those who would go anywhere anytime to see a game. There were twenty-seven men to a side and the *liathroíd*, ball, a tightly-wound sphere of woollen fibre covered with close-stitched leather so that it was both hard and resilient, was placed in the *poll na h-imána*, hurling hole, at the hostages' end of the field. Curnan stepped up to it to send it to the centre before the game began. Legs slightly apart and flexed, his left side towards the centre of the field, he reached forward with his hurley and placed the flat of the blade on top of the ball. Then quickly drawing the blade across the ball's surface towards himself, he caused it to roll a little. In one movement he slid the blade of the hurley under the ball and tossed it lightly upwards, swinging his hurley back behind his right shoulder while the ball was in the air. As it dropped he swung powerfully and the ball sailed in a fine arc towards the centre of the field.

The size of the playing field varied, but it was seldom less than two hundred paces long and one hundred paces wide. Sometimes it was larger. Much depended on the numbers playing. At each end were two poles set close together. Between them was the *barna*, or gap – the goal which was the object of each team. Beside each *barna* was the hurling hole from which the *cúl báire* struck the ball back to the centre of the field whenever it crossed the base line without scoring and went out of play. The field was divided into four sections with *grifid* lines half way between the centre of the field and each goal, and the *comrann*, the place of division, across the centre, dividing the field into two territories. The lines were marked out clearly in lime. The game began in the middle of the pitch, halfway along the *comrann*, when an official threw the ball up in the air and the forward players of each team tried to capture it or knock it onwards with their hurleys.

In the centre of the forward line of the team from the King's household was the son of the King's steward, by name Tadhgh. He was a huge, heavily-built youth, red-complexioned and round-faced. He had fair, straw-coloured hair, watery blue eyes and the reputation of being a bully. He enjoyed throwing his weight around, especially against those he considered physically weaker superiors. His size and strength gave him the kind of confidence that is prone to evaporate if opposed. He was the one who, in the normal run of play, would most often challenge Curnan and it was known that there was little love lost between them. The spectators looked forward to some lively clashes. Curnan considered Tadhgh to be a boorish upstart whereas Tadhgh saw in Curnan all he would himself like to be, and resented it. They had had more than one verbal brush, one of which might have come to violence had Curnan's wiser fellow-hostages not led him away from the other's insults when Curnan began to go white and seemed in danger of forgetting his position and rank. Now as they faced each other a self-satisfied smile touched Tadhgh's mouth briefly as he looked down the field at Curnan and he flexed his huge shoulders. His bare arms were mottled red and white like his face and other exposed parts of his body, especially just above his knees. Curnan, looking back up the field, hardly noticed him. He gripped one of his hurleys across his body, right hand low between knee and thigh, left hand a little higher at thigh level, holding it just where it began to broaden into the flat, curved, tapered blade which was thick as a thumb behind and thin as an earlobe on the inner curved edge. Then the ball was thrown in the air and the game began.

The match was like many others of its class, full of enthusiasm rather than skill, but with some fine individual play from members of both teams as the *liathroíd* swung from end to end of the field. Twice Tadhgh charged Curnan as the ball dropped towards the hostage's goal. Each time Curnan gathered it, turned away from his opponent and swung his hurley short and forcefully, clearing the ball back up the field as Tadhgh rushed past him like an attacking boar. The third time Tadhgh deliberately slowed his charge and, as soon as Curnan cleared the ball, ran full tilt into him and sent him sprawling backwards on the grass. It was a clear foul, but Tadhgh pleaded inability to stop and this was accepted although, unseen by the others, Tadhgh had also driven the butt of his hurley hard into Curnan's throat which left him dazed, sore and breathless for the better part of a minute before he recovered his feet. Several times thereafter Tadhgh tried similar tactics, and Curnan, while he cleared the ball and avoided bodily contact, did not always manage to avoid the blows from the hurley that were aimed at him rather than the ball. As they swung towards one another after one such bout Curnan warned the other: 'Don't try that again, or it'll be the last time.'

'Mind your goal, little man,' replied Taghgh, forgetting or ignoring the breadth of Curnan's shoulders.

They moved to their respective places and the next play began. Inevitably the ball curved against towards Curnan - for his team was the weaker of the two - and he moved out to take it. Tadhgh charged in on him. Even with his eye on the ball Curnan was aware of the other some ten or twelve paces from him and realised that this time there was going to be a decisive clash between them. He took the ball, wheeled and sent it out low above the sward with a sweep of his hurley. He tried to sidestep the charge, but Tadhgh's shoulder caught him and he was sent spinning. The blade of Curnan's hurley shot between the legs of the other man, tripping him. They both went down and were instantly on their feet again. Red-faced and furious Tadhgh swung his hurley at Curnan's head, but Curnan blocked it easily.

'Take it easy,' he snapped.

Tadhgh's response was another backhanded swing at Curnan's neck, which he ducked. Tadhgh then tried to hit him with the butt of his hurley, but Curnan swayed backwards and jabbed instinctively with the bronze-mounted butt of his own. It took Tadhgh full on the forehead and he fell forward on his face and lay still. It had all taken less six seconds.

Before Curnan had time to find out if Tadhgh was all right another of the King's household team ran up and knelt beside the prostrate form. He rolled him over by the shoulders, placed his fingers on Tadhgh's neck and then looked up at Curnan, his face grave and unsmiling.

'He's dead,' he said.

Now members of both teams were crowding round and a shocked gasp went up.

'He can't be!' cried Curnan.

'See for yourself. He's dead.' The other man stood up.

A voice cried, 'He's killed Tadhgh.'

Curnan wheeled. 'It was an accident.'

He felt the opposing team closing round him and stepped back. 'It was an accident. I didn't mean . . . '

'Tadhgh started it. It was his own fault.' This was Benan, a nephew of the King of Munster and captain of the hostages' team. 'We all saw what happened.' That halted the movement towards Curnan. 'One of you get an ióidhe (*eekih*), physician,' he said. No one moved. 'Quickly! He may still live.'

Several youths ran shouting towards the spectators and the *rath.* Immediately Benan took Curnan by the arm, hurrying him from the group. He jerked his head at one or two of the other senior hostages to follow. They stood in a huddle near the *barna* and Benan hissed: 'You must fly.'

'But it was an accident . . . '

Angrily Benan shook his arm. 'We know that. But what difference will it make to you? Go! Now! Or you'll be dead before sunset. Quick!' He gave him a shove with his hand. Curnan hesitated. 'Go on!'

Curnan looked back in confusion. 'But . . . where . . . ?'

Benan had no reply. He was afraid as much for himself and the other hostages as for Curnan. Vengeance could take strange courses, and if they could simply say that Curnan had fled, attention would focus on pursuit. But he could not answer Curnan's question. West, towards Connacht, he would have supposed . . . One of the others suddenly had a thought.

'Kells!' he said, pointing east. 'Colm Cille. It's only thirteen miles . . . '

Curnan looked at their frightened faces for a moment. Then he turned and started, only to look back again, his reluctance clear.

'Go on,' shouted Benan. 'Go!' Beyond him Curnan could see that the onlookers were now running towards them, some of them shouting, and he turned and began to run hard.

Colm's anger and disappointment at Diarmuid's judgement was not lessened or made any easier to bear by the knowledge that it was not only juristical but wise - even just in its own way. He had decided to remain at nearby Kells for a few days with his friend and companion from Clonard, Ruadhan, who had attended the hearing and was as incensed as Colm was by Diarmuid's decision. He and Colm were cousins, of similar age and temperament, though if anything Ruadhan was the more fiery of the two, as the red-gold hair that gave him his name suggested. They had spent a lot of time in heated talk before deciding that the only practical thing to do was offer up the losses, physical and moral, with as good grace as possible. In such matters there was in any case no appeal against the judgement of the King.

They were in the oratory when they heard a commotion outside, which was followed by the sudden appearance of a sweating and panting Curnan at the small doorway. He stood there for a moment, grasping the lintel, trying to recover his breath. Both monks stood and looked at him curiously.

'He-help me,' gasped Curnan.

'Don't I know you?' asked Ruadhan. 'Aren't you the son of Aodh of Connacht?'

Curnan nodded. 'C-Curnan,' he gasped.

They smiled at him. 'What's the problem?'

'Sit down, lad,' said Colm.

Curnan resisted. 'No – time. They're after me.' Recovering his breath he quickly told what had happened.

'Well, you're all right now,' said Colm. 'This is sanctuary.'

It was more than two hours later that some of Diarmuid's soldiers arrived searching for the fugitives. When they learned he was there they demanded he be handed over. Colm – supported by Ruadhan – refused, pointing out that he had sought and been given the safety and sanctuary of the church. Having warned them of the king's personal interest and displeasure the captain of the troop rode off with his men and nothing further happened that night.

Three nights passed. On the morning of the fourth day, when the underbellies of the eastern clouds were barely tinged with yellow, a monk hurried into the refectory to say that a chariot and horsemen were approaching from the direction of Tara. Before Colm reached the faitche (*faha*), community lawn, surrounding the oratory, horsemen and three splendid chariots clattered into the precincts of the monastery, drawing up in a shower of dust, rattling harness, and stamping hooves. As the snorting and tossing of the reined animals quietened Diarmuid stepped from his splendid chariot.

'Greetings, Crimthan,' he cried, using Colm's secular name. 'I believe you have a hostage of mine here?'

'My name is now Colm, Diarmuid,' replied Colm evenly.

The King waved an uninterested hand. 'I can never remember these things. You must bear with me. Where is he?' He strode up to Colm and Ruadhan, looking about him as he did so. 'Small place you have here,' he commented.

'It's large enough for God's purpose,' said Colm.

'No doubt, no doubt,' snapped the King impatiently. 'Now where is he?'

'Curnan?'

Slowly the King turned full on Colm. He was somewhat taller and, perhaps, ten years older. A man in his prime. He wore a full beard, forked as was proper to his rank and, even at that early hour, had clearly spent considerable time with a fear-berad (*farr-berrad*) shaving-man and hairdresser, for both his beard and his shoulder-length hair hung in carefully twisted fillets and braids fashioned by heated irons. He was dressed for hunting. His eyes were expressionless and his handsome face was immobile as he looked at Colm for several seconds. Then he smiled.

'Have you any other hostages of mine?'

'He is under my protection and the protection of the *maigen* of this church.'

Diarmuid placed both hands on his hips and turned away. He was apparently surveying the simple buildings of the monastery. With his back to Colm he asked, 'You know he killed a man?'

'Yes. He says it was an accident.'

'Does he now?' Diarmuid slowly turned to face Colm again. 'Did you know it was the son of my steward he killed? Do you know that there are witnesses who say it was no accident?'

'He has sought sanctuary.'

'And he has been given sanctuary. He has been here in safety for three nights. Now he comes with me to answer for his crime.'

'That is not the law.'

Diarmuid drew himself up. 'Are you telling me what the law is?'

Colm did not reply. He met the King's gaze.

'You are an impetuous fool, Crimthan. Your nature has brought you nothing but trouble.'

'No one,' replied Colm steadily, 'is above the law.'

'By God,' swore Diarmuid. 'By God! Now you listen to me, Crimthan or Colm or whatever you call yourself. That is my hostage you have. He has no rights on that score. He is also a murderer. He has no rights on that score. He has had the three nights of sanctuary he is entitled to. Now hand him over.'

Colm started to protest, but Diarmuid raised his hand.

'I have been very patient with you. You have no authority in this matter. You have challenged the law before me once. Will you do so now to my face in defiance of my right?'

'What right? You just want to kill the boy?' It was Ruadhan who spoke.

'Stay out of this, Ruadhan. I have no quarrel with you.'

'Isn't it true?'

'The law is the law. He is an escaped hostage and murderer . . . '

'He is in holy sanctuary.'

'Mmm. Is he now? Before I come to that, tell me what I am to say to his father, my steward.'

'Aodh of Connacht will pay any *eric* and honour price, you know that.'

'And will Curnan return as my hostage?'

'I can not permit that,' said Colm.

'You will prevent me?'

'I cannot prevent you. But let me ask you a question. Will you, the King, violate the laws of sanctuary?'

'I will not violate the laws of sanctuary.'

'Then you cannot take him,' said Ruadhan.

Diarmuid looked at them. 'When,' he asked, 'was this church consecrated by a bishop?'

Ruadhan looked at him for a moment and then, in alarm, at Colm.

Diarmuid nodded his head. 'It hasn't been, has it? And on whose lands does it stand, may I ask?'

'Yours,' said Colm, 'but . . . '

'So that the church is not in fact a church and I am the owner of the land, is that not so?'

'Diarmuid, I . . . '

'Is that not the case?'

'Yes. I . . . Diarmuid, are you going to act on a technicality?'

'Technicality? You of all people should know that the law is the law, Colm. Is that what you call a technicality?'

'I intend to have the oratory consecrated.'

'But it isn't consecrated now.'

After a moment Colm shook his head. There was nothing to say. The king was entirely within his rights. At a sign from Diarmuid six soldiers ran forward and, brushing past Colm and Ruadhan, burst into the oratory. Ruadhan was fast on their heels.

'Get out of here, you sacrilegious dogs,' he cried, pushing one of them. 'Out.'

'Take it easy, monk,' said their leader. 'We don't want to have to hurt you. Just tell us where he is.'

Ruadhan had great difficulty in controlling his temper. He almost visibly subdued it before answering with what he considered to be an effectively diplomatic reply.

'No man stands in this church but ourselves,' he said.

However, it was to no avail. Curnan was concealed in a small chamber under one of the large flagstones in the floor of the oratory and the soldiers, seasoned and experienced campaigners, quickly located the small compartment. They dragged Curnan out and threw him in front of the king, who ignored him and

looked at Colm, then at Ruadhan, nodding his fine head slightly.
'So,' he breathed.

'Diarmuid, don't do this . . . ' But the king turned away before Colm finished. The soldiers picked up Curnan and tied him behind a horse with a length of chain. They could see blood running from his head and hip where he had been struck. Ruadhan was trembling and speechless with rage, and the colour mounted in his face.

'Diarmuid,' shouted Colm, stepping forward.

From his place behind the horse Curnan looked at him and appeared to Colm like an exhausted deer about to be torn down by hounds.

'Diarmuid!' he shouted again.

This time Diarmuid, still standing in the chariot, turned and looked back.

'Save your breath,' he said, and to his charioteer, 'Drive on!' With a crash and a rattle the chariot swept out of the monastery followed by the soldiers dragging Curnan behind them. Before the dust had settled Ruadhan leaped to the bank surrounding the monastery and at the top of his lungs bellowed after the king: 'Diarmuid! You will leave Tara. I curse it. I curse you and I will fast against you until it is abandoned.'

A most extraordinary series of events now took place, in which an onslaught of fury and emotion seemed to wrench the minds of otherwise balanced individuals. It was as if a combination of accumulated political and personal passions swelled and expanded like an overfed tarn, overspilling onto the land and sweeping everything before it except those boulders or trees that were strong enough to withstand the flood. These forces were unleashed when Ruadhan, together with Colm and several other monks, began to fast against the King, the highest possible moral sanction open to a plaintiff and all the more powerful when employed by priests and monks. It could not fail to have a profound effect on the citizens, let alone on Diarmuid, whose instinct was to rush out with a troop of soldiers and slaughter the monks sitting outside the entrance to Rath na Ree.

But even in his rage he knew that if he did so it would be the end of all his hopes. So he raged and fretted while first by night and in stealth, then in a visible trickle and finally as a wailing column the citizens of Tara abandoned their white-walled city so that the streets rang hollow and the cries of birds echoed among them. They knew of Ruadhan's solemn curse against the entire royal city. They also knew of Diarmuid's contempt for their traditions and that he refused to fast himself.

'He that does not give a pledge to fasting is an evader of all. He who disregards all things shall not be paid by God or man.' As Diarmuid recalled these lines from the old law book he shuddered. Moral defeat towered over him like some terrible nemesis.

At last the city was empty except for the troops and members of his household - and they had thinned perceptibly. He endured the sense of desolation for as long as possible, but finally could stand it no longer. Eaten by a warped compulsion to do his own will at any cost, he and his remaining troops and servants followed the people out of the city. From that moment Tara began to decay. It was never again occupied by man.

Diarmuid headed north to the territory of his uncertain allies the Dal Riada who were hostile to the Northern Ui Neill, and took over a castle known as Rath Beg, the Small Castle, beside the Dalriadan stronghold of Rath Mór, the Large Castle, on the north-east shore of Lough Neagh near a settlement called Antrim.

Earlier Colm had been advised to leave the fast to Ruadhan for fear of his life. It was good advice for he was gone only hours when a king's assassin disguised as a beggar slid among them in the dark looking for the Abbot Colm. He went directly to Aileach in Donegal, a mere five miles from his own monastery at Derry and the seat of the joint kings of the Northern Ui Neill, his cousins Donal and Fergus Mac Murray.

From their own sources they already knew most of what had happened. Nor was Colm surprised to find an emissary from Aodh of Connacht also there seeking help in a war against the King. What did surprise him was the brothers' reluctance to give that help.

With the heavy sword he had worn on his journey still buckled incongruously outside his white robe Colm stood in the council chamber surrounded by the nobles of the Northern Ui Neill and the emissary from Connacht.

'What are you thinking of?' he cried. 'We will never again have such an opportunity. If we don't control this man now, when he is morally at his weakest, we may never do so, and the right of Rí-Eireann will pass from both our houses!' He turned to the Connacht ambassador who nodded his agreement.

'He is an Ui Neill, whatever else,' said Fergus, reluctant still to ally with Connacht against his own kin.

'That may be so,' Colm said. 'But you can rest assured that if he gets his way, his will be the only Ui Neill. Are you blind, or what?' he asked, suddenly passionate. 'Will you allow this man to do what he has sworn to do? Keep the Kingship for his own people. If that is what you want, I'll have no part of it. Will Connacht fight?' He wheeled quickly on the ambassador.

'Yes!'

'Whether we join you or not?'

'Connacht will not let Curnan go unavenged.'

'Then there are men in Connacht at least!' cried Colm harshly.

'Hold on, Crimthan. You're going too far . . . '

'And you're going nowhere!' Colm cut Fergus off. 'Diarmuid violated the sanctuary of the Church; he murdered a king's son and hostage; he tried to assassinate me; he has plotted to make the Kingship, if not hereditary, at least dynastic. And you're prepared to let him. I say this Diarmuid is not fit to be Rí-Eireann.' There was an audible gasp.

'You know all this?' asked Fergus.

'I know it. You know it. Don't pretend. You have your sources. I don't understand you – ' which was not wholly true. He understood the brothers' reluctance well enough. They might have the moral right for a battle (and that was debatable), they might even win it, but to overthrow the constitutionally elected King was quite a different matter. And if they lost, where was their moral superiority then? Moreover they suspected that part, at least, of Connacht's anxiety for battle was once again to become eligible for the Kingship, and that they would not permit. But Diarmuid had overturned established law and tradition to strengthen his own position. It was this that gave validity to what Colm said.

In the end it was agreed that the Northern Ui Neill would join forces with Connacht and meet the Rí-Eireann in the field at an agreed place, as was the custom. This they did just over a month later at Cúl Drevni in Sligo, not far north of where it was possible to cross the great River Shannon.

Chapter 20

Diarmuid assembled an army of more than four battalions, thirteen to fourteen thousand men in all, cavalry, foot soldiers and war chariots, and marched from his new seat in the north-east across the country to meet the combined forces of Connacht and the Northern Ui Neill, who outnumbered him by two full battalions of three thousand men each. The western allies also had the advantage of fighting in home territory whereas the King was forced to march right across the country.

The capriciousness of political loyalties had left Diarmuid as exposed as before he had been strong and secure. No longer established on the ancient throne of Tara in the white-walled Crimson City from where the lords of Ireland had ruled for twelve hundred years or more, he had no powerful, disciplined standing army at his command, but a polyglot collection of troops from wherever he could force or gather them. Some came from Meath, of course, some from Leinster, compelled to do so for the sake of their hostages, and a large contingent from the Dal Riada. He even had a battalion of Saxons. His army had no common religion for many of them were unbaptised pagans who venerated old gods and goddesses; they brought their idols with them and placed them on rocks to worship. Inevitably the battle was seen by many on both sides as between pagans and Christians, and this disturbed Diarmuid very much, for he was an avowed Christian.

Cul Drevni was a shallow valley sloping towards the distant ocean. A lake at the eastern end gave birth to a stream that wandered through the valley towards the sea. Forest filled most of the depressions between the surrounding hills, but the valley itself was bare of trees except for some isolated clumps, for they had been burned and levelled countless years before to provide open sward for grazing. Furze and other bushes clustered here and there, and a profusion of glacial rock was scattered at the feet of the rounded hills.

Diarmuid reached the east bank of the river in mid-afternoon. The autumn sky, which had earlier been clear and blue, was by then overcast and the air hot and heavy. The troops, particularly those on foot, sweated in the heat and cursed the flies that swarmed about them as they marched. It was hard to say which was worst, the heat, the flies or the fatigue; all produced a surly malaise that communicated itself even to the King. He rode in a great travelling chariot, the four wheels ingeniously sprung from the body with leather and willow. Above his head swayed a purple canopy fringed with bird feathers dyed golden with mountain herbs. With him were his ally Laib of the Dal Riada and his commanders, and all five were as surly and disgruntled as their men. All around them, in no particular order, trudged the foot soldiers, more than ten thousand of them, scattered in groups over the plain. In the distance a dust cloud showed where the more compact cavalry rode together while in the rear, baggage chariots and wagons drawn by oxen brought up the equipment and accoutrements, including the battle chariots, of the army.

Cahal Maol, Charles the Bald, the Dal Riadan commander of cavalry, lounged on a cushion against an awning pole. The only facial feature that gave an indication of character were his eyes, and they were small, mean and hard, like spots of brown lichen on a rock. Where his nose should have been was a large hole, the edges curling inwards to darkness, through which his breath sucked and whistled whenever he tried to speak, which was infrequently. The same sword cut that had removed his nose had split both cheeks, the left from the lower jaw and the right one high under the eye. He was lucky to be alive. His lower jaw protruded and the teeth were visible. All in all he was a typical example of a professional battle survivor. His chief characteristics were treachery, self-interest, and an especial viciousness and indifference to danger which made him a useful field commander. Now he wanted to go home to Antrim.

'There's nothing for us here,' he whistled laboriously, wiping sweat from his forehead with his bare forearm. 'The best we can expect is stalemate. And then we'll have to fight our way home again.'

He was right, of course. Diarmuid had few illusions. But he had worked well on Laib, promising to make the Dal Riada one of the ruling houses of Ireland – which at present they were not – in return for his support. 'If we defeat the Northern Ui Neill and Connacht nothing can prevent us ruling the country between us as we like,' he said. 'The only other effective opposition is Munster and it could not stand against us both. Help me in this and you have my word that the Dal Riada will alternate with us as Kings.'

The offer was more than Laib could refuse. With their Scottish colonies behind them . . . who could tell, perhaps in time they would rule Ireland, Scotland, and Northern Britain. Even further . . . so Cahal's suspirating comment was ignored, sound though it was, and the dispirited army trudged on until it reached Cúl Drevni. On the plain between the lake and the sea they made camp. They built an *arba*, thorn fence, round it for protection and spent the night sharpening weapons, harnessing the light, speedy battle chariots and making sure that the tackle of the horse soldiers was oiled and strong. But these activities did nothing to dissipate the general air of gloom pervading the camp.

Cahal and the chariot commander, a Leinsterman called Fionn Aosta, old, because of his white hair, came to Diarmuid's *pupall*, pavilion, where he and Laib were drinking moodily but not excessively. They brought with them a third man whom they left outside under the royal standard hanging limply in the lifeless air.

'We must do something,' wheezed Cahal without preamble.

'If we go into battle now we'll be beaten for sure,' agreed Fionn Aosta. 'The men are in no mood to fight.'

Diarmuid looked at Laib and then at Cahal, holding him with his eye. From Cahal he turned to Fionn.

'What do you suggest?'

'The best suggestion I have is that we turn round and go back,' snorted Cahal.

'I didn't ask you,' snapped Diarmuid. 'Fionn?'

'I agree with Cahal Maol,' replied the tall man.

'Go home?'

'We won't win given the mood the men are in.'

'We must change their mood then. I'll speak to them.'

Cahal and Fionn exchanged looks. Before Cahal could blunder on, Fionn, the more tactful of the two, said: 'I think you should do that, Diarmuid. But I think you must reinforce your own confidence and speech with something positive.'

'What?'

'We have a very mixed army. As you know, there is already quarrelling among them and twelve have been killed fighting. Some are Christians, the majority are not. They have no faith – if you'll pardon me – in what they are doing. They see little in it for themselves, win or lose. That's all against us. They have no reason to fight. We *must* turn that round.'

'How? Have you any suggestions?'

Fionn looked at Cahal, who was obviously impatient to speak, and nodded. Laboriously the cavalry commander snorted and grunted through his damaged face as a preliminary to speaking.

'We have a druid,' he whistled. 'Let him perform the rites. Make an *arba drua*, druid's fence, round the camp. That'll give them a feeling of security, pull them together. It'll make them feel strong. And let them make their own offerings.'

'And they must be promised something for themselves,' said Fionn Aosta quickly.

'What?'

'Cruachan is hardly twenty miles south of here. Tara has been empty nearly a year. Let them sack the palace of the King of Connacht and give them the gold . . . '

'And slaves . . . ' hissed Cahal from that terrible face.

Startled, Diarmuid said, 'Slaves?'

The two men looked at one another and then Fionn nodded to Diarmuid.

'If you want them to fight to win.'

'But . . . but . . . ' stuttered Diarmuid. This was more than backsliding. It was a rejection of the basic principles that Patrick and his own great-grandfather had made the law of the land. Slaves were not captured in Ireland . . .

'They're right!' This time Laib spoke. 'You know it as well as I do. There's no turning back. Either you want to win this battle or you don't. If you do, listen to them.'

From more than a mile away Colm and other leaders of the western allies watched the King's camp from the cover of a wooded hill. Before nightfall they saw the druid and his acolytes emerge from a temporary gap and begin the ritual for the *arba drua*.

'Look,' cried someone, 'a druid.'

Colm stared for a moment and then raised his hand and made the sign of the Cross towards the enemy camp.

'What are they doing?'

'What's the druid doing, you mean.'

'Some kind of ritual. What is it?'

An old warrior, one of Aodh's captains, whose people had resisted Christianity in each generation, grunted and shuffled his feet.

'What is it, Ferdia? You know. What's he doing?'

He told them. A protective druidic fence. And he told them

that the army itself, predominantly pagan, would be setting up idols and asking the gods of their choice for help and protection in the forthcoming battle. Indeed, now that they knew what to look for, they could see groups of people obviously performing rites of some sort – Colm shuddered to think what – here and there inside the enemy camp. They could clearly hear the chanting and the accompanying music.

'The host that marches round *carns*,' he cried angrily. 'Do they think themselves a match for the host that fights with God?'

The old warrior Ferdia coughed and Colm looked at him sharply, knowing the significance of such a cough from such a man at such a time. He was diffident, but he felt he had something important to say.

'What is it?'

'I have a suggestion . . . '

Ferdia and the men he commanded came from a broad bogland north of the conical peak of Nephin that stretched in every direction for many miles. It was criss-crossed with sluggish rivers and high banks, and the inhabitants had developed a novel method to enable them to get from one isolated field or pasture to another. The settlements were small and scattered, seldom consisting of more than one large family. Roads hardly existed, such as there were being little more than tracks through the heather, here and there reinforced with patches of corduroy. They were barely wide enough to take a chariot and then only with difficulty. Many of the tracks stopped at a dead end in the middle of nowhere, sundered by a wide brown stream, an oozing ditch or a treacherous stretch of water with bright green surface growth. The people pole-vaulted across such obstacles in the manner of the warriors of the Fianna performing the heroes' leap, but on a larger scale. This leap was most notably performed by the renowned Diarmuid O Dyna when he eloped with Grainne who was promised to Finn Mac Cumhail (*Cool*), according to the old tales of that time. The warriors used a spear – in some cases two spears – but the people of the Nephin district used very long poles and were able to clear obstructions of great height and width.

Ferdia's plan was to take his company, under cover of night, to the barricade of the enemy, pole-vault over it and form a bridgehead inside the perimeter to enable the main army to fight its way in. After some discussion the plan was agreed and it was decided to put it into effect without delay before the enemy had time to recover from their long march.

They were in luck. The night was moonless and remarkably still after the sultry day. Even the slight wind from the ocean did not dispel the low-slung clouds. It was decided to attack from the north-west where there was more broken ground and better cover. To the south the fence spanned the river and strong stakes had been driven into the riverbed to prevent attack by water. The King's army had settled down in good spirits after the druidic rituals, promises of loot and plunder and plenty to eat and drink. The cavalry occupied the southern part of the camp, the chariots the northern, and the foot soldiers were between. The camp was close to a quarter of a mile across. Within the huge thorn fence were hundreds of fires and many tents, but the majority of the troops slept in the open, wrapped in their large woollen war cloaks.

By the time Ferdia and his men were in position the fires had nearly all died down. Only the large guard fires remained. The camp was quiet except for the occasional snort of a horse or the lowing of an ox in the night. The fence was a darker rim against a dark background.

A mile away the western army was drawn up to attack. Three hundred cavalrymen were followed by fifty chariots with scythes on their axles. Behind this assault group were two battalions - six thousand men - in three formations line abreast and behind them three more formations of cavalry of a hundred men each. Every cavalryman had beside him a *gilly*, or servant, armed with a javelin. Behind these was another battalion of foot soldiers. As soon as the breach was made the cavalry and the chariots would lead the charge into the camp. The remainder of the army was to remain outside. It consisted of three groups of horsemen with their *gillas*, interspersed with two units of foot soldiers, who were to intercept and block any attempt at escape. A group of horse, foot and chariots - amounting to another full battalion - were in reserve. In the event they never saw any fighting.

Several days earlier the western allies had established a camp among the low hills some five miles away. Diarmuid's scouts had examined it and reported - as they were meant to do - that the allied army was well settled in and appeared to be in no hurry for battle. A forest of colourful méirghe (*mair-ya*), banners, each with the crest, *suihantus*, of its owner, rose above the fortifications. Huts and tents stood in orderly rows on the grass and there were special enclosures for the animals - not only the warhorses, but oxen and domestic cattle for food. Traders had erected stalls and booths and there were commodious cooking and eating places. Healing baths had been dug in preparation for the wounded, and men and women were whitening shields and sharpening weapons at leisure. A closer look at the warriors in camp would have revealed that an inordinate number were very old and the remainder had strangely beardless faces and remarkable bosoms for warriors, and that their weapons and shields were old and damaged.

The attack began in the second hour of the first *cadar*, three hours before dawn. Ferdia's company of three hundred men brought their fifteen-foot poles within thirty paces of the fence without being discovered. The main army, its chariot wheels, harness and hooves muffled, was in position less than half a mile from the enemy camp. When a 'wolf' howled twice in the valley from the edge of the timber Ferdia gripped one end of his pole and rose to his knees. The men down the line on either side of him silently did the same. This was the most dangerous moment when an alert *dercaid*, sentry, might give the alarm before they were inside the *arba*. Ferdia gently eased the pole through his hands and along the ground towards the fence until he held it about five feet from the top. When all his men had done the same he stood upright. For a second he paused. Then with gathering speed he charged at the fence, his men in a line with him, plunged the end of his pole at the ground and leaped forward and upwards, the battle cry of his clan bursting involuntarily from his throat and that of his men. The great leap carried them clear over the fence, and only three men were injured on landing. The enemy slaughter began immediately. At same time, some of the men began to slash and tear at the fence while others made for the nearest fire and returned with flaming brands which they thrust into the *arba.*

In the vicinity of the attack the uproar was tremendous. The confused enemy half-dressed and half-armed, ran here and there slashing indiscriminately at friend and foe alike. The din of battle and crackle of flame penetrated to the further parts of the camp which was now stirring. Ferdia and his men were under desperate pressure. A semi-circle of enraged enemy closed in on them and arrows, javelins and sling-stones whistled among them like hailstones, bringing them down with great speed since because of the leap they had been unable to carry shields. By the time the fence was breached more than two hundred of the three hundred who had leaped the wall were dead or dying and most of the remainder were wounded. Yet still when one man fell the ranks merely closed tighter and fought on. Suddenly the remnant of Ferdia's company scattered as the spearhead of cavalry charged through the gap in the fence and spread out, trampling the foe. Immediately behind them hurtled the chariots, scything down men and beasts as they went. Then came the foot soldiers, swordsmen, bowmen, slingers and spearmen, advancing at a run. It was a total rout. The western allies advanced steadily, mercilessly destroying all before them. The enemy on the northern perimeter were pushed back onto those in the centre, who in turn fell back towards the southern boundary and the river, stumbling over their own comrades and equipment in the dark.

Three thousand men of the King's army died in the

battle. The number that fell on the other side was slight by comparison: only the three hundred men of Ferdia's company, who perished to a man. He and his men were commemorated in the name given to the battlefield: Magh Leim, the Plain of the Leaps.

Colm did not take an active part in the battle. But in the morning light, when the tumult and the shouting had fled eastward with most of the pursuers and pursued, he went towards the stricken camp. Here and there fugitives from Diarmuid's army were still being routed out of hiding and made prisoner or killed by their captors, often with much jeering. Colm entered the camp through the reeking gap that Ferdia and his men had made. Bodies, dead and wounded, lay heaped wherever he looked. As he passed a deep and narrow cleft that in some remote age had been gouged in the terrain by a retreating glacier, his attention was attracted by a small group of laughing, shouting men standing on the other side of the crevice. He moved closer and was met with as barbarous a sight as he ever imagined. One of the fighting women of Connacht, her once braided hair tangled and clotted with dried blood, the clothing ripped from most of her greasy and grime-streaked body, was attacking a woman of Diarmuid's forces whom she had found cowering in the furze that grew on the sides and bottom of the cleft. The peculiar weapon she favoured was a long-handled iron hook. The furze was trampled and beaten flat where the two women fought and tore at each other. As Colm looked the Connacht woman beat aside the sword of the other and sank the barbed hook into her breast. She screamed and fell, blood pumping from her wound. The panting, sweating Connacht woman then seized her weapon in both hands and, bending her back and bracing her legs, began to drag her fallen victim away, to the accompaniment of cheering from the men looking on.

Nausea and an overwhelming shame smothered Colm. He staggered and had to be supported by two of his companions. He vomited again and again until nothing but slimy bile trickled from his glaucous lips, and still his body convulsed painfully. Smoke spiralling upwards in the still air added to the awful stench from the carcasses of those with belly wounds. The cries of the wounded were piteous. Ignoring the physicians helping the wounded, carrion birds and dogs moved among the dead, gorging themselves. From north to south the camp was a place of stinking desolation and Colm's spirit resembled it. He tried, but no prayer would form in his benumbed mind except, over and over, '*Mea culpa, mea culpa . . .* ' He recovered enough to see Aodh of Connacht swagger in triumph towards him, a huge smile on his grimy face. When he saw that Colm saw him he roared his battle cry and raised both hands. In one he held his bloody *claideamh mór*, great sword, and in the other, jammed on the point of his *scian*, dagger, a noseless head cleft athwart by some old sword cut, blood capping its bald crown. Colm turned and stumbled blind from the field of victory.

Chapter 21

On Colm the effect of the slaughter for which he was largely responsible was shattering. Too late he found what he had believed a just anger wanting and vengeful. The vision of the carnage he had contributed to crowded in on him and he fled as best he could from himself to penance and solitude. All that winter and most of the spring he spent alone on one of the remote islands of the west where, as an eremite, he eked a bare subsistence on what he could catch or gather with his hands. He built a stone hut, little more than an extension of a natural cavity in the rock. He drove his mind, body and spirit in continual fasting, prayer and contemplation. At first he was astonished by the noise of the island – the loud and continuous crying of the sea birds, the ceaseless sound of the waves, which rose to unimaginable crescendos at times, and the many voices of the wind which was an unending counterpoint to the turbulent ocean.

His body had wasted and his spirit was no more recovered when one skittish spring day six months later a bent sail turned the corner of his island and headed unsteadily for the bay. Only one person knew where he was: Dermot.

Colm's feelings were mixed when he saw the boat and he did not go forward to greet it, thinking it might perhaps carry merely a casual stranger – a fisherman or someone seeking sea birds' eggs. But he heard Dermot before he saw him, his voice echoing from the sea and around the rocks.

'Col-um! Coh-lum!'

Several times he called, even standing dangerously and

unnecessarily in the boat to do so. Finally Colm overcame his reserve and the impulse he felt to run and hide. With a considerable effort of will he rose from where he crouched behind a clump of long, yellow, sea-blown grass and walked to the landing place. Dermot waved when he saw him, sat down and brought the boat skilfully to the small beach. He dropped the sail and leaped out in one movement; grabbed the high bow of the hide-covered vessel and pulled it easily above the high-water mark. Then he turned and hurried to meet Colm who was coming slowly towards him. Dermot's eager expression turned to shock as he got close enough to see his friend clearly.

'Colm!' he exclaimed and stretched out his arm.

Colm's eyes were sunken and his skin was pale and unhealthy-looking under a short stubble in which some grey hairs were showing. His gums were sore and swollen and his teeth loose. His hair flowed down his back in an unkempt tangle and had become brindled with grey. His cheekbones were gaunt and high under the sunken eyes and he moved his emaciated body slowly and as if in great pain. Dermot took all this in at a glance and then dismissed it as of secondary importance.

'They've been looking for you everywhere. I've only just heard. You must come at once.'

'Come where? There's nowhere I want to go.' Colm's voice was dull.

'You must. You're on trial?'

'I'm always on trial!'

'Col-um! Will you listen? There a synod of bishops meeting at Taillte – they're there now – to try you.'

'Try me?'

'Yes.'

'What for?'

'Colm, don't play the fool. This is important. You know what for! You know what has happened. It's as much political as ecclesiastical. Diarmuid is still king even though most of his power is gone.'

'What's that to me?'

This wasn't the Colm Dermot knew and loved. It was some other, lethargic, defeated, person. Dermot wanted to grab him and shake him, but he was afraid to. This frail creature might disintegrate.

'Do you want to be excommunicated?'

A brief flash stirred somewhere in the depths of those lifeless eyes.

'They wouldn't . . . '

'They would! They will if you don't come with me. Now, quickly! Brendan of Birr, your own confessor, sent me to get you.'

'Brendan?'

'Yes. Come on.'

'I'm not going. I want to stay here . . . '

Dermot looked at the fragile figure before him and made a decision. He remembered the vibrant young man who had consoled and bolstered him long ago when he himself was drowning in despair and self-pity at Glasnevin following the ritual of *virgines subintroductae.* He reached out and placed a firm, steadying hand on Colm's arm - and was immediately further shocked to feel the wasted arm beneath and how the other swayed under the slight pressure of his hand. He looked into Colm's wavering eyes and said, 'Are you coming, or must I carry you?'

Colm returned his look with a strange expression of mute hurt and protest; but there was also resignation, perhaps even relief, lurking somewhere underneath. At all events he began to walk in silence with Dermot towards the boat and uttered no further protest as Dermot launched it, alone, and helped him aboard. On the mainland he forced Colm to take some broth at a small public hostel where he had left his chariot and some retainers. Then they set out immediately for Meath, so urgently had Brendan communicated the necessity for speed. Colm sank onto the cushions of the chariot without a word, where he remained without stirring for the entire day. It took them two nights to reach Taillte, arriving on the third day. During the journey Dermot told a recovering Colm all that he knew, which was little enough.

The synod of prelates, bishops and abbot bishops convened in the old church of Donoghpatrick, the largest built by Patrick, and remained in plenary session there for three nights. The church was over sixty feet long and could amply accommodate them. It stood overlooking the River Blackwater and only five miles from Colm's settlement at Kells. Under the presidency of Erc, Bishop of Armagh and Primate of Ireland, the tribunal had considered the question of Colm. The case might not have been brought had it not been for the desire for retribution - or, as they considered it, a sense of outraged justice - which burned with equal ardour if dissimilar motive in the breasts of Diarmuid, the King, and Finian of Moville. Finian's sense of outrage would have been no less if he himself had been in breach of his moral standards. He would have judged himself, as severely as he wished to see Colm judged. Diarmuid simply wanted Colm crushed once and for all, for he remained an important cleric and as such continued to be a threat to Diarmuid. Once excommunicated, Colm was fair game.

In spite of all the King's efforts the synod rigorously excluded from its sessions all but those directly involved and the only contribution he was permitted was to give evidence. For the first two days they heard a great deal of evidence. Unfortunately for the absent Colm his past record was against him.

Brendan of Birr, Colm's confessor and close friend, was his advocate and made his case as best he was able in Colm's absence. Cormac of Ardstraw presented the evidence against him. A judgement was expected on the third day, following the president's summary and a vote. But the pleadings took longer than expected and procedure was complicated because - although considerable efforts had been made to locate him in the preceding months and particularly in recent weeks - Colm could not be found. This made his case seem worse and his guilt clear and had it not been for the strenuous pleading of Brendan Colm might well have been excommunicated *in absentia.* Although the synod refused to grant more time on the not unreasonable grounds that there had already been ample time to locate Colm if he intended to appear, the court did allow Brendan to reply to Cormac's demand for excommunication on the grounds of Colm's obduracy, wilfullness, incitement to murder and battle on more than one occasion, and flouting of the laws of God and the Church.

Now Brendan did not know what more he could say. He had exhausted his resources. There was no sign of Colm in spite of Dermot's assurance that he knew where he was and would fetch him. It had been a faint hope anyway, and more than six nights had passed. The last thing he wished to do in Colm's absence was seek the mercy of the court with its implied admission of guilt.

He stood to address the bishops who sat in two rows either side of the central table where the president, Erc, and the Bishops of Cashel and Meath were seated in front of the altar. The interior of the large church was cool and dim in spite of the candles that flared on the pillars and as Brendan started to speak he became aware of a tired patience emanating from the assembled bishops; they were being tolerant only out of consideration of the circumstances. He realised that they took the result to be a foregone conclusion.

'My lords,' he began, 'I hope to show that between the evidence we have heard and the charges presented by Bishop Cormac there is a contradiction sufficient to establish that the charges against the Abbot Colm are neither sufficient grounds in themselves for solemn deliberation by a Synod, nor sufficiently substantiated by the evidence we have heard to reach a conclusion as to their merits or otherwise.'

He paused. He was merely repeating, and rather more cumbersomely, what he had already said. If, in fact, there was a way out, he could not see it; his only hope lay in Colm's character and the circumstances. But these were dangerous waters. He must try to establish that in conscience Colm had not rejected the law of God and yet that he was moved by secular forces outside himself which had a legitimate claim on him. He took a deep breath and went on.

'Crimthan, son of Phelim, might well have been King of the Northern Ui Neill if he had not chosen to serve God instead. It is not beyond the bounds of possibility that he might have gone further . . .' which was about as far as he could go towards indicating that Colm might have become King. 'Most of you are related to the ruling families and I do not need to tell you what that means in personal no less than in political terms. A man cannot easily set aside his birthright and ignore the stirring of his blood in times as turbulent as these.' He looked around and was suddenly appalled. What had he said? That was precisely what was expected of a cleric. Precisely what most of these men – including himself – had in fact done. Horror gripped Brendan. He was doing nothing for Colm with such a line. Could he turn his course?

He selected what he could; he made the case of the apparent backsliding of Diarmuid in making use of pagan rituals before the battle; he cited the seeming victimisation of Colm through the incident of the book, the breach of sanctuary . . .

'But was not Diarmuid's judgement in the matter of the book just?' asked one of the bishops.

'Was it not in fact the case that the church at Kells had not been consecrated by a bishop and that it stood on Diarmuid's land?' asked another.

And yet they all knew they had not yet penetrated the heart of the matter, which was the rivalry between the Northern and the Southern Ui Neill and, in particular, the rivalry between the family of the King and that of Colm. But there was one point of even greater significance to the synod. The president voiced it as Brendan finished.

'Where is the Abbot of Durrow?' he asked. 'Why has he not

come before us to explain himself? Nor has he, so far as we know, shown one sign of remorse or repentance.'

The president announced that next day he would sum up and ask for a vote, and on that sombre and threatening note the synod adjourned for the night. As they left the church Molaise, Bishop and Abbot of Devinish and an old friend and counsellor of Colm's, called Brendan aside and they strolled down to the river.

'There's little left we can do, I'm afraid,' said Molaise, 'unless he comes himself.

'Where is he? I sent Dermot O Donal for him, but . . . '

Molaise shrugged. 'I've no idea. The best we can hope for is a postponement of sentence, but I'm doubtful of even that.'

Brendan nodded. They said their office together and parted.

The president's summing up was factual, reasonable and clear. He was neither unduly lenient in considering Colm's position, nor exceptionally condemnatory. At the conclusion of his summary the bishops discussed the points among themselves. A decision was not reached until mid-afternoon.

There was a majority vote for excommunication. The president accepted it in terms that made it clear he concurred. But before he could pronounce formal excommunication against Colm, Abbot of Durrow, a loud and unexpected knocking on the locked door reverberated through the church. They tried to ignore it, but it was so loud and continuous that it was impossible for the president to continue and he asked Brendan to find out what was wrong. When Brendan opened the door, Colm, still very weak and leaning on Dermot's arm, all but fell into the church. 'Colm!' whispered Brendan as he caught him and helped to hold him upright. Then he looked desperately round towards the president. 'My lord!' he cried. And back at Colm. 'Are you all right?'

It was Dermot who answered, grimly, 'He'll do.'

Colm straightened. He stood a moment supported by his friends. Then haltingly he walked to where the president of the tribunal sat, grim-faced and silent, facing him. There were gasps as the assembly saw Colm's condition, and audible murmurs of sympathy rose here and there. He stopped at the witness stand and slowly climbed onto it.

'I apologise for my delayed appearance. I did not know of the synod until two nights ago.'

The president nodded. 'We have been trying to reach you. It is a great pity you are so late. Sentence has been passed . . . '

'My lord . . . ' Brendan was on his feet. Molaise was also standing. 'A vote was taken, my lord. That is all.'

The president held up his hand. 'I was about to pronounce sentence.' He turned to Colm. 'Have you anything you wish to say before I do so?'

Colm did not reply. His face was turned to the ground and his emaciated body was curved, seeming almost to crumble under his robe.

The president was moved to pity. 'Where have you been?'

Slowly Colm looked up, his eyes unfocused.

I asked, 'Where have you been?'

There was an extraordinary silence in the church. The assembly of senior clerics seemed to hold their breaths. Every eye was on Colm who stood, an archetype of humbled man, devoid of all feeling except faith.

'I was doing penance,' he said, his voice little more than a whisper and as he looked up they could see tears running down his cheeks.

The immediate and strong intervention of Brendan and Molaise was sufficient to prevent the formal pronouncement of excommunication against Colm, but only on condition that Brendan, his confessor, would impose a sentence both appropriate and acceptable to the synod. Brendan wrestled all night with the problem and in the morning delivered a sentence which was as harsh as it might be. On the grounds that Colm's love of Ireland – inherited or engendered – and through that his love of his own people and of power had brought about the situation, Brendan decreed that Colm should receive the punishment for a murder, which was ten years' exile from Ireland; that, in addition, he must endeavour to bring to the Church as many souls as there were lives lost at Cúl Drevni; and, most bitter of all, that he should die in a foreign country. Furthermore, he was forbidden during his lifetime to feel Irish soil under his feet again. It was a terribly harsh penance, but better suited to his nature - and to his ability to work for God - than excommunication or that of his own self-imposed eremitical penance; and this he knew himself. But it was heartbreaking nonetheless.

Later that year, 563, Colm and twelve of his monks sailed down Lough Foyle from his first settlement at Derry towards the open sea. They were in two large hide-covered sailing boats with a minimum of equipment, principally cooking utensils, food, water, tents, ropes, tools and so on. As they glided between the hilly shores covered in green sward, yellow corn and a dark cloak of forest over which small, white clouds drifted slowly, Colm's heart turned within him and he composed one of the many beautiful poems that survived in his own hand.

What joy to fly the white-crested sea;
And watch the waves break on the Irish shore;
My foot is in the little galley,
But my sad heart bleeds for evermore.

There is a grey eye that ever turns
To Erin, across the grey waters.
But never shall it see the sons
Of Erin in this life, nor her daughters.

I look over the bleak sea from the prow;
And the great tears are in my eyes when I turn to Erin,
Where the songs of the birds on the brown bough
Sweeten the soft airs of Erin.

Erin! Where the young are so gentle
And each old head is a wise head;
Where the kings and great men are so noble,
And the women so fair to wed.

Young traveller! Carry my sorrow with you;
To Congall of the eternal heart;
Noble youth, take my prayers with you,
And the blessings of my heart.

One part for Ireland, seven times blessed,
The other for Alban. I charge thee
Carry my blessing to the west;
Carry it across the sea.

My heart is broken in my breast.
If death comes suddenly to rest
On me it will be because of the great
Love I bear the races of the Gael.

Chapter 22

CONAL Gulban looked out over the sea, brooding. Life as King of the Dal Riadan colony of Albyn was as uneasy at the moment as the restless and tormented ocean, what with the Picts to the north and east, the Saxons and Britons to the south, and demands for tribute not only from the Dal Riada themselves in Antrim but also from the King. Now he had to cope with this tempestuous clerical cousin of his descending on him. If it weren't for his mother . . .

His mother and Colm's were first cousins (their own mothers, from Connacht, had each married a king: Colm's grandmother the King of Munster in Cashel, and Conal's grandmother the king of the colony - she was thought not to have done so well for herself). Now Conal's mother was behaving like an excited young girl at the prospect of receiving her cousin's son, the abbot - 'the disgraced abbot, by God,' he thought to himself, 'coming to live and spread the Gospel of Christ among us. And she moving on seventy.' And then he smiled. He loved his mother dearly, an ample woman who rarely (unless it was for a purpose) lost her self-control.

Below and in the distance the sea was blue and choppy, white manes tossing on the necks of the waves, stringed froth and spindrift riding them like a saddlecloth. He rubbed his chin with the heel of his fist, pleased with the practical sound of the rasp. Just then his mother came in and crossed to the window.

'I wonder when they'll arrive? I can't wait to see him.' She turned to Conal. 'They say he's a remarkable man. He might have been . . . ' But already Conal's head was nodding up and down.

'I know, I know. Rí-Eireann. But he isn't, *a mhathair*, my mother; he's an abbot, an exile, and a fugitive.'

'Conal! I'm surprised at you. You must welcome him here to spread the faith in Albyn as Patrick was welcomed by Laoire in Ireland when it was pagan. Apart from Whitehorn, which is almost Britain, there are no monasteries in Albyn - and certainly none among our own people. Think of it!'

'I am!' said Conal dourly. Then, 'I know my duty, *a mhathair*.' The rebuke was gentle. She drew herself up and the sentimentality dropped from her like a cape.

'Then do it,' she said. 'There is more to be gained for God and Albyn than you might think. Colm may yet be your most powerful ally.'

'You think so?' His look was quizzical and shrewd. This statuesque woman who was his mother - a fact that often surprised him since she seemed to possess no qualities of genuine affection - was remarkably long-headed. Under the gracious exterior she could be both calculating and sentimental. She returned his gaze in silence and then turned her head and looked towards the sea through the window. One might believe that those hard, shrewd eyes saw more than there was to see, even the ceaseless wind, and calculated with exactitude all that they saw. Yet her answer was oblique.

'It would be very unwise to dismiss him,' she said. 'I hope you will not be so foolish.'

In the event Conal was not unwise; neither was he generous - it was not expected of him. Colm asked for little; a place to build a monastery, the humbler the better, and when Conal offered him the small and useless island of Iona, lying off the rich and prosperous Isle of Mull, he accepted gratefully. There he and his twelve companions built temporary shelters from the bent osiers that bowed to the wind forever sweeping it. Later they built wooden huts – the first, at his companions' insistence, for Colm himself – and worked on some stone buildings.

And here on bleak Iona they also built a monastery that grew and flourished until it became one of the most renowned in western Christendom and where, it has been claimed, more kings are now buried than anywhere else on earth. During the following years additional monks came from Ireland and the simple tents and shelters of the first monks gradually gave place to more permanent buildings of stone and wood – every foot of it ferried from the mainland. From Iona they penetrated the mainland. Led by Colm they crossed to Mull and from there to the remainder of the Irish kingdom sprawling across the whole western region. Although the colonists benefited to some extent from the influence of Whitehorn further south of them and from direct contact with Ireland, they were still Christian in name only, with few churches and no monasteries.

It was typical of Colm to seek out the frontiers of civilisation for Christ. He and his monks and the people of the Dal Riada, Irish colonisers of both Church and State, carved from the Pictish wilderness the beginning of the nation that became Scotland.

Iona 573: Colm's monks built and infused life and energy into a faith that was almost dead. But Colm himself did more. During the following ten years he made his way east and north to the Picts, becoming friendly – through an interpreter – with their king, Brude, whom he converted to Christianity in spite of the most pessimistic and jaundiced forecasts.

The British monk Gildas (in truth half-Saxon), visiting Iona, characteristically expressed this view with that brand of superior ignorance which contemptuously brandishes its prejudices aloft as if they were revealed truths: 'Those Picts are all the more eager to shroud their villainous faces in bushy hair than to cover with decent clothing those parts of the body which require it.' And that was the sole comment he deigned to make about them, or their souls. In spite of such attitudes – and they were not uncommon - Colm persevered. He learned Pictish and, as Patrick the Roman Briton had done in Ireland one hundred years earlier, brought and helped establish the Christian message so that at the end of ten years and much journeying there was no corner of that savage territory, from the Grampians to the Hebrides, from the Hebrides to the Orkneys, where living Christianity was not to be found. And then, suddenly, the ten years ended and stupendous events once more altered the pattern of his life.

Diarmuid was long since dead - murdered by a Dalriadan prince within a year or two of Colm's exile. After a seething darkness of violence and bloodshed, Aedh Mac Anmirra of the Northern Ui Neill held the Kingship of Ireland, West Britain and Albyn. And Albyn! This matter now became an issue of tremendous importance.

Conal, king of the colony, was also dead and had been succeeded by Aidan Mac Gowran in that same year, 573; more, he was annointed king - in the first such ceremony recorded - by the Abbot of Iona, Colm himself (*in ordinatio benedixit*), a ceremony made all the more singular since Colm was not a bishop.

Almost before Aidan was king a wet day, as the saying has it, the annual tribute to Rí-Eireann fell due. For more than two hundred years the Dal Riada had colonised Albyn; now called Scotia Minor (just in time Ireland would lost the name of its people and no longer be Scotia Major, but Eire or Erin, and Scotia Minor alone would carry forward the name of the people and be called, simply, Scotland). Even in Conal's time the colonists felt themselves to belong to a kingdom in its own right, within a commonwealth, and resented paying tribute to the King of Ireland. Now, under Aidan, they added resistance to their resentment and when the King sent the *taurcrec* - the token gift, acceptance of which was acknowledgement to pay the tribute - his demand was for the first time returned and payment of the tribute refused.

In his courteous but determined reply to the King's

demand Aidan said: 'This kingdom is not a tributary kingdom but is an independent kingdom in its own right and we do not owe tribute to any overlord.'

Again the King demanded his tribute, this time with a scarcely veiled threat, and again it was refused. And so Aedh faced war. But it was war against the Dal Riada of Albyn, across a turbulent sea filled with their fighting ships, in alien territory where the enemy might call on help from both the Picts and the Northumbrian Saxons. Such a punitive expedition would be costly, beyond question, and might well degenerate into a war of attrition. But what choice had he? He could not afford to lose face and have his authority flouted by these colonists or his throne would be in jeopardy.

Among his advisers was the chief poet of Ireland, Dallan Forgaill, old and blind but no less sharp and wise than he had ever been. And it was he (with perhaps another motive as well in mind) who suggested a solution to Aedh's dilemma.

Like many blind men he had a habit of sitting with his head tilted back, eyelids closed, and as the council unenthusiastically debated what to do about the Scots in Albyn, so he sat, silent, listening, his head caught in a shaft of sunlight that streamed from a high window. The assembled lords and *ollamhs* came yet again to the dead-end conclusion of war or nothing, and a disconsolate silence fell like a heavy fog on the council chamber. At last Dallan spoke, and then it was in response to a weary observation from the King that they had not yet had the benefit of his wisdom.

'I have been thinking, my Hugh. It is more than thirty years since the last Assembly of Tara.'

'In God's holy name,' swore the irritated King, 'what has that got to do with it?'

'Maybe nothing,' answered Dallan, 'maybe more. But it is a fact – for you have often said it yourself – that there are many things abroad in the land that warrant settlement and discussion that might be rectified at the Feis of Tara, if we had it.'

'Come to the point,' snapped the King, listening now.

'If the Assembly at Tara still existed,' said Dallan, 'this matter of the Scots in Albyn would be a matter for discussion there, wouldn't it?'

'Of course! And the obvious thing to do,' said the king hurriedly, his interest kindled, 'is to hold the overdue national assembly.'

Dallan spread his hands momentarily before folding them on his lap and closing his eyes again. The meeting came to life and the idea was excitedly discussed for almost an hour, at the end of which a committee had been formed to make the preliminary arrangements and the King was congratulated on a brilliant solution to the impasse. Such was the origin of the great Council of Drum Ceat which was convened towards the end of that year, and lasted for more than twelve months, into 575.

Drum Ceat is about twenty miles east of Colm's first monastery at Derry near a place called Leim a' Mhadaidhe (Limavady), Dog-leap, where An Rua, the Red River, flows directly north to the mouth of Lough Foyle. Between the settlement of Limavady and the stronghold of Cahan stands a hill called the Mulloch, not far from two ancient burial mounds then, as now, overgrown and long abandoned; places of mystery, best left alone. The hill of Mulloch had been used by the Northern Ui Neill as an assembly place from the beginning of their overlordship almost two hundred years earlier. And it was here, overlooking An Rua, that the King decided to hold the national convention of Drum Ceat. The situation that now existed between the king of the Dal Riada of Scotland and the King was, naturally, one of the principal matters for discussion, but it was by no means the only important one. Substantial legal and economic reforms were long overdue; important social measures required clarification; and the relationship between secular and clerical interests was not as harmonious as it might have been. But the most pressing, certainly the most dramatic, concerned the future of the Order of Poets. Its destiny was in doubt and perhaps Dallan

Forgaill had been less than ingenuous in suggesting the idea of the council to the King at that particular time.

The crisis regarding the poets was precipitated by their unremitting arrogance and insolence which infuriated the people. They abused their power and privileges, especially in their unending demands for hospitality and lavish presents, to such an extent that most of the kings and chiefs of Ireland had condemned them out of hand as a public nuisance. Twice before, for similar reasons, the Order had been threatened with abolition and each time they were saved by the people of Ulster, who were traditional defenders of poetry (besides possessing the attributes peculiar to the North, namely: battle, contentions, hardihood, rough places, strifes, haughtiness, unprofitableness, pride, captures, assaults, hardness, wars and conflicts). But now the poets' outrageous insolence and extravagance had alienated even the nobles and people of Ulster. The disrespect reached new heights when one poet, in return for an unsolicited and fulsome piece in praise of the King, demanded as payment the Roth Croi itself, the royal wheel-brooch, a symbol of office passed from one Ri-Eireann to the next. Aedh had had the poet thrown out and gave immediate support to the public outcry against the Order, swearing that he would legislate for its suppression and have the worst offenders banished from the country.

Dallan Forgaill pointed out (to no avail) that the fault, though largely of their own making, was not entirely so. To some extent it was the result of changes in society, notably four: the hostility of the Christian clergy towards the poets, whom they saw - with some justification - as both rivals in literacy and inheritors of the druidic tradition; the poets' resentment in these circumstances of the undermining and implied criticism of their traditional moral status; an increase in the number of idle poets - poets without official function due to the greater numbers of pupils, fewer official places in the households of nobles and some places being taken by clergy; and the abuse and manipulation of poets and their privileges by unscrupulous upstarts.

The power of the Order was great. Officially they ranked with kings and at all public assemblies the place of the official poet was next to that of the king. At this time they owned vast estates and often had incomes higher than their king. Before Drum Ceat they owned one-third of the land of Ireland. But their main source of power was fear of Áer (*awr*), satire, the essential prop of all their insolence, wealth and honours. The abuses came mainly from the satirists, cynical and sinister people whose numbers were increasing. A poet praised or satirised as occasion demanded and all poets could do both. But some poets, particularly those with no official position, devoted themselves almost exclusively to the composition of Áer. They came to be recognised as professional satirists, commonly called cáinte (*coynteh*), dogs, 'because they have dog's heads in barking, snarling and biting', as one of their own Order wrote. They were classed as people of disreputable character.

It was against this background that Dallan Forgaill encouraged Aodh to hold the great and long overdue national assembly. To some it seemed strange that he, a poet himself, should at that time still be in a position to counsel the King. But the Order had not yet been abolished, which required legislation, and it was still immensely powerful. More to the point, perhaps, was that while he suffered the general odium Dallan was a court official and no satirist.

Colm was fifty-three in that year and at the height of his mental, physical and moral powers. His work in Scotland and North Britain was already being compared to Patrick's in Ireland one hundred years earlier and he was recognised as being unquestionably the most distinguished churchman of Ireland, even in an age of many men of such distinction.

He was troubled in himself about the convention of Drum Ceat. Uncertainty was not one of his notable characteristics and he was somewhat irritated by the irresolution he felt. It was not simply a question of whether or not to attend. He had every right to be there; he had a duty to be there. And yet he hesitated.

Ten years' exile. That was done. That he win as many for Christ as the dead at Cul Drevni? That was already achieved over and over. That he never again set foot on Irish soil . . . that he die in exile. Supposing he went and had an accident? If some lunatic with a desire for revenge were to murder him? What then of his penance? How in any case could he go without walking the soil of Ireland? He shook his head. These were trivial considerations in one sense, but they bound him more effectively than the major penances. It was Aidan who first applied pressure.

On a cold, grey, lustreless day when the sea heaved unbrokenly Colm was surprised when one of his monks shouted and pointed towards Mull, to see the king's personal ship heading alone towards them, the great sail and the standard showing his arms. Half an hour later Aidan himself arrived and Colm escorted him to the church. On the way they chatted inconsequentially, but once seated inside beside a hurriedly lit brazier, Colm asked in his direct way: 'What brings you, Aidan, in the middle of winter?'

Aidan laughed shortly.

'Trust you to come straight to it,' he said. He leaned back in his chair and was silent a while. Then he said, 'I have returned the *taurcrec*.'

Colm looked at him curiously. Of course he knew that. And Aidan knew he knew. 'You didn't come here in mid-winter to tell me what I already know.'

Aidan shook his head. 'I – we – need your help.'

'You have all I can give you, you know that.'

'Then you will be our advocate before the convention?'

Colm winced. This was one of the things he had feared. He was blood relation to both Aidan and the Rí-Eireann. He was an Irish nobleman. His work was among the Dal Riada, and yet Aidan was asking him to plead his case against his own King.

'You must give me time to think about it . . . ' And in spite of all his pleading, that was as much as Aidan could elicit from him.

Yet while Colm played for time, events were already forcing

his hand. Within weeks an emissary from the King arrived, pleading with him to judge the issue. After considerable thought on his part, and persuasion by both kings, he reluctantly agreed - not to plead the case, or judge it - but to state it.

The decision to return to Ireland having been forced on him he realised that even though his ten years of exile had expired he might otherwise never have returned to Ireland, much as he longed to. Indeed, although he had not recognised it before, it was the very intensity of his love and longing for Ireland, and the persistent homesickness that accompanied it, that had deterred him most.

His leave-taking was simple. Aidan wanted him to travel with him in one of his warships, but Colm declined on the grounds that he did not want it said that he showed favour. He decided instead to go as he had come, in one of the community's own leather-covered boats. With him he took some monks, among them his nephew Beheen who gave him the means of not breaking the stricture against walking on Irish soil.

To the amusement of his monks this had preyed on Colm's mind and he had fashioned two dried slabs of Iona peat into clumsy overshoes which he could strap to his sandals. They were cumbersome and it was clear they would not last long. But he was so intent about it that none of the community dared laugh outright.

The day they left a fresh westerly breeze blew, which meant a long tack down the Mull followed by a hard row westward. There were four travelling and the boat was trimmed and ready. The rest of the community assembled to receive Colm's blessing before seeing him and his companions off. He spoke to and kissed each of them in turn, then went to climb into the boat which was held to the wooden quayside by the two monks already aboard. The mast rocked slightly at the top where the sail was furled along the slanting boom, the far end of which was held by one of the people ashore.

'Come on, Beheen,' Colm said, 'get in.'

Beheen looked at him and suddenly Colm became aware of an air of expectancy in the others and looked round in surprise. From behind his back Beheen produced a pair of sandals and held them out to Colm to the accompaniment of laughter and clapping from the community.

Bemused and pleased at the thoughtfulness, Colm said: 'Are these for me? Well, my thanks. But I don't really need another pair of sandals. You should not have gone to such trouble . . . '

'You need these ones, my lord,' said Beheen. 'Look at them.'

Colm examined them and they were indeed unusual, with soles exceptionally thick and soft. They were unlike any he had ever seen, with an inner and outer sole, heavily padded between and perhaps half an inch thick all round.

'What's this?' he asked, squeezing the soles between his finger and thumb, 'padding . . . ' He looked up and they saw understanding dawn on his face followed by bewilderment and confusion so that all they could do was laugh with delight. Tears filled his eyes. Rather than permit him to jeopardise the prohibition, they had made him the sandals with Iona peat-mould stuffing between the two soles so that he could walk anywhere in Ireland without walking on Irish soil.

'Who . . . ?' he began, and caught Beheen's grin before he finished. 'You!' He took his nephew by the shoulders and shook him. Half blinded by the tears in his eyes he looked around at the others. 'I know you all took part in this.'

Their softer laughter was his only answer and he nodded, swallowing.

He again raised his right hand. 'May the Almighty Father bless you and safeguard you, my children, until I return to you in a little while.'

Helped by Beheen he stepped into the boat and they cast off, rowing from the island pier to where the chop began. The sail dropped, then quickly bellied and, with a deep oar from the stern, she was held to the wind and quickly scudded south before it.

At Limavady the town's population, its number swollen by visitors from near and far, went out to meet him and such was the veneration in which he was held that he was welcomed almost as if he were an angel of God. An avenue in the moving, clamorous multitude opened for him and closed again as he passed, a forest of arms reaching towards both his own outstretched hands. The cheers rose and fell away again as he approached and passed each place between Limavady and the Mulloch.

From a distance he saw the hill bright and alive with coloured tents and the flags and banners of every king and noble in the land. At the foot of the hill a huge open pavilion had been built within a giant enclosure where the Assembly would be held. As he reached it an enormous roar went up which carried mile upon mile, reverberating and swelling until he turned with upraised hand and blessed the entire convocation of people, and beyond, all the people of Ireland: '*In nomine Patris, et Filii et Spiritus Sancti* . . . '

And his own people of the Northern Ui Neill were almost as shaken and overcome by the extent of his welcome as he was himself. Many a spear shook in the hand that held it, many a shield was raised before a face, as throats swelled with pride and joy. Yet, in all that tumultuous excitement there were some who were not so moved, or were moved in another fashion. One of them was Caitlin, wife of the King, who feared Colm's power and influence and was jealous and ambitious for her sons Conal and Donal whom she commanded on no account to welcome - or show respect to - Colm. It is hard to fathom the mind of such a woman who had so much to gain from Colm's help and friendship. But she was of the Southern Ui Neill. What she had been told of Cúl Drevni festered with the jealousy in her impassioned spirit and made her blind to her own best interests and those of her sons. And to no purpose, in the event.

True to her command the elder boy, Conal, stood in his place and glowered under her wrathful and imperious eye when the

Assembly erupted in welcome to Colm. But Donal, moved by some impulse greater than himself, left his place at the royal end of the pavilion and, before that mighty assembly, walked towards the white-cowled figure of the man who stood alone before the benedictory host at the far side of the enclosure. Donal gave no sign that he saw anything except the lone figure who had just blessed them all or that he heard anything of the crowd – or his mother's hissed command. He neither ran nor dawdled, but strode as purposefully as his five-year-old legs would take him, his short, scarlet, yellow-lined cloak rippling behind him. Before he was halfway there Colm saw him and stretched out his arms to the child prince who went straight to them. Kissing the abbot on both cheeks, Donal took him by the hand and led him firmly to his own place. And the cheering then was mightier than before. Before the crowd, Colm blessed the child and prophesied that he would be a famous king, victorious against all enemies and – unlike most kings – that he would die in his own house, peaceably, in his own bed surrounded by his friends – a prophecy, the first of many of Colmcille's, that was fulfilled in its entirety.

Colm's place at the Assembly was assured and exceeded by no one. The respect and veneration with which he was everywhere – if not by everyone – received was tinged with awe. He was acknowledged as the man who had successfully carried Christianity from Ulster to the Scottish colonies, just as Patrick himself had brought the Faith to Ireland a century before.

The convention was opened with a fanfare from the huge, curved, decorated bronze trumpets of the nine finest *cornaire*, trumpeters, in the country. The colour and majesty of the occasion affected the whole country and raised the feelings of the thousands present, participants and spectators alike, to unusual heights of solemnity and hope. The kings, nobles, *ollamhs*, bishops, clerics, officials and, of course, poets filled the enormous auditorium as if it had been the Assembly Hall at Tara, each in his proper place under his crested banner. The whole enclosure had an air of dignified splendour. Whenever consultation became necessary within representative groups it was in whispers, heads close and bodies leaning. The King flanked by the kings of the provinces and Aidan of Albyn, with Colm and other advisers and learned men, sat on a large rostrum beneath the awning, facing south. In front of them was a clear space, in the centre of which was the *cos-na-dala.* When Aedh had formally made his opening address it was announced that the first business before the convened Council of Drum Ceat was the issue between Aedh Mac Ainmire, Rí-Eireann, King of Ireland, West Britain, Man and Albyn, and Aidan MacGowran, King of the Dal Riada of Albyn.

As was customary, the case was first to be stated by an *ollamh* and Colm came forward to do so. In that glittering throng his undyed cowl and habit looked drab - and in a way more impressive for it. He strode from his place on the rostrum and mounted the *cos-na-dála*. He gazed round for a moment or two before beginning. An almost tangible hush settled over the Mulloch. Then, in the mellifluous voice which, it was said, could be heard at fifteen hundred paces without losing its quality, he started to speak.

The entire conclave knew and understood that Colm was kinsman to both kings, one of whom he had anointed in his office. He was eminent in his own right, and might easily have been the Rí-Eireann Aidan was challenging. Moreover he had himself challenged a King, been defeated in law, and had supported - even incited - an old enmity between his people and the King by way of revenge; and ever since had been constant in his endeavour to purge his spirit of self.

'Beloved brothers and sister,' he cried, 'I ask you to pray with me while I invoke the blessing of the Almighty Father and his glorious son Jesus Christ on our work and deliberations here that we may pursue truth and justice and, in so far as we are able, through the sanctifying grace of the Father, the Son and the Holy Spirit, achieve them.'

'Amen,' came the sonorous, immense, response.

Colm stood quiet and silent for a moment while his mind ran on a tight rein. He knew what was desirable. How to present it acceptably? Quietly he began to outline the background.

The Dal Riada originated in Muskerry, near the Great Corcach na Mumhan, Marsh of Munster, where the monk Lochan - better and more popularly known as Finbar - built in Colm's lifetime the settlement that became Cork City, capital of Munster. Some three hundred and fifty years before, Colm reminded his audience, during the reign of Conaire the Second in about 220, famine ravaged Munster. One of Conaire's three sons, Riada, brought his people north to Antrim and southern Scotland where they settled and became known as the Dal Riada, the people of Riada.

'Since that time,' he went on, 'the Dal Riada of Ireland and the Fir Albyn (men of Albyn) have been one, by blood and by nature, in their laws and in their allegiances. But in some respects they have gone separate ways, as is normal and natural. Different changes of fortune affected their new and developing life-styles. The fortunes of the Dal Riada in Ireland have changed from the time when they were an independent kingdom to being tributary kings to the King. That is just and proper in Ireland. On the other hand the Fir Albyn - ' and it was noticeable that he used the form men of Albyn rather than the Dal Riada in Albyn ' - have expanded their kingdom so that it now consists of all but the remoter areas of the Picts. And they have done so on their own and at a time when the kingdoms of the Irish in Britain have either seceded or been overrun by Angles or Frisians or Saxons for want of support from Ireland.'

Colm then went on to give the origins of the present dispute: that Aidan had refused to pay tribute to the Rí-Eireann on the grounds that he was an independent king and had therefore returned Aedh's *taurcrec*, thus renouncing submission and allegiance.. Aedh, in turn, had rejected Aidan's claim to independence, regarding him as a rebellious vassal. At that point

Colm stopped. He felt the old turbulence in his blood and the explosive desire for action rising in his throat and behind his eyes. But with an effort he took command of himself and, lowering his head and swallowing, fought down the threatening eruption. 'Stand by my side, O Lord Jesus Christ,' he prayed silently, 'that I may be able to pursue justice and continue my work.' He knew well that should war occur between the King and Aidan, not only would the cost in loss of life and in material terms be enormous - in both respects one of the most costly wars that Ireland had ever experienced, he estimated - it would also hamper his own work for Christ in Scotland beyond calculation. He could see churches and settlements burned and destroyed, savage Picts, Angles and Saxons turning their backs on a Christ whose people slaughtered each other across the sea and throughout their land; all he had done and set out to do would be brought to nothing. He debated if he should say more, but, fearful of exacerbating one side or the other to intransigence, he stood down.

Advocates for the two sides pleaded vehemently, and not without bias, for the remainder of that day and the two following days. On the third night the Rí-Eireann invited Colm and King Aidan to join him in his tent at a private banquet, also attended by the Pentarchy, Dallan Forgaill, and some other members of the council.

On the surface it was a relaxed evening and the talk ranged over every subject of current importance - the affliction of the Lombards on the Empire; the rumoured madness of the useless emperor, Justin the Second; the imminent death of the frail Pope, John the Third; the devastation of Central Britain by the Angles; the price of cattle; and, of course, law reform. But nothing about the cause at issue these last three nights. One guest volunteered a light-hearted reference to the forthcoming banishment of the poets, only to be met with silence and a blank stare from the blind eyes of Dallan Forgaill, so that his face was suddenly enveloped in a hot *aonach-ruice*, blush of shame. When all were again relaxed and talking among themselves the King nodded to Colm and Aidan and the three of them moved to another part of the tent where they sat round a low, small circular table of Arabia on which were bowls of fruit, bowls of water in which to wash their fingers, and a beautiful Etruscan flagon with matching goblets in chased gold and silver. Aedh poured them each a goblet, raised his own in a silent toast and drank. Aidan did likewise and Colm smiled and raised his right hand in blessing. The King looked at them.

'Something must be done,' he said, 'or this endless arguing will get us into a situation nobody can retreat from.'

Aidan looked steadily at him. 'I will not retreat,' he said. Colm put a hand on his arm and the tension between the eyes of the two kings softened and relaxed.

'That is not the King's meaning,' said Colm. 'He didn't intend what he said as a suggestion that you should retreat' - Aidan grunted and the King looked slightly alarmed - 'while neither does he accept your position and has no intention of retreating himself. But, Aedh,' went on Colm, 'none of us would be here if we did not believe that a solution could be found.'

The King of Albyn moved his prickly shoulders. He was not long enough king to feel he didn't have to prove himself, but was king enough to know he shouldn't need to. Moreover his kingdom was in another place, across the sea, and he was strongly tempted to emphasise that while the kingdoms of West Britain were ruled by Irish kings and their descendants with small groups of retainers and fighting men, but with a population essentially of West Britons, his people, nobles and commoners alike, were principally from Ireland or of Irish descent, if you didn't count the Picts and Saxons who came under his rule. But the Rí-Eireann spoke first.

'Colm is right, *a bhrathair*, my brother. Even if you and I cannot see our way out of this difficulty at the moment, a way must be found . . . ' He hesitated. Then felt it best bluntly to bring the obvious out into the open: 'Or we must both face the terrible prospect of war on a huge scale. One thing is certain,' he went on, holding up his palm as Aidan opened his mouth to speak, 'such a war would mean death and destruction beyond anything you or I have ever experienced. You want that no more than I.'

Instead of replying, Aidan shook his head. Then said: 'Have you any suggestion?'

Aedh turned to Colm. 'Before the differences between – ' he swallowed ' – the Fir Albyn and the Fir Erin harden beyond going back, which is what could happen with all this talk – one insult . . . ' he paused, and they both knew what he meant. With tension so high and personal and collective honour involved, it would take very little to pitch over the yawning edge. 'I want you,' he went on, looking compellingly at Colm, 'to state the case.'

'But . . . ' began Colm.

'Again!'

'Of what use will my repeating it be?'

'You gave a cold and uninspired historical summary. I felt no conviction. The . . . '

'But that is exactly what I wanted to avoid,' interrupted Colm. 'You are both my cousins; these are all my people. I said I would state the case, and I have.' But he felt an unease all the same.

Aedh nodded and continued: 'As I was about to say, they need leadership.'

'Then let Colman give it in his judgement.'

'And if his judgement is not accepted?'

Colm was silent. Aidan leaned forward intently, his eyes going from one to the other.

'These are your people,' Aedh repeated Colm's words softly in his deep voice, 'we are your cousins. Do you want to see us and them fight each other in *another* war, for want of leadership?'

The oblique reference to Cul Drevni made Colm jerk as if he had been struck. He knew what Aodh was driving at. He had felt it minutes before. And he himself knew that he had reneged: that his fear of partisanship had caused him to be afraid to speak more strongly before the Assembly. If Aodh saw that, how many more saw it too? Was it his fault that the talk made no progress? He had been asked to do something, had undertaken to do it, and then tried to avoid it, even worse, he had tried to convince himself he was right.

'You have no right to give a cold cause,' went on the king, 'and allow the possibility of destruction because you are afraid of the fire in yourself.'

For a moment Colm looked at him angrily. There had been one war because of too much fire in his blood, was there the danger of another because of too little?

His face pale and drawn he said: 'Very well. I'll speak again.'

'Beloved people and children of God, listen to me. I am wracked with horror at the prospect of war among you; a conflict which could and should, and *can* be avoided. There is no need of war to settle this difference. Before the learned Colman adjudicates the issue shall I tell you what I see? I see the bloody corpses of three hundred years and more of battle fouling the plains of Meath and Leinster. What greater evil is there in Ireland than that cursed tribute? How many men, women, children not yet able to talk have died under the spear and fire and the sword because of it? Whatever the wrong, it was surely absolved long since. Are we, my beloved brothers and sisters, you and I and all of us, now going to stand idly by and for want of effort and good will bring another similar curse on the people of Albyn and the people of Erin, bring murder and death and destruction to innocent people for countless generations? No! No, I say. I beg and implore you. Let us turn to God and beseech His divine intercession. Pray that His divine grace may inform our hearts and enlighten our minds that we may avoid such a calamity. Albyn is enlarging and consolidating a new and flourishing Gaelic kingdom. The country is surrounded by powerful foes, the Picts in the north and west; the Northumbrians . . . Is it not in every way better that the people of Ireland should have this new, powerful and vigorous kingdom and its people, who are brothers and cousins, as friends and allies rather than as foes and enemies? And are not Aidan's difficulties in expanding his kingdom matters of proper concern to the Rí-Eireann in considering the question of a yearly tribute and the burden involved?'

Colman delivered his opinion the next day. Although it gave offence to and was unacceptable to many on both sides, the general opinion was favourable and it was accordingly adopted. The substance of it was that the kingdom of Albyn would henceforth be an independent kingdom within the Gaelic commonwealth and would have the same status as any of the five provinces of Ireland. It would continue to acknowledge the King, but would not pay tribute as a vassal kingdom. It would have the right to appeal to the King for certain assistance and for judgement in matters requiring superior knowledge. In war the Rí-Eireann would have the right to call on the King of Albyn to provide a manned fleet of warships. In accepting this solution, Aidan, King of Albyn, swore that his people, already blood relatives, would be allies and friends of the people of Ireland in perpetuity. And so the question was settled.

Colm planned to spend some further time at the council in order, among other things, to follow the proposed legal reforms, in one of which - recollecting with revulsion the battle of Cul Drevni - he was particularly interested; that of prohibiting the use of women warriors in battle. But over and above that was his interest in and concern for the fate of the poets, to whose Order he belonged himself, and in which he now became actively and unexpectedly involved.

The night following the day on which Colman's adjudication was accepted Dallan Forgaill went to see Colm. After initial surprise at the poet's suggestion Colm listened attentively and it was without too much persuasion that Dallan convinced him that he was the one who could best defend the Order against the formidable opposition determined to destroy it. Most of the night they discussed it: the abuses; past and possible future roles of the Order; the effect on a nation that suddenly outlaws its most encompassing intellectual and cultural heritage, and much more. Deeply moved, no less by the appalling consequences of abolition than by the fact that he was asked to speak for the Order, Colm asked: 'And do you all want me to do this for you?'

'Yes.'

'And if I were asked to give a judgement?'

'We would accept it.'

For the next several days, instead of attending the sessions of the council which discussed a variety of legal reforms, Colm prepared his brief to defend the poets against the charges which were due to be heard five nights hence. When the representatives and attendants learned that he was to defend the poets, disbelief and excitement ran hand in hand, disbelief gradually giving way to speculation as his participation was confirmed.

The hearing itself took three nights. On the third day, Colm was asked to give judgement. The prosecution had been formidable, relentless and detailed. On the vast amount of evidence against it the Order might have been disbanded many times over and the poets banished. Evidence for the defence was spirited, but lacked conviction, for those giving evidence knew that what was said against the Order was true. It was pleaded that only some members of the Order were at fault, but this was instantly challenged with several examples proving otherwise. The good that the Order had done was pointed to, to be met with clear evidence that the harm was demonstrable. Reforms and revisions were promised, and the Assembly was told that such promises had been heard before. Finally it was asked who would maintain the art of poetry if the poets were banished, whereupon a tumid bishop proclaimed that the Church would provide everything that might be needed in that respect.

For the third time Colm looked out over the vast assembly, now from the eminence of the judgement seat, and felt the silence. He was nervous and sweat filmed his body. He understood that in one sense this issue was even more important than that of the Dal Riada. He also knew that it might not seem so. Worse, he was concerned in case the natural frustration and sense of outrage of the nobles at the Dal Riada decision (contrary as they would see it to their rights) might become an additional and insurmountable barrier.

Once again he blessed the assembly and asked God's guidance. Then, carefully choosing his words, he said: 'I am an exile. By my own actions I am banished from the land I love so well. Now I ask you to listen to some lines from a poem of mine – for as you know I too belong to the Order you would banish. And I ask you to believe me when I tell you that this poem comes from my heart:

What is my power, filling me only with sadness
in a strange land?
My sorrows in exile are more than the grains
on a desolate strand.
Oh, if I could turn back the desperate years
And halt the battle of Cul Drevni, and the tears.

'For the wrong I did,' he went on, 'I was justly exiled. Yet here I am now contributing what I can to this convention, may the Almighty Father and Christ Jesus be my guide. And I ask you this. Once banished, who or what circumstance will bring the poets or poetry back again? Ask yourselves this question, is all that is Ireland, mountain and plain and forest only? Is it rivers and sailing clouds above them alone? Is Ireland complete with the people who inhabit the land? Or, tell me this: is what we know to be Ireland not also all that is gone before us? Is it not the learning and the traditions from the past that the saintly

Patrick loved so greatly and did so much to preserve? Is it not the songs of the present and the prospect of the future too?'

He turned directly towards the King sitting with the Pentarchy and Aidan of Scotland and, raising his voice, cried: 'I put it to you, Rí-Eireann that the Order of Poets should not be abolished, but be reformed. Yes, they are wrong. They are in error, arrogant and contemptuous; but they hold in their hearts the past and the future and if you abolish them, that is what you will be abolishing. And for this cause it is right that you should buy the poems of the poets and keep the poets in Ireland and, since all the world is but a story, it is better that you buy the more enduring story rather than the story that is less enduring.'

Aedh's voice was loud and firm. 'Abbot Colm, for you personally we have the highest respect and regard. But in defending the Order we must only suppose that you do it from a sense of duty. That also we respect. But this matter has been discussed over and over. It is not the first time we have been brought to such straits by the poets. It is up to us to see that it will be the last time. They have been given every opportunity to do so, and they have not reformed. They are too ungovernable. Their demands on the people are too exorbitant, and if they do not get their own way in everything, they revile and scoff at the people and scourge them with abominable satires. What you say may, perhaps, have some merit, but they have gone too far and every king and lord is of one mind. Proceed with your judgement and we will decide if it is acceptable when you have done.'

Colm remained thoughtful for a moment. 'I understand what you and the other kings feel, *Ard-Ri*,' he said quietly, 'and I sympathise with it. I also want to assure you that it is not merely from a sense of duty alone that I am here, but much more. Yes, I know they have gone too far. I know they have not been reformed,' and he laid a small stress on the word *been*. 'But listen to my suggestion. Let there now be a reformation both from without and from within for the good of the whole nation.' He turned and with an open-armed gesture encompassed the wider audience in his appeal.

'We all know that learning and civilisation have everywhere, except here, been extinguished in the west by the barbarians. Recently the Lombardians tore vast lands from the Empire and now nothing but an unenlightened wilderness lies between here and Byzantium. Angles and Saxons ravage Britain destroying the vestiges of Roman civilisation. We stand alone in this desolation. It is up to us to stop it and turn the tide of chaos. But how? you ask. We must educate. Prcvide schools that will be forges of knowledge as yesterday's smithies were forges of weapons. And who better qualified to be the smiths and anvil beaters of the future than the very poets you would banish and destroy?'

Suddenly, somewhere, someone cheered, and the response began: a sound, small and localised at first, that swelled until it was a roar that reverberated about Colm. He had to wait until it quieted before trying to continue.

'Surely,' he began as the cheering subsided, 'surely you can see that the poets were also victims of changes in society? That many of the abuses result from these changes? That is clear to anyone who genuinely looks for the truth of the matter. What were honours and privileges for the few became expectancies and rights for the many. Naturally as their numbers increased and places for them did not, abuses developed. How could it be otherwise? So to this extent it is society's responsibility.' He waved a hand and thumped the *cos-na-dála*. 'Oh, I'm not saying it is the people's fault. The poets must answer for their own faults. But, in the last analysis, it is a collective problem that won't be solved by throwing it away, which is what you would do if you abolish the Order and banish the poets. It will need a collective solution. I believe the solution to be along the lines I have outlined. Let there be schools. Let there be education for all the people. Let the poets teach the people in these schools and let Ireland reilluminate the desolation in the western world.'

His words produced a further uproar of cheering and he saw

that he had the sympathy if not the will of the Assembly. He again turned to the King.

'*A Ri*, my King, our ancestor the great king Cormac Mac Art is now nothing more than a skull to be dug out of a hill and a few letters carved on a stone. Even so, that noble, generous, beautiful memory that is Cormac is understood today as well as – perhaps even better than – when he was alive and he continues to go among us, making us all strive to follow his example. And what is it that enables Cormac still to be a pattern to all men? Not his possessions, surely, long since gone; nor his power, which died with him, nor anything that he himself has done. It is the praise of the poets that is Cormac's lasting possession and that gives him the life he still has three hundred years after his death. But if there were no poets to praise him what would Cormac be now? An unknown skull and lettering on a stone! Is that to be the future of you all? For if you banish the poets that is what it will be. Banish the poets and you banish the future!'

But the Assembly was already on its feet, cheering and shouting so thunderously that he could not continue. They converged on Colm and carried him aloft from the auditorium to the city of temporary buildings and tents beyond the Mulloch.

On the following day the King announced that a special commission would be formed under the leadership of the chief poet of Ireland, Dallan Forgaill. Its purpose was two-fold: to revise and reform the Seven Degrees of the Order of Poets and bring it into line with the requirements of the community; and to devise and instigate a system of universal education in which the poets would adopt a new and positive role and responsibilities as secular educators, along the lines suggested by Colm.

The commission eventually proposed that there should be a chief school or college for each of the five provinces, and one for Albyn, and under these a number of minor schools, one in each *tuath*. All were to be endowed with land. Every child in a *tuath* was entitled to attend the school, and those who required but could not afford to pay for their education were to receive it free. The heads of these schools were henceforward to be the poets and *ollamhes* of the Order of Poetry.

This recommendation was speedily implemented, many of the old schools of poetry and literature being converted without delay. New ones were built where necessary. A college generally consisted of three schools, each in a house of its own, and each school taught three subjects. The number of official posts for members of the Order was defined and the number of personal pupils and retainers a poet might have was reduced. More importantly, the poets' fees were fixed. In return for their acceptance of the reforms and their new responsibilities for teaching the people of Ireland, the poets were entitled to universal freedom and sanctuary in their person, land and goods. As was later written by a distinguished scholar: 'The educational establishments then endowed were national literary colleges quite distinct from the literary and ecclesiastical schools and colleges formed around individual celebrities then in operation.' The rule for teachers and pupils was as follows: 'Instruction without reservation, correctness without harshness are due from the master to the pupil and to feed and clothe him during the time he is learning. To help him against poverty and support him in old age, these are due from the pupils to the tutor.'

On the morning he was due to leave, Colm attended one of the huge temporary open-air churches provided for the great gathering. Then he and his four companions began to pack what little they possessed - he had already taken leave of the King and Aidan and other dignitaries. It was still dark in the tent although the pale light of the growing morning filled the door space, and a blackbird called happily outside.

Suddenly a soft and melodious sound seemed to be all around them. Colm stopped what he was doing, his hand holding a cup in mid-air, and listened. He exchanged looks with the others who were as mystified as he. The music continued and increased in volume and it was clear that it was a well-trained choir of many voices outside their tent. Then they heard his name in the song: '*A Choilm Cille, rí, na filí*, as a scythed chariot armed for battle goes through an enemy, so may your soul go to heaven through the battalions of the Adversary.'

Beheen's voice lit up with joy. 'It is a *coicetul aidbhse*,' he cried, 'a canticle of praise for you!'

The four of them went to the door and there in the dawn light they saw all the principal poets of Ireland assembled in a semi-circle, led by Dallan Forgaill, singing in complicated harmony a glorious composition of praise in Colm's honour. It was their tribute to the work he had done in saving them from banishment. And the words of that canticle, the 'Arma Colm Cille', may still be read today.

Colm was embarrassed by this extravagance – as much by the response he felt within himself to their praise as by the event itself – and had to endure much subsequent banter on the subject of pride from Beheen. His emotions overcame him and he saw the choir through a blur of tears as the canticle faded away on a sweet, lingering note. For a moment no one moved. Then Colm, unable to speak properly, did what for him was most natural and all he was capable of. He stepped forward, raised his hand high, and blessed the assembled poets and all the poets of Ireland.

Before returning to Iona, Colm visited some of the monasteries he had founded in Ireland, including Derry and Durrow, where he was greeted with rapture as the founder and chief abbot of all his foundations, which were linked together through him. Then he returned to Iona and devoted himself to the work which he had begun fifteen years before.

He was now fifty-four. Gradually his tempestuous spirit steadied, became calmer and more authoritative. He was never idle, but he devoted more time to writing and studying, and before the end of his life had personally made over three hundred copies of the New Testament alone. But it was during this time that he produced his most lasting tangible memorial, the illuminated manuscript which has come to be called *The Book of Kells* – where Colm had founded a monastery and to where the book was later brought for safe-keeping.

He spent the rest of his life on Iona or in Scotland and became the force that brought back the light of Christianity to Britain, ravaged and prostrate from the barbarian hordes, especially the Angles, 'the whole nation of whom', said the great Bede, 'left empty the land whence they came' to plunder and settle all of Central Britain between the Aire and the Thames.

Colm died on the ninth day of June in the year 597, seven years after Pope Gregory, (called the Great) ascended the throne of St Peter. With his death died one of the most powerful influences in western Christianity. A noble of the highest birth, gifted with prescience and power over men, he had taken the barbaric north by storm and presented it to God. The debt owed by Scotland, England and Europe to this prince of the Ui Neill was indicated by the German scholar, Kuno Meyer, centuries later: 'Ireland drew on herself the eyes of the whole world . . . as the one haven of rest in a turbulent world overrun by hordes of barbarians, as the great seminary of Christianity and classic learning. Her sons, carrying Christianity and a new humanism over Great Britain and the Continent, became teachers of whole nations, the councillors of Kings and Emperors . . . The Celtic spirit dominated a large part of the western world and its Christian ideals imparted new life to a decadent civilisation.'

That morning – a Saturday – was blue and white, the sun high in the heavens and small clouds sailing a deep sky, all reflected in the glittering sea. Even the normally raucous cries of the gulls and gannets seemed more muted than usual. Colm, still vigorous in mind in spite of his seventy-six years though his health had been failing for the past three, wrote a lengthy letter to Gregory from just outside his wooden hut of weather-worn oak planks. Finishing it, he put down his pen and writing board for a moment and stretched to get the stiffness out of his arms and shoulders. The pet crane he kept, its graceful neck coiled beneath its ruff, stretched also and silently opened its beak like a yawn. Colm smiled and reached out his hand to gentle its slender head. He stood and went slowly to the farm where most of his monks were at work, the crane following. As he made his way along the brown path, his small island glittering like a jewel that bright day, the realisation grew in him that it was his last. Gently he went to each monk, kissed him and blessed his work. Then he went to the barn and storeroom of the community and blessed it and its contents that it should ever hold and give in plenty to the ardent servants of God. When he was finished he said to those who in their concern had followed him: 'Today is Saturday, or Sabbath day, the day of rest. And so it is for me, my children, a day of rest. The last day of my life.'

He silenced their lamentation by telling them to rejoice because he would soon join Patrick and be with him before the throne of the Almighty Father in Heaven.

In far off Dublin, south of the settlement of B'lath Cliath with its new wicker bridge (replacing one that had been washed away in a winter flood), another old man was being taken home by two of his sons. He was Dermot, Colm's childhood friend, now almost wholly incapacitated by the infirmities of age which had left him virtually witless and physically helpless. They travelled slowly, Dermot in a four-wheeled chariot drawn by oxen, his sons Donal and Crimthan alternately riding on horseback or sitting with the old man. They had a long way to go. Their mother, Aoife, wanted the old man home where she could care for him, for he had been taken south to some health-giving springs in Wicklow in May. But it had not achieved anything. He was still as helpless as ever and his mind - except for very brief and occasional lucid periods - wandered ceaselessly in the disconnected past.

They were hoping to cross the Liffey and reach Swords that

night, but as they topped the low hill above the wicker bridge near the ruins of the tiny settlement attributed to Patrick, the rear, left-hand wheel of the chariot slipped from a rock, bounced off another and, in seconds, the spokes splintered and the rim and wheel sections fell athwart the hub. The chariot braked and was dragged in a semi-circle. Donal leaped off his horse and his brother, Crimthan, who had been thrown on top of his father, cursed and joined him. They looked at the damage, at each other, and then Donal said: 'There's nothing else for it. We'll have to camp here for the night.'

Gently they took the old man and made him comfortable in a hollow, wrapping his great cloak round him and fastening it securely with the old dog-headed brooch that had been in the family for generations.

That night Colm slowly continued his transcription of the Psalter, inscribing each letter with the meticulousness for which he was renowned until he came to the words of the thirty-fourth Psalm: 'Those who seek the Lord shall lack no good thing . . . ' At that point the flame of his candle leaned horizontally and then, straightening, flickered. Colm put down his pen and almost inaudibly said to himself: 'That is enough for me. Let Beheen write the rest.' For Beheen, his nephew, was to follow him as abbot and the first words after those written by Colm were: 'Come, O sons, listen to me. I will teach you the fear of the Lord.'

Colm lay down for a little on the rush mattress that covered the slab that was his bed. As always, only his cowl was between his head and the stone pillow that had lain there for over thirty years and now had a worn place in the middle. Before he slept the community of twelve came to his bedside, most in tears, all silent, and he said, 'My last words to you my children are these: be at peace and have charity among yourselves. If you follow the example of the holy fathers, God, the comforter of the good, will be your helper and I, abiding with Him, will intercede for you . . . ' They left and he prayed himself to sleep. When the bell rang at midnight he rose and went quickly to the church beside his hut and knelt beside the altar.

At that moment one of the monks, his attendant Dermot Óg, young Dermot, another son of his old friend, was on his way to help the abbot to the church. He later recounted what happened.

'As I approached the abbot's cell, suddenly the whole church lit up from inside as if from a thousand candles.' He turned to those who were listening. 'Some of you saw it!' he said, and several nodded. 'So I ran. But before I reached there the light faded and I could see nothing but blackness. I was afraid, particularly for what I might find. I called out, but there was no reply. I looked in his cell as I passed, knowing he wasn't there, and went into the church.'

His listeners, though they knew what was to come, were very silent.

'I had dropped my own light and I stumbled in the dark. But I reached the altar – I could hear you all coming – and he was there, lying in front of it. So I lifted his head . . . '

When the monks rushed into the church, many of them with their candles still alight although some, like Dermot's had been dropped or had gone out in the hurry, they found Dermot crying and cradling the abbot's old head in his lap in front of the altar. As they came in the dying man's eyes opened for a moment and Dermot, catching the movement, himself lifted the abbot's hand to bless his monks. And so he died, peacefully passing from the arms of those he loved on earth to the enduring and everlasting arms of his Almighty Father.

Immediate lamentation, an *aidbhse-cépog*, funeral dirge, rose from the monks and continued during matins and as they arranged the body of their beloved father for burial. When the news went abroad the whole civilised world mourned. And to those he had left behind the white vault of heaven manifested rejoicing at Colm's accession to the heavenly will. An immense, clear fire, illuminating the land like the sun at noon, appeared over the Fionn, White River, that flows past Gartan and enters

Lough Foyle near Derry, and a pillar of fire went from earth until it disappeared.

In the small camp above the Liffey, Dermot was suddenly awake. He did not know why but his mind was clear and he felt an unaccustomed strength and co-ordination in his limbs and bowels. He had not disgraced himself again. His first thought was to give thanks to God. Then he heard it, a beautiful and unearthly music, above and about, receding into an infinity. He opened his eyes to an extraordinary radiance. The whole sky was alight. For some reason he immediately knew what had happened. He stood and, raising his face to the brilliance, cried: 'Crimthan! Wait for me!'

He glanced around. Both his sons and the chariot driver were still sleeping. He tried to raise his arms towards the heavens, but the heavy cloak hampered him. He tore at it, but it was fastened by the brooch. It became urgent, vital, to get it off, to raise his unencumbered arms towards heaven. Desperately looking alternately up at the illuminated sky and down at his chest, he pulled at the fastening. Finally, with a great wrench that lacerated the palm of his hand, he freed the brooch and shrugged the cloak from his shoulders. Exultantly he cast the brooch away and raised his arms to the glorious sky. The heavenly music was loud in his ears. He raised his arms, up, up, and his spirit, too, soared; he could . . . he could . . . see!

They found him in the morning lying a little distance away beside his crumpled cloak. His face was more peaceful than it had been for years. But of his brooch, although they searched for it, there was no sign, and there was an inexplicable cut in the palm of his right hand.

'Why didn't he call one of us?' they asked.

Sadly they brought his body home to their mother, the still lovely Aoife, in Donegal, and on the way learned of the death of Colm on the same night as their father's.

Select Bibliography

Adamnan, Vita S., *Columbae*, ed. and trans. W. Reeves, Clarendon Press, Oxford 1857

Carney, James, *Studies in Irish Literature and History*, Dublin Institute for Advanced Studies 1955

Carcopine, Jerome, *Daily Life in Ancient Rome*, Johannes Hirschberger, London 1941

Gallico, Paul, *The Steadfast Man*, Michael Joseph, London 1958.

Gibbon, *The Decline and Fall of the Roman Empire* London 1960

Graham, Hugh, *The Early Irish Monastic Schools*, Talbot Press, Dublin 1923

Hughes, Kathleen, *The Church in Early Irish Society*, Methuen, London 1966

Joyce, P.W., *A Social History of Ancient Ireland*, 2 vols., M.H. Gill and Son 1920

Meyer, Kuno, *Learning in Ireland in the Fifth Century*, Dublin 1913

Neeson, Eoin, *The Book of Irish Saints*, Mercier Press, Cork

—— *Poems From the Irish*, Poolbeg Press, Dublin 1986

Power, Patrick, *Sex and Marriage in Ancient Ireland*, Mercier Press, Cork 1976

Rees, Alwyn and Brinley, *The Celtic Heritage,* Thames and Hudson, London 1961

Sigerson, George, *The Easter Song of Sedulius* (trans.), T. Fisher Unwin, 1922

Stokes, Whitley (Ed), *Tripartite Life of St Patrick*, Rolls Series, 2 Vols, London 1887